For my kids; Caelyn, Tristan, and Jenna. You are my purpose, my passion, and the loves of my life. Hopefully my writing can make a difference for you, and for all children – now and in future generations. And I promise – I will let you read my next series!

Earth

By Terra Harmony

Copyright 2013 by Terra Harmony

A Patchwork Press Title

All rights reserved under International and Pan-American Copyright Conventions. No part of this book may be reproduced in any form or by any electronic or mechanical means, including information storage and retrieval systems, without permission in writing from the author, except by reviewer, who may quote brief passages in a review.

The scanning, uploading and distribution of this publication via the Internet or via any other means without the permission of the publisher is illegal, and punishable by law. Please purchase only authorized electronic editions, and do not participate in or encourage illegal electronic distribution of copyrighted materials. Your support of the author's rights is appreciated.

www.patchwork-press.com

Editing Team: Jessica Dall, Cathy Wathen, and Extra Set of Eyes Proofing
www.readitreviewit.wordpress.com

Cover design by Keary Taylor
www.indiecoverdesigns.com

Forward

Earth is the fourth and final book in the Akasha Series, a set of contemporary eco-fantasy novels. This book is for mature readers only. It contains sexual content and some use of profane language. Comments and criticism are always welcome and can be sent to terra.harmony11@gmail.com.

If you enjoy the book, please consider leaving a review online at Amazon, Goodreads, Smashwords, or Barnes and Noble. Happy reading!

Terra Harmony

Terra Harmony

Chapter 1

Inside Voices

Alex and I stood outside the gated fence, trying to figure out how to break into the Cold War-era underground bunker. Buried 720 feet into the hillside of White Sulpher Springs, West Virginia, it would not be easy. Each of the four entrances were protected by large steel and concrete doors designed to withstand a nuclear blast.

"The west and east entrances are vehicular tunnels," said Alex, handing me his binoculars. "That one there is the west entrance."

I focused the binoculars in on a large "high voltage" warning sign on the door.

"Do you think Akasha can burn through that baby?" Alex asked.

"Maybe," I sighed, handing back the binoculars. "But do we really want to risk a high-profile entrance?"

Footsteps in the woods to our backs caused us both to duck down. I peered under a thick, prickly bush. Susan's feet came into view. I stood, unsuccessfully avoiding the sharp thorns.

"Ow!"

Susan jumped at my outburst.

Bee squealed with delight, "Mommy!" She ran straight for me, and the thorns.

"Oh, honey – watch out!" I scooped her up before she suffered the same fate.

She squealed again.

"More!" she demanded as soon as I set her down.

Alex cleared his throat, "Um, excuse me everyone – we are in surveillance mode here. We need to use our *inside* voices."

"Tell that to the two-year-old," I said.

In a perfect world, Bee wouldn't have been there. But this world was far from perfect, and leaving Bee behind wasn't exactly an option.

Bee took the hint and ran to Alex. "More Unka Alek, more!"

He smiled down at her. "I can't refuse my best lady. But can you be quiet when I lift you up?"

She nodded her head as fast as she could, practically hopping in anticipation. Alex lifted her so quickly her feet flew in the air above her head, then came down again.

To Bee's credit, not one sound escaped her lips. She could be quiet if she wanted; she just had to be properly motivated.

"What did you find out?" I asked Susan.

"Hotel is operational. Well, as far as hotels can be, these days. But the tours have been cancelled since Daybreak. Electricity is too unreliable to lead tourists underground."

"Either that, or the facilities are actually in use," Alex said. "All the perimeter alarms are deactivated – could be they're conserving energy for ventilation systems inside."

"More!" Bee automatically demanded at his sudden shift in focus.

I dug around in my backpack for the stash of honeysuckle I'd found the day before. "Here," I handed her the entire bag. "Let the grownups plan their break in."

"Bake in, bake in," chanted Bee, plopping down on the ground, already diving into her new treat.

I smiled, then turned back to the west entrance and frowned. "Let's camp out for a night – see if there's any activity in or out."

"What about the other entrances?" Alex asked.

"We could split up," I suggested.

Susan groaned. "I *hate* spending the night alone, outside."

"*You* won't be outside. You can go back to the hotel; find out more," Alex said.

"And you won't be alone, you'll have Bee," I said.

The three of us looked down at her, still sitting at our feet. Several white flowers already sat crumpled by her side, having been deprived of all their sweet nectar.

In a world with only intermittent power, traditional packaged goods – including candy – were scarce. Honeysuckle had long become a treat of choice.

"Let's meet back here an hour after dawn tomorrow," Alex said.

Susan stuck out her lip.

Alex rolled his eyes. "Ok, two hours after dawn. Put that lip back in before I bite it."

Susan smiled, raising one eyebrow. "Bite me and I'll bite you back." She moved a step closer to him.

"Is that a promise?" he asked, closing the distance between them.

I turned my back just in time to hear kissing sounds. The open romance between Alex and Susan was a long time coming, and I was happy for both of them, but with every passing day it made me long for

Micah more and more. He'd been missing since a few weeks before Daybreak.

The kissing noises were still coming. I sighed and squatted down by Bee. "It's rude to stare, sweetie."

The few honeysuckle that remained were forgotten. She shifted her gaze to me, stuck out her lips and said, "Kiss, kiss!"

I laughed and obliged, then gathered her in my arms. "You're going to stay with Aunt Susan tonight. Be good, okay?"

"Otay!"

I kissed her again.

"Enough with the smooching you two," Susan interrupted. "We're going to be late for girls' night out."

"More like girls' night in," I said, passing Bee over. "Make sure she gets a bath – and check her for ticks." I dug in my backpack for the only bar of soap we had.

"We'll do the usual pampering session," Susan promised, taking the bar.

"Bye, Bee," I said.

Bee waved, and I watched them walk away as she fiddled with the soap.

"She'll be fine, Mama," Alex said, slinging his arm over my shoulder.

"I know. I just wish…" I trailed off. Alex didn't need to hear all about how Micah was missing out on Bee, again.

"You wish what?" he asked.

I leaned into him, nose first, and sniffed. "I wish we had another bar of soap."

Chapter 2

Wondrous Qualities

After scouting out each entrance, Alex and I picked the two that looked the most used. Parting ways, I traded the last of the honeysuckle for one of his apples, and headed back to the north entrance. It was uphill, but I told myself it would be a few degrees cooler than the south entrance, which was where Alex was headed.

I made my way to the top of a ridge that had just enough shrubbery to conceal me. After inspecting the area for thorns and poison ivy, I chose a bush and rolled out a blanket underneath. I laid on the ground, belly down, with the binoculars glued to my eyes for the next half hour. Absolutely no movement as far as I could see.

When my stomach started to grumble, I pulled out the apple and bit into it. turned on my back as I chewed. The stars were bright and numerous, especially with no more light pollution. Directly after the electro-magnetic pulse, or Daybreak, as the general population had named it, power for most of the United States had gone out. A few months later, we heard rumors of large cities back on the grid, only to be attacked and shut down again by roaming militias claiming to work for One Less. The National Guard wasn't very effective in thwarting the attacks. In fact, as time went on, there seemed to be fewer and fewer military personnel. Hell, some of them were probably joining One Less.

Eventually, power was deemed a dangerous magnet for One Less, so people stopped pursuing it. It wasn't until we hit Washington, D.C. that we learned of EMPs going off in other major countries around the world. Before that, I had half expected to see Chinese troops marching through the country, but it appeared most countries had gotten hit even worse than ours. We had Akasha to somewhat contain our blast. Others had no such luck.

I turned the half-eaten apple over in my hand. Moonlight glinted off the dull red skin, reminding me of shiny apples in a supermarket. There were no more shiny apples. I looked at my watch; ten p.m. There had been plenty of watch batteries left over in abandoned stores, though no double A's for our handheld radios.

I sighed. Lots of time before I would be reunited with Susan, Alex, and Bee. I took another bite, hitting the core. I dug out the seeds and placed them in my pocket. Seeds made the 'rattle' in a few of Bee's homemade toys. Micah was right. *Wondrous qualities* was how he had described apples.

Or was that me, being sarcastic?

It felt like so long ago, memories were beginning to blend together. I half-considered reaching out for Micah through our telepathic connection. It was something I had practiced consistently right after Daybreak, until it led a platoon of One Less directly to us. Somehow, they'd figured out how to tap in.

The resulting skirmish separated me from Bee for a week. It was the absolute worst week of my life. Alex had her the whole time, but I had all her cloth diapers and prepared food. When we finally reunited,

Bee was practically potty-trained, and covered head to toe in berry juice.

It took another two days to clean her. Every time I griped about it, Alex would tell me how that berry bush saved their lives. Every time Bee announced she had to use the bathroom, I caught a glimpse of a prideful smile on Alex's face. It was easy to potty train in the middle of the woods where there were no actual potties around to use.

Even still, the three of us always took care to divide Bee's supplies evenly among us. I reached inside my backpack, rummaging around for food. Nothing. I laid back down with a huff. Susan would probably be able to stock up. Bee's dimples led to a lot of much-needed acquisitions, even in today's world, where it was every man, woman, and child for themselves.

My thoughts drifted back to Micah, wondering if he was underground, possibly right beneath me. I thought back to all the clues that had led us here, most of them gathered while we were in D.C. Our former senate contact told us this was where the president and his entourage had retreated just before the EMP. Since Micah's trail led directly to the White House, hunting down the president was the next step.

So there I lay, underneath a bush by myself, setting my sights on the President of the United States inside a nuclear-protected facility, all because of Micah. I rolled back over, looking through the binoculars again. I was going to have rings around my eyes come morning, not to mention a dozen ticks.

Another low growl, and I silently wished I had another apple to settle my stomach. But the rumbling didn't stop. It grew until even the leaves on the bush above me shook with vibration.

I jumped to my feet. My hair tangled in the bush. "Dang foliage!"

The blast separated me from the bush, as well as some of my hair, throwing me back into the trees. I got to my feet, slower this time, ears ringing. The earth was on fire. The entire hillside danced before my eyes, consumed in flame. A large gaping hole was in the middle of it all. Another blast, further from me but closer to Alex shook the ground again. There was no need to break in; something else was breaking out.

Chapter 3

Dancing Flames

I scrambled back to my bush, rolled up the blanket, and stuffed it in my bag. I opted for the shorter, steeper route down, rather than using the trail I took up. Rocks slid out from the soles of my boots, and my butt hit the ground, hard. I continued to slide. Shrubs hit me as I passed but did little to slow my descent. In fact, I tried my hardest to avoid the plant life. I'd rather break a limb than get another bout of poison ivy.

The dancing flames grew as I raced closer to them. Dust and rocks churned up in my path. Just after I began a tumbling routine, flipping head over heels, I came to an abrupt stop.

I groaned, "Not cool," and removed an especially sharp stick from underneath me. Another earth-shattering blast got me on my feet. I picked up my backpack – again – and ran straight into the flames.

Dizzy from the fall, I had a hard time staying upright. In moving forward my options quickly became limited, and the blaze determined my path for me. I fought down the instinct to call out for Micah or to use any of my powers. I didn't want to draw any attention; Greenbrier was beginning to look more and more like a trap.

Heat licked at my face and hands, threatening to singe my bared skin. I approached the area of the first explosion. A giant hole scarred the earth. Trees and shrubs around the hole was already charred and smoking; the fire moving on to consume more. I looked back at the hole. One hand, then another, emerged. My heart raced. A man in a suit pulled himself up. His facial features gleamed by the light of the raging fire. I did not recognize him.

I backed away until I bumped into another body. I turned, sweeping my leg wide and catching the person behind his knees. His body hit the ground. This one I did recognize.

I dug my knee into his throat, pinning the rest of his upper body down with my other leg. "Where's Micah?!"

He bucked, but was a relatively small man. There wasn't much to him, as far as muscle went. I barely shifted.

I pressed further. "Where. Is. Micah?" I asked again, through gritted teeth.

Fast-moving footsteps came up on my right, and I didn't have time to respond. The blunt force to my midsection stole my breath. I landed on my back; my head bouncing off the hard ground. Stars above me swayed with my vision. I turned to the side to see my backpack laying several feet away. The damn thing was having trouble staying on my back.

The man in a suit came into view, along with another. They hauled me to my feet.

I held my sides, recovering my breath, eying the men as I did so. Pressed suits and shiny shoes. They looked far too good to have been tromping around in the wild. "Men's Wearhouse is still in business, I see."

The small man, the one I'd leveled, laughed. "You must be Kaitlyn."

I nodded my head down, once. "Mr. President."

Chapter 4

The List

Shawn stood in the brackish water of the Great Salt Lake, looking down. His reflection was eerily still. There were no waves, no plants, and no playful fish. Practically the only life in the salty water was brine shrimp.

Shawn looked beyond the lake at the terrain, licking his cracked lips. Everything was so dry here. His throat had been parched ever since they crossed the Wasatch Range several months ago. He turned to his right, scanning the extension of the Rocky Mountains. They were hazy. "Why the heck did the Mormons stop here?"

"Sir?" asked Shawn's first in command, David, startled from his bookkeeping.

"Never mind," Shawn mumbled, returning the few feet to the shore. "Did you rotate the perimeter sentry groups?"

"Yes. Replacements were sent out this morning, but it usually takes a full day to complete the rotation. We should see the last group coming in around sunset." David snapped his ledger shut and followed Shawn. "Where do you want them?"

Shawn stopped, bent down and unrolled his pants. "Give them two days of rest, then put them on supply duty. We'll run out of batteries by the end of the month. I know these Mormons stockpile like the world is about to end."

"It kind of already did," David mumbled.

Shawn arched his eyebrow at him.

"I mean...yes, sir." David reopened the book and scribbled a note.

"Don't call me sir." Shawn resumed walking, making quick work of the sandy dunes.

"Yes, S— Shawn." David's feet kept sinking in, making it hard to keep up with Shawn.

"And find me some damn chapstick."

David wrote another note. "I'll check with supply, sir."

Shawn stopped, and was about to turn around when one of their own came riding down the road on his bicycle, waving an arm. "They're back! The mission to Easter Island – a success!"

Shawn raised his eyebrows in surprise. After more than a year, he had written off the mission. Shawn and David collected their own bikes, spray painted black, as were all the bikes with One Less, and continued on to headquarters.

"I wish we had horses," David huffed alongside Shawn. He had to stand, putting more force on the pedals in order to keep pace with Shawn on the uphill.

"We did," Shawn replied. "They got eaten."

They soon reached their camp on Antelope Island, in the middle of the Great Salt Lake, where they had set up after the show down at Mammoth Cave. Here, Shawn could run his business in relative peace while still being close enough to Salt Lake City to procure any supplies they needed.

A group of four sat in the middle of the camp, barely recognizable from when Shawn last saw them. They were much thinner, and either had too much or too little hair.

"Where's the fifth?" Shawn asked, approaching the group.

They all hopped to their feet.

The one with a beard hanging past his chin, spoke up, "Went overboard in the Pacific."

Another coughed.

There was probably more to the story but Shawn didn't care to hear it. "And the bodies?"

"Delivered."

Kaitlyn's Akasha had caused plenty of casualties; some on her side. Her infamous black-braided friend was one of them. The body of Ahi, along with those of several fellow Easter Islanders, had been collected before The Seven could claim them.

Shawn crossed his arms and narrowed his eyes. "I'll know if you're lying to me."

One of the women walked up to Shawn and placed a bag in his hands.

He opened it and several rocks fell out into his palm.

"Hardened lava from the caves," she explained.

Shawn closed his fist around the rocks, squeezing. Energy emanated from the rocks, causing his whole arm to tingle. He nodded, put the rocks back in the bag and asked, "Anything else?"

"There's more in our trailer." The man gestured to a homemade, two-wheeled contraption hitched to the back of a well-used bike.

Shawn nodded but didn't inspect. "What did they do with the bodies?"

Procuring the formaldehyde and finding someone that could embalm the bodies had taken time and resources One Less could have put to better use elsewhere, but Shawn had a list. A list that Ahi herself said must be addressed before Shawn could obtain Akasha. Shawn figured the best he could do to make amends was send the bodies back to their homeland so they could be honored in whatever traditions the islanders had.

"Burned the three Fires, gave the Air a sky funeral."

Shawn snorted. "We could've done that."

"Made us stay until the body had been picked clean by birds." The hairy man laughed. "The next morning I found a dozen dead seagulls on the shore. I tried to tell them about the formaldehyde, but they insisted."

Shawn laughed with him.

David stepped up. "Where do you want them? We could use a few more on kitchen duty."

The group groaned.

"Get them checked out by the doc first." Shawn turned to the group. "Then to the kitchens for the next month. The work isn't very physical and you get first dibs on food. You all could use it." As Shawn turned to walk away he nodded toward the hairy man. "Except you – you're with me."

The man followed.

"You were new to One Less – right before Mammoth Cave, if I remember. What was your name?"

"Clay." The hairy man had to crane his neck all the way back to look at Shawn.

"That's right. The Earth." Shawn turned to make sure they were far enough from the group. "I'm going into town on a few errands. I could use an Earth. You in?" Shawn asked.

Clay bent down, picked up a handful of dirt and sniffed it. "Not good soil; have you managed to grow much here?"

Shawn smiled. "We've learned a few tricks. So, what do you say?"

"My butt may not be able to handle the bike seat so soon."

Shawn laughed. "We're not going until next week. Until then, try to stay off the bike." Shawn slapped Clay hard on the back and left, barking more orders at David.

Clay watched them walk away, swatting at the gnats that apparently found his beard irresistible. Despite the dry heat, and the undesirable human company, Clay liked it here. He felt at home with the bitter smell of salt in the air, so thick you could almost taste it. Clay had been one of a few chosen to infiltrate One Less during the battle at Mammoth Cave. It was easy enough in the aftermath of the blast, but he had had no chance to let Kaitlyn or Susan know he survived.

Then he'd been chosen for the Easter Island mission. It took them a year and a half to deliver the bodies and make their way home, much of it done over water. After losing his sister during the battle, he didn't much care what happened to him. But several months on the water was pure torture; claustrophobic, even – at least for an Earth.

Clay walked closer to the adobe buildings at Fielding Garr Ranch. It at least had a freshwater spring. But being in camp less than a day, Clay had already heard rumors it was close to drying up. The Waters were all worked up about it. Clay walked past the water storage area, flipping open drains on the large barrels.

There was no way The Seven was going to make it past Shawn's fortified seven mile narrow causeway leading onto the island. Clay would just have to force One Less to migrate off the island, and animals always followed fresh water.

Chapter 5

Good Cover

"Micah isn't here – he's gone ahead, to clear the path for you."

"Clear the path to where?" I asked, ducking automatically as another boom sounded off in the distance.

"To Shawn."

The President's words rang through my head, merging with the percussion of the blast, still bouncing around in my brain. My head felt like it was about to explode.

"Sir – I must insist we get moving." The Secret Service agent's words barely registered. I couldn't snap out of my shock until I saw the President's back, and my only link to Micah, disappearing into the smoke and flames. I ran after him.

The three Secret Service agents that surrounded him glanced back, but ultimately ignored me. Apparently I wasn't the biggest threat out here. Now *that* was a scary notion.

Another blast, closer this time, shook the ground.

"What is it?" I asked.

All four men were already breathing hard. Over a year underground would do that to you.

"Had a security breach," said the President. "It was an insider – he has bombs rigged to go off all over the place."

I shivered, thinking of how close we had come to entering the facility. We might have set one off ourselves. I thought of Bee and Susan, slowing down, debating if I should change my route and head for the hotel. Alex would've gone for them. That was our hard and fast rule whenever the three of us were separated. The closest to Bee go for her while the other eliminates the threat. The President wasn't the threat, but he could lead me to Micah. One thing at a time.

"Shawn is in Utah – Antelope Island, according to our reports. We have no reason to think he will leave anytime soon," the President spoke to me, stopping his forward momentum.

"Sir, please." One of the secret service agents pulled on his arm.

The President ignored him. "Take the rivers. Ohio, Mississippi, Missouri, Platte. Micah is drawing One Less away from the path as he goes."

"Sorry – we cannot wait any longer," stated the agent. He hooked his arm under the President's armpit. Another copied on the other side. The President's toes barely touched the ground.

"Oh, for Pete's sake – put me down!"

The President's orders were ignored. He looked at me over his shoulder. "Ohio, Mississippi, Missouri, Platte!"

"Upper or lower Platte?" I yelled back.

A series of bullets, aimed at the ground just in front of me, was my only answer. The agent's message was clear, our conversation was over.

I threw up my hands. No argument there – I had better things to get to…like Bee.

"Ohio, Mississippi, Missouri, Platte," I told myself as I shifted directions and ran for the hotel. Sink holes were everywhere, many of them spewing flames and smoke. "Ohio." I leaped over a fallen tree.

"Mississippi." I darted around a wall of fire, using water and air to battle it back. "Missouri." I fell to the ground, flattening my body as debris from another blast flew just over my head. The taste of burnt grass and wet earth filled my mouth. I spit. "Platte."

Eliminate the threat – that was my job. But there were no people; just a lot of explosions and fire. What was I going to do, take away oxygen? I paused before picking myself off the ground. I'd battled wildfires before, and used energy to fix oxygen levels. I just might be able to contain the entire area – and stop the blasts. But to what end? Who was the security breach? Briefly, I wondered if it was me. Maybe the perimeter alarms weren't all turned off, like Alex said. I shrugged.

Better to let the attack continue. Flames are good cover.

After an hour of running a convoluted route, I sat in a treetop studying the hotel. It was still intact. People milled about on the lawn, chattering about the explosions. I couldn't tell if Susan was one of them. They all held candles – the lucky few with working batteries had flashlights.

I turned the other direction, toward the bunker, or what was left of it, to search for potential followers. My binoculars would've come in handy, but I had left them in my bag, halfway down the tree.

Now, we wait.

Every few minutes I called out, the shrill *whoit, whoit, whoit* whistle imitating a Cardinal. It had taken Alex two months to teach me that. Bee learned it before I did. I waited each time for the response, but got nothing.

Where are they?

Images of One Less snatching up Bee assaulted me. I shook my head.

Don't do that; not yet.

I whistled again. Still no response.

That does it.

I worked my way down the tree, as silently as possible. It was difficult, considering I had to go back up for my forgotten backpack. When I hit the ground for a second time, cursing about the bag being the death of me, a noise made me jump.

"Kaitlyn!"

"Argh!" I yelled, then clamped my hand over my mouth and ducked down.

The bushes shook and Alex whisper-shouted, "Unless you're using the bathroom, quit squatting and get over here."

I crawled over, cracking twigs as I went.

Once I joined him under the bush he said, "You'd make a terrible sniper."

"I'm more of a machine-gun type of girl." I looked around. "Where's Bee?"

"She's safe with Susan, hiding about two clicks away."

"I told you before, I don't know what in the hell a 'click' is."

He rolled his eyes. "They're a little over a mile, further south from here."

I popped my head out, looking in that direction as if I could see them.

Alex pulled me back down. "You were being trailed."

"One Less or Secret Service?"

He furrowed his eyebrows, confused. "I'm not sure. I had to circle a few times to be sure of their position."

Ah, so he was using me as bait while I whistled away like a jackass.

"Come on, they've dug in around you but we should be able to get out this way." He headed north.

"But Susan and Bee are south," I said.

"We'll make a loop – now, no more talking until I say. And step where I step."

I nodded, moved forward, and my heavy foot landed directly on a dried up pinecone. Alex paused to turn back and look at me with a raised eyebrow. I shooed him on, annoyed enough with myself for the both of us.

As we walked, adrenaline wore off and fatigue set in. I fought to keep my eyes open and fixed in between his shoulder blades. After another hour, things were beginning to get hazy. If I wasn't careful, I was going to run straight into a tree. That definitely wouldn't be very sniper-like.

Clouds moved in, covering the moon and extinguishing the only light we had. I lost him in a matter of seconds. "Alex?"

"Over here," he called.

I followed the voice to a row of trees and breathed a sigh of relief when I could make out his silhouette.

"There." He gestured to a clearing with a nod of his head.

The clouds dissipated and what probably used to be a well-maintained property came into view. The house was a shell, the upper floors burnt down. We'd been in houses like that before. Probably nothing remained. People got crafty when they became desperate. I'd seen pieces of staircase banisters whittled into weapons and copper piping and shower drains used in a homemade – literally – water filtration system.

"Not the house," Alex said. "The shed."

My eyes drifted to the edge of the yard. There was a small shack covered in vines. "You left them in there?" I squeaked, emerging from our hidden spot.

Alex followed me into the clearing. "What's the matter?"

"You know," I hissed, looking at him over my shoulder. "Spiders."

"You just ran through an exploding hillside, and you're worried about spiders?"

"Black widows can be deadly to a two-year-old."

Alex moved ahead, and pushed open the doors to the shed. I shoved him aside. Susan sat in the middle of the floor, cross-legged with Bee lying in her lap. I knelt before them, holding one hand to Bee's chest and the other just in front of her mouth.

"She's breathing," I announced.

"You look surprised." Susan glared at me.

I hugged her. "Thank you."

I felt her shoulders relax, and I released her. I leaned back on my heels and looked around. Completely bare – even the shelves had been pilfered.

"I found something. Here, hold Bee," Susan said to me.

Susan shooed both me and Alex back to reveal a trap door in the floor. Dust and grime covered the edges. Susan stuck her finger in a knot in a floorboard and pulled up. A staircase led down. Alex went first, disappearing into the dark.

"It's ok!" he shouted up.

Susan went next, and I followed with Bee, snoring away in my arms.

"Oh my God," Alex said, voice cracking into a higher octave. "There are batteries." In the pitch black, I heard him fumbling around, then a beam of light shot through the underground storage area.

Alex aimed the flashlight at the walls. Floor to ceiling shelves were stocked full of supplies. The image danced in front of our eyes like some glorious revelation. Canned foods, medical supplies, camping equipment, and lots and lots of batteries.

I rushed to one of the shelves. "Soap!" I could've danced a jig just then, if it weren't for the sleeping baby. I turned to Susan. "Well, is this *all* you found?" I asked with a teasing smile.

"No. There is also that." She pointed up.

I craned my neck, looking back up the steep staircase to the ceiling of the shed. Alex pointed his light up and my mouth dropped open. A canoe hung from the rafters.

Chapter 6

Pocahontas

"One, two, three, and push!"

The back wheels of the homemade canoe trailer were stuck in the mud yet again. That Alex had been able to find tires at all was amazing, but one was beginning to go flat, and we had a little over half a mile until the river. Or 'a click and a half' as Alex put it.

"One more time. One, two, three, push!" Alex repeated. Susan and I pushed while he pulled, and the tire popped free of the mud.

"Explain to me again how you were able to find the tires, but no vehicle to *drive* us to Utah?" Susan asked, picking up a can of green beans that had toppled out of the canoe. Bee continued to nap in the middle on top a pile of blankets. That girl could sleep through anything.

"Because, all the cars were blown up. Whoever attacked the compound probably hit the garage first. These were the only tires sitting around that weren't actually on fire." Alex swatted at a mosquito on his arm. His tone with Susan was short and clipped.

We were all tired. After the high of discovering the loot, I had explained my brief stint in U.S. politics. Alex went into the bunker to find some way to transport the canoe to the river, while Susan and I loaded up. We had emptied the shelves entirely. I just hoped the canoe would still float with all this weight.

"Did you find any weapons, or ammunition?" Alex asked.

"No," I said. A pistol hung at each of our hips. They had been empty of bullets for months now, but still proved to be a valuable deterrent. Travelers thought twice about going after our supplies when we looked armed.

Alex's shoulders sagged.

"Are we there yet?" Susan whined.

Alex's shoulders sagged even further. The past year and a half couldn't have been easy on him, trudging from state to state, dragging along two women and a baby.

"Where do you suppose the president was headed?" I asked, trying to keep Susan's mind occupied with something other than her sore feet.

She shrugged. "Probably another bunker. Someplace with running water and air conditioning."

"Maybe even back to D.C. While we were there, plenty of people mentioned how much better the capital has become compared to right after the EMP. Much more tame," Alex said.

His version and my version of tame differed greatly. There was still rioting when we went through, and almost the entire Southeast section was on fire. There was no sign of Micah in all that mess.

"I should've followed the President," I mumbled. "He probably has a boat – with a motor and gas."

I suppose I should just be thankful for the pair of oars inside the canoe.

A half an hour later, Susan's head jerked up, eyes going wide and face cracking into a smile. "The river is close."

Several minutes later, I heard it. We rolled the canoe to a stop alongside the shore. It wasn't very large, but seemed tame enough. We would still need to find a life jacket for Bee.

"Are we sure this is the Greenbrier River?" I asked. It was a convoluted route on West Virginia's river system, even before we reached the Ohio. There were plenty of tributaries leading in or flowing out along the way. Keeping on the right path would be tricky. It wasn't like there were road signs posted.

Alex consulted one of the many maps he acquired. "Pretty sure." He nodded twice, as if to reassure himself, then folded the map.

"Well." Susan rubbed her hands together. "Let's shove off, shall we?"

I laughed. Her mood always improved when close to water.

"Hold on Pocahontas," Alex said. "We need to make some modifications to the boat first."

"Modifications? What modifications?" I frowned. The more we stalled, the less likely we were to make it a ways down river before Bee woke up.

A rustling from the boat caused us all to turn our heads.

Too late, I groaned to myself.

Bee was rooting around in the pile of supplies. She came up with graham crackers.

"Tootie!" she exclaimed proudly.

"Okay. Modifications for Alex – cookies for us."

After two hours of watching Alex work, and trying to keep track of Bee while she searched for more honeysuckle, we were finally ready to go.

I threw a full bag of the white petal flowers into the canoe and hopped in next to Bee as Alex pushed us off.

"She can sniff those out like a pro," Alex said.

"She knows what's important," I said, putting her on my lap. There was just enough room for my legs, which was far better than before. "Where did all the batteries go?"

"Hidden under the seats," he said, steering us away from the banks.

My heel hit wood underneath the bench.

"Hopefully it'll appear to just be part of the canoe. If we can hold onto them long enough, we might be able to trade our way into anything we need."

After Daybreak, batteries became the new currency. It was sometime during our last leg in Tennessee when seeing people tend their makeshift car greenhouses while listening to their iPods no longer seemed unusual.

"Picking up anything?" Alex asked Susan.

She was at the front of the canoe, with her hand in the water. "A lot of disturbance upriver."

"Could it be whatever tore apart the underground bunker?" I asked.

"Maybe. It's powerful." She paused, skimming her fingers along the top of the calm river. "But nothing downstream so far as I can tell."

"Micah doing his part?" My question was rhetorical.

"Well, let's just get through this while the coast is clear, and hopefully whatever is behind us doesn't catch up," Alex said, rowing hard with his oar. "Kaitlyn, I could use a little manpower here."

I nodded, closing my eyes, tuning into the frequency of the air. A little downwind wouldn't hurt.

"Nope," he interrupted by tapping a wooden handle on my shoulder.

I took the other oar and frowned.

"He's right," Susan said, turning around. "We don't want to attract any unwanted attention. Only physical energy from here on out, unless it is an emergency."

I grumbled, angling my oar toward the water. I had literally never rowed a boat before. "I don't see you with a paddle."

Susan smiled, turning back to the water. "I'm the navigator."

Alex snickered. I looked back at him; his oar dragged in the water.

"What?" he said. "I'm steering."

The canoe jolted forward, and a small boulder hidden just under the river's surface scraped against the entire length of the boat.

"I just thought of a good name for our new ride," I said as I plunged my oar into the water and pulled back. "The Titanic."

Chapter 7

Dropping Anchor

Susan and Alex had their communication skills down to a science, and all potential icebergs were avoided. Around midday, Alex and I stopped banging our oars and settled into a coordinated pattern worthy of any high school row team. Bee took several naps, lulled to sleep by the rocking boat.

We pulled over to the side of the river by nightfall. Alex created an anchor by tying a dozen D batteries together with 550 cord. Extra blankets underneath and over me made for a more comfortable bed than I had in a long time. If every day went like this, I would be a happy camper. I kept my eyes peeled open as long as I could. It had become my evening ritual; less sleep meant fewer nightmares. But I was no match for the gentle rocking of the canoe on water, or Bee's comforting warmth.

* * *

"Easy there, princess." Shawn's words echoed through my head. His blue eyes floated in front of me. Fire surrounded us like a ring, blocking off any hopes of retreat. I could still hear Bee snoring in my ear. This was a dream. No – a nightmare. One I had already seen through to the end. But here I was again because there was some unresolved business.

I looked around; there was no one else.

Shawn held his Athame up, pointed at my neck. Something danced at my back, taunting me. But the knife held my attention.

"Where's the baby?" he asked.

I flinched, and the thing behind me flickered like a strobe light.

"Kaitlyn." My name on his lips, my *real* name, sounded foreign. "The baby is mine."

The light behind me started to rise. I knew I could stop it if I wanted. There would be consequences if I did, there would be consequences if I didn't. What outcome would be worse?

My insides shook with anxiety. I had to make a decision fast. I focused on the tip of the knife. Behind it, Shawn's lip curled up in a smile. "It's already too late."

Blood dripped down the flames surrounding us, turning them more red than orange.

"Now!" The scream came from nowhere and everywhere at the same time. I had to make the decision.

* * *

My eyes flew open, heart pounding from the nightmare. I blinked, calming my body, as the morning sun peeked out above the trees. My arm was numb from Bee's large head laying on it all night. I was sore and stiff from a day of rowing, and I was covered in bug bites. If every morning started like this, I was not going to be a happy camper.

"Alugh," I mumbled. No one in the boat stirred. I cleared my throat and licked my cracked lips. "Alex!"

"Huh?" a sleepy voice sounded out from the back of the canoe.

"Are the water bottles back there?" I looked up just in time to see one being lobbed in my general direction. It landed on the bench. "You could've hit Bee."

"Mommy?" Bee asked, stretching her limbs in the small space she had. I sipped water, watching her run through the usual morning routine. A frown while her eyes searched new surroundings; rarely would she wake up in the same location two days in a row. Then reaching out with her hand, feeling for a reassuring warm body. Finally she would turn her face up to the sky. Even if the trees weren't what she remembered before going to sleep, the sky would always be there, hovering over her. She really didn't do well indoors any longer.

Next would be her first word of the day. Generally, it would be a word repeated throughout the morning ad nauseum. This morning's word was, "Itchy."

I leaned over, peering at her face a little closer. Bug bites covered her, too. One was still feasting at her hairline.

"Get away you bastard." I swatted at the mosquito.

Bee smiled. "Bashterd."

Why is it always the bad words they pick up?

Behind us, Alex moaned and sat up.

"It was a fine spot you chose to pull over," I told him.

"Bashterd!" Bee chimed in.

Alex looked at me. "And you are a fine source of vocabulary, Katie."

I rolled my eyes. "We need to find some netting. I got eaten alive last night, as did you."

Alex peered over the boat at his own reflection in the water. "I can't see anything in this muck."

"Susan awake yet?" I asked.

"Susan." Alex shook a lump next to him. "Susan."

The lump stirred. "Five more minutes."

"Nope – up and at 'em. You're rowing today."

That got her moving. "What? But I'm…freaking Pocahontas! The navigator – remember?"

"Yeah but another day of this and I won't be able to move my arms. At all," I said, rolling out my shoulders.

Alex nodded. "Me too. We switch every day. Besides, we *all* need to learn how to steer the canoe. Your turn to learn, Susan. Katie's up front."

"Fine," Susan said, sitting up and pulling back her hair.

I gasped. "Susan – your face!"

"What?" She ran a panicked hand over her smooth skin.

"It's…it's…perfect."

"Huh?"

"You have no bites."

Susan peered at me and Bee, then looked at Alex. "You guys look terrible."

"Bashterd," said Bee.

Susan glared at me.

Alex sighed, "Come on, ladies. We need to find a mosquito net today."

After a small breakfast of canned peaches and beans, we lifted anchor – or battery – and began rowing. That day we reached the tip of Bluestone

Lake, then made our way up New River. Paddling upstream, I was thankful that it wasn't me with an oar.

An hour passed on New River when I felt a trickle of energy behind me. I turned and glared at Susan. "I thought you said no magic."

Her shirt was drenched in sweat. "Believe me, I'd be the first to do it if I thought it was safe."

"If it isn't you, who is it?" I looked behind the canoe, toward Bluestone Lake. "Do you think someone is following us?"

"I don't feel anything," said Susan.

I furrowed my eyebrows, glancing down at Bee. She hadn't had an incident since her fire at the Chakra. Granted, we were very careful not to get her too excited, since that was how the fireball had appeared. At the moment, she sat with her back to me, decorating her leg with the Band-Aids out of one of several first aid kits. She wasn't excited, or anxious, or mad – none of the tell-tale emotions that sent my powers out of whack.

I turned back to the water, guiding Alex through a tame set of rapids. By the time we were through, the energy was gone.

I'll have to pay more attention to Bee.

Further upriver, homemade filtering systems dotted the bank on one side.

"Should we check it out?" I asked Alex.

He eyed them. "Those only filter enough water for ten people or so, and that's if they don't use it for growing food."

"We can handle that…" I said. Approaching people was always tricky. Though most were helpful, we had run into our fair share of undesirables.

Alex guided us over to the shore. Instead of dropping anchor, he tied us off to a tree.

"Susan, stay here with Bee."

"Gladly," she grumbled, stretching out her arms.

Alex handed her a knife. "If you hear our whistle, just cut the rope and get upstream as fast as you can. They'll expect us to go down."

Alex bagged a few different types of batteries and first aid items for trading. The canned food wouldn't go far, by now people had learned to grow for themselves. Those who hadn't were already dead.

Bee was napping again.

I threw a light blanket over her. "Keep her covered."

Susan settled down next to her, yawning. "We'll be fine. Take your time."

Alex and I disappeared into the woods, walking quietly, listening for others. Before long we heard the ominous sound of barking. Alex and I looked at each other, eyebrows raised. We would've liked to observe the camp before our presence became known.

I turned and let out a shrill whistle in the direction of Susan and Bee. Alex transferred his hunting knife to inside his boot and threw the sheath in the bushes just before the dog came crashing through, with the owners right behind him.

Chapter 8

The Captives

"Hands up. Turn around, slowly."

Alex and I obeyed, following the same protocol we might have ordered if strangers walked into our camp.

"Have any weapons on you?" All three men wore dirty overalls, no t-shirt underneath. The question was directed at Alex.

"None," Alex answered evenly.

"Search them."

The two that had yet to speak stepped forward, and patted us down. They didn't check Alex's boots. They never check the boots.

The first man didn't lower his guard. "How did you get here?"

"Came from upriver, and we saw your water filtration. We're hoping to trade a few things."

The man eyed Alex. He was older, maybe early fifties, but he was well built. Taller than all of us, with wide shoulders. Two fingers were missing on his right hand, the stumps smooth and healed over, which meant it probably happened before Daybreak.

He turned to one of the men who had the same nose and the same sandy blonde hair. "Check it out."

I stepped toward the retreating man as he headed in the direction we came, toward Susan and Bee.

"Stop," the farmer commanded, reaching behind his back and producing a bow and arrow. He nocked it and took aim.

Alex stepped in front of me.

The farmer's bow and arrow wavered, then lowered. "We have to be careful, you understand."

I moved back to where I had been, hoping Susan had heard my whistle, and wouldn't be caught napping away. No matter what kind of men these were, if they saw our stockpile it was unlikely we'd be leaving with all of it.

The tension deflated, and Alex and I lowered our arms.

"What do you have to trade?" the farmer asked.

Alex gestured to our bags. "First aid supplies and batteries."

The farmer didn't even glance at the bag. "Got any food?"

Alex and I both looked at each other, confused.

"You don't need any food," Alex said.

The farmer's mouth tipped up in a half-smile, but before he could respond, his son came crashing back through. "No sign of more – and no boats." His chest heaved, out of breath.

The farmer raised his eyebrow at Alex.

"You understand," Alex said, "we have to be careful."

"Who was it you whistled to, just before we came?"

I rolled my eyes. *Let's get on with it, people.*

I moved out from behind Alex and spoke for the first time, "Something we need to protect – much as I believe you are doing. Now – are you interested in trading or not?"

The farmer snorted, that half-smile lighting up his face again. He rubbed the back of his neck, and looked at the two men behind him. "Well, come on then. Let me show you what we got."

We followed the three men deeper into the forest. Alex's knife still hidden in his boot, and my magic, were our only weapons. After pushing aside an insanely thick amount of foliage, we stepped into a clearing. There were five tents, some reinforced by sheet metal on one side, some with duct tape patched holes. Several gardens grew behind the tents, and behind that was the thicker forest again. The entire clearing wasn't more than 50 paces across.

As they led us closer toward the tents, women emerged. Ten in all; half had small children clinging to their legs. They wore clothes made of the thicker jean material. Cotton t-shirts didn't last very long in these conditions.

"How long have you all been here?" Alex asked, looking over the gardens and judging their growth with a practiced eye. You could normally tell the productivity of a commune by the health of their gardens.

"Long enough," the farmer answered. He rooted through our bag of supplies. "What do you want in exchange?"

"We need mosquito netting. And bug spray, if you have it. Maybe something for bites," I said.

He looked at me. "That's it?"

Alex spoke, "Maybe one of those water filtration systems, if you can spare it."

The farmer looked at us, eyebrows furrowed. "Are there more of you? A child, maybe?"

My blood ran cold. "What?"

He shrugged. "Just seems like if it were the two of you, you wouldn't be so concerned about bugs." He walked over to a pile of supplies under a tarp and pulled out a mosquito net. "We ran into someone a few weeks back. He traded some things, then said to be on the lookout for another group coming this way. Said they'd have a child with them. So I ask again, do you have a child with you?"

I looked around at the women and children. They looked back at me, eyebrows raised, hands fidgety. They painted a picture of reserved excitement and anticipation.

They must have Micah somewhere, I thought.

Alex came to the same conclusion more quickly than I did. The knife appeared in his hand.

The three men backed away.

"Whoa, whoa – hey. It's not what you think," the farmer said. He retrieved the bow on his back.

I reached out for the wind, sending a strong enough gust their way to throw them all on their backs. The bow and arrows went flying. I disintegrated the bow with a well-aimed fireball. Tightening my weaves around the arrows, I managed to catch them mid-air. Carefully controlled, it took a lot of energy. The arrows moved position, first up then down, settling into place. They wavered in front of the men's faces. Out of the corner of my eye, I watched Alex's shoulders sag. Properly out-gunned, he put away his knife.

"Where is he?" I took a step forward, fists clenched.

"He...he left. Safely – I swear!" the farmer stuttered.

I released one of the arrows at the farmer's son. It shot just past his head, nicking his ear. A trickle of blood ran down his shoulder.

"I ask again, where is he?" Now I aimed all my arrows at his son.

The farmer's eyes went wide, "He told us to follow you. He said there would be a child named Bee. And that there would be more allies, along the river. He went ahead, recruiting for you." The words tumbled out of his mouth, "And he said if you didn't believe me, to tell you…"

"What? Tell me what?" I wanted to strangle it out of him.

"Dirty boots."

My eyes widened, and a small burst of adrenaline shot through me, settling at the pit of my stomach like a heavy weight. That phrase struck close to home; too close.

I looked at Alex. "I think he's telling the truth."

Alex stepped over to my arrows, still hovering in the air. The longer lengths of his hair blew, giving away what held the arrows in place. "Okay, but we're keeping the weapons for now." He plucked them out of the air and I released the energy.

Alex walked over to me, hissing in my ear, "Where did you learn to do that?"

I glanced at him. "I've been practicing." Truth was, I slept very little. Practice kept the nightmares away. I turned to the farmer, who was picking himself up off the ground. "What's your name?" I asked.

"Robert. And this is my son, Robert Jr. – we call him Bobby. And this is my cousin, James." Each of the men nodded as they were introduced. Bobby held his ear with a rag. He avoided my gaze.

"What about all the women and children? You have collected quite a few." I studied them again. Their eyes were still wide, but not with shock or surprise. It seemed more like…approval.

And then I noticed the higher levels of energy that buzzed within the small clearing. "They have powers, don't they?"

"So I've been told." Robert grimaced.

I looked at the gardens behind the tent again, growing with more intensity than I'd seen in the past year.

"They're all Earths. This here's my wife, Margie." The eldest of the women stepped forward and nodded her head. "And her two cousins – and their kids." Robert pointed down the line. "Micah brought the rest. Said he's been *collecting* them along the way."

I flinched as I realized Micah had been doing what I had just accused Robert of.

But why just Earths?

Earth magic was slow, steady, and ran on much lower frequencies. It was very hard to detect. Perhaps it would easier to sneak past whatever detection rings Shawn set up.

"And what about the children?" I asked. There were several, ranging from infants up to teenagers. "Do they have powers?"

"Some of the older ones do – we're not sure about the babies."

I nodded. Still none of the women spoke. Robert ran a tight ship. "How long ago was Micah here?"

"It's been three weeks now."

I chewed at my lip. I supposed I could begin to forgive Micah for his absence. He was clearing our path to Shawn, making it safe for me and Bee – and giving me the tools I needed to defeat Shawn once I got there.

Still, I could use a good foot rub – like the one Alex gave Susan every night. I longed to be touched by Micah again, and even more so to laugh with him. I missed my partner.

I rubbed my temples, swallowing the hard lump fighting its way up my throat. "Well – you still want to come with us?"

Robert hesitated, looking back at his son. "What if we don't?"

"I'll take the women and kids anyway, along with whatever can be reaped from your gardens." We had plenty of canned food, but now I had an army to feed.

He looked at me sharply. "We'll starve come winter."

"Okay then – start packing up and let's get on the road," I said.

As the camp whirled into action, the women moving faster than the men, Alex stepped closer to me. "River."

"What?" I asked.

"Let's get on the river – not road."

"Oh, shut it." I pushed him toward the tents. "And go help. We're going to need more mosquito netting."

Chapter 9

No Rhythm

Fortunately, Robert's group had several kayaks and canoes, enough for the people and their supplies. Alex, Susan, Bee, and I stayed in our own canoe. I needed to get some of the women alone; none of them seemed to want to talk much, especially with Robert nearby.

Halfway through the second day with our new crew, Robert paddled up to me on his kayak. "We need to talk about supplies."

"What about them?" I pulled my oar out of the water, glancing up at him.

"They won't last us long; maybe another two weeks."

Alex continued to row behind me. "And who knows how many more we'll collect along the way."

"Maybe we need to be foraging – a little bit each day, and when we stop for the night."

Robert snorted, "I ain't no gatherer."

"So adapt." My words were clipped. "We've been doing it the past year and a half. How have you managed to get by?" I made a pointed glance at some the women in a canoe next to him.

He grumbled, but didn't answer.

I took a deep breath, backpedaling. It wouldn't do to chase Robert away now; or not yet, anyway.

"How will we know where Micah has people stationed?" I asked. "I'm sure they won't want to advertise who they are in case One Less comes their way."

Robert paddled deep twice, then rested his double oar in front of him. "He said there'll be signs you recognize. Oh, and the water filters. They were his design. Said to look for them along the path."

I looked over at another canoe holding two women, including Margie, and the bulk of the group's supplies. "Can you get me one?"

He nodded his head, slowed and angled his kayak over to the supply canoe. Why he wasn't in there with his wife, helping, was beyond me. He retrieved a water filter and paddled it back to me.

"Thanks." I looked at the contraption, turning it over in my hands before attempting to disassemble it. "Did he make these using your stuff or did he have these with him?"

"He had them with him. Said it came from another camp. But he showed us how to make them."

I'd seen several versions of water filters; they had quickly become the most essential personal item anyone could own. They ranged from complicated contraptions filled with rock, sand, and charcoal to a basic water filter of plastic bags suspended over pans of mucky water. It took forever for the condensation to drip off into smaller jars, but it was the purest way to retrieve water and it could be done from basically anything letting off condensation. Micah's seemed to be a combination of the two.

I dismantled the filter as Robert kept talking. "There will be Chakra Centers along the way; places that supposedly have an abundance of food and other resources. Wiccans teaching people how to live off the land or something."

I nodded, still inspecting the filter and shirking my navigational duties. Bee was doing a good enough job of that, pointing out every fish and rock she saw over the clear water. I searched the inside of the contraption, and each side of the material for a message. An 'I love you' or 'thinking of you' would have been enough. There was nothing.

I analyzed every small nick, scratch, and dent, piecing them together in my head, searching for a pattern. Still no luck.

"Kaitlyn," Susan said behind me. "Put it back together. I think his message to you is pretty clear."

"Yeah? What would that be?" I asked, with more bite in my voice than I intended. "Just keep paddling?"

"Something like that," Susan mumbled.

I reassembled the water filter and tossed it back to Robert, feeling sick to my stomach. I had been in a boat too long, and my old motion sickness was beginning to resurface. At least Bee didn't have that problem. I watched as she leaned over the side, swiping at fish that came close. She had been born on a boat – she was right at home.

"I think that Micah knows what he's doing, better than the three of us, at least," Alex spoke from the rear of the boat.

No one responded because we all knew he was right. But it wasn't what I wanted to hear. I was tired of straining my neck around each bend of the river, hoping to catch a glimpse of Micah waiting on his boat. I was tired of counting the days that passed since our handfasting ceremony. A year and a day was the agreement, then we tie the knot for good. That had come and gone. We should have been married by now.

Shawn's voice echoed through my head, "You can't have your cake and eat it, too."

Chills ran down my spine. I was pining after one man, who was leading me straight to the only man I never wanted to see again. And I was dragging everyone left in the world I cared for with me.

"This is so stupid," I said aloud.

"Stupid!" Bee repeated gleefully. "Stupid basherd!"

"That's it," Alex said. I heard him plunge his oar into the water and the entire canoe lurched toward the bank. He whistled, motioning for the boats ahead and behind to do the same. "Quick break," he yelled at them.

Once the bow hit soil, he jumped out and jerked the canoe to shore. He threw his oar back into the boat, narrowly missing Susan's head.

"Hey!" she shouted.

He took a deep breath. He was pissed. "I'm sorry. Could you please take Bee to use the restroom while I talk to Kaitlyn for a minute?"

Oh, crap.

Susan lifted Bee out of the boat, and started for the woods.

Bee started to squirm. "Fishies! I want to see fishies!"

Susan started to point out different tree species, making it seem far more interesting than it really was. I had to give her credit. No matter how much Alex and I treated her as a punching bag, she was always great with Bee.

Another canoe came ashore, the women gravitating toward Bee. "Wanna sing a song, little miss?"

"Yes," Bee squeaked. "Stupid basherd song!"

I cringed, watching the group walk off into the woods. After they disappeared, I turned to Alex and crossed my arms, "What?"

He waited for two more canoes to come ashore and their occupants to disappear into the woods before speaking, "Do you remember when you first came to the Chakra? You were a brand new addition to our team that had been together for years. You hadn't even known you had powers until we told you. But within months, you had us all standing behind you – willing to do anything for you."

"Except one," I mumbled.

He rolled his eyes. "Besides Shawn." He picked up a rock and skipped it across the river while we waited for the last of the boats to pull in. "And with the Athame, full of Shades. You had your own little army right there in the blade, teaching you to do more things than any Gaia in history."

I stayed silent, willing him to make his point.

"Which brings us to Easter Island. When we found you there, the entire island was standing ready to fight for you."

"For Bee," I corrected him.

"For *both* of you. Then your triumphant return to the Chakra turned out to be not so triumphant. But you worked at it, and won each Elemental over in your own way. In a way Susan, Micah, and I hadn't been able to do ourselves. What I'm trying to say, is if all of this has taught you anything – it should be to have confidence in yourself. Cut the bad mood, quit wishing Micah were here, and act like the Gaia you really are!"

By now, Alex's fists were clenched tight by his side.

I sighed. "Alex, I know I can do this – that isn't the problem. I just…"

"What?" he asked.

"I just don't *want* to do it by myself. I mean, I know I have you and Susan, but I need more. I need Micah." I kicked at the rocks at my feet. "I'm…you know, lonely. It's like this empty feeling in my chest that won't go away."

He put his hand on my shoulder. "You'll get him. But let him do his thing – let him help you in his own way. Deal?"

I didn't respond.

He lifted my chin up with the crook of his finger. "Come on, Katie. Is it a deal?" he asked, raising his eyebrows.

I smiled. "Deal."

"Good. Now let's go find Bee. I think she's this way. I hear curse words."

I laughed, letting him lead. He was better at spotting the infamous three leafs and red tinted stem of poison ivy than I was. We walked to a group of three women, clapping their hands and stomping their feet in rhythm. One sang a country western song. Susan stood off to the side, stretching out her limbs and watching the show.

I walked around the women and found Bee in front of them, squat-dancing in time to their music. She kept with the beat, but about the only dance move she had thus far mastered was bending her knees, then straightening them again. She'd mix it up a little by throwing her hands over her head for a few squats.

"Mommy, watch!" she squealed when she saw me.

"I see you, honey. Very good!" I began clapping my hands, joining the circle of the other women.

Bee looked up at me, a proud smile on her face that matched mine.

"Wait." Susan walked into the circle, raising her voice to be heard above us. "What is that?"

"It's our insane rhythmic beat," I said, stomping my feet now.

"You have no rhythm, Kaitlyn!" she shouted back. She wasn't teasing, her eyebrows were furrowed and lips pursed, the way she always did when she was concerned.

I stopped stomping and clapping, and noticed the ground vibrating beneath me. "Stop – stop!" I yelled at the women.

They abruptly stopped their routine, looking at me confused.

"Something's happening."

"Earth magic," one of them said. "But not from me."

"Me either," the other two chimed in.

"No, no. It's from Bee." All of us looked down at her. She had given up her squat dancing and was now spinning in circles, expending all of her pent up energy from being stuck in a canoe for days on end.

"Bee, honey. Come here – give mommy a hug."

She ignored me, continuing to spin.

"Bee, stop it now." I used my stern voice, lowering it a pitch.

Bee stopped and looked at me. Her lower lip quivered, embarrassed to be chastised in front of an audience.

Crap, if she throws a fit now, the earth vibrations might get worse.

I took a step toward her, tripped on a tree root, and fell smack onto my face. Now I had the audience. I rolled over onto my back, groaning and feeling my nose to make sure it wasn't bleeding.

Bee laughed. "Stupid Bashterd!"

The rest joined in her laughter.

Susan helped me up whispering, "Nice save."

I raised my eyebrow at her. "That wasn't on purpose."

"Wasn't it?" she asked. "Sometimes I wonder about you."

Alex returned from relieving himself in the woods. "Come on ladies." He zipped up his fly. "Time to get moving." He took Susan by the hand and looked at me. "What happened to your face?"

Chapter 10

Afternoon Dip

We were back on the Ohio, in separate canoes, with a new game plan. Lots of shore leave to allow for Bee's 'energy breaks'. I hadn't really thought of it until now, but the past few years had to be exhausting for her. We had constantly been on the move, and as soon as she had learned to walk, she did a lot of the hiking herself. She expended her energy in a physical sense, and as soon as that wasn't possible, she'd found another outlet.

"Why Earth this time?" Susan was obviously mulling it over, same as me. "The last time this happened, at the Chakra, it was with fire."

I shrugged. "I don't know. Maybe she channels the magic of the people around her."

"Was there a fire around her in the library that time?" Susan asked.

I thought back – it was a long time ago. Almost two years. Bee had been only four months old. "I think so. But Fire may be her best element. The Elementals on Easter Island thought she was a Fire."

Susan pushed our canoes apart with a paddle, glancing at my boat's other occupant. "I'll give you some privacy."

On our way back to the boats, I worked out a riding plan with Susan and Alex. We would split up to take turns riding with different people in order to discover the extent of their powers, and to look for any signs to pinpoint spies from One Less. Bee would stay with me or Susan; I had yet to get her a life jacket. Right now she was sleeping.

I looked at the back of the head of the woman in front of me. Margie's hair was wrapped in a tight bun with hardly a stray hair. I looked around for her husband, Robert. He was in his kayak, sticking close to the food canoe. Constantly accusing people of eating too much, he cautioned the supplies wouldn't last nearly long enough. He was probably right, but in a world with no modern conveniences, the sooner we learned to live off the land, the better.

"She's a good sleeper," Margie said, looking back at Bee.

"It's the water." I smiled. "Practically puts me to sleep every afternoon."

Margie pulled her oar out of the water and laid it across her lap. Ahead of the pack, we could spare a break. I kept mine in just to steer.

She turned around so we were facing each other. "Had you been on the river long before reaching us?"

I shook my head. "Not really. We came from West Virginia. It has been quite the goose chase, looking for Micah."

The hollow feeling grew in my chest every time I mentioned his name. It must have shown on my face. Margie asked, "Her father?"

"Yes." I didn't hesitate. Not by blood, but by all rights, at least in my opinion. "How was Micah, when you saw him?"

"He seemed…distracted. Perhaps even conflicted. Very antsy. Gave us the feeling there wasn't much time left."

"Until what?"

Margie shrugged. "We don't know. He never actually said."

I frowned. As far as I was concerned the worst already happened. Shawn's EMP went off, throwing much of the world back into the dark ages. One Less was quick to shut down any signs of progress. He still had to be stopped, but I was not sure what else Shawn could be up to, besides maintaining status quo.

Bee's snoring caused us both to look down.

"My daughter used to..." Margie trailed off.

That's interesting.

"You have a daughter?" Bobby was the only one introduced as their child. It dawned on me, "Oh. You *had* a daughter," I said, in a much softer voice.

She nodded.

"I'm sorry," I said. I wasn't going to be making any friends by bringing up people's dead children.

She took a deep breath, and stretched out her neck. "Robert and I only recently got married. I did it more out of necessity than anything else. He is a good...protector. Well – at least until you scorched his arrows." The corner of her mouth turned up in a teasing smile. "Anyway," she continued, "Bobby's my stepson. My husband of fifteen years, and my eight-year-old daughter, both died after Daybreak."

"Were they on a plane?" I remembered the one that had almost fallen on us, right outside the caves in Kentucky.

She shook her head. "No. We all got sick. Some kind of infection. I survived; they didn't. It was long enough after Daybreak that the pharmacies and hospitals had been wiped clean. Medicine was horded by those hoping to profit. I gave away everything I had, including my body, to try to get what they needed. Problem was, I had no idea what would help. I didn't find out fast enough."

My mouth hung open. Here she was, losing her family because there was no medicine to cure what might have been a basic infection, and we complained about no running water. "I'm so sorry," I said again. There really wasn't much else to say.

"It's not your fault," she said, looking down again at Bee. Little did she realize, it was my fault. Partially, anyway. I had the power to stop Shawn, but I had gotten there too late. My stomach lurched. I didn't want to be in this canoe anymore, sitting face to face with a woman whose husband and child I had killed.

I looked up at her again, for the first time seeing the subtle red streaks in her hair. I imagined them on a little girl in pigtails. Acid rose up into my throat. I leaned over the side and threw up. The edge of the boat tipped dangerously close to the surface of the river. Margie threw her weight to the other side to compensate, rocking the canoe even further. There was a split second of heart-stopping realization, and then we were all tossed into the icy Ohio River.

I reached for Bee, latching on and squeezing as tight as I could. We went under, but my head popped above the surface almost right away. I pulled with my arms, dragging Bee's weight up. Several agonizing seconds later, the bag of potatoes my arms were wrapped around came up.

"SUSAN!" I screamed at the top of my lungs. I heard splashes and shouting above the ring of panic in my ears. Susan was already in the water, by my side. She paused, closing her eyes and concentrating. Without a word, she jumped, piked her body and dove under. I tried to follow, but the water was murky. The sight of Susan's kicking feet disappeared in no time.

I came up for air. Margie hadn't resurfaced either. A horrible thought hit me. What if she did know how responsible I was for her husband's and child's deaths, and she was seeking revenge?

Without thinking, I sent blasts of air into the river. They were strong enough to create large but temporary divots in the water. There was still no sign of Bee – or Susan or Margie. I continued to tread water, shooting more divots and pulling at the river.

Out of the corner of my eye, I saw Alex's canoe pass. He searched the water, then paddled forward and searched again.

"You dumped a quarter of our food!" Robert's gruff voice was just behind me. "And my wife!"

My lip curled in a snarl. I shot another hole in the river, trying to tune him out.

I scanned the river. A few of our supplies had popped up to the surface, much further downstream. Despite the calm surface, the undertow was strong. It was possible Bee had gotten picked up by it. Alex was still in his canoe. He threw his oar into the boat, and reached down into the water, grabbing at something.

Robert continued pestering me. "You want to throw me in too? How can we follow you? How can we trust you? You have no idea what you are doing." He angled his kayak so the tip of it moved in front of me.

The river pushed me into the side of his boat. I put my hands on it, trying to pull my head far enough out of the water to see what was happening.

Alex had come up with Susan, who held a limp Bee in her arms.

"Hey!" Robert yelled. "Get off." He raised his paddle, aiming at my already slippery grasp of the side of his boat.

I pulled, yanking on his kayak. As the edge submerged, I ripped the paddle from his hand. Robert went upside down just as the river turned rough, reacting to my energy. I got pulled under without having the chance to suck in air first. My body somersaulted until I was so disoriented I didn't know which way was up.

Bee would have never been able to hold her breath through this. My elbow hit hard rock. I forced my feet against it and pushed off. I swam until my mouth breached the surface. I got a quick glance of Alex's canoe, now parallel to me. He already had a bag valve mask out.

"Bee!" I managed to shout until I got sucked back under. I floundered around again. My limbs were growing tired and refusing to do what I wanted. I didn't go nearly so deep this time, and popped up again without hitting the bottom first. Now the canoe was upstream from me. Susan leaned over Bee. I could see water particles being pulled from her mouth and returning to the river. Could her tiny lungs even hold that much water and still function afterward?

Another surge of adrenaline hit me. I tapped into the air element, weaving a windstorm just above my head. Clouds rolled in, thundering at the disturbance in the atmosphere. I raised my arms and lifted myself from the river. It required more control than I had ever used with the air element; ten times as much as I used with Robert's arrows.

Water dripped as I flung my body forward. It was a hard landing in Alex's canoe, but he and Susan managed to keep it upright. I turned to see Bee's blue lips, water still trickling from them.

"That's enough," Alex said to Susan. "Let me do the chest compressions again."

I was frozen still, too scared to move. My unfortunate reaction to facing down my worst nightmare. Susan and Alex were focused, determined to bring Bee back to life. Alex placed his hands at her sternum and pushed, counting out loud. "One, two, three."

Susan squeezed the bag valve mask, forcing air into her lungs.

"One, two, three."

In contrast to my frozen over limbs, my stomach felt like it was on fire. It grew as I stared at Bee's blue lips, obscured when Susan placed the mask back over them.

"One, two, three," Alex said again, his voice cracking.

The fire reached my chest now, and my cheeks were going hot.

One, two, three. I counted inside my head with Alex, willing him not to give up. Too much time had passed. The fire was molten hot, consuming me.

"You bitch, are you trying to kill everybody?!" Robert yelled, bobbing up and down on the other side of the river.

I released my fire directly above his head at a tree on the bank. The tree cracked and fell forward into the river. Robert went under just before the tree hit. The huge wake rocked our canoe. We all came a few inches off the seats, including Bee. When she landed, a splash of water was forced from her lungs and she began coughing.

Alex rolled her on her side, patting her back. "There, there," he said. "Get it all out."

As soon as she had the breath, she began to cry. I dropped to my knees, my eyes also brimming with tears. Across from me, a drenched Susan sat back, hands shaking.

Alex pulled out several blankets and wrapped all three of us, then retrieved his oar and steered us toward the bank. I glanced back. Robert clung to the fallen tree trunk; both making quick progress down the river. Beyond him, on the opposite shore, I spotted Margie pulling herself up onto the bank. She turned just in time to see her husband go floating past, still cursing me. She shook her head, then placed her hand on the ground beside her. Seconds later, vines tumbled down from branches hanging over the water. Robert and his trunk became tangled. His forward momentum stopped until another canoe could catch up and retrieve him.

Before I could look back at Margie, we were jolted forward as our canoe hit land. Alex helped us each out; we all shook with exhaustion and cold. Bee's crying had subsided. She clung to my neck, hiccupping. Susan and I stood, side by side, saying nothing while Alex tied up the boat then started a fire. Half of the rest of the convoy pulled up on our side of the river; half on the other.

Alex intercepted them as they came ashore, keeping them clear of us despite their concern to see if we were ok. He suggested everyone start setting up camp for the night. We sat around a fire, bare under blankets while our clothes dried nearby. Alex passed out portions for dinner, but I was too upset to eat. Bee was ravenous; she finished mine for me.

An hour later, the sun sank behind the trees and Bee fell asleep in my lap. My eyes had barely left the fire since Alex built it. Alex was still running around, setting up camp, getting people organized, and making sure boats and supplies were secure. Once it was full dark, he sat down at the fire beside me and Susan.

He poked at the fire, glancing up at us. "Everyone okay?"

No one answered. He addressed us individually, "Susan?"

"I'm fine," she said, tight-lipped.

Was she mad? I suppose she had every right to be. She was hard at work saving my child while I was busy flying around, knocking down trees, and dumping more people in the river.

"Kaitlyn?"

"Huh?" I said. My eyes flitted from Susan over to Alex.

"You okay?" he asked.

I looked down at Bee, and pulled the blanket tighter around her. "I'm not getting back in the river until we get her a lifejacket."

"Agreed," said Alex and Susan at the same time.

More silence, and more poking at the fire.

"Did *you* eat anything?" Susan asked Alex.

"No. I'm going to take a canoe across the river; make sure the camp over there has everything they need."

"Eat something first," she said. It wasn't a suggestion; it was an order.

"Yes, ma'am." Alex stood up and went over to another fire they were using to cook food.

Susan picked up Alex's stick and assumed fire duty.

I stared into the glowing coals. "Susan..."

She paused poking.

"I just wanted to say...that if anything ever happens to me—"

"Don't," she interrupted.

I glanced at her.

"There isn't any need to have that conversation because nothing is going to happen to any of us. Micah, Alex, you, Bee, and me. We're all going to be just fine."

It really was wishful thinking, considering I was thrown into the mix.

I leaned back, adjusting my legs under Bee. "You guys have really been great to her. Thanks for saving her today, and thanks for...well, just everything."

She sighed, put the stick down, and scoot closer to me. "You're welcome." She wrapped her arm around me, laid her chin on my shoulder, and looked down at Bee. Susan straightened. "Our pants."

"What about them?" I looked over at them drying across a log.

"Didn't Alex say they can float?"

He had.

"Sure weren't floating for me today," I said.

"You have to take them off," Alex said, entering our clearing while eating an apple. He wiped juice off his chin. "Tie off each leg, then cinch down the waist."

I stood, and handed Bee to Susan.

She asked, "What are you—?"

"Geez, Kaitlyn," Alex cut off Susan's question as he turned his back to me.

The blanket was already on the ground at my feet.

"A little warning next time?" Alex mumbled.

"Oh, please. We're all adults here." It wasn't like he had never accidentally walked in on me when I was changing, or using the bathroom – in the woods.

I put on my oversized shirt before I grabbed my pants. Under Alex's direction, though he still refused to look, I tied each leg off.

"Now hold them at the waist, and bring them up, then down quick, catching the air. Cinch the waist straps down," he said.

It took me a couple tries.

"It will work better when the waist is in the water," Alex said, having turned around.

"By the time she is in the water, it will be too late," Susan said.

I studied the pants, "We could seal the waist up, instead of tying it off."

Alex picked out the seeds and threw the core of his apple in the fire. "I'll check with the other side if they have anything for that." He handed me the seeds.

"Thanks. Oh – and Alex?" I looked up at him. "See if anyone can spare some pants."

Chapter 11

Nightmares

"Easy there, princess." Shawn's words echoed through my head. His blue eyes floated in front of me, but they were familiar. I was able to ignore them. It was the same dream that always plagued my sleep. The circle of fire surrounded us, Shawn held a knife, and there was something at my back.

This time, I would make a decision. Maybe it would end the repeating nightmare. I turned, leaving my back vulnerable to Shawn and his knife.

"Where's the baby?" I heard him ask behind me. I ignored him.

The thing at my back was a large ball of light, steady and strong. It didn't flicker like in the last dream. When it began to rise, I pulled at it, willing it back down. It didn't stop; but it slowed. I did have some control over it, but my grasp was slippery, making the task difficult.

I pulled again, and the light ceased its upward momentum. I worked, struggling as though my fingertips were barely holding on.

I took a deep breath and tried again, aware of Shawn breathing down my neck.

"Come on!" I shouted at it. The ball obliged, falling the rest of the way toward me. I extended my hand, and the ball grew smaller, fitting in my palm. Within seconds, it winked out, extinguishing itself. I smiled.

The circle of fire around us roared in reaction. Blood mixed with the flame and it grew higher and thicker, closing in on us.

I turned to Shawn.

He was smiling. "Too late."

* * *

The next morning, after a rough patch of unintentional head-butting by Bee, I woke to Alex and Susan talking together by the fire.

Did they even sleep?

Susan's hair told me yes. Alex – I wasn't so sure.

Bee snored; her head heavy on my arm. Pins and needles raced through my limb from the weight. I had to pee, but I wasn't quite ready to rouse the little one. The smell of coffee tempted me. I turned to look at Alex and Susan. Their backs were to me, but I could see them working together to pour boiling water over crushed beans. The steamy liquid ran through a filter and into a camp cup. They took turns sipping from it.

"I miss cream," Susan said, voice low.

"We had some a few months ago, when we came across that dairy farm," Alex reminded her. Susan stuck out her tongue in distaste. He pretended not to notice. "At least you had that – I haven't seen sugar in over a year."

Susan took another sip, "We should save some for Kaitlyn."

"These beans can be used again," Alex placed another pot of water over the fire for boiling. "And here, let's warm up these canned peaches for Bee. She'll be hungry as soon as she wakes up. She deserves a treat."

"Do you think she'll be scared to get back on the river?" Susan asked.

I hadn't thought of that.

"I don't know. I'm a little more worried about how Kaitlyn will act."

Susan nodded. "Have you noticed the bags under her eyes? They are getting darker by the day. I don't think she sleeps much anymore." Susan kept lowering her voice.

"Hell, her nightmares are keeping me up now," said Alex. "Good thing Bee is a heavy sleeper."

Heavy head, too. I flexed my arm muscles. Come to think of it, last night was the best night's sleep I had in a while. Maybe it was just pure exhaustion.

Alex started analyzing my nightmares, "Do you think it's because of what happened?"

What happened? I strained to hear them.

Susan shrugged. "She hasn't mentioned anything leading up to Daybreak. Maybe it's a sort of memory loss."

"Or maybe just a subconscious block, but one day the memories are going to catch up with her and it won't be pretty." Alex threw his head back, finishing the drink.

They couldn't have been talking about what happened when I was kidnapped by Shawn; Susan and I had had a few conversations about that during the past year. We knew we had to face him again, and talking about him openly let us fear him less. It was extremely therapeutic.

Bee whimpered, and both turned to look at us. I closed my eyes, feigning deep breaths of sleep.

"Come on, they'll be up soon. Turn the peaches so they don't burn. I'll pour more coffee," Alex said.

Thanks, Bee. I would have to discover the source of the mystery nightmares on my own.

Chapter 12

Thunder

"Earthquake in Huntington," Alex said as we pushed our canoe into the river.

"Huh?" I asked, preoccupied with the balancing act of moving to the front, with Bee in one arm and an oar in another. It wouldn't do to immediately dump Bee in the river on her first day back in.

"The camp across the river linked up with someone from Huntington last night on their ham radio. They said there was an earthquake three days ago." Alex pushed the canoe into deeper water, then jumped in himself without a wobble. His learning curve with this whole canoe thing was much steeper than mine.

"Wasn't that the big city we just went through?" Susan asked, sitting in the very front, playing navigator. We decided to stick with the fab four after yesterday's incident; no more splitting up.

"Yep," said Alex.

"So what are you saying?" I asked.

"I'm not saying anything, except that maybe we ought to reach out. See what information we can gather about places we left, as well as our next destination. Whether the natural disasters are caused by someone in our group or not," he cleared his throat, "we don't want to be leaving a trail."

Susan glanced at me over her shoulder. "Could just be a coincidence."

"Could be," I agreed. Desperation crept up my chest. She was finding excuses, trying not to be obvious about the truth.

So was Alex. "Could be a spy from our group, leaving bread crumbs the only way they know how," he suggested in a much lower voice.

"Maybe..." I said. I looked down at Bee, busy organizing her play area for the day. *Oh fine, I'll just say it.* "Or it could be me and Bee."

Bee looked up at the mention of her name and shot me a smile. I touched her dimple with my finger, "You are trouble; you know that?"

"Let's just see how it plays out," Alex mumbled from behind me.

Very shortly, we'd be in Louisville, Kentucky. As the morning hours passed, the trees that dotted the riverbanks became sparse, replaced by wide open parks and fields. Buildings, many just showing the first signs of neglect with plants growing out of gutters and broken windows, began outnumbering the trees. There were people, at first just one or two, then larger groups of a dozen or more, working along the riverbanks. Washing clothes, filtering water, or bathing – they all stopped their work to watch us row past. Bee waved to every single one of them. Several waved back, smiling.

"A different perspective from our hiking trails," Alex said from behind me.

I nodded. "When we started to see fewer and fewer people, I thought we were dying out. Turns out everyone was just flocking to freshwater sources."

"And thriving," Susan chimed in, staring at a fenced off area full of chickens. "Remember all the bones we found?"

I nodded. On our way from Mammoth Cave to D.C. then West Virginia, we saw countless remains of dogs and cats, sometimes even horses, lying exposed by a snuffed out campfire. "People had to eat something once the packaged food ran out."

I touched the bag of canned vegetables at my side. The chickens, even scratching around in the mud as they were, looked far tastier.

A dog ran around the pen, playing. It was one of the lucky ones.

We passed under a series of bridges, and all at once the groups of people grew in number – so much so they couldn't be classified as groups. It was just one, large mass.

"How are all these people surviving?" I wondered aloud.

"The rivers support the masses," Alex said. "Look Bee!" He pointed to five horses tied up by the river, drinking.

Five horses! I never thought I'd see another horse.

"Big dog!" Bee shouted at them.

We laughed. "Horse, honey. That's a horse – neigh!"

Bee spent the next two hours practicing her horse sounds until one loud, horn blast drowned her out. She jumped into my lap. "Thunder!"

I brushed the hair out of her face and kissed her forehead. "No – not thunder. Some kind of horn." I turned around and looked at Alex, my eyebrows raised in question.

He shrugged.

We slowed the canoe, and motioned the rest of the group to do the same. Robert and Margie, now in a double kayak, were the exception. They pushed forward to investigate, both looking at me as they passed. Robert had a set chin and narrowed eyes, Margie glanced over me from head to toe, then Bee.

Looking for injuries, perhaps? Would she be relieved or disappointed that we had none?

I didn't get a chance to find out. They rounded the river bend before I could read the expression on her face. Their kayak disappeared from sight. A long silence seemed to last forever, all eyes just beyond the trees, seeking out the tip of their red kayak. Another horn blast. This one put me on edge. The energy in the atmosphere heightened as Elementals put their powers at the ready.

I wanted to shout out to hold fire, until we saw the whites of their eyes or something, but the truth was I was a hair away from blasting down those trees myself so I could see what was happening. Finally, Robert and Margie came paddling upstream. Robert waived his arm, gesturing the rest of us forward. They both looked excited.

"Susan, can you tell what it is from here?" I asked as we put our oars back in the water.

She put her hand in the water, too. "Something big."

"Care to be more specific?"

"Can't." She looked back at me. "Fill Bee's lifejacket, just in case."

I looked down, it was nearly deflated. Our stitching job wasn't holding the air very well.

"Careful, Kaitlyn – we don't want to attract any unwanted attention," Alex said.

I rolled my eyes. I was *always* attracting unwanted attention; it was inevitable. I used energy to inflate the pants hanging around Bee's neck. She didn't notice, still staring at the direction of the horn.

As we rounded the bend, the horn sounded again and the source revealed itself. I craned my neck up to see a large steamboat barreling down on us. Four stories high, with black and gold steam columns and red, decorative trim; the ship was straight out of the 1920's.

I blinked, then rubbed my eyes.

"Row!" Alex shouted. "Row, row, row!" Our convoy of canoes split down the middle as everyone scrambled to get their oars in the water. Our canoe shot forward.

I looked back; everyone appeared to make it out of the way in time.

"Sorry!" Someone from the top deck of the steamboat shouted apologies. I gave them a dirty look, then did the same to Robert, who was laughing.

Something else caught my eye as the steamboat passed. Dragged alongside it was several large water filters. "Look!" I shouted.

Susan turned, and a wide grin spread across her face.

"Micah's been here," I breathed.

They were exactly the same as we found near Robert's camp.

"Let's pull in over there," I said, pointing to a large, cemented area that sloped down into the water. "We need to check it out."

The other boats followed our lead. As Robert came closer, I resisted the urge to dump him in the water again. Just barely. He was still laughing when they pulled ahead of us. As soon as our canoe hit cement, Margie was there, pulling us in.

"Sorry," she said, voice lowered. "I had no idea that thing could pick up speed like that. I don't think they heard my warning shouts."

I put Bee on my hip and took Margie's extended hand for help out of the canoe.

"Are you guys okay after yesterday?" she asked. "When I came up and saw you, but not Bee, my heart skipped a beat. I went back under and almost got caught in the undertow and I just got scared—"

"Margie, come help with the boat," Robert growled at her. Their kayak was completely out of the water. What help he needed was beyond me.

She rolled her eyes and turned back to me, smoothing out her hair. "I should've kept looking—"

"No," this time I interrupted her. "It wasn't your fault; don't worry about it."

She nodded. "I'm glad everyone is ok. Thank God for Susan."

"Margie!" Robert yelled again.

"I'm coming." Margie squeezed my hand, wiggled Bee's bare toes and walked away.

I turned, watching Susan pack a small bag with Bee's toys, a change of clothes, and extra food.

Yes, I thought. *Thank God for Susan. Susan and Alex both.*

Chapter 13

The Spirit of Evansville

"Welcome aboard your ship," the captain held out his hands in a grand gesture as we walked up the gangplank. I paused in the middle of wiping grime from Bee's cheek to look over my shoulder. There was only Alex – standing off to the side with his arms crossed. The captain was, in fact, addressing me.

"My...my ship?"

He smiled, nodding his head with enthusiasm.

"I don't follow."

"Come, come. Let me show you around. I'll remain to drive you down the river, of course."

"No – me drive!" Bee shouted, kicking to be let down.

As soon as I set her on the ground she ran for the captain's outstretched hands. Alex stepped in between the two, swooping Bee up in his own arms.

The captain shrugged. "Looks like I've got myself a co-pilot." He tousled her hair and walked away with a skip in his step, leaving me like an idiot, with my hand in the air and speechless.

I glanced at Alex, who was glaring at the captain.

"Come on," I said, nudging him forward. "Let's at least hear him out."

"Now this ship wasn't a steamboat until after Daybreak," the captain waited for us to catch up. He reached over and pinched Bee's cheek. "No it wasn't. We had plans, but weren't motivated to put them in effect until the diesel stopped coming."

We followed him down some stairs. The elevators had a large 'out of order' sign posted.

He continued, "Daybreak was good in a lot of ways like that."

It was the first time I'd heard anyone refer to Daybreak as a good thing. Bee leaned over to pull on the captain's beard.

"Honey, be careful." I said.

"She's fine. I'm Captain Carl, by the way." He stopped suddenly and stuck out his hand in delayed introduction.

"Oh, I'm Kaitlyn." I shook his hand. "And this is Alex, and…well – I guess everyone else is busy."

"Yes, yes – I'm having them load the canoes and all your supplies on the boat. Eventually we may reach a point where the steamboat is too big for the river. Anyway." He turned down the stairs again. "Took us over a year, but we got her ready just in time for Micah to come along."

"I'm sorry – if you could explain how exactly he purchased the boat?" I couldn't imagine what Micah had traded.

"Well, for one – this entire community owes him and The Seven. Under their guidance, the Wiccans were able to build our own Chakra Center."

"Chakra Center?" I looked at Alex, eyebrows raised.

He shrugged.

"Community-based farms that are able to support any who come. Permaculture at its finest," touted the captain.

"What else did he give you?" I asked.

"A promise."

"What kind of promise?" I narrowed my eyes, taking Bee from Alex.

"I get to captain one of the new hybrid power stations. They are under construction just off the coast of California, and in the Gulf, and at the Great Lakes. After I drop you off, I'll be headed to California to take up my post."

We were just outside a large steel door now. Alex paused. "And you believe him?"

Captain Carl turned, crossing his arms. "Why? Is there a reason I shouldn't believe him?"

Hybrid power stations? I glanced at Alex. He looked just as lost as me, though I wasn't willing to call any of it into question. I just wanted Micah to pop out from behind the door.

Captain Carl pushed his glasses up on his nose. The frame was duct taped together. "I'm a Coast Guard vet, I'll have you know. Twenty years. Just because this boat has never been more than a mile from the dock, doesn't mean I'm not capable."

Alex held up one hand. "I'm sorry, I'm just confused."

"Well." The captain spun the dial on a padlock and opened the door. "Allow me to enlighten you."

My shoulders sagged; no Micah. Instead, three huge boilers took up the entire room.

"Cast iron and bronze. Thankfully we had these babies built before Daybreak. Basically, we boil water straight from the river inside, and the resulting steam powers the boat."

"How do you boil the water?" Alex asked, walking around one of the boilers.

"By burning trash, mostly. Oh – and office furniture. No one needs it anymore."

I stepped closer, and Bee reached out to touch the shiny cylinder.

"Don't touch!" I snatched her hand back. "It's hot!"

She looked at Captain Carl for confirmation.

"Nope," he said. "The outer shell stays cool to the touch." He leaned against it with one hand to demonstrate. "Although, they have been known to explode."

I looked at him, mouth open.

"No incidents with these particular boilers yet. Top of the line, they are!" He patted it.

"Okay. This room is officially off limits for anyone under the age of, well – me." I said.

"Ohhh," Bee let out a disappointed sigh, as if she knew what I meant.

"Come on." Captain Carl shut the door to the boiler room as we exited. "I'll show you the captain's bridge next."

Last time I was in one of those, I thought, *I...well...I met Bee.*

Alex was quizzing the captain about the hybrid power stations.

Captain Carl held open the door to the captain's bridge for us. "They've been building them since before Daybreak, preparing to run the country on renewable energy. A combination of solar, wind, and hydro-power; eventually there will be enough power to support the population."

"What about One Less?" Alex asked. "I thought they were shutting down any attempts at energy."

The Captain shrugged. "I guess not renewable energy. I've heard almost all of Germany is powered on solar and wind, and has been since Daybreak. They've had no issues with One Less."

A man, standing at the wheel inside the captain's bridge, perked up at our conversation, inserting his own two cents, "Hungary is powered by its nuclear reactors. They were at thirty-nine percent before Daybreak but almost the entire country has power now."

Captain Carl rubbed his temples. "Here we go again." He addressed my raised eyebrow. "This is Arnold, the First Mate."

Arnold looked at Carl with crossed arms, "You only prefer renewable because you've been promised one of those hybrid thingies."

"Hybrid power stations," Carl almost yelled. He threw his hands in the air. "I prefer renewables because there is no chance of nuclear meltdown!" He glanced at us. "Sorry – we've had this conversation more than once."

Arnold didn't notice. "Renewables are inconsistent – you know, those pesky clouds and all. And wind doesn't blow constantly. Besides, too much land needs clearing for wind and solar farms."

Carl rolled his eyes, then turned to us to explain. "And the hybrid power stations resolve all that. Wind farms do typically take up a lot of space, which is why they are being installed in the ocean. The stations are basically large floating vessels that patrol the wind farms. Plus, they are outfitted with solar panels and hydro-electricity pumps. The three renewable resources combined allow for more consistent power. Developments in energy storage let us store more power, accounting for dry spells."

Alex interrupted, "The Seven itself has had this debate for some years. Nuclear vs. renewables; which way does the world move forward?"

I rubbed my temples. "And the consensus?"

He shrugged. "Never came to one. Susan was all for hydro, of course. Cato seemed to be for nuclear."

"What about you and Micah?" I asked.

"We just sort of heard out each argument, then tried to keep the peace."

I cleared my throat. "And Shawn?"

"He never really stuck around for the heated debates." Alex walked over to the large windows. "Um, Captain Carl?"

"Hmm?" The captain flipped switches at the helm.

"Are we leaving already?"

I joined Alex at the window, Bee still on my hip. Most of the open decks were taken up with our convoy of canoes and kayaks, along with our supplies. Someone was lifting the onramps up.

The captain nodded his head. "Gotta keep on schedule."

I sighed. I could've used a few days on land. The buildings, even overgrown with vines as they were, were a welcome site.

The captain tapped one of the steam output gauges. "Barrel two is only at half capacity again. Check it out after we get underway," he told his second in command. "Have you ever considered that mining for uranium could create just as much damage to the earth as mining for natural gases and coal?"

Arnold was undeterred, "Solar panel construction consists of no less than a dozen minerals, all mined in various places across the world. Cadmium, copper, titanium dioxide—"

"Well what about radioactive waste?" Carl interrupted.

"Miniscule at best. A soda can's worth of waste over the entire lifetime of each person. Can be buried with insurances of a million years of safe storage."

"Still not worth the risk, in my opinion," mumbled Carl.

They both paused in their work and glanced at me over their shoulders, as if they wanted a final ruling on the issue.

"I'm still on the fence, guys. Sorry." Actually, I was on top of the fence, standing on my tiptoes, searching for Micah. I looked at Alex for support.

"There are advantage and disadvantages for both." Alex was turning out to be quite the diplomat.

The vessel jumped forward and Captain Carl sounded the horn. Bee kicked to be let down, and ran to the captain. "Me, me!"

He laughed and scooped her up. "Wait for it…wait for it…"

I exchanged a confused glance with Alex. Arnold had a smile on his face. Carl continued, "wait for it…and…there! We are officially further than I've ever taken the boat!"

The two men cheered. Bee pulled the horn.

"Oh, man." Alex brought his hand to his face, shaking his head back and forth.

"Seriously?" I asked.

"Yep. Before 2002, we had to move it four feet from port every few months. A state requirement. But after that – no need to sail it unless there was an emergency."

"Like this?"

"Yep," he said, "like this."

"Too bad we couldn't take *that* boat." Alex pointed out the window. A large battleship-looking boat sat in the water close to shore, the front half almost completely submerged. The number 325 painted white on the bow stood prominent out of the water. The only redeeming quality of the steamship compared to the navy vessel was the fact that is was river-worthy.

The captain's shoulders sagged. "Yes, well. Lots of other people wanted to take that boat somewhere. After all the fighting, turns out what they should've been looking for was a driver." He smiled to himself. "We're lucky the LST was there, though – kept everyone away from good 'ole *Spirit of Evansville*, here." He patted the instrument panel.

I smiled at the irony as we passed the navy warship. I was charging into yet another battle with Shawn, this time on a gambling steamboat with the potential of exploding on its own.

The captain leaned over and said in a low voice, "Toddler life jackets are in that bin, there." He glanced over his shoulder, motioning with his chin.

"Oh, well in that case…" I walked over to the bin and pulled one out. I glanced at Alex. "Looks like we're staying."

Chapter 14

Thirsty?

"Did you get him?" Shawn asked the guard posted outside the building. Shawn, Clay, and a small contingency of Elementals rolled up to the state capitol building.

"Inside, sir." The guard took their bikes.

"Don't call me sir."

"Yes, S...Shawn."

Clay's short legs had to work twice as hard to match Shawn's pace up the steps and down the length of the building. They were directed underground by various guards posted, and into a small storage room.

"Shut the door," Shawn ordered once everyone squeezed inside. Shawn plus four Elementals, one of each power, hovered over a man tied to a chair in the center of the room. Clay sweated profusely, as did the man in the chair.

Shawn removed the duct tape from the man's mouth. The captive rubbed his cheeks against his shoulder, but didn't speak.

"Gentlemen – this is the CEO of the building company for Utah's first nuclear power plant." Shawn circled the man, then stopped in front of him, bending down to the captive's eye level. "What are you doing in Utah, rather than your posh headquarters in New York?"

The man cleared his throat, eyeing the rest of the group. "I was here when Daybreak hit." He looked around. "Who are you? What do you want with me?"

Shawn didn't answer his questions. "And so you decided to hang out; mooch off the Mormons."

"I...I..." the man stuttered, then trailed off.

"Understandable. Most of them were more than prepared for an event like Daybreak."

The man sighed. "I've been tied to this chair for days. I am sitting in a puddle of my own piss and I am thirsty as hell. What do you want?"

Shawn stood, moved behind the CEO, and massaged his shoulders. "I want to know where you have been storing all the supplies for your new facility."

"Why would you—?"

Shawn's fingers, digging into the CEO's wiry muscles, cut him off. "Let's just move past the bluffing stage, shall we? You said you're thirsty?"

Shawn stepped back and nodded to the Water Elemental. He opened a bottle hanging from his belt loops. Small droplets appeared in the air, joining together to form a fist-size globe of sloshing water.

Every last Water at The Seven had more control than that, Clay thought.

The CEO's eyes shifted from the globe of water to the Elemental. "What *are* you?"

Clay slapped his forehead. *Wrong thing to say.*

The Elemental's stare went cold. He reared his hand back, then forward, shoving the water straight down the CEO's throat.

Clay stepped forward, hands extended to help. Shawn pushed Clay back. Clay swallowed hard as Shawn's eyes bore into him. They almost glowed blue in the dark storage room.

The CEO gagged and choked. Every time he managed to expel bits of water, it was redirected right back into his mouth. With one hand still on Clay's chest, Shawn checked his watch. "Stop."

The Elemental extracted droplets from the CEO, but it wasn't fast enough. His face was going white.

"I said stop!" Shawn shouted at the Elemental.

The Elemental narrowed his eyes in concentration, and extended both hands using physical motions to pull the water out. Sweat beaded on his forehead. The CEO went limp.

Shawn pushed the Elemental out of the way, and pressed his hand to the CEO's pulse. "Alive," he nodded. He slapped the CEO hard across the cheek. The man jolted awake, and took a deep breath.

Clay let out a sigh of relief. The CEO's eyes darted around the room, as if he had just woken up from a nightmare.

"Welcome back," Shawn said. "Where are you keeping the storage supplies for your nuclear facility?"

"We…we don't. There was a chance the permits wouldn't be approved. It wasn't worth the risk."

"Bullshit!" Shawn turned on him and the CEO leaned back in his seat. "You suits had enough money to push anything through. Although…there are always shortcuts to be had." He tapped his chin. "What were your planned shortcuts?"

The CEO furrowed his eyebrows. "I don't know what you mean."

"Hmm," Shawn mumbled. "You've met our Water."

The CEO automatically leaned away from the Water.

"Wanna see what our Fire can do?"

Flames lit up the room.

The screeching sound of metal against metal made Clay cringe as the CEO backed his chair away.

"Fort Calhoun," he said in a panic. "Nebraska. Right on the Platte River. It was being decommissioned, and we arranged to have a majority of the parts and materials refitted for ours."

"Now we're talking," Shawn said, rubbing his hands together. "How far did it get?"

"The first—" he cut off, leaning away further as the Fire came closer. "Can you get that out of my face?"

The Fire backed off.

"The first shipment was ready to go, but then…"

"Then what?" Shawn looked like he wanted to strangle him.

"Then Daybreak. The shipment is probably still sitting there on the river."

The Fire released his element, and the tension in the room dissipated.

Shawn turned, putting his arm around Clay and escorting him out. The Air and the Water followed. Heat licked at their backs. Shawn paused. "You, too!" he yelled over his shoulder.

Clay tried glancing back, but Shawn kept a tight grip on Clay's arm.

The heat had gone away when the Fire followed the group, but the man was left behind – still tied to the chair. Clay hesitated, indecision racking his brain.

"You with me?" Shawn asked.

Now is not the time, Clay thought. "Yeah," Clay followed Shawn and the rest of the group outside.

They retrieved their bikes, and headed back for their island. Shawn kept a slow pace.

"A nuclear facility – here?" Clay asked, angling his bike next to Shawn's.

"Country has gotta run on something," Shawn said.

Clay glanced at the Wasatch Mountain Range. They were not hand-carved; they were thrust together over time. Whatever fault line did that was still there, which meant the potential for earthquakes. And their fearless leader wanted to build a nuclear power plant right on top of it.

Shawn watched Clay eyeing the mountains. "Lake Utah is the largest, natural freshwater lake West of the Mississippi. Nuclear stations need tons of water to cool down the core, and I plan on building a really big one."

"Why not saltwater? You can build this thing in the middle of the ocean, away from the population."

"Saltwater corrodes the lines and valves. Besides – look at this place!" He gestured to the Wasatch and the much smaller range to the west. "It is completely protected."

Clay ran a hand down his beard.

Shawn continued, "No one cares about Utah except the Mormons, and they're used to being pushed around. I'm not too worried about earthquakes; that's what I have you for." Shawn patted Clay's shoulder, hard.

Clay steered back and forth, thrown off balance. By the time he had his bike under control, he had to pedal hard to catch back up.

Shawn was still talking, "Though, I can't say the same for some of the other facilities I have planned."

"There will be more?" Clay huffed.

Shawn shrugged. "As many as there needs to be to power the world."

"How are you going to mine for the uranium?"

"What – you can't find it for me with all your 'Earth' magic?" Shawn smirked.

"Sorry – I'm not powerful enough for that." Clay grimaced. He'd only seen one person with that kind of power, and she wasn't with One Less. "So…" Clay peddled harder to keep up with Shawn. They approached a hill. "How are we gonna get to Fort Calhoun?"

Shawn looked down at his bike. "The rivers will be the fastest."

Chapter 15

Patterns

Ohio, Mississippi, Missouri, Platte. I ran through the list of rivers again. It worked better than counting sheep when I was trying to fall asleep. Sheep reminded me of fluffy pillows; something I had too long gone without. Bee stirred next to me. If I wasn't careful, I'd wake her too. Then there'd be no sleeping for anyone on the deck. I slid out of my sleeping bag and made my way to the back of the steamboat, out of view of the night watch and away from the sleeping mass that was my new army. I leaned over the railing and watched the churning water left in our wake. I was partly relieved to be on a boat powered by something other than my own arms. Perhaps we could outrun whatever was chasing us. I glanced behind me at Bee.

Or maybe not.

At the same time, we were approaching our destination much faster, and we weren't nearly ready to face Shawn and One Less again. I squeezed the railing, thinking of our last battle with them. I'd almost won. I was seconds away from destroying his EMP with Akasha, but something caused me to release too early. Something horrible had happened...

Ohio, Mississippi, Missouri, Platte. I interrupted my own train of thought with the familiar chant.

"You okay?"

I jumped at the sound of Susan's voice. I turned, rubbing the rail imprint out of my palms while I willed my pulse to slow. "Yeah...couldn't sleep," I mumbled.

"Me neither," she commented, joining me at the railing. "I keep thinking…"

"About how you've gone from Pocahontas to Mark Twain?"

Her tight smile revealed a few new wrinkles around her eyes.

"What?" I prompted.

She looked at me. "I'm scared."

I nodded, taking it in. "Me too. It's probably because of the two-ton boilers sitting beneath us. They keep propelling us closer to Shawn, but I don't think we're ready for him."

She agreed, "It feels like it has mostly been a draw. He doesn't come out on top, but neither do we." She took a deep breath. "It can't be a draw this time; we have to finish it."

"How do we win?"

"That's the question of the year, isn't it?" She smiled at me. "When we were back at the Chakra, we were talking about all of his advantages. He has his knowledge, his locations of power, and his Athame."

I recalled our conversation. "We have our own knowledge – and our own locations of power; the Chakra, the forest in Indonesia Micah and I planted, and Easter Island."

Susan nodded her head.

"But what counters his Athame?"

She stopped nodding, her hand touching something at her hip. "Do you know what the Great Rite is?"

"No," I said. "Is this another Wiccan thing?"

"It's a ceremony, used to raise magical energy. It's a spiritual practice that involves sex, either literally or symbolically."

I eyed her. "What are you getting at?"

She continued fiddling with something at her hip. "In the symbolic sense, during the ceremony a knife, or Athame, represents the male half. A cup, or Chalice, represents the female half."

I finally understood. "So we are the Chalice to Shawn's Athame."

She shook her head. "No. This Chalice...is the Chalice to Shawn's Athame." She held it up and we both leaned away as if it were the devil itself.

"Is that the one from Bee's Wiccaning?" I asked.

"Yep." She turned it in her hand and light from the moon glinted off. It had come in handy at Mammoth Cave, but only because Susan used it as a physical weapon. It had left a mean lump on someone else's head.

I swallowed. "Does it hold Shades like Shawn's Athame?"

She shrugged. "I don't know. I wouldn't have the ability to find out, anyway."

But I do. We both sat in silence. I could most certainly try, but these things never seemed to work the way I intended. I wasn't sure if the risk was worth it. I sighed, and took a step back. Sitting on the deck, I really took in the view for the first time in a while. With our passing from the Ohio to the Mississippi earlier that day, thick groves of tall trees along the banks of the river had given way to shorter shrubs and opened our view to the horizon.

The night was cloudless, and fluorescent green swirls streaked across the sky. The aurora borealis had been visible in the lower latitudes ever since Daybreak, like a constant reminder of my failure.

Susan sat down beside me. "Remember when Bee got that pack of crayons and paper?"

I nodded. We had had a lot of luck with wild berries that season and plenty to trade for frivolous extras.

Susan smiled. "She held up the green crayon, and said, 'sky'. Then she ran around for an hour, holding up her crayon trying to trace the green lines, trampling the paper into the ground."

I laughed with Susan. I guess the magnetic fields weren't all bad.

Snoring from the front deck reminded us to keep our voices down. We lowered our gaze from sky to inky black river, and all at once I was reminded of the experiment in Spain when Susan and I had stood alone at the end of a long pier in the Mediterranean.

"The green reminds me of phytoplankton," I said.

She smiled. "Yeah – it kinda does. Funny how nature has a way of repeating itself."

"Just like history." The words were out of my mouth before I could stop them. I cringed, half expecting another tidal wave to take us out.

Susan's hand on my shoulder brought me back to reality. "We've come a long way since that night. And we have plenty to go on to ensure history doesn't repeat itself this time." She held out the Chalice for me to take. "Have you ever held this before?" she asked.

I shook my head. "No." I extended my hand cautiously, letting it hover over the cup. It was definitely powerful. This close to it, I could feel the energy coming off in waves. "Was it ever used for the same purpose as the Athame?"

Susan nodded her head. "Yes – though not in my time. During a saining, the inductee would bleed into the cup until it was full."

"Lovely." I stood and walked around the cup, studying it. "Do you think I need to consecrate it first, like I did the Athame?"

Susan shrugged. "Probably not; this was never cursed to begin with, and never corrupted, so far as I know."

I moved my hand closer, and a static shock jumped from the cup to my finger. "Whoa." I pulled my hand back. "That doesn't bode well."

Susan looked like she might drop it. "Maybe we should consecrate it." Susan stood just as the boat lurched to the right. Knocked off balance, Susan stumbled then tripped. The Chalice went straight up into the air. I caught it.

Just as I had done with the Athame, part of me went forward, falling to the deck unconscious. Another part fell back, and I watched green streaks rush down to meet me. One bright flash, and I was falling, or rather flying. Instead of plunging into a deep cave, I was thrust into the air. It was just as uncontrollable. My arms and legs flailed, trying to slow my momentum.

Give in to it, I told myself.

I heard Susan call my name in a distant echo. My face stung. She was trying to slap me awake.

Just give me a minute, I thought.

I extended my hands in front of me, and angled my body one way then another. Just like S-curves on a ski slope, it allowed for some control. Blackness opened up to a small sliver of light. My eyes adjusted to the brightness as I came closer and closer.

Blurry, dark forms dotted the edges of the circle of light. As their outlines came into focus, I realized I was looking at lean muscle. And very few clothes.

Arms rose, pointing to the center of the circle simultaneously. A small pinpoint of light emanated from each of their fingertips. Before my lips could form the word 'wait', their light joined and shot toward me. I was blasted back. My eyes flung open. I sat up, catching Susan's arm mid-slap, and gasped for air.

"Kaitlyn! Are you okay?" she sounded frantic.

I nodded my head, swallowing.

"What did you see?"

"Men. Lots of men."

Chapter 16

Ladies' Night

"It makes sense," Alex said. We sat at the bar at one end of the large, open ballroom below deck. Bee was at our feet, playing with clay poker chips.

"What makes sense?" I asked, taking a swig of my pint of Tang.

"The men would be less excitable. Possibly more organized," said Alex.

"How would you know?" Susan and I squeaked at the same time.

"Haven't you ever been to a strip club?"

"No," Susan looked offended, her eyes shooting darts. "Have you?"

"Of course."

She punched him in the arm.

"What?" Alex rubbed his arm. "I was in the military!"

"Our tax dollars hard at work?" Susan glared.

He narrowed his eyes right back. "You never paid taxes."

"Touché," she mumbled. She buried her nose in her own pint.

"Men at a strip club are relaxed, calm, and very businesslike. Ladies' night, on the other hand, is completely out of control."

I almost choked on my Tang. "You've been there on ladies night?"

"Well, yeah." His cheeks turned red. "I worked on stage; the military doesn't pay very much."

Susan punched him again. This time, her hand lingered near his bicep. "I think he does have the body for it." Her eyes flickered to me. "Don't you?"

"Oh, please." I rolled my eyes. "As if you didn't know. I've shared the same campfire with you two for a loooong time."

Now her cheeks turned red.

I looked at Bee. "But why would they just…push me away like that?" Many of the female Shades in the Athame befriended me; trained me, even. Granted, I had to bargain away control over my body, but they never tried to oust me – not as a coordinated group, anyway.

I rubbed my eyes, trying to ward off sleep and the inevitable nightmares. After my brief fling with the land o' plenty men, I worked off my adrenaline rush by charting the rest of our course with the captain, and comparing its timeline to an estimate of how long our supplies would last. Once Bee woke, I spent the rest of the morning tending to her and trying to avoid First Mate Arnold's persistent arguments that nuclear was the way to go.

"Not enough sleep?" Alex asked.

"Not in months."

I caught Alex and Susan exchanging a glance. "What—?"

Bee spilled her drink, cutting my question short. The already dirty carpet was now tinted a bright orange.

"Dang it!" I stooped to grab the cup. "This is how we get ants."

"Is that even possible in the middle of a river?" Susan asked, searching the bar's cabinets. "Where would they keep the towels?"

"Why do you need them anyway?" Alex asked, refilling a cup for Bee.

What we needed was sipper cups.

"Why do we need towels?" I was on the floor on my hands and knees, doing what I could to clean up Bee's mess.

"I mean the men – in the Chalice."

"Oh – ow." I bumped my head underneath one of the chairs. "Because it matches Shawn's advantage with the Athame."

Alex handed Bee the new cup. We all straightened at the same time. Susan eyed the forming bump on my forehead, sighed, filled the towel she found with ice and handed it to me.

"Thanks," I mumbled. "Wait – we have ice?"

"The fridge and freezers are powered when the boilers produce excess steam," Alex said, chomping on something hard. I looked at his glass, failing to realize until now their pints of Tang contained refreshing, cold, cubes of goodness.

I immediately dumped the contents of the towel into my glass and took a sip. "Mmm, that's the stuff. By the way – no Tang for Bee tomorrow. We have just enough for one glass a day for everyone on the ship. No going over."

Susan frowned into her empty glass. "I think we need to put someone else in charge of food storage."

"Fine by me; it'd give me more time to figure out this Chalice." I looked at the cup in question, sitting on the bar.

"So, with the Chalice and Athame pair, the two location pairs, and the Book of Shadows..." Alex was counting out on his fingers. "That makes six points of power that balance each other out," said Alex.

"And?" I asked, not following.

"They sort of correspond to six of the chakras on the human body. Maybe together they'll reach The Seventh – Sahasrara. This is, in a way, just like Akasha. It is the state of pure consciousness, transforming the divine. The 1,000-petalled lotus."

"Buddhist much?" I asked.

"Yes, yes," Susan chimed in. "That might be just what we need to beat Shawn."

Now my mouth hung open. "What – meditation?"

She rolled her eyes. "Maybe there's more to the names—'The Seven' and the Chakra—that we've been missing all along." She turned to Alex. "These seven vortices on the human body are focal points for receiving and giving energy."

He nodded.

She continued, ignoring my raised hand. "What if there can be such a thing on the body of Mother Earth, so to speak."

"Oh, I get it," I said.

"Congratulations." Susan smiled, turning back to me.

I cleared my throat, and all eyes traveled down to the cup still sitting on top of the bar.

"Drink!" Bee exclaimed.

"Not from that thing, honey. Not ever." I glanced at Alex. "So what are the chakra points on the body?"

"Let's see – there is Muladhara, set at the base of the spinal cord and associated with the element of earth. Then there is Manipura—"

"Okay," I said, cutting him off. "You lost me at Mu…Mula…"

"Muladhara," he helped.

I shook my head. "We're going to have to come up with code words or something."

"What, like 'head, shoulders, knees and toes, knees and toes'?" Susan began singing the song and going through the motions. I put Bee down so she could join in.

"More like head, throat, stomach, and prostate," interrupted Alex. He snorted, the only one laughing at his joke.

Bee was still singing, but now substituting 'puh-state' when she touched her toes.

I glared at Alex. "Well that wasn't very Buddhist of you."

Susan picked up the Chalice and tucked the stem under her belt. She took my arm. "Come on, let's go see if we can find a real Buddhist on board."

"Why?" I asked.

"So they can teach you how to meditate."

"I know how to meditate; my mom taught me."

"Not like this, she didn't," Susan mumbled. She looked over her shoulder at Alex. "You have prostate duty!"

He sighed, looking down at Bee now doing a squat dance. "Puh-state, puh-state!"

Chapter 17

One of the Guys

Our search around the ship for a Buddhist provided none. Apparently, we didn't attract the type. Susan left to put Bee down for a nap while I stayed to help in the kitchen, peeling the last of the potatoes uprooted from Robert's farm. Speaking of the devil, ten minutes into peeling, Robert entered the kitchen and everyone else left. Most preferred to avoid him if they could; I refused to be chased away that easily.

Robert eyed me, picked up an unwashed carrot, and started to chew, loudly. I took a deep breath.

Meditation would come in handy right about now.

"Not many trees around here anymore," he said.

I paused, setting my peeler down on the counter, but didn't retort. By now, he surely didn't think lightning and trees were the extent of my power.

He took another bite of carrot. He pointed the nubby end at me and said with a full mouth, "I'm warning you, if you ever do anything like that again—"

"Let me ask you something, Robert."

His eyebrows rose in shock at my interruption, but I'd thought of a use for him, which was just as shocking for me.

"If I wanted to break into a group of tightly knit men; be one of the guys – so to speak, what would be the best way to do it?"

He resumed chewing, mulling over the question, probably trying to figure out where I was going with it.

"Not *your* group, Robert." I rolled my eyes. He didn't have a group.

"Well." He cleared his throat. "I suppose you'd have to prove yourself to them."

"Prove myself? How, exactly?"

"Equal them. Show you are one of them."

Equal them? I snorted; that might be kind of hard. *Any woman who seeks to be equal with men lacks ambition.*

"Don't get all high and mighty," Robert said, as if he knew what I was thinking. He pointed the nub at me again. "If they catch on to that attitude, they'll never let you in. And don't show them up. That'll just piss 'em off." He stopped himself. His eyes opened in surprise again, then his brow furrowed. He'd caught himself helping me with a problem.

How did that happen? I smiled to myself, picking up the peeler and resuming my work.

"Anyway, as I was saying…" he trailed off when I raised my eyebrow, looking at him. "Oh forget it." He threw the rest of his carrot stick on the table in front of me and left the room.

* * *

"Susan!" I shouted across the deck.

She turned, putting her finger to her lips. "She's still asleep," she whispered as soon as I was close enough, gesturing to a snoring lump at her feet.

I lowered my voice to a whisper. "Do you still have the Chalice? I want to try again."

"Right now?"

I looked at her. "We're running out of time."

Bee's eyelids fluttered. She was dreaming. Hopefully about something good.

"Maybe not this close to her, but somewhere high – I feel like the higher the better."

Susan nodded to the captain's bridge on the other end of the deck. "How about on top?"

"Looks good to me."

"Here." She removed the Chalice from her belt and wrapped it in one of the smaller blankets surrounding Bee. "I know I don't have to say it, but-"

"But you'll say it anyway," I interrupted.

"Be careful."

As I took the wrapped Chalice her nose crinkled. "You smell like potatoes."

"Thanks." My mouth tipped up in a smile. I darted off like a teenager with the keys to mom's car.

I poked my head into the captain's deck before scaling the ladder to the top. I sighed, Arnold was at the wheel. "Hey, First Mate." I cleared my throat. I really didn't know what to call him. "Er… Arnold. If you hear anything up top, it's just me. I need some privacy."

He smiled. "Well, hell. Feel free to hang out in here. I won't bother you none."

"Oh, thanks. But I'm going to try to…meditate. It'll be easier alone." I took my leave.

"I hear ya, I hear ya," his voice floated out before I could close the door. "Oh hey, Kaitlyn!"

I poked my head back in, sighing. I'd almost gotten away. "Yes?"

"Did you know the Antarctic has their own nuclear power station? McMurdo Power Station on Ross Island. You can build these things away from the population."

I frowned. "Antarctica? That anywhere near Heard and McDonald Islands?"

Arnold smiled. "Yes, actually. The nuclear reactor was shut down in the early 70's, but the infrastructure is still there."

He went on, citing the potential for various nuclear reactors located in desolate areas. I tuned his voice out. One of Shawn's bases of operations was awfully close to that reactor. That couldn't have been a coincidence. Was that his plan? To run the world on nuclear?

"…take Russia for example," Arnold continued, unabated. "They built the first floating nuclear station. It's not in danger of earthquakes like Fukushima, and in a worst case scenario, the entire station could be sunk. Cold sea water cools the core and prevents atmospheric release." He paused, laughing. "I don't mean to talk your ear off on the matter, but that McMurdo plant—"

"How would they transport energy to the rest of the world?" I asked, interrupting him.

"What?" He looked dumbfounded.

"Floating stations are a good idea, but you still have to bring danger to nearby populations in order to transfer the power. How do you safely transport energy to the population with Antarctic nuclear stations?" I asked again.

"Well…you could…I mean I would just…" he stuttered out no solutions.

"You think on it. Listen, I need to get my meditation done before Bee wakes up." The door swung shut behind me and I scurried up the ladder before he could protest.

Positioning myself in the middle, I waited a few minutes to make sure he wouldn't follow me up. I unwrapped the Chalice partly, balancing it in front of me without touching it.

"Equal them, but don't better them," I said to myself. My conscience sneered. *At least not to their faces.*

I took a deep breath and grasped the cup with both hands.

Chapter 18

Righting the Wrong

"Sir?" David asked, pen poised over a notebook. Both highly prized processions, as they were hard to come by these days.

"Don't call me...never mind." Shawn sighed, putting a few handfuls of dirt into the bowl he held. If they hadn't gotten it by now, they never would. "We're going to St. Louis via river. I'll need you to find several motorboats and gas, and anything else that is sea-worthy that we can slap a motor on. Much of it is upriver."

"Yes, sir." David wrote furiously in his notebook.

"Bottle up what you can of the well water – and do the same for anything edible in the gardens."

David paused writing, then cleared his throat. "Sir, the water source has dried up."

Shawn sighed again, standing up and wiping his hand on his pants. "Just do what you can. Oh, and David?"

"Yes sir?"

"There is a man tied up in the basement of the capital building. Send word to the Wiccan camp. They'll go release him, and we'll be long gone."

"A man, sir?"

"Just do it." He didn't need his list to get any longer. Shawn walked into his tent, bowl in hand, zipping the door flap up behind him.

He set down the bowl of earth, right next to the one of water. Further away was burning incense to represent air, and a lit candle for fire. Shawn took out his Athame, and sat down in the middle of a pentagram drawn on the nylon tent floor with chalk. He turned the black, worn handle of his Athame over in his hand, thinking about his father.

My father.

Shawn had never pinned those words to Cato until after it was too late. As a boy, ever since Cato had passed the Athame to Shawn on his thirteenth birthday, Shawn had studied the magical history of the Athame ad nauseum. He'd adhered to guidance from the book of The Order of the Golden Dawn. According to the book, the consecration needed to happen on the day of Mercury, meaning Wednesday, and the knife needed to be tempered 'thrice' by fire and dipped into the blood of a black cat and juice of hemlock. It had taken some time to find hemlock, and even longer to find a black cat. Eventually, both were procured through local Wiccan covens.

It was doubtful the Shades would give him their power of Akasha willingly; he was on his own with that. But Shawn knew exactly what he had to do to obtain it.

Make amends with all those you have wronged.

Ahi's words flitted through his head in a whisper. Shawn sighed again, thinking of the one at the top of his very long list. *Sarah.*

She was long gone, but her Shade remained. The only thing he could think to make things right was to release her. First, he need the Athame back – allied with him and not Kaitlyn.

He took a deep breath, and began the spell, "I cleanse and purify this tool from all my past negative energies. Spirits of Earth, bless this Athame. Lend your strength and stability to my magic." Shawn sprinkled the briny earth, direct from the bottom of the Great Salt Lake, onto the blade.

"Spirits of Air, bless this knife with the power to direct my magic on my journey, penetrating through space and time." Shawn waved the blade through the rising, smoky incense.

The tent flap opened, intruding Shawn's circle with light and a breeze that doused the flame on his candle.

"Did you say something, sir?" David asked, poking in his head.

"Not to you," Shawn hissed over his shoulder. "Please don't interrupt until I come out. And make sure no one else does either."

"Yes, sir!" David closed the flap.

Shawn took another deep breath, trying to release his anger. He relit the candle and continued the spell, "Spirits of Fire, who forged this blade, bless my Athame to be the instrument of my will, pure in its direction of my energies." Shawn held the blade over the flame, turning it so both sides grew hot.

"Spirits of Water, bless this magical knife to be a tool used with love, and in respect for the Shades." Shawn dipped the blade in the bowl of water, cooling it. "I bless this Athame in the true will of my spirit."

He touched the blade to his forehead, giving in to the consecrated knife and his subconscious. He fell forward, but didn't stop at the chalky outline of the pentagram. He floated right through it. His feet drifted down to the ledge of a platform inside the cave. Shawn looked around him. Gaseous forms of Shades flit around, filling the cave and the water below in deep, shimmery blues, golds, and reds.

One single form descended from a far corner of the cave, placing herself in front of Shawn and taking form.

"Hello, Arianna."

She nodded her head once.

Shawn looked past her, stepping toward Sarah's cove – the entrance high on one of the cave walls.

Arianna blocked his way. "She knows why you have come, Athame Wielder, and she has a demand."

Shawn narrowed his eyes at Arianna. "Let her tell me herself."

Arianna shook her head. "She refuses to see you until the task is performed."

Shawn moved to step around Arianna. She placed one, solid hand on his chest. "To force yourself in would be bad. It would nullify the consecration, and the blade's magic would become useless to you – without the possibility of restoring the relationship."

Shawn's jawline tightened, and he released a slow, controlled breath. "What is her request?"

Arianna lifted her chin, looking Shawn in the eyes without blinking. "To release every one of the Shades here before Sarah. Only then will she see you."

"And your powers will go with you?" Shawn asked, wondering what would be the point of having the Athame at all in that case.

"Yes," Arianna said. "But to find what you seek, you must let go."

Shawn resisted the urge to roll his eyes. He crossed his arms. "Fine – who's first?"

Arianna stepped to the side, revealing a long line of Shades waiting patiently on the stairs.

"All of them? Now? That would take all night!"

"Have somewhere to be?"

Someone in the line cleared their throat, bringing Shawn's attention back to them. They had all taken solid form now. Shawn grumbled, lifting his hand over the first Shade in line.

Arianna grasped his wrist, "Make sure to do it right, Athame Wielder. Not only are we connected to the Athame, but we are connected to each other. We'll know if our sisters do not end up with the Goddess."

Shawn ripped his arm away from Arianna, glaring at her. He turned back to the first in line and forced his fist to open. "In love and in trust, in peace and in wisdom, I release you, so mote it be."

The woman smiled, shimmering from head to toe. Parts of her went translucent, then opaque again. Shawn frowned.

"Try harder, Athame Wielder." Arianna's voice echoed around the cavern. She was in her ethereal form, floating above him.

Shawn repeated the chant. The Shade shimmered more violently this time, and Shawn poured some of his energy into her. She brightened, enough to burn Shawn's hand. He pulled back with a hiss, and she lifted from the ground then disappeared in a puff of smoke.

Shawn shook his hand, trying to stop it stinging.

Laughter floated down from above. "A release always comes at a small price."

Quiet waves of chatter drifted through the line of women, and the air charged with excitement.

Shawn cleared his throat and wiped his palm on his pants. "Next."

Chapter 19

Meditation

I jettisoned through space, holding my breath, though I probably didn't have to. Instead of flailing limbs, I kept my arms and legs rigid and straight. Wind caused my eyes to tear up, but still I spotted that tiny pinpoint of light and angled for it.

The shapes were still there. Just as their blurry outlines came into focus, I saw them raise their arms. This time I was ready for it. I spun a web of elements, creating a shield in between me and them. I left my weaves loose, ready to absorb the ball of light now racing toward me. It worked like a charm. My shield shivered; silver waves of energy pulsated.

I moved closer to the men. Their arms rose again, shooting another blast at me. Again, I absorbed it. The shield was growing more solid and steady with the added energy.

I was close enough to hear their voices now. One loud, commanding tone followed by several shouting their consent. I needed to find the one in charge. I lowered my shield and turned my ear toward the group. Another shout, and smaller but numerous blasts flew by, narrowly missing me. I dodged some and absorbed the others. I had to remind myself my body wouldn't tire here, just like it didn't need to breathe. But the mental exertion was exhausting. Soon, they were going to catch me off guard.

Come on guys, I thought. *I am taking everything you're dishing out. Give me a break.*

The entire right side paused their attack long enough to build momentum together. I turned, using my shield to block their blast just in time. The left side did the same seconds later. Their aim was slightly off, but caught my arm nonetheless.

I looked down, a searing blade of light slashed across my bicep. I flexed, confused that it actually hurt. I forced myself to ignore the pain. Instead, I focused on the group of men. Self-preservation mode apparently wasn't convincing them; I had to try something different.

I held one hand to the back of my translucent shield, and drew some of its energy. I felt the men's signature on the elements; lots of air and fire. I weaved it together, trying to emulate their power, with a personal touch of my own. As soon as my weapon formed, I looked up and took aim.

I almost stumbled back at the sight. They all lowered their hands and took a step back.

Except one.

He launched himself forward, meeting me in the inky black atmosphere. I positioned myself, keeping him and the other men to my front, with the shield in between us. As soon as he stopped, I released a little bit of earth from the shield, making it transparent.

Well-defined muscles covered his abdomen and chest, over his shoulders and down his arms. He wore nothing except a loincloth covering the essentials. Very barbaric; he probably had a name like Conan, or Thor.

"I am Ted," he said in a higher voice than I would have suspected with that chiseled jawline. "We are Shades, and although I understand you currently wield the Chalice – you are not welcome here."

"Why not?" My voice was also slightly higher than I wanted it to be.

His eyes narrowed, as if debating how much to tell me. "Why have you come?"

"I need your help."

He didn't respond.

"Earth needs your help."

That might've done it; I could swear his jawline softened. I glanced down at my arm, the wound seeping blood.

He blinked a couple of times. "Why do you think we could help?"

"I've visited the Shades of the Athame; they were able to share their powers with me. I am trying to defeat a threat to humanity."

He tensed, retreating back to his circle. "Our sisters are rapidly disappearing! It is you?!"

"No!" I followed him forward, refusing to let him go that easy. "I don't wield the Athame! It is the one I spoke of, the threat – he must be doing something to the Shades!"

I don't think he believed me. He turned his back, flying faster toward his group. I could see them beyond him, preparing their light again.

I increased my speed, aiming for his back. Just before I hit him, I yelled, "Hey!"

He turned, eyes wide. I expanded my shield, encircling us both. Before he could react, I closed the shield, tying off the ends.

He beat at it, caught inside. He turned back to me, balling his fist. I glanced at it; light emanated from between his fingers.

"I wouldn't do that in here; you would destroy us both," I said. It seemed likely enough.

He believed me, releasing the energy. It hovered in between us until I drew it into the shield. He watched it merge, then looked through the shield at his men. They wavered in indecision. They certainly couldn't target the very thing that held their leader.

"Okay." He crossed his arms. "You have my attention."

I took a deep breath. "I'm not going to harm you, but I think we can help each other. The same man I intend to destroy has the Athame. He alone is responsible for what is happening with the Shades. Teach me, and I'll find the Athame."

"What do we get out of it?" he asked.

"You mean besides helping your sister Shades?"

"Yes."

"And helping Earth?"

"Yes," he repeated.

I huffed. "What do you want?"

"To be released."

"I can do that?"

"I believe so."

I thought for a minute. It was worth a try. "Deal." I extended my hand.

He just looked at it.

All right. I let it drop.

"So I'm ok to come back?"

He nodded. "Yes – and next time, you will be releasing at least one of us."

"I will?"

"To prove that you are both reliable and capable."

"Okay, until next time." I released the shield and we separated. I didn't turn my back until I was sure I was out of firing range.

Back in my body, I sat upright, taking a deep breath. "Ow!" I looked down at my arm. It bled profusely. "Shit!"

I slowly made my way down the ladder, off the captain's bridge. As soon as my feet hit the deck, the door opened.

Arnold poked his head out, eyes drawn straight to my arm. "What kind of meditating did you do?"

I just smiled, riding the high of my victory. A bleeding arm wound, or Arnold, couldn't bring me down. He handed me a first aid kit. After wrapping the wound, I walked to the back deck then slid in under the blankets with Bee. I was in a good mood. No nightmares for mama tonight…

* * *

"Easy there, princess." Shawn's words echoed through my head, annoying me. Blue eyes stared through me. The fire was there, as was Bee's snoring – my only grounding.

My shoulders sagged, but I looked around; still no one else.

"Where's the baby?" he asked.

I looked back at Shawn, there was no Athame this time. Instead it was a gun, cold and dark against his white skin.

I blinked, feeling Akasha at my back. Before, I destroyed Akasha, letting Shawn have his way. That wouldn't have been the right decision.

"Kaitlyn – the baby is mine."

I mirrored his words with my own lips. He didn't seem to notice. He continued with the same words, and the same motions as before.

The light behind me started to rise. I walked around Shawn this time. His back was now in front of me, and I could see Akasha beyond him.

He continued talking as if I were there, "It's already too late!"

I raised my arms with Akasha, forcing it to go faster; to go higher. The light increased with power, and I had to shield my eyes. Just as blood tinged the flame, Akasha breached the top of the wall and my insides shook with anticipation. This was what I was meant for; I was fulfilling my purpose.

"Yes!" I shouted. This had to be right.

I released Akasha over the whole of the world. The sky fell, smothering the fire and throwing us to the ground. After the explosions stopped, I lifted my head to look at Shawn.

His clothes had caught fire, but he made no move to put it out. Instead, he lay on the ground motionless. Bits of bone poked through his cheek. The rest of his face was scorched, like the ground he lay on. He rolled his eyes toward me. "Too late."

Chapter 20

The Great Rite

"Captain says we're going to have to pull ashore tonight," Alex said.

"Why?" I asked. "Hold still, honey." Bee's hair was long enough to braid, if only I could keep her still long enough.

"One of the boilers stopped working. They don't want to attempt fixing it while everyone is on board. We'll camp under the trees – you know, like we used to." He nudged my shoulder.

One of the braids came loose. I sighed, brushing out her hair again then letting her go. I'd try another time. She squealed then ran off, circling the deck.

I glanced at the shoreline. "There are no trees." It didn't matter, I had missed camping ever since we'd gotten into the canoe in West Virginia, like I was homesick for solid ground.

"Oh, cheer up, Katie. I'll round up some trees for you."

I smiled as he walked away, busy sorting out which supplies would come on land with us in case of a catastrophe. I followed his lead, but on a much smaller scale. A change of clothes for me and Bee, my mom's charms tethered together by fishing wire, and a few blankets. All of it fit in the pack I had been carrying the past year. Hopefully Susan had the Chalice with her; maybe I could pay the Shades a visit again tonight.

Later that afternoon, I watched the shore go by as we moved from the Missouri River to the Platte. The captain joined me at the railing.

"How goes it?" he asked.

"Good," I said. "Will you be joining us tonight?"

"Part of it. I'll oversee some of the repairs but they'll kick me out eventually. I'm no engineer."

I laughed, and we both turned back to the shore. We passed a large building standing right on the bank of the river. Completely dark, the place looked abandoned, most of the windows broken.

"What is that?" I asked.

"Fort Calhoun's Nuclear Power Plant. It was shut down about a year before Daybreak because of some damage caused to the reactors during a flood."

I raised an eyebrow at him.

He shrugged. "I keep tabs on what happens on my rivers. And Arnold, Mr. Pro-Nuclear, keeps tabs on the plants closest to us."

"And those?" I gestured at two long boats with stacks of storage containers on top. They looked like miniature versions of some of the huge shipping barges that used to go up and down the river.

"That…is new," said Captain Carl. He put the binoculars hanging around his neck to his eyes. "There are people manning the decks."

I straightened, body going tense.

He lowered the binoculars and put a hand over mine on the rail. "Just relax. They are probably observing us, too. As long as we act natural, there won't be any problems."

I closed my eyes, taking a deep breath and opened up to the energy in the area. No Elementals in that direction; or at least no one using their powers. Still, we attracted some attention; the number of bodies on the decks of the boats doubled. Their movements remained steady; they weren't panicking.

We passed without incident.

Captain Carl scanned ahead. "I was going to pull over soon. What say we wait until the next dock, just to be on the safe side?" He winked at me.

The next dock turned out to be another abandoned facility; this time it was a ship storage warehouse – without the ships. The captain pulled *The Spirit of Evansville* up to the dock and several people jumped off to tie it up. We waited until the ramp was lowered and then there was a mad scramble to find the best camping spots.

"We leave two hours after sunrise – with or without a complete body count!" Alex shouted after them.

"Hopefully everyone has watches," I mumbled.

Alex shrugged. "I've heard potato clocks are a thing again."

I stepped to the side with Bee, unwilling to thrust her into the melee of people leaving the boat. As we hit dry ground, dusk was approaching. I walked through the small pockets of campers already starting their fires and pitching tents.

"Hey, Kaitlyn!" Margie called, standing on the outskirts of the forming circles. "You and Bee can spend the night near us. Robert found a clear spot, no roots or rocks—"

"Margie! We need dry wood!"

Her shoulders sagged at Robert's rough voice.

"Thanks, we'll be okay." I smiled at her.

"He's not all bad you know, he's just—"

"Margie!" Robert shouted again.

"I'm coming, hold your horses!" She walked away, turning back to send an apologetic grin.

I walked to the opposite side of camp, stopping no less than ten minutes after I saw the last of the tents. Bee had fallen asleep on my shoulder, and stayed asleep when I laid her down on our blankets. As soon as I had a fire going with canned baked beans and corn heating over it, Susan and Alex came up behind me.

"It's about time." I scooted over on the large log to make room, "I think I have enough wood for the night but did you guys bring something for breakfast?"

They exchanged glances.

"What?" I asked.

Alex cleared his throat, "We were sort of hoping…well – if you don't mind…maybe we could—"

"Spit it out, Alex," I said.

"We're going to branch off for the night," Susan said.

"Oh, okay." I tried not to look disappointed. Truth was, I was looking forward to it just being the three of us again.

"We won't go too far – you'll be alright?" She glanced at Bee, still fast asleep.

"Oh, yeah, we'll be fine." I swallowed and forced a smile. "Have fun. Oh, and can you leave the Chalice?" I gestured to the cup tucked into her belt.

She hesitated. "You're going tonight? Maybe we should stay…" She glanced up at Alex as disappointment flickered across both their faces.

"No, no. Just hand it over and go do your…thing." I stood up and held out a small blanket for her to wrap the cup in.

She obliged. "Be careful."

"Yes, mother." I winked at her.

They disappeared into the woods; Susan's giggles floating back to me.

I sighed, and held the wrapped cup up in my hand. *It's just you and me, and our male harem. You'd think I'd be more excited.*

Bee snored, then sleep-laughed.

And you too, of course.

I passed a few hours by overcooking my food, eating it, tending the fire, checking on Bee, and pacing our campsite. I wasn't ready to visit the men again. They wanted me to release one of them, and I had no idea how to do it.

Eventually, I found a large boulder jutting out of the hill leading up from our campsite. I clawed my way up to find the top smooth and mostly flat. Below, I had a perfect view of Bee. Above, I had a perfect view of the full moon.

I sat, taking off my boots and socks, stretching my bare feet out in front of me. Memories of my saining with Cato, then my handfasting with Micah flashed in front of me. Both had been done in bare feet with a full moon.

The full moon allows us better control over our powers, Cato had once told me. I rubbed the back of my neck and tried to work out the kinks in my shoulders – those days were so easy compared to this. I took off my pack; something inside thumped against the hard rock. I searched through our spare clothes to take out the culprit. I found it in a small pocket on the side of the pack. It was the rock Micah and I had used in the cave on Reunion Island. I had kept it with me all this time; our own personal, inconspicuous sex toy.

I squeezed it in my palm remembering that night. An ache ran through my chest, and I quickly put the rock down beside me. I busied myself with the rest of the bag's contents, folding and refolding our clothes. I brought out my mother's charms, the ones that had protected Bee during our fight at Mammoth Caves. I lay them down beside me, opposite the rock. I unwrapped the Chalice in front of me, standing it upright.

And that was it. There was nothing else left to distract me. With the moon large and bright above me, its light enveloping me like a warm blanket, the tears flowed. I grabbed the rock again, holding it to my chest as if it alone could fill the hole and stop the pain caused by Micah's absence. My blurry view of Bee only caused me to cry harder. He should be here with her, not out gallivanting around, trying to save the world from Shawn.

The rock grew warm in my hand. I placed it against my cheek, drawing strength from its heat. Hiccups replaced tears and memories of that night in the cave with Micah raced through my mind. It had to have been the most gratifying sexual experience of my life, enhanced with elements as it was. Wind blew in, tousling my hair, enticing me. The rock vibrated in response.

Oh, no, I thought, glancing down at Bee. *I couldn't.*

The rock vibrated harder. If it could talk, it would convince me – *Why not? What do you think Susan and Alex are doing this very moment?*

Heat blossomed in my stomach.

The rock tried harder, and so did the elements. The wind brought in a female moan from the distance. My womb clenched in response, remembering what it used to feel like to be loved.

A male groan answered, "Hold still."

His mouth was on something. *Her lips? Her breasts?*

My hand automatically moved to my already hard nipples, pinching them. My body sparked to life with the sensation. I lay down flat on the rock allowing my knees to fall apart. I placed the rock in between my legs. Even through the material of my cargo pants, the vibrating rock was strong enough to cajole my hips into movement.

"Mmmm, faster!" the female voice said.

I obliged, pressing the vibrating rock against me, over and over again. My lips parted in shock as I already felt my climax building. I turned my head to the side. The charms were glowing bright. I squinted then looked away. No time to think about that now.

"Yes, yes!" the man yelled.

Yes, I thought. My muscles tensed, and the skin on my shoulder stretched, then split. Shawn's mark was tearing open. I ignored the pain because the pleasure building was greater. Besides, I didn't want to think about Shawn just then.

Elements raged, swirling above me in blue, gold, red, and shimmering brown. My legs straightened and my hips thrust up as the rest of my body was paralyzed with waves of pleasure. The climax lasted forever, straining my muscles to the point of snapping.

I dropped the rock before I hurt something, and my palm involuntarily closed around something hard and cool. When I realized what, it was already too late.

The Chalice.

I shot up, still riding waves that propelled me even faster. Within seconds I had arrived at the pinpoint of light that was all too familiar to me now. Only this time, I was a giant compared to the men. They turned toward me, caught off guard and in shock.

I lifted my arm and waved my hand across a small group standing closest to me. Each man disappeared in a tiny poof of smoke. Not murder; release. Mouths opened, the rest turned to me. Everyone paused; aftershocks still rocked my body. I squeezed my eyes closed, riding them out. When I opened them again, it was my turn to let my jaw drop. They were all bowing down to me.

The leader was the first to rise, a smile on his face. He nodded once to me. I nodded back, then returned to my body before I could do anything wrong. For once, I had managed to do something right.

I sat up on the rock, gasping for breath. I set the Chalice down and looked around me. The charms were losing their glow, and the elements above were dispersing. Still, energy hummed throughout my body.

I slowly lay back down with my hands behind my head when the notion hit me. "Damn, the Great Rite really does work." I rolled to my side, flush with contentment.

Chapter 21

Pieces

"Easy there, princess."

I rolled my eyes and crossed my arms. "You again?" The sleep I was getting wasn't worth this.

He smiled, his gun aimed at my chest. "Where is the baby?"

I stepped forward so that it pressed against my shirt. I closed my fist, reared it back, and then forward. I connected with Shawn's jaw. His head lurched to the side, but he kept his balance. He rubbed his jaw and looked at me again. "Kaitlyn, the baby is mine."

I threw my hands up in frustration and stepped around him. Stopping Akasha wasn't the right decision, but nor was releasing it. Killing Shawn outright wouldn't have an effect; he was just a figment of my imagination – part of the dream, just like the landscape.

The wall of fire seemed real enough. I held my hand up to it. Searing heat greeted my palm, but the skin didn't blister. I bit my lip, then stuck my arm all the way through. After a few seconds, I pulled it back. My skin was unmarred.

I took a deep breath, stuck my foot straight out in front of me, and stepped forward. Two large strides with my eyes closed. On the other side of the wall was a gray, desolate landscape as far as I could see. I walked around the wall, still blazing with flame. The sky outside the wall was a dull blue. I kicked at the chalky dirt. A vast desert of nothingness. This wasn't where I belonged. I stepped back through the wall of flame.

* * *

Susan and Alex joined me by the fire the next morning. Still unsure if they were the pair I heard last night, I avoided eye contact anyway. At least until Alex said, "We have to tell you something."

I locked eyes with Susan. With what had occurred last night, I jumped to conclusions. My eyes traveled down to her midsection, looking for telltale signs of pregnancy. I hadn't noticed her morning sickness yet, but some women didn't get it – the lucky ones, anyway. I could definitely see Susan falling into that category.

Susan flinched, then turned to Alex. "We need more wood, would you mind?"

He looked confused; this obviously hadn't gone the way he expected.

"And take Bee with you?" Susan asked, fixing him with a pointed look of raised eyebrows.

"Come on, peanut, let's see if this state has any honeysuckle." He held out his hand for her and she hopped up, tempted by promises of dessert for breakfast.

After their voices were out of earshot, she turned back to me. "I'm not pregnant."

"Oh," was all I could say.

"If you must know, I have an intrauterine device for birth control, put there before Daybreak. The relationship between me and Alex has obviously…escalated." Her cheeks went red. "And we have definitely discussed kids; at least after this whole 'Shawn' thing is over. But there haven't exactly been any gynecologists running around the woods, or on gambling steamboats, and I'm too afraid to remove it myself." She took a deep breath and looked at me, "Satisfied?"

I nodded quickly, like I had just barely escaped a chastising. Time to change the subject. "I'm...so sorry, Susan. I had no idea. I haven't had my period since – well, since before I met The Seven. I'm not sure I can even get pregnant anymore." I dug out a small divot of dirt with the toe of my boot. "I guess that's a good thing."

Susan looked at me, eyes wide. "Oh, yes – I suppose. You know, it happens to a lot of Gaias, very shortly after they start using their powers. Though normally women don't become Gaias until after menopause; you were a rare exception."

I raised one eyebrow at her. "So I've been told."

Time for her to change the subject.

She turned, scanning the woods for Alex. "I suppose I should just tell you, Alex would muck it up anyway."

"Tell me what?"

She picked up a stick and poked at the fire, all of a sudden avoiding my eyes.

"Susan?!"

"Okay, okay." She threw the entire stick into the fire. "Just...try not to get mad. Have you meditated yet this morning?"

I stamped my foot.

Her lips went tight.

I huffed. "Just spit it out before I—"

"There was a tornado in Evansville."

Her interruption rendered me speechless.

She continued, "An F3, they think; wiped out half of the town, including the Chakra Center."

"That…is terrible." Weak response, I knew, but I was preparing myself for what was to follow.

"There are too many incidents for it to be considered coincidence any longer," Susan said.

My eyes flit to the woods around us, seeking Alex and Bee. I stood up, looking harder, my heart skipping a beat.

"Kaitlyn, don't freak out." Susan stood now too. "We need to decide what to—"

Before she finished the sentence, I bolted into the woods. "Bee?" I turned and turned. Still no Alex, still no Bee. "BEE?!"

Out of everyone on the planet, Susan and Alex were the two people I trusted the most. They would do anything to keep Bee safe, including keeping her away from me, if that was what it took.

"Kaitlyn!" I could hear Susan running after me, and I bolted again. She continued to try to reason with me. "What happens when the disasters catch up with you? What happens when you and Bee stay in one place too long?"

Blood pounding in my ears worked to block out Susan's voice. I felt her hand on my shoulder.

"I'll tell you what happens," she started, but didn't finish.

An explosion shook the ground, and knocked us both on our asses. My eyes went wide as I looked at Susan. *Was it catching up with us already?*

She shook her head. "That came from the river."

A second later, shards of white and red painted wood rained down on us. A piece of the *Spirit of*

Evansville metal railing bounced on the ground a few feet away.

"Oh, God." I got to my feet.

"What was that?" Alex's voice boomed behind us.

I turned; he approached, arms full of wood.

"Mommy!" Bee yelled, running up behind him with two small sticks in her hand.

I dropped to my knees and scooped her up in a bear hug. "Oh, honey. I thought..." I trailed off. It didn't matter what I thought now. She was here, and that was all that mattered.

It was a moment before I realized Susan's arms were around the both of us. I raised my head, looking at her with tears in my eyes. She looked to be on the verge of waterworks herself.

"We would never take her away from you," Susan said. "We will work this out together."

I nodded, and buried my head back in Bee's hair. She trembled.

Alex set his pile of wood down with a clatter. "There could be people hurt. I need to check it out. You guys stay here until I know it is safe."

We nodded, uncoiling ourselves from each other. A half an hour later, without Alex's return, we ventured forward. People were wading into the river collecting anything they could from the disaster; wood, supplies – useable or not – pieces of metal from the ship. People in canoes in the water were doing the same. Whole sections of the *Spirit of Evansville* were nowhere to be seen.

Captain Carl saw us and stood from scouring the ground. He was in his briefs; nothing else. "Boiler exploded. Ship is now at the bottom of the Platte River." He hung his head. "The captain did not go down with it. Thankfully, it happened after they had quit work for the night. No one was on board except..."

"Except who?" I swallowed hard.

"Except Robert." Captain Carl nodded to a figure hunched over the ground, Bobby Jr., his shoulders shaking with sobs. Margie kneeled next to him, rubbing a hand over his back. Her eyes completely dry.

"What do we do now?" Susan asked.

"Now – we walk," I said.

Chapter 22

New Energy

The marching party was reluctant, at best. We only packed what could be carried on our backs, which meant much of the supplies were left behind. People had a hard time giving up their Tang. But Susan, Bee, Alex, and I had spent the last year and a half walking. For us it was like returning home.

"Do we stick by the rivers?" Alex asked.

"Yes," Susan and I said together, probably for different reasons. I glanced at her, continuing, "That's where Micah expects us. He might be leaving other groups of people or supplies along the river – or *he* might be there…"

I trailed off and Alex arched his eyebrow. "Waiting with open arms?"

"Something like that," I mumbled.

Susan walked up to us, cinching her backpack down on her shoulders. "Just so you know, I'm not happy about this. I'd rather be on the water. It's faster, and less physically demanding."

I put my arm around her. "Well, you are welcome to swim your way there."

She looked at me sideways. "Ha, ha." She took a deep breath. "We divided the group. Half will stay back to finish the burial ritual and clean up the mess. They'll follow in a day or two."

I craned my neck to look around Susan. "What about Margie, is she staying?"

"Well, the deceased was her husband, so I assume so," Susan said in her grumpy voice.

I rolled my eyes. "Wait here, I want to talk to her a minute."

I found Margie inland, gathering wood for the funeral pyre, whistling.

"Margie?"

She stopped her tune and spun, eyes wide, like she had gotten caught with her hand in the cookie jar.

I narrowed my eyes. "Are you okay?"

"Yeah, um…" she looked around, then set down her pile of sticks. "Look – I know what this might look like."

"Like what?" I asked, playing dumb.

"Like, maybe that I'm not sad enough after what happened." She brushed bits of leaves and dirt off her skirt.

"Are you sad?"

She paused, actually thinking about it for a moment. "For Bobby, I am. His father was everything to him. But…" She paused again, and scratched her arm.

"But what?" I prompted.

"But he was going to lead that boy astray. He was not the best role model."

I furrowed my brow, testing her. "He was your husband."

"I accepted the union because I thought I needed him to survive. I was lonely, and scared, and destitute."

Now I was reeling with confusion. "You can do some pretty powerful stuff; I didn't even know Earths could control plant life like that," I said, thinking of the vines that saved Robert on the river.

She ceased twisting her hands to wave one in the air, "I don't know about at all that. I had to save him. I mean, I caused the mess in the first place."

Funny, I blame myself.

I sighed, and sat down on a large log a few feet away. She joined me.

I nudged her. "Maybe we both need to stop being so hard on ourselves."

She smiled.

"I'm serious," I told her. "You're totally powerful – and smart. You could live off the land by yourself for years if you had to."

"Well, what about you?" she asked. "The energy practically comes off you in waves. I've felt it strengthen every day since I've met you. Especially today."

"Oh." My cheeks went red. "Last night I, um, meditated." I cleared my throat, looked at her, and smiled. "You know, I think we're going to be okay. We've been through…a lot. But we're still here."

She nodded. "Alive and kicking."

"Exactly…" our voices were almost at a whisper now.

"You and Micah saved us, you know." It was her turn to nudge me.

"What? How?"

"Robert and his son were in charge of the camp, as you probably guessed. When we started to grow food successfully, our small group thrived. They became more and more protective – to the point that it was becoming more of a cult than anything else." She picked up a stick, scratching it aimlessly in the ground. "It was getting ridiculous. He…hit…me a couple of times when I tried interjecting." She shrugged. "I made excuses for him, thinking it was just because he had so much on his shoulders, protecting us and all."

I stayed silent, letting her get her story out.

"When we went more than a month without seeing other people, Robert claimed we were close to the last humans. He even 'accidentally' destroyed our radio. He said it would be up to us to repopulate."

My hand went over my mouth as I gasped.

She kept her eyes forward. "They were coming up with a schedule – a rotation at nights. And that was the exact moment when Micah walked into our camp." She smiled to herself. "There was a fight, of course. But it was no contest. Robert was way out of his league."

"But, how did things not go back to bad as soon as Micah left?" I asked.

"Somehow, Micah detected my abilities and he made me demonstrate to Robert. I had never revealed them before; not even to my first husband." The words caught in her throat.

I took her hand and squeezed it.

She continued, "I thought, people might fear me. Single me out – you know, like a modern-day witch hunt." She shrugged. "So I hid them. But Micah spent three days with us, and spent a lot of time guiding me to believe in myself, and in my powers."

"Yeah, he is good at that," I said, the words almost choking in my throat.

"It wasn't instant confidence, of course. But it helps to see you – leading all of us, making decisions, working toward a goal that is going to save the planet, and all with a baby on your hip." She straightened her back and smiled at me. "Makes me believe I don't need someone like Robert."

"Margie." I squeezed her hand. "I have to ask you something, and please don't get upset."

"What?"

"Did…you…cause the boiler to explode?"

She stiffened for a moment, settling her gaze on me. "I saved Robert, in the river. You saw it. I would never resort to murder. Not even when he was beating me."

"You're right, okay. I'm sorry. It was just on my mind, after your reaction to his death, is all."

She relaxed her shoulders. "I know. It's not like his death hasn't brought me some relief, after all. I really don't care what people think. I just need to concentrate on Bobby Jr. now; undo everything Robert planted in that poor kid's mind."

"Fair enough," I said. *Time for a change in subject.* "I need to leave soon, got a long walk ahead of us."

She laughed.

"I was hoping you could show me how to move the vines like you did on the river."

The corners of her mouth went up in a smile. "I'd love to." She released my hands, cleared her throat, and stood. "It really has everything to do with the energy of the plant; and much of the energy is active during photosynthesis."

She walked over to a small, budding plant in the ground and squatted down. I followed.

"You're aware of the laws of ecology?" she asked.

"Not necessarily," I said. *Not at all.*

"I won't give you a lecture here, but one of them is that energy cannot be created, nor destroyed. In photosynthesis, plants simply convert solar energy into chemical energy. I tap into the byproduct, enzyme-modified electrodes. It works much better when the plant is actually absorbing sunlight." Margie looked up, frowning at the cloud-covered sky.

"Oh, I got this." I stood up, closed my eyes, and whispered a spell Vayu taught me shortly after we met. "*Sol iustitiae nos illustra* - sun of righteousness shine upon us."

I tapped into the frequency of the wind, guiding it to carry my words higher. I shivered as memories of the man who killed Cato, and my parents, assaulted my brain. But his spell was good magic. The clouds above us parted, and the warmth of the sun raced to chase away the remaining chills in my body.

Margie and I both lifted our faces, inviting the sun in. A small wave of energy tingled at my fingertips. We glanced down at the plant.

"See?" asked Margie. "Do you feel that? There is an increased electrical current in the plant. And with stronger illumination the process accelerates, creating more and more energy. All you need to do is tap into it."

Above us, the clouds moved with the wind, and the beam of sun slowly shifted down the forest. Margie extended her hand toward the beam, following it with soft footsteps in the soil. Large leaves on the plants dipped and rose; the stems on taller plants leaned to the side.

"Are you doing that?" I asked.

"Hmm." She nodded. "It isn't exact. I can't manipulate them to do move exactly how I want. The vines over the river were more of a fluke; made me look better than I am." She gave a nervous laugh. "You try."

I was still riding the high frequency of air. Earth was much lower. Slow and steady. I made the transition, tapping into the soil.

"A little higher," Margie coaxed. "Remember, it is a mix of solar and earth energy."

I tried again, melding the two elemental properties together, remaining sensitive to what responded. Finally, a frequency hit, the waves parallel to those I was managing. I followed it back to a plant. I almost got bogged down in it. "Sticky – like syrup."

"Glucose," Margie said. "You got it."

I sent my own energy to intertwine with that of the plant. The weaves buzzed and the plant leaves moved, like it was waving to me. I smiled, waving my own hand in response.

Margie laughed. "Good! You're a quick learner."

The clouds closed up again and the combined energy fizzled out. We lowered our hands.

"Could this be a power source? For electricity?" I asked.

She nodded. "Biofuels. I was following research on the concept before Daybreak. It is totally possible, but there was a lot of development needed on the technology back then. Not sure if anyone pursues it anymore. Too many distractions nowadays, like…"

"Surviving?" I interjected for her.

"Yeah, something like that."

"Well, if plants give off their own frequency – does everything?"

She furrowed her eyebrows. "What do you mean?"

"I mean, do people emit a certain frequency?"

"Yes, I suppose everything does. But you can't use a 'people frequency' as an energy source."

"No, no." I laughed. "I was thinking it might be useful for more of location purposes. Like finding someone."

"Kaitlyn?" Alex's voice startled us. "Ready? We want to cover some ground before we lose daylight."

"Sure." I turned back to Margie, trying to wipe Micah from my mind. "Thanks and…be careful. I'll see you in a couple days."

"You be careful too. Good luck, and kiss that baby for me." Margie hugged me.

"Okay." I turned away with an unexpected lump in my throat. Had I not spent so much time suspecting her, we might have had a chance to become good friends.

Alex glanced at me as we walked. "You okay?"

"Yeah, fine. In fact, really, really good." I took a deep breath. "Looking forward to keeping my feet on dry ground for a change."

"You and me both," Alex said.

Chapter 23

Theories

By the third day of walking, my feet were covered in blisters.

"Those boats made me go soft," I told Susan as she helped bandage them. "I never had this problem before."

Susan shoved a canteen in my face. "You don't drink enough water."

"What does water have to do with blistering feet?" I asked.

"Water has everything to do with your body." She put the last bandage on. "There – that should get you a few more miles."

I finished half the canteen under her watchful eye, then handed it back. As I laced up my boots, Alex joined us. He stopped, setting a large, clunky radio next to his feet on one side, and Bee on the other.

Bee popped up on her feet, hopped over the radio, and got busy pushing buttons and turning dials. She picked up the handset. "There? Over – come in. Over."

Alex beamed. "She uses better radio etiquette than you."

"Oh, shush." I tied my second boot and stood. "Trying to track down the other group?"

We had expected them to catch up with us by yesterday morning, but there was no sign of them. Not even this afternoon when Alex had backtracked to search for them. I looked up at the sun, slowly sinking behind the trees. It would be time to stop for the night soon.

"Yeah. They were supposed to be the faster group; I purposely divided them up by physical...prowess," said Alex.

Susan and I laughed, covering our mouths trying to hold in the snorts.

"Prowess?" I mocked him.

"You know what I mean," he grumbled. "Little Miss Bee, can I see the radio now?"

She shook her head 'no' and turned her back on him. "Over, over."

Susan and I were still laughing.

"That's just what I need; someone else to ignore me." Alex rubbed his temples. "You know what? You two try – I'm going to scout ahead."

He stomped off before we had a chance to apologize.

"Should we go after him?" I asked.

"Nah," said Susan. "Let him walk it off. He needs it."

I glanced at her. Of all of us, Alex had been doing the most walking. Constantly scouting ahead, and sometimes behind, he probably covered more than twice the distance we did.

A muffled, distorted voice came in over the radio. "Who is this? Over."

Susan grabbed the handset from Bee, and I grabbed Bee, searching my bag for honeysuckle to keep her quiet.

"This is..." Susan let go of the handset, then whispered to me, "Oh, geez. We didn't come up with call signs."

I rolled my eyes, taking the handset from her. "Margie? This is Kait—"

Susan ripped the handset right out of my palm. "Don't use your real name."

I took the handset back. "What else should I use?"

"Give that to me!" She yanked it back.

I lunged for it again, but tripped. I fell into her and we both ended up on the ground, wrestling for the handset.

Margie's voice continued to come over the radio, "Kaitlyn? What's happening? Are you okay?"

We both stole glances at Bee, ensuring we wouldn't roll over her. She did the right thing, backing away.

"Stop it, Susan! She's already used my name anyway!" I snaked my arm around Susan, grabbing at her shirt, trying to pull her off me. I wasn't really motivated to hurt her, unless she kept pushing her luck.

"I refuse to sit by and keep letting you put us in danger!"

I froze; so did she.

She recovered first, standing up and backing away. "Sorry; that came out wrong."

I stood as well, not bothering to brush off bits of dead leaves. "No it didn't."

"What?"

"You said exactly what you wanted to." I picked up Bee, who looked like she might cry, and put her on my hip. "What did it mean?"

Susan's face crumpled at Bee's pouting lip. "The disasters that have been following us…"

"What about them?"

"Oh, come on, Kaitlyn. I don't want to do this now."

Not without Alex, I thought. *So they can gang up on me.*

The handset laying on the ground between us sparked to life again, "Kaitlyn?"

"Look, we don't know for sure what's causing them." I walked to the radio and picked it up. "And until we do, I'm not going to be separated from my child on a theory." I pressed the talk button. "Sorry, Margie. I'm here – everything is fine." The bite in my voice would tell her otherwise, even over the air.

"Um, ok. Things here aren't so good; there has been an earthquake."

My eyes opened wide; so did Susan's. Without breaking our shocked stare at each other, I put the handset back to my mouth. "Say again?"

"Earthquake, over."

I shook my head. "Impossible, we're not that far away. We would've felt it."

"I was able to contain it. Did some damage to our immediate area, though. We lost most of our supplies when the river surged. Half our group doesn't want to continue; we've been arguing back and forth. What should we do?"

"Um…" I trailed off.

"Say again?" asked Margie.

"Hold tight. Don't go anywhere. I have some thinking to do. Over and out." I dropped the handset, and brushed by Susan.

"Kaitlyn?" I heard her ask behind me.

I half-turned my head. "I said I have some thinking to do."

***

"Not now, Arnold."

He had been trying to catch my ear all day. Unfortunately, being with the slower group meant being with Arnold. For the most part, I was able to avoid him by using Bee as an excuse. Bee needs to pee. Bee needs to eat. Bee wants to be at the front of the pack. But now Susan had Bee, and I had no more excuses.

"I just wanted to talk about Fukushima."

I sighed. "You mean the nuclear meltdown in Japan? The tsunami that caused the release of radioactive material into the ecosystem."

"Yes – that was an example of our worst fears with nuclear power. And you know what we discovered?"

"What?"

"That it really wasn't that bad. Losses were minimal—" He tripped over a root sticking out of the ground, caught himself on my arm, and almost brought me down with him.

I smiled to myself. *Was that Earth trying to tell him something?*

When we both caught our footing, he continued like nothing had happened, "Scientists also agree there will never be an observable cancer increase in the Japanese population attributable to Fukushima."

"Way too early to know that." I didn't say what we were both thinking…because of Daybreak, now we'd never really know.

"But nuclear is just…dangerous," I said.

"Oh." He clicked his tongue. "That's just fearmonger talk. More people die each day from coal pollution, or did before Daybreak, than have been killed by nuclear power in 50 years of operation."

"But we're not talking about coal. We're talking about renewable energy."

"Listen, in another time, I might have been all for renewable energy. But we just aren't there yet – we don't have the capability of supporting large population masses on just that. And now, thanks to Daybreak..." He gestured up to the night sky and the green streaks of the aurora borealis. "We really don't have the chance."

I sighed. He was right – and it was because of my failure to stop Shawn. "Okay, so say we go the nuclear way—"

"You mean the *right* way," he interrupted.

I glared at him.

He cleared his throat and said, "Sorry."

"If we have nuclear power plants running all over the world, we still need uranium to power them. How do we find that without gas to run the machines, or power to run the instruments?"

"Well, for starters – I think some of you magical folk can do it. I've been talking to some of your Earths—"

"Earths?" It was my turn to snort. "I've never seen an Earth powerful enough for that; not even Margie – I don't think."

Oh, shit.

I stopped dead in my tracks. The person behind me ran into me. It was definitely getting too dark to continue, but we hadn't yet found a good camp spot.

"Hey, you okay?" Arnold asked, pulling me forward again.

"Yes...I...it's just..."

It's just I know someone that might be able to find uranium underground – me. Hell, I had managed to find iron sulphate at the bottom of the ocean, and that was back when I was new to the Gaia business. The problem was, if I knew that, Shawn definitely knew it. He was going to use a Gaia to run his nuclear power plant. And if he has more than one plant...

I cleared my throat. "It's just the same as with renewable energy – we aren't there yet. I'm not sure us 'magical' types have developed that ability."

"But you have to agree, it's probably easier to attain than a ramp up of renewable energy would entail."

I stayed silent – I would never, ever admit that.

The quiet chattering ahead of us stopped as the entire line of people was coming to a halt. I tried craning my neck over their heads. "What is it?"

Arnold stood on his tiptoes. "It's Alex."

The line ahead parted, as people began diving into the tree line on either side of the trail.

"What the—?" I stopped, mid-question, as soon as I saw Alex. He was flashing a signal with his hands; the one signal I didn't want to see. *Enemy coming. Hide and stay down.*

A flutter by my side and Arnold was gone, disappearing into the trees on the side of the trail. I had not thought he could move so quickly. I stayed put until Alex made his way down the entire line to me.

The panicked look in his eyes said it all, but he told me anyway, "Elementals. About 50."

He grabbed me at the waist, ushering me into the tree line.

"One Less?" I whispered back.

Just as the shadows enveloped us, we heard boots on the trail. Alex had me out of view just in time. We both crouched behind a thick bush. "There are so many. Oh my God – Bee!"

I tried to jump up.

Alex gripped my shoulder, hard. "She's with Susan. I saw them hop off the trail on the other side."

"The other side!" I hissed. "Then why didn't *we* go that way?"

"I was just getting you off the trail—"

I put my hand over his mouth. The front of the column had just reached the trail in front of us, when someone put their fist in the air and shouted, "We'll stop here. Fifteen minute break."

Alex and I looked at each other, each mouthing the word, "Shit."

Chapter 24

Fresh Scars

The long column of Elementals broke rank. Most of them started to make their way into the tree line and we heard a series of zippers echo throughout the forest. Considering there were hundreds of people in the immediate area, the silence was deafening.

Alex and I leaned further into the bush in front of us. Already pitch black outside, the tree cover made it even darker. I pulled my hands into the sleeves of my jacket, and closed my mouth and eyes, eliminating the whitest parts of my body. I prayed Bee was still asleep.

Footsteps approached the other side of the bush. My heart jumped to my throat.

Please don't come around, please don't come around.

He didn't. We heard a buckle, a zipper, then a steady stream of liquid spray across the bush and ground. Alex's hand stayed on my shoulder – my hand still covered his mouth. We refused to move anything.

It was the longest pee in the history of man. They must have just come across a freshwater source. I slowly opened my eyes, and could just make out the silhouette of legs in front of me. The stream inched toward the toes of my boot, which were shoved so far under the bush they almost came out the other side. The sound of his urine took a higher pitch when it moved from dirt to my boot.

I whimpered, looking at Alex. His grip on my shoulder tightened. His eyes bore into me. His creased forehead all but told me, *If you move, things much worse than a little pee on your boot will happen.*

Then I heard it. Bee cried out.

Her whimper sounded strangely out of place, almost otherworldly, even to me. A murmur of confused whispers followed it.

The stream in front of us stopped. The man turned and said to himself, "A baby?"

Alex and I shot to our feet. The man on the other side of the bush whipped back around. His jaw met Alex's fist, and he fell to the ground, unconscious.

Bee was still crying, but her voice was drifting further from us. Susan was on the run.

Short bursts of scuffles, scattered on both sides of the trail, brought the forest to life. Some of my people were running, some attacked. One Less responded more quickly than I did.

"Got one!" I heard down the way.

Someone responded, "Cuff 'em. Group them together!"

With hands bound behind their backs, people were dragged to the trail. I squinted my eyes in the dark; we were losing. A small contingent of guards set themselves up around their captives.

"Do something!" shouted Alex.

I resisted the urge to roll my eyes. *He* was the man of action. Besides, I was doing something. I was finding Susan. I blocked out the noise around me, tuning into the telltale frequency of plants. I had meant to explore finding people's frequencies with Margie – but her group had never caught up.

Now was not the time for experiments, but how else would I find Bee? I raised my pitch, disregarding the plant life and searching for humans. I found heartbeats – everywhere. Most were racing, beating frantically during the fight. I chose one and delved into it, mentally dissecting the body down to individual cells. They each vibrated at a certain frequency. Brain cells were faster. Those in the stomach were slower.

I looked closer. Each cell held its own anomaly. An additional type of energy emanating. This was a Fire. I moved to the next body – there were a lot of Fires.

It barely registered that two men had approached us. Alex intercepted them. They wrestled on the ground, similar to what Susan and I had done over the radio earlier. I hoped Alex had better moves than us.

He finally pulled out his knife, finishing the fight with two clean cuts.

I went more quickly now, pinpointing Waters. I found one, moving fast and away from me. A significantly stronger signal accompanied her, which caught my attention. Bee.

"Straight that way!" I caught Alex by the arm, hoisting him off the ground. I pointed the way and he took off running.

Two more men approached. I raised my pitch to the frequency of air, sucking it toward me then shooting out. I ducked to avoid my own gust, and the men flew back into the trees. The gust continued toward Alex. I flattened it to give him a push, increasing his speed and a better lift over obstacles.

I moved forward, making it back to the trail. The group of guards surrounding my people turned toward me, each pointing something at me. Few had guns with ammunition these days, but I wouldn't put it past them.

With one hand extended toward Alex, still pushing him forward with air, I shot my other toward the guards. Flames volleyed at the group, flying over my guys, who had been forced to sit. The smell of burned hair and singed skin permeated the air.

I left the trail, running again. I kept trying to use my own air to propel me up and over – an arc straight to Susan and Bee. It didn't work. Twice I was shot down by branches I didn't see. The third was a hard knock to the head. The fall took my breath away.

By the time I recovered, I was completely disoriented. My head pounded, and my ribs ached with each breath. I could set up a shield around Bee, if I could just get close enough. I closed my eyes, seeking her out again. It was easier this time.

She wasn't too far; maybe ten yards away. Susan had stopped moving. And Bee wasn't crying. My stomach dropped.

Are they okay?

My heart pounded in my chest as I struggled to stand. Right away, I realized why they were quiet. Three members of One Less stood in front of me. Two men, one woman, all Fires. They had me back on the ground, face down, with my arms behind my back before I had time to think. If only my head would stop pounding.

Behind us, a twig snapped.

"What was that?" I felt a pair of hands come off me while one turned to investigate.

Bee, no!

I struggled, attempting to get my legs underneath me. "I'm one of you!" I shouted.

That caught their attention. I felt Susan backing away slowly. She needed to get further. "I mean, I'm with you. I'm part of One Less."

Someone tugged at my arm. "You're not wearing the band."

I craned my neck to see a bright blue piece of material wrapped around his bicep. Uniforms were hard to come by, without direct shipments from factories in China and all. "Got torn off while I was just scuffling with an Air. Got her good though – her nose will never look the same," I laughed. It sounded fake to my own ears.

I heard rustling a few feet from my face. I looked up to see Alex peeking out from some foliage. I shook my head, then motioned for him to go around. He nodded once. The three behind me were oblivious to the entire exchange.

The woman grabbed me at my collar and yanked me to my feet. She was stronger than she looked. "Yeah? Prove it." She had a British accent.

Damn – is there a secret password? A code or sign or something?

Susan was far enough away now to move more quickly. Alex was catching up. Bee would be okay. All I needed to do was get rid of these guys. Air would do the trick again. As I started to call for it, a searing pain shot through my head. Had it not paralyzed me completely, I'd be on my knees throwing up.

I let go, and the pain dissipated in waves. My hands went to my temples.

"Well, prove it fast or it's into the cuffs you go," said one of the men, waving a plastic zip-tie in front of my face.

A new sensation of pins and needles took me, as I realized magic would not get me out of this one. "Okay, okay," I mumbled. "Just give me a second."

I dropped my backpack and turned away from them. I pulled down on the neckline of my shirt, exposing my right shoulder blade.

"I can't see it; it's too dark. Can you see it?" one of them asked.

"No – wait, I have a flashlight." Material rustled as hands searched pockets.

I looked over my shoulder. "No need to waste batteries."

"Shush, you. We have to be sure."

I sighed, keeping the shirt yanked down on one side. It didn't matter, the more time we wasted, the more time for the others to get away.

"Here it is."

Light flashed over my shoulder for a brief second while they studied the scar Shawn had left with his Athame.

"Ok, yeah. You're clear."

I pulled my shirt back down. "Oh, goodie," I said, mustering as much sarcasm as I could.

"Come on, they're regrouping on the trail." The three of them started walking opposite the direction of Susan and Bee.

"You go ahead, I think I lost my…my…" I had to think quick, some excuse to separate from them.

"Your what?" the woman asked.

"I think my armband must be here, somewhere. Don't want to be baring my shoulder every five seconds." I managed to muster a nervous laugh.

There was a click, and a beam of light darted around the ground at my feet.

"Nope," she said. "Here, I have an extra one."

My hand went to the air to catch the piece of blue material she tossed. I grimaced at the pain in my ribs and managed to turn it into a smile. "Thanks, lady." I bent to pick up my backpack.

"The name is Laura," she said. She put her arm around my shoulder, leading me back to the path. "You must be new here – that scar looks fairly fresh."

Chapter 25

Muscle Memory

For the next two hours, we walked the way I had just come. Every step was one in the wrong direction. My head still hurt, as did my ribs; all compounded by the fact that the woman next to me with short brown hair, continued to talk my ear off—mainly about the men around camp.

"…but then he started to bed down with Sheila. Mike told me they went through several condoms a night. Tent mates couldn't handle it so they moved out – one of them was Jack and I offered room for him…"

In five quick minutes I had learned enough to know that camp at One Less was sexually active as long as two rules were obeyed; condoms and no rape. There was no way that could be one of Shawn's; at least not under his direct control. My ears had strained, trying to catch his voice among the quiet chatter of fifty people, with no such luck. I relaxed a little.

"…but he was a Water and believe me, opposites do not attract. With them it's so gentle and soft and they always want to talk after, and I'm like 'Bugger off – I need my three hours of sleep 'cause I got sentry duty in the morning'."

I smiled, nodding my head, and regretting it instantly. My hand went to my temples again.

"Hey, you okay?" Laura asked.

I tripped over a rock.

She steadied me. "Be careful or you'll be arse over elbow!"

"Thanks. I'm fine." I risked a sideways glance.

She looked at me, expecting more.

"It's just – you know – *that* isn't my thing."

"Ooooh, I get it." She removed her hands from my arm.

I sighed, relieved that she could understand sex wasn't top priority in everyone's mind. But no.

"Then you must be part of Erika's group. No wonder I didn't recognize you. You all do keep to yourselves; don't catch you around the prophylactic distribution tent, if you know what I mean." She laughed, nudging me with her elbow.

I forced a laugh in return.

Oh great, I have just come out of a closet I didn't even know I was in.

But it worked. Her chatter ceased until she found someone else to 'talk shop' with. There were no protests when I began to fall behind. As soon as I was clear to concentrate, I reached out, searching the electrical waves around us, honing in on those with the telltale signature that screamed human. I could do that much without causing an earthquake in my head.

Bee was behind us, accompanied by a Water and a muggle. I smiled. They were alone putting a safe distance between them and One Less. I fell back further until something else caught my ear. Crying.

I picked up the pace, making my way forward among the ranks until I was almost to my very hetero female companion. Just ahead of us were ten or so Elementals they had caught from my group. I recognized the one crying, an eighteen year old female who had joined us in Evansville.

"Shut it, will ya?" One of the guards grabbed her arm, pulling her into him as they walked. "Once you get to camp, there'll be plenty more to cry about."

She recoiled from his breath. He laughed and shoved her away. The rest of the prisoners instinctively crowded around her, shielding her from more bullying.

"Quit messing with them," another guard whispered to his coworker. "You're just jealous because the prisoners eat better than us."

The man grumbled, but didn't outright protest.

The girl stopped crying, but her hiccups and deep, shaky breaths continued to float back to me. I couldn't just abandon them. It was because of me they were here. Apparently, they weren't the only prisoners. How did One Less manage to hold Elementals?

Somewhere up ahead, a dog barked. I flinched at memories of my penguin guard dog on Galapagos Island. The feeling of my power drained, heavy limbs, and the bitter taste of hopelessness raced through my body. Whether there was a place like that close by or not, I couldn't let that happen to anyone else, much less my people.

Without thinking, I reached for my powers. By now it was muscle memory. They didn't come, only pain greeted me. My head spun, splitting open as I fell to my knees. I just managed to crawl to the side of the trail when I vomited, spewing my insides all over the flora and its annoying, consistent buzzes of electricity.

Desperate, I reached for my powers again. Like a drug locked away from me, I panicked at the absence of magic. I felt hands on my back, but the voices around me were drowned out by the roaring in my head. I threw up again, dry heaving stomach acid now. The puke-covered plant life raced up to meet me.

* * *

"Easy there, princess."

I took two steps forward and manipulated the gun out of Shawn's hand in a lightning quick move Alex showed me once. I turned off the safety, took aim, and pulled the trigger.

Chapter 26

Camp

A mullet swayed in front of me. All business in the front and a party in the back. The mullet disappeared as a head swiveled. Overgrown eyebrows and a square chin greeted me.

"You must be Erika," I said. My mouth was sticky and dry at the same time.

She smiled. "They brought you in yesterday, and you've been asleep since. Must've been one helluva fight – wish I'd been there."

"No you don't." I tried to shake my head; a sharp stabbing pain shot through it.

"Here." She held a canteen of water to my lips. I took a drink before she eased it away. "Doctor said not too much."

"The prisoners." I tried sitting up. My head felt like it would split open.

"Whoa, whoa, easy there." She pushed me back down, it didn't take much.

I blinked away the pain.

When Erika came back into focus, she was looking over her shoulder. She turned back to me, whispering, "What business do you have with the prisoners?"

I didn't answer. My hands went to my head, making sure it was intact.

"Listen," she said, "I don't care – but other people will. All I'm sayin' is be careful who you say things around."

I tried to nod, but then thought better of it. "Sure, thanks."

She put a blanket over me. "They said you was one of mine when they brought you here. I went along, but I ain't never seen you before – at least not in my camp."

She stared at me, unblinking. I was going to have to tell her something. "It's...I'm new here – and there are...things...going on in camp that I don't want to participate in."

She held up her hand. "Stop right there – no need to go any further. Several of us that run with a different crowd, but the majority of my group is just seeking shelter. You're welcome to bed down with us. There are just a few rules."

"Okay." I could handle rules.

"First, we follow the rules of camp. Everyone pulls their duty – I can't protect you from that."

"Okay," I repeated.

"Second, no drama."

I liked her already. "Is there a third?"

"I think the second rule covers pretty much everything else. Now, I've got clearance to keep you on bed rest for another two days, but then I gotta put you back on rotations. What were you on before?"

"Um..." I couldn't think clearly. What duties was the camp likely to have? "Kitchen." I pressed my lips shut. *Kitchen?* I couldn't think of a worse duty – which was why it probably popped into my head. "But I hate it." I added.

She raised an eyebrow. "Could be worse – could be latrine."

I crinkled my nose.

She sighed. "I'll see what I can do – someone will be in every few hours to check on you. In the meantime, stay put."

Erika left before I had a chance to thank her.

I surveyed my surroundings. I was in a large tent, but just how large I had no idea. My small corner was blocked off by a sheet draped over a clothesline. I heard activity outside the tent, and kept my hearing on alert for the sound of Shawn's voice. Three hours later, and no Shawn. Instead, I caught clips and phrases of other helpful information.

I heard a working party returning for the day.

"The river was choppy today – gear kept rolling around on the boats."

"Good thing half the plant was disassembled before we got here."

"Job will be done in a week. Then we can head back to Utah."

"Only half of us will fit on the boats, the rest have to walk."

I racked my brain, and came up with Captain Carl's voice, *Fort Calhoun's Nuclear Power Plant*. The activity we'd seen was One Less. I shivered at how close we had come to Shawn. I shivered at how close I was to him now. And if he ever found Bee...

Bee!

Where was she? I closed my eyes and reached out. The sounds around me dulled and the barely audible buzzing of electrical signals became more prevalent. I followed each one, systematically eliminating each Water I came across. Finally, I found them – almost too far to detect. They were on the other side of a hill, sheltered by thick brush. Safe for now.

Do I run to them, or stay?

I opened my eyes and the buzzing in my head disappeared. I took a deep breath. Someone came in, smiled at me, and set an aspirin on the table next to me.

Aspirin?!

I hadn't seen aspirin in months. I sat up. Waves of pain gripped my head again. I reached for the aspirin and swallowed, without the water. As she left, pushing back the hanging sheet, I caught a glimpse of shelves and shelves full of medication.

I lay back down, taking more deep breaths until the pain passed. I'd be no use to Bee this way. Maybe I'd stay until they could help my concussion; maybe even help me get back my powers.

The more I thought about it, the more it made sense. Perhaps putting a little distance between me and Bee would help with the energy. No more earthquakes; nothing to tip off Shawn. Then we could regroup and figure out what to do.

* * *

My first trip out of the tent was necessitated by my full bladder. The late morning sun was blinding after two days of sleep and a dimly lit tent. I stumbled forward, feeling awkward and out of place, like the word 'spy' was tattooed on my forehead.

No one seemed to notice. I adjusted the blue band on my arm, spreading it out. Slightly more confident, I took a deep breath, and followed the smell to the latrines.

I watched the Elementals as they worked around camp. They all looked like normal people. Fat, skinny, old, and young. Diverse nationalities; I even heard several languages. All were intent on some task. And all were...happy, or seemed so, anyway.

There were hundreds of them. Shawn had been busy. I passed a tent with a dozen or more people standing in line just outside. "New recruits, stay in line! Have an ID ready if you have one. You will be marked—" The man barking out orders cut off at the screaming inside the tent. All eyes shot to him, people straightening their backs and fidgeting, on edge.

He held up his hands. "This is the price of admission. It will be clean and quick. You'll get a local anesthetic before and an aspirin after."

More than I got, I thought.

I kept walking, strangely more secure with the knowledge that One Less had several new recruits. Maybe it wouldn't be so hard blending in.

"Whoa, there." I felt a hand pull back on my upper arm. "Don't want to be stepping in there."

I glanced down at my foot, hovering over a ditch. I threw my arm over my nose and mouth. "Oh, man – the smell!" I turned to face my savior as he pulled me back to even ground.

"I know. They're behind on their digging." He nodded to a dozen people with shovels a few yards away, excavating more ditches.

Latrine duty. Suddenly the kitchen didn't sound so bad.

"The women's bathrooms are over the hill." He pointed in the opposite direction. "Much nicer facilities from what I hear." He smiled.

I forced a laugh. "Yeah, well – thanks for the rescue."

He shrugged. "No biggie. Maybe we could meet up later – eat chow together?"

"Oh." My eyes went wide. I hadn't had to turn a man down in a long time.

"I'll come find you – where do you camp?" he asked.

"I'm – well, I'm over there." I pointed in the general direction we had both come, fumbling around for an excuse – an answer – something. "I'm with Erika. Er, not *with* her – but I'm from her. Camp, that is."

I groaned. *Screwed that one up.*

I put my hand on my hip and said a little louder. "I'm part of Erika's camp."

"Oooohhh," said the man. "Sorry – didn't realize. Well, have a nice day!" He turned and walked away.

That was easy. Already Erika was proving useful.

The sound of his zipper and a steady stream of liquid hitting dirt got me moving. Up and over the hill, another ditch greeted me. There was at least privacy from the camp. I chose one end of the area and hesitated. My bladder, aching with the need to empty itself, suddenly turned shy.

I waited until the women that were there left, then relieved myself. No splashing – score. I stood and zipped up my pants. I turned, planning a route back that avoided my puddle and any other suspicious wet spots, when a procession of prisoners crested the hill.

Tethered waist to waist with actual shackles and chains, they were all Earths, guarded by other Earths at a ratio of two to one. I recognized the one on the end as the girl crying after she had been captured in the forest. More specifically, she was one we had picked up in Evansville.

After they made their way down the hill, finding their spots in the ditch as best they could, I walked over to them. I jumped, pretending to avoid a nastier part of the ditch, and ran into her.

"Oh, sorry." I put my hands on her shoulders, steadying her. Under my breath, I whispered, "Are you okay?"

She turned, eyes going wide when she saw my face. "You!" She glanced down to the blue band of material on my arm. "You're with them?!"

"Hey – no talking to the prisoners!" One of the guards pointed her finger at me.

I smoothed my face over. "I ran into her – I was just saying sorry."

"Fine. You said it."

"And now I have to pee – again."

The guard put her hand on her hip and looked me over.

"I have a big canteen," I said, pulling my zipper down.

The guard shrugged and walked away.

"You. Bitch."

I turned back to the girl; her eyes were on fire, face flush with anger.

I grabbed her arm pulling her down so we were both squatting. "Shh! Please, I'm not with them." I glanced at my armband. "Well, I am. But as a spy."

She raised an eyebrow. "We followed you here; we trusted you! And now look where we are."

"Listen, I'll work on it. I've lost my powers but I'll find some way to get you out of here. Remember—"

"All I remember was your baby screaming; giving us all away. Once the fighting started, I got a quick glimpse of you hurling a fireball toward me, then running after your kid without a second thought for us!"

She stood and glared down at me. "You remember who you are, and why you're here."

"Prisoners up!" The rest of the chain gang stood at the guards command and were ushered away before I could get in another word.

Who I am? I'm a mother for Christ's sake! What mother would've done it differently? I pulled up my own pants for a second time and walked away with crossed arms, kicking rocks as I went. I took in a deep breath and cleared my head. I tried to put myself in her position. I couldn't very well pick up people along the way and abandon them at the first sign of trouble.

I sighed. *Maybe I'll be here longer than I thought.* Besides, Bee was safe for the moment, and I could always check up on her.

With my bladder taking up significantly less room in my midsection, my stomach began to rumble. Erika had deprived me of food for fear of it coming back up all over one of her tents.

I followed my nose again, this time to the kitchens. There were several fires going. On top of them lay pieces of meat, skinned and splayed out. Unidentifiable from where I stood, but probably rabbit and squirrel for the most part. Maybe some birds. It smelled delicious.

I stretched, biding my time to observe how exactly food procurement worked. A long line of Elementals held empty plates. They stopped at one table, spoke to a woman sitting behind it, and she checked lists marking something off.

Dang, they're keeping track. If my name isn't on the list, how am I going to get food?

I made my way over to sets of long logs laid in parallel rows. Several groups of people were eating. I picked up an empty plate, then sat on a log one group just vacated. They left behind several scraps of food. Dirty or not, I put them on my plate.

I walked back over to the lines where they dished out food, skipping directly ahead to the servers, and squeezed my way in between two others in line. "I'm sorry. Excuse me." I looked directly at one of the servers. He wiped sweat from his forehead with his shirtsleeve and frowned.

I cleared my throat. "I dropped my plate – is there any way I can get another serving?" I displayed the dirt covered roll as evidence.

He glanced at the roll, then back at me. "No seconds."

Someone down the line shouted, "Come on lady – no cuts!"

Another person shoved, and the entire line, ending at me, was pushed forward. "Please?" My eyebrows rose in desperation. "I missed chow last night and I'm on a working party today."

More shouting down the line.

The server clenched his jaw, and huffed. "Fine, but half-rats." He slopped a large pile of stew with meat chunks on my plate and added a clean roll. It was burned on the bottom.

I gave him my best smile, showing plenty of white. "Thanks!"

I returned to the eating logs, finished my meal alone, and went back to Erika's camp. I was going to have to figure something else out for food. I couldn't keep feigning clumsiness.

When I returned to the tent, I found my corner cot occupied. A girl, with an ankle swelling up to the size of a softball, lay there groaning.

Erika walked up behind me. "Sorry. You've been relocated due to the uneven ground the night guard gets to patrol on."

"Okay…" I wasn't looking forward to another day of staring at the fabric roof anyway. "Where should I go?"

She turned, motioning me to follow. We walked back outside. "My perimeter is marked off by the blue tents in a sort of semi-circle. No one crosses into them unless they're new…or desperate." She looked me over.

I'm both, I thought, in case she was wondering.

"Anyway, this one is yours. No tent-mate for the time being, but that might change."

I peeked inside. A sleeping bag and pillow were there. Other than that, it barely looked large enough for another person. I couldn't complain – I'd been sleeping in open air the past year. At least this way there would be no mosquitos.

I straightened back up and looked at her, "Thanks."

"I've also got your assignment."

I swallowed, hard, as the smell from the latrines wafted over.

"Admin. Specifically, an assistant to an admin clerk."

"Oh – ok." I relaxed, having prepared myself for the worst. "What does that entail, exactly?"

She crossed her arms. "Sitting at a desk, reporting on numbers of Elementals, supplies, or whatever around camp."

That sounded like a headquarters sort of deal; might make for a higher chance of running into Shawn.

Erika continued, "They keep pretty close tabs on the prisoners. You know, in case you were curious about that sort of thing."

My eyes widened, and before I could stop myself, I threw my arms around her. "You are the best."

She stumbled back, her cheeks red. "Okay, okay. Just remember – I may need the favor returned someday."

Chapter 27

Tonight

"Reporting for admin duty," I announced to the first person who looked my way once I walked into the cordoned off area. He surveyed me from head to toe.

Should I salute or—

"Are you new? They don't usually send the newbies to admin duty." He stood from behind two pushed-together crates that made a makeshift desk. It was covered in papers.

"I'm not that new." I put my hand on my hip. "I've been assigned as Jason's assistant. They said he needed one."

"Oh, well – unfortunately Jason was injured in that last battle. He's in the sick bay for at least two weeks. Which means…" The man turned back to the crates, searching under the stacks of papers for something. "Jason needs a temporary replacement."

I caught a few sheets that floated off, and gave them back.

In return, he handed me a red armband. "Which means you've just been promoted."

I glanced around the area. Everyone working there wore a red band above their blue. I took it from him and ran it up my arm. "Thanks – I think."

"You probably won't be thanking me after your first day. Here – you can get started with these inquiries." He handed me a new stack of papers, and pointed to an unoccupied crate.

I nodded, took my place and began my new job. In a way, it was more exhausting than covering thirty miles a day. Inquiries kept arriving – and I had to answer them, or find someone to answer them for me. The kitchen needed to know how many days' worth of tomatoes our mobile garden had. The guards needed to know how many more days we were staying at camp so they could work out a sentry schedule. The medics needed more cloth bandages.

Jason was also apparently responsible for daily reports which included Elemental counts, prisoner counts, food storage, fresh water tracking, and more. But for a spy, there was no better place to be.

Someone set several lists in front of me.

"What's this?" I asked.

"Daily chow roster. You need to double check names and add new recruits; then deliver to the kitchens."

I nodded. "Okay, thanks."

Score!

I scribbled my name in between two others. After adding several new Elementals to the end of the list, I left the admin tent to deliver the lists.

I also needed to take the time to check on the prisoners. I weaved around the camp, spread across at least ten acres, keeping an eye out. I waved to the woman who had helped check on me when I was still on bed rest. She had laundry duty. I peered at her hands, wrinkled and white from too much time in the water. I nearly crashed paths with a group coming over the hill, each carrying a shovel on their shoulder. None of them looked happy. I had certainly dodged a bullet with my assignment; so far I hadn't come across a better alternative.

"Watch out!" someone yelled.

I jumped out of the way of a panicked pig, squealing as two men chased it. Someone else shouted for help to repair the pen the animals had broken out of. Behind the pen, in between a staggered row of tents, something caught my eye. I paused, taking a step back and craning my neck. A row of guards stood around a larger tent. The prisoners!

I walked toward the tent, blocking out the sound of squeals and grunts, forming a plan in my head as I went. As I neared, I realized there were two layers of guards I would have to talk my way through. I approached the first, flashing my list of names and folding them back up. "I have new orders for the prisoners."

I have no idea what that means, I told myself. I kept my chin up, fixing him with my stare.

"I'll take them." He held out his hand.

I crossed my arms, tucking the papers out of his reach and displaying my already prominent red armband. "Sorry, has to go directly to the head guard."

I really, really hoped there was one.

He sighed, then miraculously, stepped aside. "Fine." He gestured to another guard on the inner circle, near the opening of the large tent.

I waited until I passed him to let out a sigh of relief. It was short lived; there was still another guard I had to get past. How could I possibly convince him to let me in alone with the prisoners?

Excuse me, we're conducting a short survey with all camp prisoners. Excuse me, don't you know who I am? Excuse me, I'm the cleaning crew.

My confidence was quickly waning as I approached the head guard. He was bent over, fiddling with the leather straps around his boots. I adjusted my red band to make it appear larger and cleared my throat, still having no idea what to say.

The guard straightened, or at least I could've sworn he did. He was shorter than me by a full foot or more.

Then he turned, and my mouth dropped open in shock. "Clay?!"

His beard was definitely longer, and his eyebrows definitely thicker, but there was no doubt it was Clay.

I took a step forward, bent slightly, and hissed, "What are you doing here?" If he had been spying for Shawn all along, I would strangle him right then and there – with his beard.

"Kaitlyn, please keep your voice down," he hissed right back. "If you recall, I was one of the few who volunteered to hook up with One Less after the battle at the caves."

I went silent while I racked my brain. It was so long ago – and the preparations went by in such a whirlwind I wasn't aware of half the things that occurred. "I think…maybe…I—"

"What are *you* doing here?" he cut me off.

I cleared my throat again. "Spying." Might as well be forthright about it, if he was with Shawn, Clay would turn me in no matter what I said.

Clay's mouth twitched. "So you decide to show up at the most watched place in camp?"

I crossed my arms and narrowed my eyes. "I have friends inside." I moved to step around him.

"So does Shawn."

I stopped in my tracks. "What do you mean?"

"He keeps his own people in there, playing them off like real prisoners. They're meant to keep an eye on things; get what information they can from the others."

I rubbed my temples. "Oh, great." Like playing a game of chess blindfolded, this was all getting too complicated.

"Keep it down, will ya? You're attracting attention." He motioned to the circle of guards; a few were looking our way.

I straightened, and handed him the papers, trying to play off my role. "Some of the guys in there are mine. Are they being treated okay?"

He pretended to look over the papers. "Of course – I'm the head guard."

"Are they getting enough food and water?"

"More than the working parties do." He crossed his arms.

"No physical abuse?"

He huffed part of his mustache away from his mouth. "I am doing the best I can here, Kaitlyn. I've been with One Less for almost two years now, sabotaging what I can, passing info when I can. I haven't been caught yet." He handed the papers back to me. "Now you need to go before you ruin all that. I'll catch up with you at chow tonight."

"Fine. Tonight, then. And I want to know *everything*."

"Fine."

I turned on my heel.

"You might want to consider changing your name, at the very least. *Miss Spy*," he said from behind me.

I glanced down at the papers I held. Right where I scribbled it, *Kaitlyn Alder* stood out like a sore thumb. My cheeks grew hot, and I was glad my back was to Clay. I walked off, erasing the name as I went.

Chapter 28

Kaitlyn, Left Behind

"Lucy Evermore," I repeated the name to the admin clerk set up just in front of the kitchens. She put a checkmark next to the name I'd inserted to replace my own. I moved forward in line, not bothering to hide the triumphant smile on my face. The meal rations list was delivered to the kitchens daily. Thankfully, it was always copied over from the previous day – the admin clerk adding or subtracting names as necessary. Sometimes the exact same list was resubmitted. My "name" would forever be on the list. Unless I died.

I shivered as one of the servers slopped unidentifiable stew on my plate.

"It ain't that bad," she mumbled.

I moved on, finding space on the crowded logs. Loud groups of people surrounded me, everyone buzzing with excitement over the gala tonight. Already I saw condoms being passed around. The women were hiking up their pant legs and rolling up their sleeves, baring as much skin as possible.

I hunched over, with my plate balanced on my knees, keeping my head down.

I'll eat and leave, I told myself. *If Clay isn't here by then, I'll catch up with him another time.*

Tonight was not a good night to be waiting around. I needed to be hiding out in my tent. I scraped the last bits of stew into my mouth with the crude, wooden spoon. I moved to stand when a heavy hand clamped down on my shoulder, stopping me cold.

"Have a partner yet for tonight, sweet thing?"

I brushed the hand off my shoulder. "Yes, as a matter of fact…"

I drifted off at the laughing, and turned, craning my neck up. I didn't have to crane it that far. Clay stood behind me, nearly spilling his plate of food his shoulders shook so hard.

I held in my growl. "Careful, there are no seconds."

He squeezed in beside me on the log. "Sorry, couldn't resist. You looked so worried." He shoved a roll in his mouth and his beard moved up and down with what I could only assume was chewing. "You need to relax. Look at everyone around you – happy, excited. Then there's you, hunched over your plate, eating like it's your last meal."

He was right; I needed to be better at this. *Starting now.* I took a deep breath, leaned back, and put a smile on my face. "That better?"

He paused to look at me. "Getting there." He went back to his food.

I rolled my eyes. "What's the matter, not interested in the wares on display?" Both our eyes followed the bared, glistening abdomen that passed in front of us.

He grunted. "Better things to do. What about you?"

I smiled. "Didn't you hear? I'm in Erika's camp."

He nodded. "That'll do. Maybe you're not so bad at this."

I snorted. "Yeah – we'll see how long I last." I watched him sop up the rest of the stew on his plate with bits of roll.

Clay swallowed. "So, what's your plan?"

I shrugged. "I don't have one."

"Can't you just, you know, level the place? Take your people back?"

I took a deep breath, forcing back the lump rising in my throat. "I've lost my powers."

Clay started choking, spewing out food. I patted his back. He recovered, and looked at me.

"I hit my head pretty hard a few days back, and now I black out when I try to use them." I looked down, concentrating on spreading dirt around with the toe of my boot. "Hopefully it is just temporary."

Clay nodded. "Probably a concussion. Happened to one of the Fires a while back. Go see Sabrina; she is the doc specializing in 'power' issues." He paused, burping. "And the baby?"

"Safe," I said.

We leaned back, allowing room for a couple glued to the hip and making out as they passed. I rolled my eyes. "What's with all the sex?"

Clay set down his plate and wiped his mouth with the tip of his beard. "Shawn encourages it. They are briefed on expectations when they arrive and even rewarded for the behavior."

A flying condom hit me in the shoulder. At least it was still in its package. I kicked it away. "Obviously not many babies are produced. What does Shawn get out of it?"

Clay laughed. "Come on – I'll walk you back to your tent."

We walked back, avoiding the larger groups of people.

"Energy," Clay said.

"What?"

"Shawn gets energy out of it."

I thought of the Great Rite, and how it had worked for me. "How?" I stopped, looking around, eyes wide. "Is he here now?"

Clay took my arm and propelled me forward. "Remember what I said about relaxing? He hasn't been back from the boats in days. Busy protecting his stash. But trust me, when he is about to come back, the admin guys will be the first to know – you positioned yourself well."

The tension left my shoulders. "So if he is not here – how does he collect the energy? And what exactly does it do for him?"

Clay shrugged. "No one really knows the specifics. But he has increased his strength significantly since the galas have started. Trust me, if I knew I would've found some way to sabotage it by now. As it is, the most I've done in that department is dispose of all the strawberries in camp."

I laughed out loud. "Strawberries?"

"They're an aphrodisiac, you know."

"So they say."

We stopped at the perimeter of Erika's tents. "Well, this is as far as I go," Clay said.

I bent down to hug him.

"What was that for?" he asked.

"I'm glad to have you, is all." I smiled. We had to untangle my hair from his beard before we could part fully. "Why do you keep that thing?"

He ran his fingers through it. "Warmth, mainly. And it makes a handy napkin."

I ran my fingers through my own hair.

"Besides, if I ever need to ditch camp, a quick shave – maybe some thicker shoes for height, and no one here would probably recognize me."

I nodded. "Your hair is pretty recognizable."
He raised his eyebrow at me. "As is yours."

* * *

Before returning to my tent, I sought out a pair of scissors.

Erika was able to produce them. "You're not going to cause problems with these, are you?" She twirled the scissors on her finger. I had a flashback of someone flourishing a two-fingered salute. I shook my head, now wasn't the time to explore forgotten memories.

"If you think I'm going to harm myself – or someone else, no. I just want to change up my look." I held out my hand.

She placed the scissors in it, handle first. "I have some former hairstylists; probably can do it up right."

I smiled but kept my gaze down at the metal in my hands. Moonlight glinted off the sharp blades. "No thanks, I need to do this on my own."

I turned, then stopped and asked over my shoulder, "But do you know any tattoo artists?"

She nodded. "A few."

"Maybe send them my way tomorrow?"

"I'll see if I can pull strings – get one of them off their working parties."

I turned, facing her. "I'll need all of them."

Once in my tent, I zipped up the door behind me and fell to my knees. No need to delay the inevitable. I snipped off a brown and gold curl toward the front.

That one always got in my eyes anyway, I told myself.

Outside, music started up at the gala. Drums, strings, and even a flute gave their all to the party. I snipped another piece.

And that one had some grey in it. Good riddance.

Unexpected tears sprang to my eyes, watering the growing pile of hair below me. Bee loved playing with my hair. As a baby, she would wrap her fingers around and around my strands while she fed. Once a little older, we would twist each other's hair on top of our heads and pretend they were crowns.

Forest princesses, her small voice echoed in my head.

Would she even recognize me now?

My hands moved quicker, cutting away without hesitation. Try as I might to block them, the memories came flooding back. Frozen locks breaking off in my hand after I saved Alex from the Chakra's icy lake. Holding my hair back while Micah clasped the butterfly necklace around my neck. Golden brown tresses rising with static electricity when I forced lightning to destroy the handfasting location Shawn desecrated.

Between sobs, I shouted out loud, "Damn it!" *Why is this so hard? It's just hair, for Christ's sake.* I moved to the final few curls at the back.

One more memory came; Micah in bed with me, smoothing back my hair and calling me 'mop head'.

The scissors snipped my finger, and I dropped them. Holding my bleeding hand, I still cried. Blood, tears, and hair swirled together, making one messy pile of Kaitlyn, left behind. I crawled into my sleeping bag, cocooning myself off from the world and hiding from the building energy within the camp.

* * *

"Easy there, princess."

My shoulders sank. I'd never had a recurring dream that was so damn frustrating. I looked into Shawn's cold, blue eyes. If my nightmares had done one thing for me, it had made those eyes less intimidating. I leaned to the right. His eyes followed. Then I leaned to the left, going a little further. He watched to a point, but then his eyes drifted back to where I should have been standing. I returned to my position.

"Where is the baby?"

"Safe," I responded. He had a gun in his hand, pointed down this time. I stepped forward, counting until I reached him. Five paces away. His gun now pointed at my knees.

Why there?

I stepped back once, and mist swirled around my ankles. Something was there, in front of him. The harder I looked, trying to piece it together, the more it evaded me.

"Kaitlyn, is the baby mine?"

I blinked, now *that* was different. He asked instead of declared who the baby's father was. Was that how it actually went down? I couldn't even remember anymore. Akasha burned bright behind me, trying to distract me. But the puzzle was right in front of me. I just needed more time…

Chapter 29

Tainted

"What a waste," Shawn said.

"Sir?" David trailed Shawn, notebook open, pencil at the ready.

"All that energy last night, left to disperse on its own."

"Did you lose the Athame?" David asked.

Shawn continued walking the old, dilapidated power plant for the last time, checking to see if anything else could be salvaged before their trip home. "No."

"Then why did you order the gala last night, if you weren't going to absorb the energy?" David tripped over a piece of laminate, curling up from the floor.

"Last night was a test. The energies in the area lately have felt off, and I needed to know why. If anyone significantly strong was nearby, that energy would have naturally gravitated toward them."

"So did it work?"

"We are clear." Shawn nudged at a door. "Why won't this open?"

David flipped through his notebook, as if the answer would be there.

Shawn rolled his eyes, took a step back, and drove his shoulder into the door. It still didn't budge.

"Oh, yes – I have it here." David held up the notebook, pointing. "This door is locked."

Shawn looked at the notebook, then back at David. He turned away before he followed his better instincts to strangle the man. Shawn drove his shoulder into the door again.

David closed the notebook. In between Shawn's pounding, he asked, "So do you want to go back to camp before we leave?"

Shawn paused, rubbing his shoulder. "If I have time tomorrow. We need to focus on breaking camp and getting everyone on the move before that storm gets here."

Shawn turned, and aimed for the door with his left shoulder. The door sprung open into a dark room. Shawn lit a match and stepped inside.

The small flame glinted off large, metal barrels. Bright white lettering along the side of them read, 'Fuel Oil'.

David stepped up beside Shawn, "Enough to get us to Denver – I dare say, sir."

Shawn nodded. "Get a working party; put all the barrels down in the engine room. I'll be in my quarters, and I'll need some privacy. No interruptions."

* * *

Shawn stood on the platform once again. This time there were no shimmery forms flying through the air, nor swimming below. They were all in solid, human form, waiting in line patiently on the stairs. It was eerie. Shawn held up his hand, tightly wrapped in bandages from his experience two days earlier. The skin was trying to mend itself, but every time he moved his fingers, barely-healed wounds tore open.

He sighed, rewrapping his right hand. He lifted his left, gesturing the first in line forward and said, "Come on. Let's get this over with."

She was an Earth Shade – and Chinese. Energy swirled around her feet as she stepped forward, revealing her unchecked excitement. Dust and grime from the dirt floor lifted to join the fray.

Shawn coughed, covering his mouth with his bandaged hand. "In love and in trust, in peace and in wisdom, I release you. So mote it be."

The Chinese woman nodded once at Shawn, and her silky-white skin grew even brighter. Shawn grimaced as the familiar burn touched his good hand. He wasn't going to be able to hold on to his bike handlebar for weeks. Was this Sarah's way of delaying his plans? If only he could talk to her…

As the Chinese woman disappeared in a puff of smoke, Shawn glanced up at the cove high on the wall. It was dark.

A sudden blast of wind hit Shawn. He squinted, protecting his eyes from the sting as his hair and clothes flapped.

Once the wind died down, someone giggled. "Oh – sorry."

He opened one eye, then another. An elderly woman—an Air, obviously—stood hunched before him.

"I have been waiting a long time to return to the open arms of the Goddess," she said.

Shawn ran the back of his hands over his hair, trying to tame it. "May your return join together body, spirit, and Shade, giving back to the Earth what was borrowed."

The woman grinned from ear to ear and the wind started up again. Shawn stuck out his hand, turned his head and said the chant quickly before he was blown off the ledge.

As she floated away, Shawn heard a distant, "Thank you, young man."

Shawn rubbed his face with his arm and grumbled, "Happy to oblige."

"Margaret always was excitable."

Shawn jumped at the voice over his shoulder. Arianna stood there, smiling at the puff of smoke the old woman left behind.

"You going to miss them? Because we don't have to do this."

Arianna narrowed her eyes at Shawn. "This Athame was never meant to be tainted. The wrong must be made right again."

Shawn huffed; righting wrongs was a lot of work.

"Next!" Arianna called for Shawn.

Chapter 30

Inked

"Are you awake?"

The voice called me from my nightmare. I opened my eyes and was greeted with pitch black.

I clawed my way out of my sleeping bag. When the fog cleared from my head, Erika stood at the flap to my tent, staring at my pile of hair from the night before. She stepped in, picked up the scissors, and then looked at me.

I sat up, running my fingers through my hair. They hit air way too quickly.

"You certainly did a number on yourself. Mind if I take some of it?" She bent down, sweeping my hair into a tighter pile with her bare hands.

"Why?"

"We can add it to our mobile compost piles. Hair takes a long time to decompose, but it is a rich source of nitrogen."

I scooted out of my stifling hot bag, rubbing my face. "Sure." I looked away. My eyes were puffy enough as it was.

Erika collected all my hair in a small canvas bag and stood. "I've got the tattoo artists. Ready for them?"

I nodded, still turned away. Three women entered and set up a cot in the middle of the tent. There was barely enough room for everyone.

They put down their bags. The tallest one stepped forward. "Hi Lucy – I'm Layla." She had a slight accent, maybe Dutch.

I nodded my head at her.

"What you see here," she gestured to our bags, "is the last of our ink."

Behind her, one of the women's lips went tight. The other glanced at the bags, then swallowed.

Layla continued. "If we do this for you, we can no longer continue our art."

Her words hung in the air. Behind me, Erika cleared her throat. She wanted me to say something; she wanted me to answer the unasked question. *Why should they use the last of their ink on me?*

I looked at each of the women. None gave away any clues as to what the right answer might be.

Erika spoke up. "She is interested in the prisoners."

One of the women stepped forward, standing next to Layla now. "What business do you have with the prisoners?" Her whole body leaned forward, her hand on her hip.

Layla put her hand on the woman's shoulder.

To calm her or hold her back? I couldn't tell. Maybe both.

"This is Marissa," Layla said. That was all she said, but her hand stayed on Marissa's shoulder. They stood together, waiting for me to respond.

I looked back at Erika. Her eyes widened only slightly. *Respond carefully*, is what she should've said to me.

I looked back at the women. "I want the prisoners gone." *There, that leaves me open to go either way.*

Marissa tensed. Layla's grasp on her shoulder tightened.

"Gone, how?" Marissa asked.

I stood, body going as tense as Marissa's. My hands twitched at my side, ready for a fight.

Time to gamble, I thought. My heart beat so hard I could feel it in my throat. "Gone as in set free."

My eyes darted to each of the women, even to Erika, expecting an attack. But Marissa sank back, releasing a breath.

Layla's mouth turned up in a smile. "Marissa's sister is being held there. But she can't get close enough to even talk to her, much less figure out how to free her."

My eyes flitted over to Marissa. "Have you tried the latrine area?"

She furrowed her eyebrow.

I sighed, "Here – use this." I removed my red arm band and tossed it to her. "It'll get you to the head guard. His name is Clay and he is a friend of mine. Tell him Kai—" I cleared my own throat. "Tell him Lucy sent you. He can at least maybe give you time with your sister."

"Can I trust him?" she asked, looking at the arm band.

"Can he trust you?"

She nodded, then slipped the arm band on.

"He will do what needs to be done to help your sister."

"Thank you," Marissa said. She looked to be on the verge of tears.

She turned to leave, but Layla stopped her. "First, we repay the debt. Okay?"

"No, no." I interrupted. "It's okay. Let her go."

Everyone looked at me. I shrugged, "I know what it is to be separated from family."

Layla nodded, and Marissa left after another round of thanks.

Layla turned to the bags, "Well, let's begin." She nodded to the other woman. "This is Sheri."

Sheri nodded. I recognized her as an admin worker. She helped predict weather patterns. "What kind of ink can we slap on you today?" she asked.

I sat on the cot, meeting their eyes. "I don't care. Just keep them where people are most likely to see them. Arms, face, neck. Maybe shoulders. That tree looks nice." I gestured to the tattoo on Layla's upper left arm.

They both exchanged glances. "Let's take a look." Layla reached for my hands, surveying several small scars up my arms. "We can cover these up, if you like."

I nodded, and removed my shirt, baring my shoulder. "What about this one?"

They peered at my back. "That one looks too fresh."

I snorted. It was a couple of years old, at least.

"We don't want to mess with it too much, but we'll see what we can do."

Erika was still at the tent flap. "Can I straighten up your hair a little? You are uneven in the back."

"Sure."

The tattoo artists set up a makeshift table, preparing their ink and needles. The tattoo guns were altered to run on battery power. Thank goodness they still had batteries for them. Erika began snipping away at my hair.

"Do you know someone named Sabrina?" I asked her.

"You have some sort of medical problem?"

"More like a power problem."

Erika turned my head. "That's what she is good at. I'll see if I can get her here today – you'll probably be at the mercy of these needles until dusk at least. Your debt is starting to stack up, you know."

"I know." I sighed.

"What's your power anyway?" She turned my head the other way.

I froze – I hadn't though this one through yet. I very well couldn't say all of them. Hello red flag. No matter what I chose, they may be able to detect their own element within me. I could always play dumb if it came to that.

"Guess," I said.

"Well, she ain't an Air." Sheri glanced at me. Layla agreed.

One down, three to choose from.

Erika wasn't offering any information.

"What are you?" I asked.

"Fire." She snipped at my hair again.

Earth or Water, which one? I went with the former. "I am Earth."

"That probably explains it," Erika said.

"What?" I asked.

"That I can't detect your magic. I usually can, no matter what the element. But Earths are tricky. They operate on a lower frequency."

I thought of Susan's words, 'Earths rarely know they possess the ability themselves.' Still – all of them should've been able to detect their own elements within me. Probably another side effect of my concussion. I wondered what else my injury was shielding me from.

"Ok, ready?" Layla turned on the ominous tattoo gun in her hand. "Back or front first?"

I lay down on my stomach. "Back."

She started in right between my shoulder blades while Sheri extended my left arm for an ink bracelet on my wrist. I turned away. A few sharp stings here and there, and my bones felt like they were vibrating, but the pain wasn't nearly as bad as I had expected.

Erika finished cutting my hair and went to collecting the rest. She came around to the front of the table, opened my hand, and placed a small braided section of my locks in it. It was tied together on both ends with a thin ribbon.

"What's this for?" I asked.

She shrugged. "I don't know – your hair seemed significant to you, so I thought you might want to keep a bit." She turned, exiting the tent. I was left to the mercy of the tattooists.

I closed my fist around the hair.

An hour later, Layla moved on to my shoulder blades. Here, the pain was worse. It was four men, pulling at each limb while Shawn carved his symbol into me all over again. It was his knife piercing my skin, leaking its poison into my body. I needed more of a distraction than my own thoughts – or my own hair.

"So – how's the weather been?" I asked Sheri. She moved from one wrist to my other.

"Weird." She pulled the gun away, blotting blood away from my wrist. The pile of reddened rags in front of me was growing.

"How so?"

"There is a derecho coming." She put the gun back to my arm.

I looked away. "A derecho? Sounds like a cowboy thing, or something."

"It is a huge, drawn-out line of thunderstorms. This one's going to have hurricane-force winds."

"Will the camp be safe?"

"Probably not – we'll need to move out soon."

I need to warn Susan and Alex.

"How much time do we have?" I asked.

"Not even a day – we'll probably leave this afternoon."

I wondered what that meant for the prisoners; and for Marissa. I closed my eyes and reached out, searching for Clay. He was standing with someone – an Earth. Her heartbeat was racing; his was slow and steady.

Sheri was still talking. "You might have some pain with fresh tattoos on the march. But there ain't no stopping that storm – too powerful. It really is too late in the season for derechos, and the developing patterns were all wrong, but it's coming."

My eyes widened. Bee was still near, and the freak storms were still following us. We couldn't fool Mother Nature with even a little separation.

Scalpel-like sensations dragged across my shoulder. I twitched as fire went down my spine.

"Stay still," Layla, standing behind me, mumbled.

Above us, clouds moved in and the entire world seemed to go a few shades darker.

"We might need to move this outside – for the light," Sheri suggested.

Rain drops drizzled over the tent.

She sighed. "Guess we'll just have to make do."

My shoulder was finally going numb to the pain. I barely noticed when Layla stopped.

"Done with the back and neck."

"Done here, too." Sheri said.

They pressed clean gauze against the new tattoos and secured them with medical tape.

"Want anything on your legs?" Layla asked.

"No." I mostly wore pants, anyway. "Something on my face, though."

Layla's eyebrows rose, "Do you have anything specific in mind?"

"No," I answered. "I just don't want to look like me."

I caught them exchange a glance.

Layla smiled. "Kind of hard to do, unless we perform minor surgery." Stepping to the side, she surveyed me. "But we can do something subtle with your profile. And maybe some permanent eyeliner, and a darker lip shade…"

"We can continue what I did on her shoulder," Sheri suggested.

They both stepped around, discussing the canvas that was my body. When the needles came back on the two women worked alternately, tying in the pattern on my shoulder over Shawn's scar with another design on the side of my neck, going up to my face. It burned and pinched; cat scratches on a sunburn.

I stared at Layla's shoes as she worked. Her hands remained steady, but she tapped her foot like it was a nervous tick. Her tattoo gun felt like a sharpened pencil, scraping off my skin, cell by cell. I tried to concentrate on the beat of her tapping foot.

The side walls of my tent blew in and out, so far holding strong against the growing wind. Voices outside went from groggy, still recovering from the festivities the night before, to concerned. Shouts to break down the tents and secure loose items sounded around us. Inside, my two artists barely spoke, intent on their work.

"I'm out of black," Sheri said.

"Finish outlining in dark purple," Layla mumbled. But one by one the colors were beginning to run out.

After working on my eyelids, eyebrows and lips, they moved on to the detail work alongside my cheek and temple, ending on the side of my forehead. I gritted my teeth. My entire head vibrated as if they were inking directly onto my skull.

I wasn't sure I could let them finish, it was too much. "Wait—"

"Someone need a doctor?" I was cut off by a small form at the opening to my tent.

The needles stopped. *Thank God.*

"Yes, are you Sabrina?" I started to push myself up off the cot.

"No need to get up, I can work on you from there."

"Oh...okay," I reluctantly laid my head back down. I couldn't even rest it on my arms, covered in fresh, still bleeding tattoos as they were.

She came around the cot, set down a small stool near my head and took her place. Without asking, she began running her fingers through my hairline, pressing into my scalp. She glanced at the tattoo artists. "You may continue."

Darn.

The needles started back up, but the newcomer's fingers were distracting enough. "Erika told me you were having an issue with your powers. Did you hit your head?"

"Yes." One of the needles pinched extra hard as I spoke.

"Damn it," Layla mumbled.

Sabrina took no notice. "Any other symptoms?"

"Headaches, and my ears seem to be ringing a lot."

The needle pinched again.

"Ugh, no more talking!" Layla said. She wiped her brow, flexed her hand a few times, then continued.

I shut my mouth. I needed this to be over with about two hours ago. The wind was picking up even more and I needed to get word to Alex and Susan.

"Okay, I'm just going to poke around and see what I can find out," Sabrina said.

Isn't that what she has been doing?

I glanced up to see her close her eyes. I didn't dare try to tap into what she was doing. The last thing everyone in the tent needed was to be puked on. My head tingled, and the ringing in my ears started up again.

It stopped all at once when her eyes flew open.

"What's the matter?" I asked. She was staring straight ahead, eyes still wide. She didn't answer me. She just got up and started for the tent flap like she had a sudden case of small bladder. "Wait!" I yelled after her.

She stopped just outside, turning her head to address me. "Not much we can do for a concussion. Take some aspirin when the pain gets bad; in time it will heal."

I stood up from the cot. "I mean, what about my powers?"

Thunder rolled overhead like an ominous warning.

Now she turned to face me full on, and cocked her head. "You said powers, not power."

Chapter 31

No More Tears

Sabrina left in a rush, leaving the tent flaps unzipped. They fluttered in the strengthening wind. The low buzzing of tattoo guns ceased all at once. Layla and Sheri wiped down their instruments and stowed their now empty jars of ink.

"Are we done?" I asked.

Layla looked up at me, putting away the last jar. "It's all gone."

"Oh, right," I said, furrowing my eyebrows. "Can you get more?"

Layla rubbed the back of her neck. "Not unless we come across a very talented Earth to sniff out Iron Oxide, Cadmium, and the dozens of other metal salts used to make ink."

Both of their eyebrows went up. I did just declare myself to be an Earth.

"Sorry – power problems, remember?"

Sheri mumbled under their breath. "Figures - Earths can't do all that much, anyway."

I don't think I was meant to hear it, but I answered anyway. "We can do enough."

"Like?" she asked. It wasn't a challenge, more like a distracting conversation for her as she placed her tattoo gun back in its case, perhaps for the last time.

Layla stepped forward, bandaging up the side of my face. "Keep these on the next couple of days. We'll find you and check back in – see how they are doing."

I nodded, then addressed Sheri's question. "I can tell you where Marissa is, right now. And I can send help for her and her sister."

Sheri turned around, putting her hand on her hip. "Okay, I'll bite. Where is she and how can you send help?"

Layla answered before I could. "She is probably with your friend Clay, where you sent her."

"No," I shook my head, standing up. "No – she's with the prisoners. They're all running. And..." I closed my eyes, concentrating. "They aren't being followed. Clay probably has the guards distracted."

Sheri and Layla stopped what they were doing, staring at me.

"How can you know that?" Sheri asked, her hand dropping from her hip.

"It's an Earth thing," I said.

"Maybe we should go see," Layla glanced at Sheri.

Sheri nodded, slowly. "Just in case she needs help."

"Okay," Layla said. She zipped up her bag and pointed at me. "You – you take care of yourself, and those tattoos."

Sheri followed Layla outside, and I followed Sheri.

"If you find them, they need to go northeast. Tell them Alex can help!" I yelled after them.

Layla waved her hand over her shoulder, acknowledging me as her pace quickened.

"Thank you!" I yelled louder, but they were already over a hill.

I grabbed my backpack and raced for the perimeter of Erika's camp. It was difficult to establish, now that most of the tents were rolled up. I had been keeping tabs on the only non-magical person the past few days; Alex. They were still nearby, and so far each of the patrols had missed them. I paused, making room for three large guys pulling a truck bed with no cab. Crops and vines stuck out the top and hung over the side.

Behind them were barrels, each pushed on a dolly. As one came near, the top blew off. The convoy stopped as everyone raced to catch the apparently irreplaceable lid. I stepped toward the barrel, peering inside. A pile of gold and brown curly hair sat on top of rotting vegetation. *Erika doesn't waste time.*

The lid was replaced, plunging what was left of Kaitlyn into darkness and stench. I swallowed hard, and continued my sprint, reaching out for Alex as I went. I found him, much closer than he had been before. And Susan and Bee weren't with him.

Oh God, I told myself. *Something went wrong.* A strong headwind picked up, working against me; like running through mud. Despite the wind and rain, my skin felt like it was on fire. The elements scraped across fresh wounds as my physical exertion stretched them tight.

I crashed through a set of bushes, and ran right into Alex. We both bounced back and hit the ground, hard. I pushed myself up, straight into the barrel of a pistol. Alex turned off the safety with a steady hand.

I glanced up at him. "You haven't had bullets in that thing since D.C."

"Oh my God – Kaitlyn?"

His other hand replaced the pistol. I took it and he yanked me to my feet, embracing me in a bear hug.

"What did they do to you?" His hands ran through my hair and over the gauze covering my tattoos.

I winced, pushing his hands away. "Nothing, I did this to me. I had to change my appearance."

Lightning struck dangerously close. Screams came from the camp.

Alex licked his lips, glancing toward the screams. "I was coming to get you. Susan says a huge storm is coming."

"I know – which is why you have to leave me behind." I stepped back.

"What? No – come on. Bee and Susan are waiting for us."

He tried pulling on my arm, but I pulled back. He raised his eyebrows.

"A group of prisoners escaped. People from Robert's camp, and some we picked up in Evansville. Also – someone named Marissa, and her sister. Can you make sure they are taken care of?"

"Why don't *you* make sure? Come on." He turned, but I didn't follow.

"She's going to be okay, you know," I raised my voice at his retreating silhouette.

He stopped in his tracks, hunching his shoulders like I just knifed him in the back.

"Bee is…" I paused, swallowing the lump in my throat. "She's going to be fine. As long as she is with you and Susan."

He turned, his face contorted in pain. "Don't do this…" I could barely hear him.

"Go north – or maybe east. Get to the hybrid power station on the Great Lakes so I'll know where to find you. I'll go west with One Less; until I've done what needs to be done. Then we can reconnect."

He stepped forward. "We can figure this out, these storms. It'll be dangerous to separate." He put his hand on my shoulder.

I winced again, ducking out of his grasp. He was left holding his hand out in midair. "What is happening to you Kaitlyn?!" He yelled above the wind.

I placed the braid of my former locks in his hand. "I'm not Kaitlyn anymore. I can't be if we're going to survive this." I closed his fist around the hair. "Take care of her, Alex."

I turned away, forcing one foot in front of the other as fast as they would go. There were no tears, no more aches in my chest, and no more heavy stomach. My world had gone numb.

Chapter 32

Finish It

The pads over my fresh tattoos were soaked, many hanging off my skin. As I walked, I ripped them off. The rain helped to take the sting away. I shut down the electrical signals I used to pinpoint people. I couldn't be witness to a retreating Alex, Susan, and Bee. Shawn had managed to take them all away after all.

I skirted the perimeter of the camp. Most likely, my stuff had already blown away.

I'll just keep walking until everyone else is ready to move. It was mindless work, one foot in front of another.

A flash of yellow on the trail in front of me broke me out of my trance. A rain jacket. Someone was moving quick and staying low, keeping between the largest shrubs. I followed.

"Stop!"

I froze in my tracks, racking my brain for an excuse as to why I was out here.

"What are you doing?" the voice demanded.

I turned, opening my mouth, still unsure of what was about to come out. Twenty feet in front of me, the yellow rain jacket person stood, arms in the air. A guard stood in front, pointing his weapon at them.

I ducked behind a tree.

"I said, what are you doing? Everyone should be back at camp, packing up."

A woman's voice answered, "I have information to deliver that can't wait. I need to catch Shawn's group before they leave."

I know that voice. I crawled closer.

"Do you have clearance?" the guard asked.

She held up a note. He snatched it out of her hand, unfolded it, and read. "Is this for real? You've found the one he's been looking for?"

My heart jumped up into my throat. I peeked around another tree and saw Sabrina, nodding.

"Very well then." He handed back the note. "Did you report to admin before you left?"

She shook her head. "No. Admin is compromised. But the issue will be resolved soon."

He lowered his gun and motioned for her to pass. I crouched down behind the tree. The guard walked by on the other side, continuing his rounds. As soon as he was out of sight, I stood and sprinted in the direction Sabrina went. I slowed only when I found the yellow.

I had to stop her, at all costs. She probably detected my powers when she attempted to heal me. She already knew about my hair and tattoos. It would all be for naught if I let her get to Shawn.

With the storm getting louder and louder, sneaking up behind her was easy. I matched her steps, closing the distance between us. I picked up a large, round rock. My fingers gripped its curves as I held it up and back, preparing for the strike.

Thunder cracked overhead. I swung, connecting with her temple. She crumpled and lay still on the ground. I threw back the yellow rain jacket, revealing a thin line of blood trickling down her face. I pawed at her body until I found the note. Just as I unfolded it, the sky opened up in a downpour. The paper, and all the words on it, melted in my hand.

"Goddamn, handmade paper!" I threw the note down, stomping it into the ground, finishing it off. My backpack fell off of me, its contents tumbling out.

I stopped stomping; the note didn't matter, I knew its message. I just had to make sure no one else did. I looked down at Sabrina. Her chest still heaved with the steady up and down of breath. I wiped my nose, squeezing the rock in my other hand for reassurance.

Limbs still heavy with the numbness that had overtaken my entire body, I raised the rock again. This one struck her cheekbone. Another one higher – on her scalp. Bile rose in my stomach. I fought it down, striking faster now, trying to finish the job before my conscience came knocking.

I walked around the body and kicked at her face to turn her over. I started in on that side. *I've killed before*, I told myself. *This is nothing.*

But it was something. It was murder with my bare hands. Up close and personal – with no powers to do my bidding. Her face caved in. She was no longer recognizable as Sabrina the Healer.

The wind beat against us, flapping her annoying coat in my face. I tore it off her. Thunder boomed overhead every few seconds, it seemed. I continued to strike, each one landing home. My arm ached. I hit and hit and hit until a strong gust of wind blew me back against a tree. My head bounced against it, hard.

Lightning struck the tree I was against. I looked up, just in time to see a burst of electricity and huge branch, tree-sized itself, fall. I dove to the side, covering my head with my arms. The ground reverberated with the crash of wood on ground.

I peeked out, the lower half of Sabrina's body hung out from under the branch.

Get up, I told myself. *Make sure it is finished.*

I pushed myself to my feet, and climbed over the fallen branch. Her head was still visible. I blinked away the fuzziness and stared at my masterpiece. She looked at me, one eye open. The eye blinked. I gasped.

I jumped over the rest of the branch. My feet hit something solid and round. The Chalice.

I leaned over, and put on a glove that also came out of my bag. I picked up the Chalice with a shaky hand. I closed my eyes, taking a deep breath. My fingers traced the rim of the cup once, then down, closing around the stem with a solid grasp.

I opened my eyes and looked at Sabrina, raising the Chalice above my head. I gritted my teeth, met her eye, then brought the Chalice down hard. It only took one blow; her temple shattered.

I turned and doubled over, vomiting. I stayed crouched for several minutes, emptying my stomach. Finally, I stood, wiping my mouth – hands still shaking.

Trying to avoid looking at the body, I collected everything that came out of my bag. The Chalice lay near her head, splatters of her blood dotting the interior.

I felt dirty all over, itchy. I wiped my hands on my shirt, leaving dark red streaks on the white cotton. Shivers ran down my spine. I tore off my shirt, used it to wrap the Chalice and threw it and everything else in my bag. Even my naked skin felt wrong. It was pulled too tight, stretching further with every movement as if it would tear any minute.

I picked up the backpack and continued to walk through the storm, only pausing to brace myself against the stronger wind gusts. Trees and branches crashed down around me. Between the soaking wet ground, lightning, and hurricane force winds, I wasn't sure there would be a forest left come morning. I decided to let fate work its magic, expecting at any moment to be crushed by a tree or blown away by the winds. But fate brought me something different. Fate brought me a cave.

By the time I reached the entrance, I was stumbling over my own feet. I forced myself to go as far back as the shallow shelter would allow. No sign of a vicious wild animal.

Darn.

I tucked my knees into my chest and hugged them, shivering. The world outside was destroying itself. Water seeped in, creating a small pool that reached the tips of my toes. I pulled them back further. I closed my eyes, taking in deep breaths and trying to ignore the fact that I had just committed murder. I reached out for human forms around me. The storm interfered. Electrical signals bounced around.

I extended my reach and finally located two large groups. One on the river, one on land – both headed west. I went in the other direction, seeking Bee, Susan, and Alex. They were eastbound, walking slowly, their faces would be turned away from the wind. Everyone was fleeing, leaving me alone. No distractions; I had to come to terms with what I'd just done.

Still, it wasn't too late to join either group. A quick run and I could catch either of them. I just had to make a choice – which direction to run? East or west? Bee or One Less? With Bee, I would spend the rest of my life running and hiding, trying to protect her from Shawn and the storms we apparently created when we were together. With Shawn, I could face my fears, but risked never seeing my daughter again.

Indecision kept me firmly planted on my butt. I reached into my bag, and my fingers brushed something hard. I gripped at it and pulled out the Chalice. I held it up. It was my only company – the only real and solid thing left in my chaotic world. I removed the shirt wrapped around it and grasped the bare stem of the cup.

Chapter 33

An Unlikely Ally

I shot up, leaving my body and the storm behind. I spotted the telltale circle of light and aimed for it. Instead of hanging back, I landed on their platform. My toes tingled as they touched down on glowing, not-so-solid ground. I looked up at the men that were left. They huddled in a group. They weren't alarmed, just...expectant.

Ted approached. "What have you done?"

I met his eyes, but didn't answer.

He continued, "Look around you. The power of the Chalice is becoming tainted."

I turned, surveying the atmosphere. It was grainier than I remembered. I looked down at my toes, the floor beneath us was losing color.

"If you continue down this same path, it will only get worse. And the power of Akasha will no longer come to you." Ted crossed his arms, glaring down at me.

"I know, but I did what had to be done." As soon as I said it, the atmosphere around us went a little grainier, and we sank a few inches into the floor. Everyone there had to make the effort to levitate, myself included.

"That is the wrong mindset," Ted said. "You need to make it right."

"How?" I asked.

Ted stepped to the side, as did the group of men. Their circle opened up, revealing two people in the center. I gasped as they walked forward. Sabrina moved toward me, face intact and a blank stare in her eyes. Her arm was wrapped around that of another – Cato.

Ted explained, "We've never had a woman here before. The Chalice itself represents female power, which is why only male Shades come. But now, the balance is off." Ted lowered his voice as they came to stand before us. "You must right your wrongs."

I blinked at Cato. They were the same dull, blue eyes, surrounded by wrinkles that I remembered. My tongue grew thick in my mouth. I didn't know what to say to him, so I turned to Sabrina. Her eyes were wandering.

"I killed you," my voice echoed in space.

She looked at me, forehead creased. After a few moments she replied, "Yes. Now I remember. Why?" Her eyes rolled up and to the left until she gasped. Now they were wide with surprise. "I was about to do something to put you at jeopardy. Something I knew about your powers—"

"She is the Gaia," Cato interrupted. My eyes shot back to him and he continued, "And she is out to stop my son."

"Your son needs to be stopped," my voice rose several decibels. "Your son deserves to be killed." I turned to Sabrina. "You did not deserve it, and I'm sorry for what I've done."

Her lips pressed together. She took several deep breaths through her nose.

Someone should tell her she doesn't need to do that anymore.

Everyone remained silent, waiting for Sabrina to speak. She never did.

Ted leaned into me and said, "You know what to do."

I looked at Sabrina, and raised my hand above her head. She didn't stop me. I closed my eyes, recalling a small meditation chant my mom made me do anytime I was overly stressed or upset. "In love and in trust, in peace and in wisdom, I release you, so mote it be."

Sabrina shimmered, growing brighter. A wisp of smoke rose up from the palm of my hand. I yanked it away. Sabrina was still there.

I looked at Ted. He lowered his head, but didn't say anything. My hand shook with pain. I held it steady with the other, and put it back over her head. "In love and—"

"Wait!" Sabrina interrupted me. "Your powers."

"What about them?" I asked.

"I just wanted to tell you, they'll come back to you. Start small, a little at a time. Once you rebuild, they'll be stronger than ever before." Her eyes were wide, unblinking. "Baby steps."

"Thank you," I said.

She nodded her head once.

With a much softer voice, I began again, "In love and in trust, in peace and in wisdom, I release you." My last words were barely a whisper, "So mote it be."

In a flash, Sabrina disappeared. My palm singed with pain, but the ground beneath us hardened. We lowered our feet to it. I turned to Cato. "Are you next?"

He shook his head. "No."

We continued to look each other over. It was so very hard to read him. Like always. "So, your son has created a destructive organization, One Less. Susan has taken over The Seven, or what's left of it. Which side are you on?" I asked.

Cato's lips turned up into a half-smile. "I'm with Team Kaitlyn."

Chapter 34

Hero

I woke in the cave, drenched and shivering. The entire floor was two inches deep in water now. The rain continued outside – though the thunder had died down. I stood, shaking out my rigid muscles, and began to pace the small cave. I walked away the chill, one step at a time, until I could think about something other than the cold.

Cato was an ally I had not expected, and I had yet to decide if he could be trusted.

Powers first, I told myself. I remembered what Sabrina said. *Baby steps.* Shawn and One Less continued to march east; Bee and her protectors west. I was here, riding out the storm, still with a decision to make. Just me and...Cato. I glanced back at the cup, lying in the pool of water on the ground.

I picked up my sopping wet shirt, and used it to wrap my burned palm. Then I held my other hand above the pool of water.

I closed my eyes, tuning into the frequency of the element. Its composition revealed itself to me and I slowed the molecules, bending them to my will. A small teardrop of water lifted from the pool, pausing in front of my eyes. It was miniscule, but more controlled than I had ever managed before. I twisted it this way and that, marveling at how it reflected images around it, distorting them as though they were part of some other, fantastical world.

I returned the drop of water to the puddle, and stepped through it to the entrance of the cave. Rain fell in thick sheets. I held my good hand out, palm open. Water pooled up, spilling over the sides. I inhaled the thick scent of pine, and stepped into the downpour. My already damp hair soaked through, and wind whipped the short, wet strands against my face. I threw my hands above my head, palms out. Rain drops directly above me froze, suspended in midair.

I looked up at them. Wind continued to blow my hair, and the rain fell just outside of my bubble, but the ice-cold, torrential shower was paused above me. I smiled, splashed through it with my hand, and walked back in the cave.

My powers are back.

I ran my fingers through my hair, and the wrist tattoo caught my attention. It was hard to see in the darkened cave. I realized I had yet to really see any of the tattoos. Outside, the thunder started up again.

I spun energy, weaving it into the pool of water at my feet. Once it was infused, I lifted the molecules, and spread them into a thin plate. Tilting the oval shape so it stood upright, I created a makeshift mirror. When lightning flashed behind me, my image lit up in the glass clear water. It was blurry, moving unnaturally like an apparition, darkening when the lightning stopped.

A tree, I thought. *My face is a tree.*

A cherry blossom vine, snaked around from the tattoo on my back, up my neck and along the side of my cheek. Small, pink flowers bloomed along the dark brown branches. I thought of the tree at the Chakra, and me and Micah sitting in the swirl of pink and white petals.

Did they know? No – it has to be coincidence.

I stepped closer to the mirror, raising myself higher to meet it. During the next lightning bolt, I caught a flash of my permanent makeup. It did a good job transforming my face. Darkened eyebrows and golden eyelids. Eyeliner on the top and bottom. My lips were bright red, the double arches on top more pronounced with a significant dip in between.

In the next few flashes I surveyed a series of leaves down my arms. They really went all out with the plants.

Fitting for an Earth, I guess.

I turned in the dark, baring my back to the mirror, and waited for the next streak of bluish white light across the sky. This one lasted forever. Right over Shawn's scar was an intricate compass. A combination of swirls and straight lines covered the wound. I ran my hand over it and winced. The raised scar tissue could still be felt, if I needed to validate my affiliation again.

"It's...perfect," I whispered to myself.

The lightning petered out, but not before I caught the cherry tree that covered almost the entirety of my back. Above it, in the dip of my shoulder blades, rising up my neck to my hairline were four words. Earth, Air, Fire, Water. Stacked on top of each other, they created the shape of a diamond.

My shoulders sagged. *That one might give me away.* I shrugged. *I could always grow out my hair; and find turtlenecks.*

My powers weren't strong, but they were coming back. The wind outside was finally dying down; the storm was passing. When the rain stopped, I'd have to make a choice. Which direction to go? East or west?

I sighed and looked down at my feet. I gasped. The water below me had changed form; I was standing on top of it, even though the rest of the puddle swirled and vibrated with the wind and rain. I extended one toe out, dipping it in. Icy cold raced up my leg, and I shivered. I walked forward, out of the puddle. Each time I took a step, the water hardened, supporting my weight.

The magic was subconscious; I hadn't even realized I was doing it.

I am literally walking on water here. Probably means there is a right choice to make.

But I still didn't know what it was. I stepped to the entrance of the cave. Dawn approached, and the rain was petering out. I stayed still for quite a while, breathing in the chilly air. When the sun crested the treetops, I held my hand up to shield my eyes. My wrist tattoo caught my attention again. What I had thought was just a detailed, Celtic knot, was actually words. I turned my wrist as I read them.

I am the hero of this story.

I dropped my hand. "Damn straight I am."

I looked to the west. It was time to relearn the element of air.

Chapter 35

What is it Worth?

Shawn landed in the cave once again, this time with two useless, bandaged hands. He came barefoot. Arianna stood on the ledge, waiting for him.

She glanced at his feet. Her hands went to her hips and her lips pressed together in a snarl. "You *will not* be sending these women off to the Goddess with your feet."

Shawn almost shrank back. He held up his hands in defense. "Not sure how else it can be done."

Arianna roared, going partly translucent and growing in size, "I am not without knowledge of the pain you have caused others. A few minor burns are the least of it!"

Shawn took a step back, and his foot slipped off the ledge. His arm shot out for something stable, but it went straight through Arianna. She caught him at the wrist, but did not pull him back right away. Instead, she ripped at the bandages. Tearing them off, she took bits of freshly-healed skin with them.

Shawn's yelp was barely heard above Arianna's roaring. Shreds of white bandages, tinged with Shawn's blood, floated down to the pool below. Arianna quieted, slowly returning to her full physical manifestation. She pulled him back firmly on the ledge and released his wrist, throwing it down to his side. Shawn resisted the urge to curl his hand up into his chest.

Arianna stepped to the side, revealing an even longer line of women than before. "You may begin, Athame Wielder."

By the time Shawn had released five Shades, he was on his knees fighting back tears. Yellow pus oozed out from the exposed, shredded meat of the palm. If any more burned away, bones would be visible, Shawn was sure of it.

Arianna glance over his shoulder. "How badly do you want Akasha? What is it worth to you?"

Shawn didn't respond.

"What is she worth to you?" Arianna repeated.

Shawn glanced up at Sarah's cave, then slowly got to his feet. He held up his other hand, "Unwrap this for me."

Chapter 36

Favors

Erika stood from readjusting her backpack. The group was covering thirty miles or more a day, walking at breakneck speed. Well, breakneck speed for Erika. Her shorter legs took two strides to the men's one. She rubbed her shoulders. *These dang straps keep digging in*, she thought. *Another few miles and they'll start bleeding.*

"They're ready, got everyone in your camp accounted for?" The annoying little man with the notepad asked Erika.

"Yes, David." She mumbled, readjusting her straps once again. She watched him turn on his heel and walk away. Perhaps she couldn't account for Lucy, but given the uproar over Sabrina's disappearance, not to mention the prisoners, Erika would never fess up to it. Besides, Erika had enough people owing her favors – they could cook the books.

Erika heaved the bag back on her shoulders as the wind picked up behind her. A yellow rain coat flapped away on a stray gust. Someone else chased it down. Good material was hard to come by, after all. Erika turned. "Oh – hello Lucy."

Lucy was smoothing out her shirt. It looked as though it had just been through a tornado.

Erika cleared her throat. "Your tattoos are healing nicely."

Lucy smiled. "Water does a body good." She stepped forward, reached behind Erika and pulled on two straps. A hard jerk, and the waist buckle cinched in.

"Oh – wow. That really helps!" The shoulder straps no longer dug into Erika's skin. "Thanks!"

Lucy shrugged. "Well, I do owe you."

From the front of the line, Erika heard David call the group back on the trail. "So..." Erika asked as they fell into line. "Where have you been? I was about to report you missing."

"I've been around; hanging out in the back mostly."

"Hmmm." Erika didn't buy it. She'd been to the back several times in the last few days. "Well, try to stay more visible, if you can. I may need to call in one of those favors."

Lucy smiled again. "Like a piggy-back ride?"

Erika laughed out loud. "Something like that. A 900-mile march in a month does not do a body good."

"Why the sudden rush, do you think?" Lucy asked.

"We're headed back to Utah." Erika nodded west. "We need to make it over the Rockies before winter hits. If we don't, we're stuck in Denver for the season."

"Oh, come on. Don't tell me you don't want the break. Spending some time in the mile high city? Could be fun." Lucy nudged Erika.

Erika let out a nervous laugh. *Of course it is fun; I grew up there.*

Erika slowed her pace by a hair, then a little more. The group would only go as fast as their slowest walker.

Chapter 37

Slow Ride

"Hey, Clay – wait up!"

Clay halfway turned. "I can't. If I go any slower I'll end up at the back of the pack or further, then they'll be no catching up!"

I ran up to him. "They wouldn't leave you behind, would they?"

Clay shrugged. "Not sure. But that wouldn't be keeping a low profile, now would it?"

I looked down at his feet. His strides were even shorter than Erika's. "Don't worry; I'm working on the pace for you."

Clay looked up at me, raising one eyebrow. "You certainly did a number on your hair," he touched my chin, forcing my head to the side. "And your face."

"What can I say?" I lowered my voice. "I'm a good spy."

"Not if you keep saying that, you aren't." His moustache moved up. He was smiling underneath all that hair. "Besides, I recognized you."

"You recognized my voice before you looked at me," I corrected him. I would need to work on keeping it a pitch lower, or higher. "Anyway, you aren't so bad yourself – thanks for helping with the prisoners. Hopefully they've met up with Alex by now."

Clay's boots pounded against the ground with each labored step. "Marissa stayed with them. There'll be hell to pay when Shawn finds out. We need to come up with a good excuse."

"What we need to do is stop Shawn before he gets to Utah."

Clay looked back at the ground, concentrating on the pair of boots in front of him, keeping up. "We needed to stop Shawn years ago."

"I know, but...we're here now, and this is what we have to work with. I'm thinking we make a stand in Denver." I adjusted my shirt over my tattoos. The skin was still tender, like I had rug burn.

Clay began to pant.

I fell in behind him, unstrapped the sleeping bag and tarp from the top of his backpack, and held them under my arms. Maybe he'd do better if his load was lighter. "We need time to organize. If we slow the group down, they won't be able to pass over the Rockies in winter. We'll have a few months to coordinate. What can we do to slow the march?"

Clay ran his fingers through his beard. "Sicknesses, disease – an outbreak of some sort. Or weather, maybe. How are your powers?"

"I got some of them back. Air and water, though I can't go too extreme with them." I smiled, thinking of my wild ride over. The rain jacket plus a few old rods made a makeshift hang glider; just add air. "Besides, manipulating the weather could give me away."

"You're right, it would need to be something subtle..." he said.

"What did you have in mind?" I asked.

Clay rubbed his chin. I glanced behind us. As the pace slowly picked up, the column of people became more strung out. I saw someone shift to the edge of the trail, and a steady stream of people began to pass her. Erika. Two women stuck with her, taking a few items to lighten her load and give her what encouragement they could. But how many miles could that last? How many more miles did David have planned for us today?

I grumbled, then hopped out of the column, feigning a cramp and falling to the ground.

Clay followed, crouching next to me. "Well this isn't exactly subtle."

"Shut up and call for a medic," I mumbled through my lips.

He turned, opening up his throat. A deep voice rolled up to the front of the line, "Medic!"

The line stopped, curious faces turning my way. Three men came trudging toward me; two carried the extra gear of doctors. The other was David. "What now?" he asked.

I put my hand at my side. "I've got cramps."

One of the medics handed me his canteen of water. "You're probably dehydrated."

I pushed the canteen away. "Not those kind of cramps – female cramps."

"Oh." The medic scratched the back of his neck. "I don't think...well, we don't have anything for that."

The other stood, looking at David. "Maybe we should take a five minute break?"

"We just took a break!"

The medic shrugged, glancing at me. "I don't know what else to do; we're running low on aspirin."

David's faced turned red. "You don't know? You're the medic!"

As they argued, Clay slipped away behind the growing crowd of people.

The other doctor rooted in his bag. He held up a foil-wrapped bar. "I've got chocolate."

I buried my face in my hands, shaking my head, trying to keep everyone from seeing the smile I could not get rid of.

David's whole body shook, but clearly for a different reason. He stomped toward me. "Get up – we don't have time for cramps! That's not a real medical condition, anyway!"

"What's not a real medical condition?"

David turned to address the questioner.

Erika stood in front of the crowd, arms crossed, clearly not amused. "Well?"

David stuttered, "I didn't mean…" He gestured toward me. "She just…"

"She just what?" More women, many I recognized from Erika's camp, emerged to stand around David.

David pushed his glasses up on his nose. "Listen – we have a schedule to keep." He held up his notebook, pointing to an open page. "I'm just following orders."

"You aren't going to make it if people start dropping like flies; female problems or no." Erika dropped her pack. "Break time!" she shouted.

Her announcement was met with a few approving whistles, some claps, and a 'Hallelujah'. She stepped toward David, and snatched the notebook out of his hand.

"Hey!" he protested.

She glanced at the open page. "I'll be making a few adjustments to the schedule. If you want the group to get there as a whole; I suggest you follow it." Erika walked past David and took a seat on the ground next to me.

I handed her a pencil, no longer bothering to hide the smile on my face.

David was still stuttering, "You...you – I'm going to report this. Give me back my—"

"We've got flats!" A bellow from the back of the line cut David off.

"Oh, for Christ's sake. Flats?! As in more than one?" David shouted as he headed toward the truck bed gardens.

"As in all of them!" the voice answered back.

"How in the world? Get some Airs over here!" David ordered.

My eye caught a short figure slinking away from the truck beds. Clay. My smile grew wider.

Chapter 38

The Best Thing

By the time we reached Denver, one month from when we started, David was a hot mess. After the first few incidents, Clay, Erika and I had very little to do with it. People caught on, making a game out of trying to drive David insane.

Very quickly our thirty miles a day had dropped to twenty, often falling even below fifteen. Half the camp developed the stomach flu – something I still couldn't determine was real or fake. We were now two and a half weeks behind schedule.

Shawn's river group had long since reached the mile high city, or so said the scouts. He sat waiting not-so-patiently for the rest of us. Word of the prisoner's escape also reached him. Something else for David to deal with.

Train would be the transportation of choice over the Rockies, and word on the trail was Shawn needed certain people from our group to help with steam technologies.

Excitement buzzed up and down the long line of people as we entered downtown Denver, and the 16th Street Mall. It was an outdoor mall, running the length of several blocks with stores on either side of the cobble-stoned street. Despite the self-created slow gait of the rest of the march, everyone was now picking up the pace – many had an actual spring in their step. This was home for some.

I gravitated toward Erika.

"I can't believe how much I missed this weird place." She wouldn't stop talking. "Every year at Christmas the entire capital building was lit in color. I never missed the Parade of Lights – every float, band member, and clown was decorated in actual lights lit by portable battery packs."

Despite the lack of batteries, 16th Street Mall was alive and illuminated, cutting through the dull, black night with a light all its own. The promenade of red-and-gray granite, running through the center of Downtown, wasn't cracked and crumbling. It wasn't run over with plant life as we had seen in the concrete jungles of most big cities. Except for the glow of lanterns lining the path, it probably looked much the same.

"It's almost like Daybreak never happened, here. Look how happy everyone is," I said aloud.

Erika smiled. "Come on, let me show you." She took my arm and we broke rank, crossing the pedestrian path to the other side.

I looked back to the rest of the group. People noticed, but no one cared – Erika could do what she wanted, after all. The rest of One Less turned right, off the street and in between two glass-walled skyscrapers.

"You might appreciate this as an Earth." She winked at me. We approached a large planter in the middle of the sidewalk. "These are up and down the length of the mall. They used to hold decorative trees, shrubs, and flowers – you know, useless stuff."

I ran my hand through the leafy greens, blossoming over the side of the planter despite the cold weather.

"After Daybreak, the community came together. Stoners, college kids, the rich, the homeless, families with kids – we all created a food system that works, and feeds everyone. It was really the agricultural knowledge of the large Hispanic population that saved us."

I looked down the way at another planter. A woman and a child were pawing through it, picking out ripe squash. "How do you ration the food?"

Erika shrugged. "We don't. People know that if the vegetables are over-harvested, there won't be any seeds for next year. Besides, a lot of hard work goes into it – and there is plenty to go around. Some leftover, even, that is used for compost or shipped off to neighboring cities in exchange for other supplies. Look over there."

She pulled on my arm until we approached a rectangular, stepped enclosure. Chicken wire hung from a railing on one side, infused with vines.

"Writer Square. This used to be a fountain. We took any space we could and turned it into a food source."

As she talked I turned around, mouth dropping open. Buses facing both directions of the street sat where they had probably stalled out during the EMP. The tops were torn off and the windows knocked out. Corn stalks grew out of one, a row of fruit trees from the other. The words 'free mall ride' were still visible on the sides of the busses.

Behind us, the mall was lined with what had previously been bars, restaurants, and retail stores. On the left, all of the infrastructure was still intact. People entered and exited the building with baskets of supplies, sleeping bags and more food – like they were out for their daily shopping trip. Across the way, every single window was broken out. There were even holes in the brick and mortar façade of the buildings. Plants and herbs, growing inside, were packed in where dresses and shoes used to be.

"Brings a whole new meaning to window shopping," Erika said, nudging me. "Beautiful, isn't it?"

I smiled at her enthusiasm. A man passed, whistling. He tipped his hat at us. I nodded back. Further up the outdoor mall, a large group sat around a pair of teenagers playing a guitar and banjo. In sync clapping sprouted up and people got to their feet to dance.

Erika waived at one of them, then turned to me. "Daybreak is the best thing that could've happened to this place."

The smile froze on my face, and my ears rang with her words. I was shocked - because she was right.

Chapter 39

Expediting the Process

"It's been awhile; we had almost given up hope," Arianna greeted Shawn on the platform.

"Burns take a long time to heal," Shawn said.

Especially with no more skin graft surgery, he thought to himself.

"Let's see." Arianna gestured to his hands.

He held them up for her. The swelling had gone down. Yellow puss was replaced by angry red and pink tissue.

"Any infections?" she asked, gesturing to his unwrapped hands.

"We have medicine, for now," he replied, looking at the women assembling on the stairs. "How many will there be today?"

"As many as you can handle, Athame Wielder." Arianna moved to stand behind him.

"What about you? Aren't you anxious to be released?" Shawn asked. Without her there, maybe he could find some sort of shortcut.

She cocked her head at him, almost smiling. "I will go right before Sarah."

Of course she will. Shawn huffed.

He turned to the first waiting in line. A Water this time. He craned his neck around her, and motioned for another to step forward as well.

"What are you doing?" Arianna asked.

Shawn held one of each of his hands over the Shade's heads. "Expediting the process. My second crew just reached Denver – I need to go greet them."

Chapter 40

A Little Crazy

"Erika, wait!"

She paused and turned as we headed to where One Less set up camp.

"I have a confession to make."

She raised her eyebrow and waited.

I cleared my throat. "I…um. Well, the reason I hid in your group…um—"

"Just spit it out." She crossed her arms.

"Well, I had a thing with Shawn, and I can't see him again. I don't want him to see me."

She stepped forward, gesturing to the side of my face now caked with ink. "With the number you did on yourself, I doubt he'd recognize you."

"Maybe…" I ran my fingers through my short strands, trying to convince myself of the same.

"Look, if you want to disappear – this is the place to do it. I can make it look like our camp numbers are still whole. But you gotta make a decision. In or out."

"In, definitely in." I didn't walk all that way just to quit now. "But I thought, maybe I could stay away, just for tonight. That way you can let me know if he is there – and where he hangs out. I could just avoid those areas."

She crossed her arms, looking me up and down. "Okay, meet me back at Writer Square tomorrow around dusk. That should give me enough time to find out. But don't leave the mall. Things aren't so nice in some parts of the city."

I nodded and watched her walk away. I turned in the other direction, watching the people around me as I strolled. As night, and the cold, set in – there was less and less activity on the streets. I looked closer at the stores. Starbucks had grain sprouting out of its broken out windows. Ann Taylor Loft was now a trade post specializing in sleeping bags; they even offered repairs. Banks, oddly enough, were still banks. They advertised safety deposit boxes with around the clock guards. What did people store in them now? Certainly not cash. Maybe batteries. Or matches. Or medicine. Everything we had taken for granted until Daybreak.

I stopped at the next intersection, glancing down a darkened street that ran past an old movie theatre. I hesitated, drawn in. I needed to prove Erika and Shawn wrong. I needed to prove Daybreak was not the best thing for humanity; otherwise – what was I here for?

I soaked in the glow from the lantern above, as if it would keep me safe through the darkest parts of Denver. I left the populated, outdoor mall. My steps echoed in the deserted concrete jungle. I passed in and out of the long shadows cast by buildings. I twisted and turned through the streets, coughing, humming, and occasionally banging on car hoods or kicking glass and rocks across the street, sure to make plenty of noise.

An hour went by with no human contact. I pulled a thin jacket out of my bag, wishing I had stopped and traded for a thicker one. I zipped it up to my chin, sighed, and turned to head back.

"What do you want?!" I jumped at the screech behind me. I spun on my heel, and stepped back.

The man was tall, and very thin. He smelled as though he hadn't bathed in a year – he probably hadn't. I stepped into the light cast by the moon peeking through the clouds.

He backed away, waving his hands in front of his face as if to fend me off. "Don't like people, don't like people."

"Wait, I just want to—"

"No!" He retreated, his scream echoing down the alley.

"That one probably could've done without Daybreak," I mumbled to myself.

The smell of old, burnt out wood drew me to a metal trash can sitting at the entrance to the alley. Just outside of it stood a pile of fresh wood, and a piece of flint. Old blankets, a chair missing its back, and a hollowed out computer sat close by. This was his home.

I put a few pieces of wood in the trash can, and glanced down the alley. No sign of him. I held out my hand.

Time to find my fire.

A growl behind me caused me to pause.

My shoulders sank. *Not another one.*

I turned, bracing myself for another dose of crazy. Instead, three wild dogs snarled at me, posed to pounce. My heart jumped to my throat

I squared my shoulders, racking my brain to remember how to treat the animals – challenge or submit? In the first few months, Alex had quizzed us on the subject, covering a range of beasts. We had never run into dogs; too many had been eaten before they had a chance to go wild. Of course, I had to run into the three exceptions.

"Sit."

The one in front of me laid his ears back, and shifted his weight to his front paws.

"Sit!" I said again, louder.

They weren't sitting. Another growl.

Mumbles echoed from the dark alleyway behind me, "Don't like humans – dogs are worse."

I rolled my eyes, then held out my hand, praying the art of fire found its way to me. One of the dogs pounced. I ducked, trying to roll under him. His jaws snapped, catching my thin jacket, tearing the sleeve right down to the wrist. Another dog went for my opposite wrist, clamping down on it with his razor sharp teeth.

I screamed out loud. They pulled and growled until I was on my knees, staring straight into the eyes of the third animal.

"I could use a little crazy, here!" I hissed into the dark alley behind me. Only whimpers answered my plea for help.

Looks like I have to find my own crazy.

I flicked my fingers on my left hand, desperately calling out for the element of fire. The fingers on my right hand refused to move. Fire never came. The dog in front of me curled its lip up, baring his teeth. I was out of time.

Producing my own growl, I leaned forward and opened my mouth. I bit down as hard as I could, right on the dog's nose. The taste of wet canine and coppery blood filled my mouth.

He yelped and backed up, pawing at his face. One of the others let go of my jacket sleeve, circled around, and leaped. I cringed, covering my face with my good arm. Mid-jump, the attacking dog let out yelp. It crashed into me and we both went to the ground.

Instead of another melee, all I felt was dead weight. The dog was not moving. I reached up and around the body on top of me, and felt the long, solid shaft of an arrow protruding from its hide.

The pressure from my right wrist let up. Sharp teeth retracted, leaving behind searing pain. There was a flurry of growls and barking as I struggled to push the dead dog off of me. As soon as I made it to my feet, all I saw was the tail end of two animals retreating into the dark.

"You shouldn't be out here," a male voice chided me as he ripped material in half.

I recognized that voice.

My throat went dry as I croaked out his name, "Micah?"

Chapter 41

Meet Fido

The familiar body in front of me froze for a brief second. He pulled on my arm – my good arm, until I was out of the shadow of the tall building behind us. Moonlight spread across my face.

"Kaitlyn?!" He squeezed me. Eyes wide, Micah's breath caught in his throat. "Oh my God. What are you doing here? I thought you'd be in Utah by now. Is Susan here, too? Where's Bee? What happened to your face?"

His other hand brushed the tattoo along my cheek, then ran through my hair. I moved to stop him, wincing at the throbbing in my wrist. He halted the interrogation long enough to wrap my wrist in the strands of material he'd torn from his own shirt.

He looked at me again. "I barely recognize you."

I smiled. "That's sort of the point."

He almost returned the smile, until his brain got in the way. "Hell - I could've accidentally shot you with that arrow. Why didn't you just fire bomb those dogs?"

I shrugged. "I got a concussion a while back and lost my powers. I've managed to get water and air again, but not the other two."

His mouth dropped open. "You are powerless?"

"*Half* powerless," I corrected him.

He shook his head, as if he couldn't believe it. "We need to get you out of here. Shawn's here—"

"I know – I came with One Less."

I didn't think it was possible, but his mouth dropped open even wider.

I rushed on, "We have a lot to talk about. Where are you staying?" I laid my hand on his arm, and static shock jumped from him to me. Our eyes met. "I can't tell you how much I've missed that," I whispered.

He stepped forward, closing the distance between us, and kissed me. I opened my mouth and closed my eyes, drawing him in and melting into him all at once. My hands crept up behind his neck, pulling at him. His arms went around my waist. We kissed until my lips cracked and we were out of breath.

Even when we stopped, we didn't pull away. We rested our foreheads against each other.

"You don't have fire because you were missing passion." His lips went to my forehead, then followed the trail of cherry blossoms down my neck and over to my ear. "Try now," he whispered.

I shuddered at the sweet sensation that warmed my body. Without looking, I flicked my good hand toward the tin trash can. Flames sprung up from the wood piled inside.

I felt his cheek pull back in a smile.

His stubble scratched my face. "See! I told you—"

My lips on his cut off his gloating. I needed more of him, all of him. He obliged, allowing me to run my hand up under his shirt and my tongue over his teeth.

Heat licked at our faces as the fire in the metal can grew.

He pulled away. "Take a deep breath, Kaitlyn, before you burn the city down."

"Right," I said, "baby steps."

We broke apart, and I held my injured wrist to my chest.

"Come on, Kaitlyn. We should get that checked out." He put his arm around me, leading me away. "Speaking of, how is the baby? Is she here?"

I stopped walking, causing him to turn around into me.

"What?" he asked.

I looked at him, forehead creased. "She's not a baby anymore, Micah."

"Right, I know." He rubbed the back of his neck. "What is she now…two?"

"And I'm not Kaitlyn anymore." I held my wrist to my chest as it throbbed.

"What do you mean?"

"I'm Lucy. And Susan and Alex had to take Bee away from me…" My throat constricted. "And you've just missed so much." I focused on the wrappings around my wrist, trying to hold back tears. Blood was already seeping through, enough to drip on the ground.

"You're losing too much blood," Micah said, voice lowered. "I don't have anything to help you. You're going to have to get that looked at by One Less. They have all the best doctors."

I thought of Sabrina. "They have one less of those, too," I mumbled.

"What?"

"Not important." Where would I even start with that one? "I'm going to need to explain what happened."

Micah nodded and walked to the dead dog. He pushed the arrow through the rest of the way and hoisted the body up on his shoulder. As he passed the alley he paused at two beady eyes peering out. "Those dogs shouldn't bother you anymore, Felix."

The crazy man stepped out, warming his hands at the fire. "Don't like dogs, don't like dogs."

We completed the short journey back to the mall in an awkward silence.

"You're going to need to walk this in from here. I shouldn't go any further without some sort of disguise." Micah lifted the dog up, and settled it around my shoulders. "Keep your wrist above your heart." He pushed it in the air, pausing to kiss my fingers.

I pulled them away, stumbling under the weight of the dog. "I know about basic first aid." I was starting to feel lightheaded.

He narrowed his eyes. "Maybe I better go with, I just need—"

"No," I interrupted him. "You would be too hard to explain. I, at least, have a place in the camp. Let me go back, get this stitched up, find out where Shawn is exactly – and then we can come up with a plan."

He blinked, then nodded. "Okay, I'll find you. Don't come back out here. It's not safe. Take care of yourself, Kaitlyn."

"It's Lu—" I tried shifting the weight of the dog and it caused me to lurch to the right. Micah steadied me. I got my footing, and took a deep breath. "It's Lucy, thank you."

I turned and walked away. All this time, chasing after him. Years trying to catch up. And here I was, walking away.

No, I told myself. *Lucy is walking away. And if I could walk away from Bee, this should be a piece of cake.*

I made my way the length of the mall, refusing to turn around. If I did, I'd probably tip over. I walked through Writer Square and down the alley to which One Less disappeared. They weren't hard to find, once I got past the skyscrapers. A ring of smoke signaled the cooking fires. I pulled the carcass around my neck even tighter. The chunk of meat was hiding my face better than the tattoos ever would.

I walked up to the sentry, pressing my bicep out to display the red and blue ties.

"I thought everyone was accounted for," he said, pushing aside fur to look at my face.

"Apparently not."

"No unauthorized entry; you'll have to wait until morning when we get the new rosters."

My wrist wouldn't wait until morning. "Fine. I don't mind sharing my catch with someone else." I turned.

"Wait!" he called.

I paused, smiling, and turned back around. Meat was not easy to pass up, roster or no. I walked past him straight to the fires. I heaved the dog off my shoulders, right at the feet of one of the cooks. "Meet Fido. Tell everyone Lucy sent him." I turned around and stopped, but the world around me did not. It was still spinning. My head felt so heavy.

Oh, right. Keep my hand above my heart.

I thrust my fist in the air and shouted, "Did you hear that everyone? I am Lucy!"

I hit the ground.

Faces appeared above me. "Get her a doctor!"

"No, no," I mumbled. If only the faces would stop spinning. "Erika. Get Erika."

Erika always knew what to do.

* * *

"Easy there, princess."

I stepped forward with purpose, then dropped down on my knees in front of Shawn, running my hand through the mist there. It dispersed for a moment, but gathered back in the same spot. I turned around, still on my knees, and backed into the mist. It swirled around me as I occupied its space. I backed up a little further until I felt Shawn's pistol aimed directly at the back of my head.

My blood pounded, roaring in my ears. In response, the dark, red liquid oozed down the wall of flame around us. Akasha had already risen, too far from my grasp.

"The baby is mine."

I heard the click of the gun behind me, and a red haze descended.

Chapter 42

Morning Mullets

I cracked open my eyes. The first thing to come into view was a mullet. "Morning, Erika."

She turned and nodded. "Hello again, sunshine."

I was afraid to look at my wrist. "What's the damage?"

She touched my shoulder, her eyes pinned to the floor. "I'm so sorry to have to tell you this, but we had to amputate."

"You…what?!" I held up my arm. My wrist was wrapped, but my palm and all five fingers were there.

I glared at Erika.

She snorted she was laughing so hard. "Sorry, couldn't resist."

I checked my other hand, just to be sure.

She started laughing all over again.

I growled and pushed myself up with my good hand. Nothing went spinning out of control.

"We put some stitches in, is all. There was no tendon or bone damage. You were lucky." She looked at me, one eyebrow raised. "I told you not to leave the mall."

I shrugged. "My catch was worth it." I stretched, yawning.

Wonder if they're still serving breakfast.

"Am I clear to go back to work?" I asked as I stood up.

"Not to admin you aren't."

"What? Why not?"

Erika walked me over to a desk and pulled out a pencil and a piece of paper. "We need a meals roster. Start with your name."

After a sideways glance at her, I fumbled with the pencil, trying to pick it up with my right hand. It wasn't happening. The bandages were way too thick and my fingers weren't cooperating. I picked up the pencil with my left hand and attempted to write my name. The word 'Lucy' was readable, but it took forever.

"Now write 250 more names. And oh, by the way, you have only ten minutes."

"Fine." I straightened up from the desk. "I get it. So what am I supposed to do now?"

She removed the pencil from my hand and replaced it with a spade. "Gardening duty."

"Seriously?"

"What?" She put her arm around me, leading me outside. "Most Earths pine for the chance. Working all day in your element – what could be better?"

"It's just…my wrist hurts." We turned in between two buildings and emerged into a large parking lot, or what used to be one, anyway. Where the asphalt was not dug up to make way for plants, you could still see the painted parking space lines. Twelve rectangles of dirt, evenly spaced from each other, stood waiting for me.

"Digging will take your mind off the pain," Erika said. "I'll have you back on admin duty as soon as you can write. Today you guys are planting the mobile gardens."

We stepped back as the trucks carrying vines and plants were pushed in.

"Why can't they stay mobile?" I asked.

We both waived at Clay, one of the workers.

"Because our plan worked," whispered Erika. "We can't make it over the Rockies before the first big storm – or so says the weather girl." She smiled down at me. "We're riding out the winter in Denver."

"Cool." I spun the spade around in my hand.

Plenty of time for planning. And planting, apparently.

"Well." She stepped away. "I gotta go. Things to do. Favors to fulfill."

"Or vice versa," I mumbled under my breath.

"I'll be back later to check on you!" Erika disappeared back in between the two buildings.

I chose a truck and hauled myself up onto it. Pumpkins – very seasonal. My stomach rumbled, but I passed on a trip to the kitchens. I needed the time to think. Besides, it was unlikely Shawn would be by here. Hard labor wasn't his thing.

I borrowed a pair of shears and cut the larger, ripe pumpkins from the vine and loaded them into a wheelbarrow.

I could start recruiting, I thought. *Between Micah, Clay, and me we might be able to have a significant force within a few months. Erika said there were plenty of Wiccans here. But would they leave One Less for me?*

I scooted the pumpkins that still had growing to do over to the side of the truck bed and hopped down. As long as I balanced them in my inner arms, they didn't hurt my wrist too much. I started transferring them to the ground, pulling their vines with me.

Maybe I could just kill him. Make it look like an accident and hang around to find out if someone else takes over. I paused. *Then what? Go down the line, killing one successor after another?* No, I couldn't do that.

I finished with the pumpkins and left to help with the broccoli. I was replanting my fifth crown when a woman about my age with waist-length, dark-brown hair knelt in the dirt beside me. I paused, wiping the sweat off my forehead. She planted her crown and rocked back against her heels. She closed her eyes, and I felt the energy in the air shift. I tensed, but her face was peaceful; not like she was preparing to attack. A few seconds later, the broccoli leaves slowly unfolded from their withered curls.

I squinted at them – they looked greener.

"There," she said, looking at me with her grey-blue eyes and a smile. "The roots are a bit stronger – it'll help them last through the colder nights."

"That…" I hesitated, running the pad of my finger across one of the leaves. "Is probably the most useful magic I've ever seen."

She laughed. "You should see what I can do with squash." She held out her hand. "I'm Kassandra."

I shook her hand, looking at the Chinese symbols on her forearms. "Lucy."

She caught me glancing. "This one means 'Acceptance of Fate', and this one means 'Karma'." She looked at me again. Her eyes were calculating. "What do yours mean?"

"Oh." I touched my finger to the side of my face, at the cherry blossom branches. I racked my brain for an answer – one did not simply tattoo their face with insignificant symbols. I thought of the tree's short blooming period. "This is for mortality. A reminder of the nature of life, and those we lose along the way."

She nodded her head. The way her eyes bore through me was almost unnerving.

We both turned as someone cried out behind us. An older man held his hand aloft, a pair of blood-smeared shears on the ground next to him.

"It's ok." Kassandra glanced at my outstretched hand. "I'll go help."

She rushed away, looking back at me once. It wasn't until I glanced down that I realized I had automatically called the elements. They were just beginning to merge above my palm. I released them before Akasha could take shape. *Did she know?* If she was an Earth, that would be the only element she would recognize.

I watched as she helped the man wrap his hand, then lead him away.

Should I follow?

I just sat there, full of indecision. In the end, I stayed. Most likely because of her tattoos – acceptance of fate and karma. Something bad might happen if I did follow.

Besides, I turned back to the last crown of broccoli, *I have one element left to recover; earth.*

Chapter 43

Stalkers

I ignored the sounds of workers around me. Soon the heavy clunk of spades hitting dirt, idle chatter, grunts, and laughter dulled into background noise. Vibrating clacks, high whistles, and low tweaks echoed in my head. These were the sounds of the Earth.

I smiled, letting the music guide me until first molecules, then atoms revealed themselves within the individual grains of dirt. I expanded my own energy field out from my hands as they speared through the soft ground. A small hole formed with perfect depth for my broccoli, and I didn't even get dirt underneath my fingernails.

I set down the plant and pushed the dirt back in around it. My hands fell to my side, brushing a pile of broccoli heads that had gone to flower. Bright yellow petals sprouted from many of them. As I peered closer, one of the leaves dropped off. Tiny seed pods hung underneath. I scooped up a pile of fresh dirt and attempted to pick off one of the seeds with my other hand. My fingers still refused to cooperate. A quick look around to ensure no one was looking, and I used a gust of air to detach the seed from the rest of the crown. It landed square on my pile of dirt.

I squeezed the dirt, concentrating on burying the seed in the deepest part. It was like I was back in the Chakra's walk-in freezer, forcing a seed to grow before I froze to death. This time, it was far easier. Inside, water from the soil rushed toward seed. I squeezed tighter; warmth from my hand soaked through. I felt the seed unfolding, revealing roots and leaves.

I opened my hand, palm up. A few flakes of dirt fell from the sides. The shoot emerged from the surface of the soil until it formed a tiny, budding plant. I touched one of the leaves with my fingertip. The vegetable quivered. Movement drew my eye down the long line of each of the broccoli I had just planted. Leaves were spread wide, and I could swear they were greener. They were all definitely quivering with energy.

My eyes darted to the right and left. So far, no one had noticed. "Stop!" I hissed at the vibrating plants. They didn't, not until I consciously drew back the energy I hadn't realized I was spreading – at least not on such a wide scale.

I took a deep breath, and risked a glance over my shoulder. All backs were turned, except one. Micah's eyes were as green as the broccoli leaves, staring me down from across the lot.

My heart leapt into my throat. He glanced down at my hand. I still held the new seedling.

"Damn it," I huffed to myself. I buried the plant in the row of broccoli, allowing my heart rate to return to normal, then scooped up a few of the overripe, flowering crowns. I walked to the compost bin halfway in between me and Micah and waited for him to join me.

He was wearing an oversized sweatshirt, with a hood pulled up over his head.

"Is this what you call a disguise?" I flicked off his hood as soon as he came close enough.

"Is that what you call a low profile?" He gestured to my patch of broccoli.

"I am an Earth, so that is perfectly explainable."

"And what about the water, or the air that you used?" He dropped his own stash of vegetables in the compost bin.

Someone came up behind Micah for their turn to dump. We both turned and walked away. I grabbed another few handfuls of flowering broccoli.

"Is your wrist okay?" He asked when we both returned. Fruit flies buzzed up from the bin.

I swatted at them. "Yeah, just a few stitches."

"Good," he said, lips pressed tightly together. "We need to get you out of here. It's too dangerous."

I shook my head. "I don't think I should leave. I could get more intel while we come up with a plan."

He leaned forward. "You're not going to get any intel playing around with broccoli!"

"I'm not, am I?" I dropped the broccoli down in the bin and put my hands to my hips. "I'll get a hell of lot more than you."

He bent over, squeezing the sides of the bin. His knuckles were turning white. "You're so goddamn stubborn, Kaitlyn."

"Lucy," I reminded him.

Someone behind me cleared their throat. I took a deep breath and moved away. Who knew the compost bin would be such a popular place?

Micah grabbed my upper arm, stopping me. He bent down to my ear. "Fine. Spend your days here – until we have a plan. But your nights are with me."

"I'll spend tonight with you. The rest we'll see about."

He nodded, I swallowed hard.

"Meet me at Writer Square at dusk," he said. "And I want Kaitlyn, not Lucy."

He turned back to his garden, and I did the same. My whole body tingled. *Your nights are with me.* His words reverberated through my head.

The chills dulled the further I walked away from him. My feet stopped at one last flowering broccoli left behind. I picked it up, smiling.

Maybe I can get him to touch me. Just a spark to keep me warm until tonight.

As I turned, a new group of people were walking into the parking lot. The one barking orders stopped me dead in my tracks. I squeezed the head of broccoli; yellow petals floated to the ground.

"Throw plastic sheeting over the gardens at night – make them last as long as we can in the ground." Shawn's voice grated at me.

My neck twitched.

"We can plant cover crops - grasses or small grains will help shade the soil and prevent weeds from growing over the winter." David stood by Shawn.

Shawn stopped. "I know how a garden works, David. I've been feeding these people for two years now."

Shawn started walking again. The group of people followed. I turned my back, and stripped off my jacket and my shirt. My sports bra could pass for appropriate hard labor clothing, and reveal as much of my new ink as possible. My disguise.

I risked a glance over my shoulder. Behind me, Micah had blended in with a group of workers. He pulled his hood up over his head.

Shawn surveyed one of the mobile gardens that had yet to be replanted. "This looks better than when we rolled out of Fort Calhoun. What'd you do different?"

One of the workers stepped out of his group; an Earth, by the feel of her. "We started using human hair in our compost a while back. We also—"

"Whose hair?" Shawn asked, cutting her off.

I cringed, ducking down trying to make myself as small as possible.

"Well." She looked down at her toes, smiling. "Mine, for one. And—"

"Let's get some of these potatoes out for dinner tonight." Shawn, always impatient, was already moving on. "Make room for more from the mobile gardens. I want everything in the ground and covered up. Nothing goes to waste. We have to last the goddam winter, here."

"Yes, sir. Potatoes will go well with the wild dog that was brought in last night."

"Who caught a wild dog?"

I sucked in the slow sigh of relief I was letting out. The tension in the air increased, and I risked a glance at Micah. He had already turned around, fists clenched, ready for a fight. I made a shooing motion at him behind my back with my good hand.

"Lucy…" David's voice trailed off as he searched the parking lot that seemed to be growing smaller by the second. "Oh, there she is."

I tucked my hair behind my ear and turned my head. My face tattoo was in full view. Along with my bared shoulders, partially bared back, and wrapped wrist – I hoped Shawn would be thrown off. I could feel his eyes boring into the back of my neck. The scar on my shoulder itched.

"I don't think I've met Lucy…" Shawn's voice was cold.

Footsteps. *Oh God, is he coming over?* I wasn't ready for a fight. My powers weren't nearly strong enough – unless he was allergic to broccoli.

"Hey, baby. You're all dirty – why don't you come take a break?" It was my hero, Erika. She wrapped one arm around me, pulling me into her and blocking my face from Shawn.

She motioned with her eyes. *Play along – if you want to get out of this.*

My turn. I tried to relax into her. "Sure, as long as it's with you."

I let her pull me away. She rubbed my arm with the back of her thumb and I played with the hem of her shirt. I risked a glance at Shawn. He was still watching; our flirting with each other wasn't doing the trick.

I laid my head on her shoulder. "Where have you been all morning? I've missed you."

"Tease," she said. She tilted my chin up and toward her with the tips of her fingers. Before shock could register, our lips brushed. I went with it. Better this than pull everyone into a fight. My arm snaked around her waist and I pulled her in tighter, opening my mouth.

Might as well give those boys a show.

We continued to walk, heading out of the parking lot. Out of the corner of my eye, I saw Shawn raise his hand. It was covered in bandages. He took a step toward us. I sucked in my breath.

"Keep walking," Erika mumbled into my mouth.

A large crash stopped Shawn. It stopped everyone except us. As we disappeared in between two tall buildings, I glanced back. Clay was in the middle of the lot, an entire mobile garden tipped over in front of him.

"Oh, geez. Sorry about that Shawn. Don't worry, I can get this cleaned up before dark." Clay was bumbling around the tipped over truck bed.

My second hero. All three of them; Micah, Erika, and Clay had come out of nowhere. *Do I have an army of stalkers?*

"Well, what is everyone staring at? Help him!" Shawn ordered. He knelt himself, brushing the dirt into a pile with his bandaged hands.

The only one not distracted by Clay's aversion was Micah. He openly stared at me and Erika, mouth hanging open.

Chapter 44

Romance

I sat on the black granite wall at Writer Square that used to contain a fountain. Now it held much more. Soil, seeds, growing plants, hope, life. I thought of Felix and his trash can of fire. *How did he survive? Does he tend his own garden?* It would be hard to find space for one amidst a jungle of concrete. I laid my hand down in the rich soil of the fountain. Then again, maybe not.

"Hey." A hand extended to me.

I took it, rising up to meet Micah's eyes. "Hey, yourself," I said back, smiling. "I brought us dinner." I motioned to two large lettuce leaves – the new plate of choice – wrapped around full servings of delicious wild dog meat and potatoes.

"Perfect," he said. He held up a canteen. "I brought us wine."

A pair of Fires walked by, whooping and hollering about how awesome they were. I turned my head. I had already removed my blue band identifying me as One Less, but the infamous Lucy and her wild dog was spreading like wildfire; especially among those that wielded the flame – they loved a good story.

"Come on, I know of a place we can go to eat in peace."

We walked the length of the mall. As we passed the final lantern, I paused. "Should we take it with us? Denver is…dark."

Micah took the wrapped food from me, then held my good hand. "There are more lanterns where we are going. Besides – look, a full moon."

We went the opposite way of Felix and the dogs. After ten minutes of walking, we turned east, passing several large, burnt out buildings.

"University of Colorado." Micah nodded to one of them. "The city fell to looting and fighting after several nights of darkness. Some thought they might be safe here – what's in a college to steal? Desks? Normally nothing of any worth - but refugees brought supplies."

"Oh, my God."

Micah nodded. "Whole families—"

"Don't tell me anymore. I don't want to know." I turned away from the shell of the building.

He squeezed my hand. "I'm just glad you weren't in a big city right after it happened."

We walked through an expansive parking lot, stepping over cracks and weeds in the asphalt, before skirting around a large stadium.

"The city set up a command center and temporary housing inside the Pepsi Center," Micah said, pointing at the stadium – also half burnt. "When it became apparent the power was not coming back on, the cops left to go protect their own families – and there was more fighting over food and blankets that were brought in."

I looked up – the moon was a far prettier sight. "Our food is getting cold," I mumbled. "How much farther?"

He looked down at me. "You've walked thousands of miles in the past few years, I think you can handle another few steps."

"Much of that was rowed," I corrected him. "But, it's like – you make me weak."

I stopped, stunned that I had just said that out loud. But it was true. When he was around, I checked out. I relied on him too much.

He sighed. "Come on, Kaitlyn. We'll talk about that later."

We stepped over a large, red, plastic 'E' lying on the ground. I looked up at a rounded entrance. The outline of several more letters could be made out, "Elitches? An amusement park?"

Micah smiled. "The new whimsical home of the Wiccans."

"And this?" I touched a painted pentagram with the words, 'Devil Worshippers' inside it.

"Put there by some that don't understand." He shrugged. "We leave it there because it seems to keep people away. The stupid ones, anyway."

We walked through what used to be the ticket booths. A group of guards, or at least what seemed to be guards, sat in a circle playing cards. There were no weapons.

"Are they Elementals?" I asked as Micah waved to them.

"Some are; mostly Earths. Come on, I want to show you the observation tower."

I craned my neck up, looking at the building just inside the entrance.

"We're going to the top," said Micah.

I groaned. The thing had to be 250 feet tall. "Wouldn't you rather show me the Ferris wheel? Or the carousel?"

"The view is worth the climb," Micah said. We passed the useless elevator and started up the stairs. "Besides, this is where I sleep."

"You do this every night?" I asked.

"And now, so will you." He paused, waiting for me to catch up. He took my hand and pulled me along behind him.

My butt is going to be so sore in the morning.

By the time we made it to the top, my legs were on fire, and I was breathing hard. Another guard greeted us at the round platform. This one I recognized; an Elemental from the Chakra.

"Natasha?" I squealed, lunging for her. I scooped her up in a hug. "You made it! The last I remember you were being chased into the woods by those Fires."

She detached herself from me, smiling.

"I'm sorry I didn't go back for you." I took a step back, looking at Micah. "Why didn't I go back for her?" My mind began reconstructing events from a day I tried not to think about for over a year. It was like racing down a dark tunnel, knowing something bad was waiting at the end.

Micah interrupted my thoughts, "She left for one of the several rally points we agreed upon. Something you should've done, too."

I narrowed my eyes. "I was searching for you. I thought—"

"I know," he cut me off. "I know..." He put his forehead against my own.

We pulled apart when Natasha shuffled by us to leave.

"It is so good to see you!" I called after her.

She turned slightly and nodded.

I looked at Micah, confused. "She didn't say one word. Is she mad at me?"

"She rarely speaks, not since Daybreak," he whispered back. "She has the ability, but she is still suffering from the battle, mentally and…physically."

I looked back. As she turned, descending the first of the stairs, moonlight glinted off one side of her face. Raised, pink scar tissue ran the length of it. Her ear was non-existent, and one nostril almost closed off. Her eye couldn't open all the way.

My hand went to my mouth as tears stung my eyes. "Burn scars." I stepped forward, wanting to hug her all over again.

Micah put his hand on my shoulder. "She doesn't like attention."

I swallowed, hard, and hugged him instead. When Natasha's footsteps faded away, Micah led me around the elevator shaft to the other side of the tower.

"The tower isn't necessarily manned 24-7. Just when we have the time." He pulled back a curtain. A mound of blankets and pillows sat on the other side.

"Oh my God – you have pillows?!" I dove into the pile, and rolled. "They smell so clean."

He sat next to me, taking off each of our shoes and pulling the bedding aside to lay out our dinner. "I was busy last night, getting ready for you."

I cleared my throat, fiddling with the edge of a pillow. Thank God I had managed to borrow a razor from Erika. "So…aren't you worried about being so close to One Less?" I nodded in the direction of the 16th Street Mall.

He handed me the canteen of wine and laid out our wild dog and potatoes. "We were here long before them, and they have yet to venture out of their camps. But…"

"But?" I prodded him, unscrewing the lid to the canteen.

"But it will be a long winter, and they'll probably get restless. We've started moving supplies and personnel to an underground silo, fifty miles east of here. Within a month we'll all be gone."

I paused with the canteen halfway to my mouth. "All of you?"

His lips pressed into a tight line and he rubbed his temple. "Let's talk plans later – now, we feast." He picked up his lettuce-wrap. "Cheers."

We touched lettuce to canteen, and I took a deep swig.

Rich, black fruit flavors danced along my tongue to the back of my throat. The aftertaste held a hint of vanilla. The sweet liquid warmed my entire body as it went down. "That is…so good."

"Picked it up in Virginia; been saving it ever since." His lettuce wrap was halfway gone.

I passed over the canteen and sampled our kill. "What if it had rabies or something?"

"Then you'd probably show signs of it. Was that not dog blood and snot I tasted on your tongue when I kissed you after?"

I laughed, spewing potatoes out of my mouth. "Well, romance is a specialty of mine."

"Oh, there is no doubt." He wiped the corner of my lips with a blanket.

We finished our cold food, washing it down with much better wine.

"Kaitlyn, I want to ask you something…about Lucy," Micah said.

I brought the canteen from my lips, a half smile lighting my face. "Ok."

"Is Lucy – gay?"

Now I was in a full out grin. "What do you think?" I teased.

He didn't notice. "Look, everyone does what they have to do to survive. I'm not going to hold anything against—"

"I'm not a lesbian," I said, cutting him off. I put the canteen in his hand and scooted closer. "Erika is a good friend." I took a pillow, hugging it to my chest. "There are good people in One Less. We need to consider that as we are figuring out what to do."

He leaned into me, nudging me with his shoulder. "I told you – we'll talk plans later."

"Okay." I straightened my back, the smile returning to my face. "What else do you want to know about Lucy, since we are on the subject?"

He turned the full brunt of his glowing, green eyes on me. "I want to see Lucy's tattoos. All of them."

Chapter 45

Control Freak

I took the canteen back from him, before he even took a drink. I downed the rest of the wine. My head swam in pure delight. I shifted in front of him on my knees and removed my shirt, then my bra. When I glanced at him again, he lifted up to his knees to look me in the eye.

His hand went to my cheek, tracing the outline of the cherry blossom branches.

"Maybe a little too obvious, don't you think?" he asked.

"I didn't ask for it – they just did what they wanted."

"Permanent makeup, too?" His hand traced over my eyelids and across my eyebrows.

I nodded.

"And your back…" He drifted around me, running his hand down and around my waist. "Almost all of it is covered with ink."

I stayed silent, letting him explore.

"The scar is almost completely invisible. The tattoo artist really knew how to shade." His hand hovered over my shoulder.

"Artists," I said.

"Hmm?"

"There were two of them."

His hand drifted up my neck, mumbling the words, "Earth, air, fire, water. That's a popular one with Wiccans."

He came around in front of me again, pulling me up so we were both standing. He held my good wrist in the air, reading the bracelet of ink to himself. His lips moved with the words. He curled his fingers into mine. "I got a tattoo, also. Want to see it?"

"You did? Yes, of course I want to see." I looked up at him with wide eyes.

He stepped back, taking off his shirt. A dark splotch of ink over his heart was just visible.

"It isn't nearly as intricate as yours..." he trailed off.

I pulled him into the moonlight streaming through the windows of the observation tower. Light lit his chest, showing a small, fat bee. My throat constricted as I placed my hand over the symbol of the daughter I left behind.

"It's beautiful; thank you." I stepped in to him, meaning to bury my face in his chest.

Instead, he lifted my chin, guiding my lips to his. I opened my mouth, allowing him in.

He pulled the rest of me into him. "You're not going back, I can't let you leave again. Kaitlyn...and Lucy, stay here with me." His fingers dug into my waist.

"Shut up," I mumbled. "We'll talk plans later."

His hands moved down, then lifted me up. I wrapped my legs around his waist. He stumbled forward until I was pressed against the glass window. His hips pinned me in place.

"People will see," I protested.

He held my hands out to the side while he ran his tongue up my neck. "Let them."

My entire back tattoo was on display. Shivers raked up and down my body, paralyzing me. Finally, he released me and my bare feet touched the floor. He unzipped my pants, slowly sliding them down my thighs until I stepped out. I did the same for him.

We paused apart, our eyes running up and down the length of each other's bodies.

"It's been so long," I whispered, folding my arms over my midsection.

He stepped in. "It's still me."

"I know." I ran my hand over the stubble on his cheek, then let it drop. "It's just – I'm not sure how much of *me* is left."

He took my hand, entwining our fingers. "I don't have any protection. Maybe we shouldn't. I mean, what if you—"

"I can't get pregnant again." I swallowed hard. "At least, I don't think I can."

"Okay," he whispered. "Then let's find out how much of Kaitlyn is left." He took my arm at the elbow, guiding me to the pillows. "Lay down."

I obeyed, biting at my lip.

He followed me down. "Stop that. I'll do the only biting tonight." He ran his tongue the length of my lower lip, then nibbled at the corner. His knee snaked up in between my legs giving him access. I melted, relaxing my legs. It felt good to let someone else be in charge of my destiny; especially when destiny ended in an orgasm.

His hand made small, teasing circles. Around my nipples, down my stomach, and in between my legs. He pressed his fingers in until they came out wet.

"Ready?" he asked, positioning himself over my entrance.

"Stop stalling." My whole body clenched in anticipation.

He leaned in slow, pausing just as I felt his light touch. "Promise me. You have to promise me you'll stay. Don't go back to him."

I looked up, his eyes were pleading. So were mine. "Let's not do this now."

"I have to, I can't lose you ever again."

I lifted myself up on my elbows. "No."

"What?" He rocked back on his heels.

I sat up. "I left her, Micah. Can you grasp how big that is? I abandoned *my* child."

He shook his head. "You didn't—"

I held up my hand, cutting him off. "As long as I am close to Shawn, I know she is safe."

He reached out and pulled on my wrist until I joined him on my knees. He traced my wrist tattoo with the pad of his thumb.

I am the hero of this story.

"You can't save everyone, Kaitlyn."

"You're right." My eyes flitted over to the window, seeking the glow of the 16th Street Mall. "But I can save her." I looked back at him. "Are you done bribing me with sex?"

He smiled. "Are you done being a control freak?"

"Hardly." I pushed on his shoulders and he fell back on the pillows. I climbed, positioning over him, and lowered myself. Slowly.

He tried sitting up. I pushed him back down. "Stay still," I hissed. I lowered myself a few more centimeters. He was stretching me out unbearably wide.

"Kaitlyn..." He gritted his teeth. "I can't wait, I need you now."

I lifted myself up a little, threatening to release him completely. "I waited two years for you. You can handle this. Now, don't move."

He looked at me, narrowing his eyes, debating. Finally, he relented and laid his head back against the pillows.

He was going to pay for his hesitation. "Put your hands behind your head."

When he obeyed, I lowered myself a little more.

"Please," he groaned. "Let me touch you."

"No." I caught the hand he extended by the wrist, then leaned forward to hold them both down. The movement opened me up, and I slid the rest of the way down. We both sucked in our breath. It was almost painful…almost.

I scooted my knees forward, getting them under me. I raised myself all the way up until we were about to detach, then lowered again. Four slow counts up, four slow counts down.

Micah groaned again. Still holding him down, I turned his head with my chin until his ear was exposed.

"Shhh," I whispered. Four up, four down.

"Kaitlyn—"

"Shut up." My lips stayed at his ear. My tongue snaked in and out. I felt him shiver underneath me. "Do you know what I had to do without you?"

He didn't answer.

Good boy. I moved faster now. Three counts up, three counts down. "I had to pleasure myself."

He shivered again. I bit down on his ear lobe. "I did it with our toy rock. I worked it without you." Two counts up, two down. My knuckles were turning white around his wrists. My hips pivoted back and forth as I moved up and down his length. My whole body began to tingle with energy.

"Oh my God." My back arched, head tilting back. One up, one down. "Now, Micah. Touch me now!"

As soon as I released his hands, he was against me – turning me over. Pillows scattered; my back hit hard floor. His hips went into motion. He thrust forward, faster than I could do it. I would've been shoved back, if it weren't for his lips pinning me into place. He forced his tongue into my mouth. It was my turn to groan.

I wrapped my legs around his waist and lifted my hips, encouraging him. The energy still flowed. I took it in, swimming in it. Wine in my head, adrenaline in my veins.

One final, deep push, and we climaxed together. Our muscles vibrated with tension, until he collapsed over me. Full of renewed energy, I pushed him off, then sprung to my feet. My hands practically glowed with light; I needed to return the power before I exploded.

I spun in a circle, holding onto it for one last second, then raised my arm up and out. Akasha burst out of one of the windows. An unstoppable stream of light. The glass shattered, littering the pavement 250 feet below.

"Stop! He'll see it!" I felt Micah's hand on my ankle.

It didn't take long, Akasha expended in a matter of seconds. I looked down. Micah was still on the floor, breathing hard.

I bent down next to him. "What's the matter?"

He shook his head. "Help me to the pillows."

I put my arms under his shoulders and pulled until he was on top of blankets, one pillow under his head. He was much lighter than I remembered.

He was starting to shiver. I threw another blanket over him, then crawled under, wrapping him in my own body heat.

"Did I do this?" I asked.

He nodded, finally getting his breath back. "I think you stole my energy."

My hand went to my mouth. "Oh, man. It was the Great Rite."

"What?"

I turned on my back, staring up at the shattered window. Two years of anarchy, and the observation tower remained intact. Until I arrived. "It was what Shawn did to me on the Galapagos. It wasn't just rape – he was absorbing my energy; my magic, through the Great Rite." I sat up. "I can't believe I just…Shawned you!"

His hand went to my shoulder, pulling me back down. "You didn't *'Shawn'* me. This was consensual. Totally different."

"Was it?" I wasn't sure.

Neither of us spoke for several minutes. The moon crept into view outside.

"It gave you power," Micah finally spoke.

I nodded. "Instant Akasha."

Neither of us said it in the open, but the possibility was there. The Great Rite would give us what we needed to defeat Shawn.

Chapter 46

Giving More

I watched the sun rise from the other side of the observation tower. All around us, the park was slowly waking up. Dozens of people exited the park buildings with packs on their backs and push carts in tow. They headed east, toward the rising sun.

I heard Micah cough. His heavy footsteps made their way around the circular tower to me.

"Did you sleep at all?" he asked, joining me at the window and rubbing his temples.

"Maybe an hour," I answered. "I kept seeing Natasha's face."

He put an arm around me.

I leaned into him, "How about you? Are you doing okay?"

"I feel...hung over. Probably just need some food." He yawned, then looked at the stream of people leaving. "Heading to the silo; first group of many. I'm supposed to go with the last of them."

I stiffened. I wasn't ready for this conversation yet. I had thought there'd be other things to do first – like breakfast.

When I didn't respond, he continued, "But I won't. I'm staying – I'm going to camp with you during the day."

I looked up at him. "You'll be recognized."

"No." He shook his head. "Nobody from One Less knows who I am. I wasn't at the battle at the caves, remember?"

"What about Shawn?"

"Yeah – that is the one we'll have to look out for. But I think we can handle it."

"But—"

"Not up for discussion," he said, interrupting. "If you're there, I'm there."

I sighed, running through all the implications in my head. None of them ended well.

"What river is that?" I asked, nodding to my left.

"South Platte."

"Ohio, Mississippi, Missouri, Platte," I whispered. The list of rivers ran through my head; my mantra to keep me sane on my road to Micah. Now I was here, and I had failed miserably in the 'sane' department.

"What?" Micah asked.

"Nothing." I sighed. "I have to say, it's awesome being up this high – until you have to pee."

He laughed, then shuffled over to the wall, "Every penthouse comes with its own amenities." He held up a large, round pan.

I put my hand over my mouth. "I am *not* peeing in that thing. Is that an old oil pan?"

He smiled, reached in, and pulled out a funnel.

I laughed, stepping toward him. "I don't think so, guy." I nudged his shoulder as I passed. "I'm going to go down, are you—" I stopped when I turned back to look at him. "Are you okay?"

He was leaning against a railing. Had I knocked him over?

"I'm fine. You go ahead. I'll get dressed and meet you down there." He shooed me away with one hand.

Under my scrutiny, he straightened up, pulling his shoulders back.

"Okay, don't take too long." I stepped into the stairwell.

When I turned back around, he was slowly sinking to the floor. I hesitated, and then I did what I had to do. I walked away.

* * *

Micah sat there for several minutes, using his hands to hold up his head.

It'll get better, he told himself. *I just need to get some food.*

There was no energy left. His limbs were weighted. Walking to Kaitlyn, then holding up an oil pan had left him shaking with exhaustion.

I can't make the walk back to the mall, but I can't let her go alone.

He'd just need to stall; time might bring him some strength. He crawled back to the other side of the observation tower. It was painfully slow, bringing a dull ache to his knees. Micah swore the path of the sun was moving faster than he could. Once back at the blankets, he rooted through the few bags he owned, pulling out crackers. He laid back, breathing hard. Before he could unwrap them, he closed his eyes.

When he came to, the sun was glaring down on him.

Shit – did I pass out?

He shielded his face, and pushed himself up off the ground, crackers in hand. He ate as he limped to the stairs. He stood at the top, wondering how many there were.

Too many, and I've already taken too long.

Micah turned, approaching the elevator shaft. The doors were wedged open, though the elevator itself sat at the bottom. A long rope dangled down the dark passage, one end of it tied off in a loop. Micah swallowed the last cracker, and untied a pair of thick gloves tethered just inside the shaft. He put one foot through the loop and squeezed both sides of the rope before transferring his body weight inside.

His other foot pushed off, and for a heart-stopping moment he dangled in the darkness, praying his hands held enough strength to squeeze. He loosened his fists and began his descent.

When his feet hit solid ground, he let his breath out, flexing his hands. He'd have to reset his escape route later. He took one step outside, then another. The crackers were already taking effect. When the sun hit him again, he stretched.

"Where is she?" he asked the guard by the tower, waiting his turn to go up.

"Went to the river." The guard stood, slinging a backpack over his shoulder.

Micah nodded. "We need to start manning the tower 24-7. Plan on having someone there nights, even when I'm there. They can go up top."

"It'll get difficult as more of us leave for the silo."

"I know, let's make it a priority though – until the last group is gone. We're way too close to One Less."

"I'll put together a schedule," the guard said, as he headed up the stairs.

Micah started for the river. When he approached, Kaitlyn was helping several women with laundry.

"What took you so long?" she asked.

Micah raised his eyebrow. She hadn't even turned around yet. "Sorry…I was rotating guards, and made a schedule. They'll be up there all day and night, now."

"Even when we're there?" She turned around with a teasing smile.

"There's another level," Micah said. "Guess we'll find out how soundproof it is."

Kaitlyn wiped her face with the inside of her arm. Her hands were dripping wet with cold river water. "I can give it back, you know." Her voice had lowered, forehead creased. "This energy thing goes both ways."

He looked at her pile of already-washed clothes. It was three times the size of any of the other piles. Before he answered, she turned back to her work like she couldn't sit still. Kaitlyn bent over the river, shoulder and back muscles flexing as she ran a blanket up and down the grooves of the oak washboard. Micah remembered making the thing out of a door.

"Slow down, girl. You're making us look bad." The woman next to her nudged Kaitlyn.

Kaitlyn smiled. "I don't really have my own stuff to wash, anyway." She only wore a sports bra on top. The intricate tattoo compass contracting and expanding as she moved. She turned, throwing the blanket on top of her pile. The sun glinted off her shoulder, revealing the raised tissue. Shawn's mark.

The smiled died from Micah's face.

She is going to need as much help as she can get; and if this is the best way I can help her…

Kaitlyn scooped her hands under the sopping wet pile of material and lifted, carrying it over to the drying area. Micah followed, hands empty. He watched as she threw blankets and clothes, positioning them over the lines. Pieces of metal track from one of the roller coasters were lashed together and balanced from one tree limb to the next. Wind over the open river would help to dry the clothes. Their days of using Airs were over. They couldn't risk One Less detecting them now.

"Well?" Kaitlyn asked.

"Well what?"

She turned, hand on hip. "Do you want it back?"

Micah shook his head,. "No – I want to give more."

It was Kaitlyn's turn to shake her head. "I don't think you'd survive it."

"We'll figure something out," Micah said, bending to pick up a cotton shirt from the pile. He raised it slowly, his hands heavy as they moved above his shoulders.

Kaitlyn took the shirt from him before it touched the line. Micah's hands dropped to his sides. He wasn't used to be being so…useless.

He took a deep breath. "We can find a way for more to lend their energy to you. There is an entire army here. Let's tap into them."

Kaitlyn shook her head. "No, I'm—"

She cut off as someone passed. Natasha, carrying a load of new laundry to the river, the scarred side of her face bared to Kaitlyn and Micah.

Kaitlyn waited until Natasha passed, then hissed, "I'm done with armies." She hung the last of the shirts, smoothing it out on the line. "If Shawn wants to destroy hundreds of lives, let him. I won't do it again."

Micah nodded, then walked over to a park bench. They had all been torn up, and repositioned near common work and rest areas. Kaitlyn joined him, drying her wet hands on her pants. "You're not going to make the walk to the mall today, are you?" she asked.

He shook his head.

"Are you going to tell me to stay?" she asked. They sat down on the bench together.

Micah intertwined his fingers with hers. "I know well enough I can't make you do anything."

She rested her head on his shoulder. "I'll stay."

He kissed her on the head and whispered, "Thank you."

"Just for today. We can use the time to plan. But seriously, I need to be in the camp every day starting tomorrow. Whether you join me or not."

"Deal," Micah said. A cold wind blew. He put his arm around her. "Winter's coming. Do you even have a coat?"

"I had a yellow rain jacket," Kaitlyn said, almost giggling underneath her breath.

Micah narrowed his eyes at her, but let it go. "Come on. The arcade serves as a storeroom for extra supplies. Let's see if there are any in there."

As they stood, the wind blew again. Some of the last leaves still hanging onto the limbs above detached. Kaitlyn caught a reddish-orange leaf midair. She pinched the stem, spinning it around. "I miss our cherry blossoms," she said.

"Me, too." Micah put his arm over her – his legs were heavy, like he was walking through mud. "But we couldn't hide out at the Chakra forever."

Micah watched as Kaitlyn's hand squeezed into a fist. The dried out leaf crumbled, bits floating to the ground.

"Nope," agreed Kaitlyn. "Not if we are out to save the world."

Micah took her hand, wiping the rest of the leaf bits off. "What happened, here?" He pried her palm the rest of the way open. "It looks like you burned yourself."

"I did…using the Chalice. Long story."

"Both of Shawn's hands were wrapped in gauze. Did you notice?" Micah glanced at Kaitlyn sideways.

"Yeah I…oh my God." She froze in her tracks. "I know what he's doing."

"What?"

"It ain't good – for us, anyway. Come on."

Chapter 47

Working Party

"Easy there, princess."

I shuddered at his voice, remembering what happened at the other end of his gun. This time, I moved out of its way. I surveyed the rest of the large circle, looking for clues. My eyes kept getting drawn back to the mist in front of Shawn. It was brighter than before, and moved faster around and into itself, shimmering with speed. It appeared to be trying to take shape, but it lacked something – more elements.

I turned away from it. Could there be more I had been missing this entire time? I kept my eyes low to the ground, searching for the telltale swirling.

"Where is the baby?"

I rolled my eyes, trying to ignore him. I searched around and behind Akasha, finding it easier once it rose, taking its searing light with it. I squinted, huffing in frustration. The mist very well could've been tricks of light caused by the dancing flames around me.

"Is the baby mine?"

I moved to the area behind Shawn, waving my hands in front of me, hoping to agitate any clumps of mist, making them more visible. With Akasha rising, I didn't have much time left.

I bent lower, searching for the slightest shimmer, waving my hands in a frantic panic. Blood was descending over the flames around me. Finally, I found something. Once I zeroed in on it, I was amazed I had missed it all this time. Four more distinct balls of mist, also low to the ground. I squatted down to examine them, willing them to materialize. The mist swirled faster, until I thought I could distinguish body parts. A hand here, a head over there…

Shawn's words boomed through the area, "You are too late."

* * *

The next morning we made our way back to the mall. Micah was almost fully recovered, almost. He had insisted we try the energy exchange again last night, but fell dead asleep before he had a chance to counter my refusal with an argument. We walked down the long alleyway leading to One Less, donning our disguises. Micah pulled on his hoodie and I removed extra layers of clothes. I shivered, wondering how long the weather would let me bare my skin.

"I'll be close by the entire day," Micah said, voice low.

I nodded, handing him a blue arm bandana and slipping on my own. We walked past the guard without a word. He looked at us, yawning.

"I need to find out who is in charge of training," I said. "I'll have to ask around at admin."

"Shawn could be there," Micah said, laying his hand on my arm. "Let me go."

"No. They know me there – besides, who do you think is more recognizable. You or me?" I smiled, pulling on the strings to tighten his hood.

He didn't respond. I think he was still too tired to argue. One Less headquarters had set up shop in what used to be a deli on the ground floor of a thirty-floor building. It was inconspicuous, other than the large blankets covering the windows, but it made me wonder if Shawn stayed in one of the offices above it. I would have if I were running the show.

Micah and I knelt behind a planter, surveying those coming and going. Every time the door opened, we scanned the inside.

"I think it's clear…" I said, standing up from my crouch.

"Wait – we need to be sure."

"We don't have all day; we've already lost enough time," I snapped back at him.

He turned his gaze to me and my cheeks heated.

"Sorry," I mumbled. He was right, I couldn't go charging in there and chance Shawn. There had to be another way.

It hit me. "Duh." I smacked my palm into my forehead. I closed my eyes, tapping into the atmosphere and the electrical signals around me. I waded through the information, eliminating the plants we hid behind, then the stray cats stalking the gardens. I ignored the low, steady buzz the earth beneath us gave off and focused in on the Elementals walking around.

"What are you doing?" asked Micah.

"Shh," I barely responded. This had been so much easier without him next to me, giving off his own, distinct signal.

Inside, I counted them out. Plenty of Fires, Shawn was always big on the Fires. No Earths; they would all be in the gardens. Three Waters, two Airs…

"And a partridge in a pear tree." I opened my eyes to find Micah looking at me, one eyebrow raised.

"He's in there," I said. "Three floors up and moving."

"How do you know?"

"New trick. He gives off a signal similar to yours."

Micah didn't ask any more questions.

"Look – why don't you find Clay? I might need his help," I told him.

Micah shook his head. "I'm staying with you."

I sighed. "I'll blend in with that work group until I see Shawn leave. I'll be fine."

He continued to stare me down. His eye tricks had little effect on me anymore. I turned and walked toward a group chopping up furniture for the fires. I picked up an axe, glancing at the sweaty men and women swinging their sharp blades at a large couch.

I turned toward a lone armchair. Sunlight glinted off my axe, and at an angle, I could see Micah's reflection. He still stood where I left him.

I grimaced, readjusted my grip on the handle, and raised the axe. I pulled, using my hips to drive it down. It went straight through the seat, hitting the cold asphalt below. I smiled. This was going to be therapeutic. I pulled my blade out of the punctured fabric, metal, and wood, glancing behind my shoulder. Micah was no longer there.

Now I can concentrate.

I closed my eyes, reaching out for Shawn again. He was in between the second and third floors, descending. I swung the axe again, aiming at an arm. The axe didn't go all the way through this time, but the footrest popped out, startling me. I jumped back, laughing.

Shawn was on the second floor.

I swung again, blade swiveling on a level, horizontal plane. The top half of the backrest toppled to the ground. I bounced it off the top of my toes, then kicked it away.

Shawn was close to the ground floor. Time to blend in.

The backrest landed at the feet of a group of people; all of whom were staring at me. Shawn was on the ground floor now, walking toward the door.

Shit.

I shrugged. "It's just...it's fun." I decided to go with the truth.

There were a few smiles and a few eye rolls but everyone turned back to their work.

I ducked behind what was left of my armchair, feigning an untied boot just as David walked out. I peered out from the faux-leather seat. Shawn walked into the sunlight, shielding his eyes. The hand he held up was heavily bandaged. My eyes flit down to his other bandaged hand, then over to the sheathed Athame hanging from his belt.

He stopped to monitor the plants growing from the beds in front of the building. Then he said something to David and walked off. David almost tripped trying to keep up, writing all along in that notebook.

Once they rounded the corner, I stood, tapping my lower lip.

I took in a deep breath, and let it out slow. I walked around the armchair and sat, propping my feet up on the extended footrest. People were looking at me again but I didn't care. I sank into the chair, head falling back with nothing to catch it. Today, the sun was spectacular.

* * *

"Clay," Micah hissed.

The shorter man didn't turn.

Micah raised his voice, "Clay!"

Clay looked, his beard catching on the barbed wire he was unraveling. "Dag nabbit!"

Micah waited patiently for Clay to untangle himself. Micah squinted. *Is that hair…coming out of his ears?*

Clay stood. "Not safe to talk here – let's go get some lunch."

"No time to eat."

"Hmpf," Clay guffawed. "There is always time to eat."

"Kait—" Micah cleared his throat. "*Lucy* is back at camp."

"Is the girl crazy?"

Micah's step faltered. "In the literal sense – yes. I think she's headed that way."

"Well, nothing beats crazy." Clay gestured to a group of One Less. "Like more crazy."

Micah furrowed his eyebrow.

"What I mean to say," Clay continued, "is what I've witnessed being with One Less the past couple of years – well, it's just gonna take a madman to take them down." Clay lowered his voice, "Or a madwoman."

Micah put his hand on Clay's shoulder. "I know it's been rough, but you've been invaluable for us. Thanks for sticking with it."

They turned off the mall toward the headquarters building.

"Don't thank me 'til it's over," Clay said. "Let's just hope you guys have a plan."

"We do…" Micah trailed off and the men stopped walking.

There, off to the side of a working party was Kaitlyn, sprawled out in a beat up armchair. Her arms behind her head, eyes closed, in plain view of headquarters – not to mention the entire street.

"Is that part of the plan?" Clay asked, arms crossed.

Micah didn't answer. He walked toward Kaitlyn, his shadow falling over her, blocking out the sun.

She opened one eye, looking up at him – then over at Clay.

"What are you doing?" Micah asked.

"Working party," Kaitlyn answered, closing her eyes again.

The group nearby was disassembling a couch with their axes. They were glancing her way, whispering. Micah was positive he heard the phrase 'wild dog'.

If Kaitlyn is going to develop eccentric characteristics – fine. Time to put them to good use.

"Come on, then. I have an idea." Micah held out his hand.

Kaitlyn stretched, yawned, and sat up. She picked up the axe leaning against the armchair and slammed the handle inside a gaping hole. The footrest snapped back into place. Kaitlyn stood, swinging the axe to rest on her shoulder.

As the trio walked away, someone from the working party – a tall male – stepped forward and cleared his throat. "Excuse me, miss."

Kaitlyn paused.

Micah looked at her out of the corner of his eye. Her lips were moving, counting to three. Micah smiled – if there was anything Kaitlyn could do well, it was drama.

She finally turned, staring down the man.

He flinched and took a step back. "You know – that's ok. Keep it."

Kaitlyn nodded once and left the area. "What?" she asked Clay as soon as they were out of earshot of the working group. "I like the axe."

He snorted, "Your wrist is bleeding."

Kaitlyn looked down at the seeping bandages. "Totally worth it."

"So what's the plan?" Clay asked.

"We've gotta shake things up a bit—" Kaitlyn started.

"*After* we get new bandages," Micah interrupted.

"Okay." Kaitlyn winked up at him. "First aid first – then the show."

* * *

Sue, the town healer, unwrapped my bandaged wrist and asked, "How long ago did this happen?"

"Um, maybe a week."

"Your wrist isn't healing nearly as quickly as it should be." Sue got up from her seat at the table and began running her finger over the line of jars behind her. Clay and Micah stood behind me, patiently waiting.

I glanced at Clay, and whispered, "Why didn't we go to the One Less medics?"

Clay mouthed a word.

I rolled my eyes. "I can't read lips through all that hair."

He cleared his throat, leaned in, and hissed in my ear, "Shawn."

"Oh…" I glanced at Micah for confirmation. Micah held up one hand, pointing to his palm. Right. Shawn must've been getting treatments for his hands.

Outside the camp, Sue had taken up residence in a small coffee shop on the mall. The hand-painted sign out front read, 'Alternative Medicine'.

I narrowed my eyes at the lady, still scanning her shelves. Thanks to Shawn, I was stuck with her and her jars, and her—

A fat, white feline jumped on the table.

"Cat!" I jumped back.

Two heavy hands gripped my shoulders, holding me in place. Micah and Clay pushed me forward, back to the table.

"Geez," I huffed, pushing hair out of my face. "I'm not going to bolt."

"Hmm," mumbled Clay.

Suddenly I felt claustrophobic.

The cat turned to me, blinked once, then jumped off the table. She made herself comfortable on top of a stack of books in the corner.

"Abby likes you," Sue said, sitting back down at the table across from me and placing a jar filled with reddish-orange flowers, soaking in a liquid, in between us.

I read the label out loud, "Calendula. What is that?"

"Marigolds in olive oil. One of my most effective home remedies. It's an anti-inflammatory, and an antiviral. Helps with cuts, scrapes, chapped or chafed skin…"

She drifted off as her cat meowed at her. "Ok, ok." She smiled at me. "Abby is telling me to shut up."

Sue unscrewed the lid and dipped a thick cloth into the jar. She spread the healing ointment across my wounds while my eyes scanned some of her other jars. White willow, cayenne, rosemary, plus an entire shelf of peppermint.

"Do many people come to see you?" I asked.

She shook her head. "Not yet, though as the manufactured medicine runs out, there'll be more and more." She made one last pat on my wrist with her herb-infused rag and said, "There. Now – do you want me to take a look at this?" She turned over my hand, displaying a burned palm. "I've got an aloe plant."

"No thanks." That wound was at least healing faster than the scar at my shoulder.

She rewrapped my wrist. "Well, at least take a leaf with you – in case it gets worse. Or if it happens again." She winked at me, then walked over to a potted plant behind Micah. Snipping off one of the thick, fleshy leaves, she wrapped it in bandages, too.

She stood to hand it to me, but hesitated. Instead she turned to Micah and said, "A few drops of the oil a couple times a day should do it."

I huffed, sinking down in my seat and crossing my arms.

The door to the shop swung open. "Sue! We've got more burns. Bad ones! Some kid passed out over a cooking fire."

Sue brushed past me, the entire aloe vera plant already in one arm. She stopped to scoop up her cat in the other arm. As she bustled out the door, the cat turned to meow at me once before they disappeared.

"Look, here." Clay walked toward a barrel full of rolled maps and pulled one out, unfurling it on the table in front of me.

"That's not ours – maybe we shouldn't be messing with it." I kept my hands off, lest someone fingerprint the crime.

Clay made a pointed glance at the axe leaning against my side.

"They said I could keep it," my argument was not very compelling. I cleared my throat and pointed to the map in front of me. "Why do we need a map of the world?"

"Because; it's about time to come up with a plan," Micah said, stepping forward to run his hand across the continent of Africa. The tip of his pinky touched the tiny spec of Reunion Island, just off the coast of Madagascar. My heart lurched at the memory of the small house he had bought for us there.

I wondered what's become of it since Daybreak. Probably occupied by squatters. Maybe even that maid.

There was some satisfaction in knowing the maid would not be able to get to Micah now.

"Kaitlyn, please pay attention," Micah said.

I shook my head, focusing.

"Ok, so if we are equating places on the Earth to chakras on the body – where do they lie?" Clay obviously had been paying more attention to Micah's lecture than I had.

"Alex mentioned Muladhara," I said, finally getting my head in the game. "The root chakra associated with the element of earth. He thinks The Seven headquarters in Simuelue is the representation."

Micah leaned over me. I inhaled his scent. Cinnamon and pine.

"So if they are each balanced by something else, the next would be Galapagos, halfway around the world," Micah said.

"Manipura," I mumbled. "The stomach of the human body. Radiates willpower and achievement, and is associated with the element of Fire." And that was the last of my knowledge on chakras.

"Two down, five to go," Clay said.

"What about the forest we planted?" asked Micah.

"Indonesia," I pointed. "Ariel reforestation. Could represent the element of Air. I don't know what any more chakra points are though. Where would the balance to Indonesia be?"

"Easter Island," Clay pointed out.

"Easter Island?" I asked, confused. "What—?"

"Down to three," Micah interrupted me, barreling through to a conclusion. "What about Heard and McDonald Islands?"

Clay leaned over the map, brushing the tip of his beard away.

I almost offered to hold it back for him.

"The balance to the island set would be just about where we are now. It's not exact, but..." Clay trailed off.

"But very convenient," I said.

"That leaves one left," Micah breathed, voice low. "Where could it be?"

"Nowhere," I said, leaning back in my chair. "The Seventh is Akasha. You tap into each of these points of power and that is when you attain the most powerful Akasha you could possibly have."

"Look – just like the chakras on a human body, the places are in one straight line." Clay ran his thumb across the equator, his forefinger touching Indonesia, Simuleue, the Galapagos, and Easter Island. "A few locations, like here, don't follow the line exactly, but if you take into consideration their balance, it all equals out."

"Ok." I stood from my chair, rolling up the map. "We've got our points of power – but how do we access them?"

First Clay, then Micah turned to look at me.

"That part is up to you, Gaia," Micah said.

Chapter 48

Dinnertime

We approached the open field, east of the city, with a group of Earths behind us. Clay and Erika were an invaluable resource when it came to rounding them up and finding an excuse for us to be out here, away from prying eyes and away from Shawn.

"This is our winter wheat crop." One of the head gardeners, Mike, stepped forward. "It got a slow start, but we're hoping it recovers. Depends if we get enough moisture this winter." He turned his head toward the sky. The rest of us followed suit. The sun had already gone down, leaving behind inky black without a cloud in sight. I surveyed the wheat field. The moon was bright enough to see the frosty white etchings across the leaf sprouts of the wheat plants.

I bent down, running my hand across one. "What is this?" I pulled back my hand, looking at the beetle. A red body with metallic blue-black wings.

Mike leaned over me. "A cereal leaf beetle. They're destroying our winter wheat crop. They cause the leaves to go white."

I placed the beetle back on one of the wheat stems and wished him luck. He was going to need it. I turned to the group behind me. A small, dark form fluttered just over the heads of the group.

I smiled, and raised my voice to ask, "Where are the nearest caves?"

"Just a few clicks north; near the river," a voice from the back shouted out.

A pang ran through my gut as I thought of Alex and his 'clicks'. I forced myself to nod at the group, then sat down, making myself as comfortable as I could on top of the cold, dry soil. Behind me, the bristled wheat began swaying, and the low buzz of hundreds of beetles taking flight from the disturbance filled the air. The energy pulse I sent out kept them confused, flying in circles, not straying far from the wheat field. I needed them for the demonstration.

Next, I lay one hand on the ground. I glanced up at Clay who took position by my side. "I'm aiming for the caves, but we can't let the vibrations get too strong in the city."

"I'm on it, but no guarantees."

I felt Clay send his energy out; an underground block running right in between the city and the fields.

I went soon after, tying off my weaves to maintain the signals with the wheat and the beetles, and pushed energy north. It went low, the surface of the ground cracking along the way. The entire field rumbled. I left it at one short burst and refrained from sending more. I pulled back my magic, nodded for Clay to do the same, and waited.

We didn't have to wait long. The buzzing of the beetles behind me grew more frantic. Predators approached. At first it was just a few. A fluttering shadow here and there, dipping down to the field and up again. The group of Earths turned their gaze from me to the north, then to the field, and back to me again.

I continued to wait. Finally, the hoard came. The moon and stars – always bright since the rapid decline of light pollution, were broken by gray strands of tiny creatures in flight. The bats took over the wheat field, picking off beetles left and right.

The Earths squealed. Several women ducked, covering their heads. I glanced down – even Clay had begun to roll up his beard.

"They aren't going to roost in it." I rolled my eyes.

"How do you know?"

"Because." I gestured to the field. "It's dinnertime."

He snorted, but let go of the beard.

I addressed the Earths before some of the squeamish decided to take off. "The beetle population will have been decimated within a matter of a couple of nights. No pesticides needed. Nature always has a way of taking care of itself – sometimes it just needs a little push." I stepped toward the group, lowering my voice and forcing them to lean in to hear me. "The magic you possess can do more than just…earthquakes."

"Can you teach us?"

I shook my head 'no'. "I want to…and I've asked Shawn. But he said no. Said we were put to better use in the gardens and fields."

A few cries of outrage.

"It's those Fires – he gives them all the best training!"

"And lets them slide on their duties when we do hard labor all day long to put food on the table!"

Mike stepped toward me. "If we could figure out how to do it in secrecy – would you train us?"

I rubbed the back of my neck. "I don't know…"

"We could keep it small – a few people at a time. He would never know."

I looked the group of Earths over. They weren't all that One Less had, but certainly enough to spread the word. As I studied them, I released the signal I had been sending out to the field and the beetles. What was left of the pests fell to the ground, quickly burying themselves under foliage. Bats began sauntering away, and the night went still.

"Okay – but I'll be sticking my neck out for you, and I'm going to need that favor returned."

"Have something in mind?" Mike asked.

A small smile lit my face. "As a matter of fact, I do."

Chapter 49

A Fragile Grasp

"Weather gir—" Shawn cut himself off at her glare.

Damn, what was her name again? She had told him dozens of times.

"Sir?" She smiled sweetly, but there was a gleam in her eye. That 'sir' was intentional.

He itched his ear and glanced at David standing behind him, buying time to think. "Mary?" He extended his arm, palm up and open, in an unsure gesture.

Her smile turned genuine. "Thank you. What is it you need, Shawn?"

He crossed the small room of the deli/headquarters to her workstation at the countertop. Her maps had spread out in every direction.

"Let's go over these storms you mentioned," Shawn said.

"Sure." She shifted on her feet. "I can only pinpoint the anomalies as the information comes to me."

"I thought you could read the atmosphere?" Shawn leaned forward over the other side of the counter, glancing at the map she pulled out.

Her shoulders stiffened. "My readings only go a dozen miles or so, as the crow flies."

He glanced up into her fiery eyes, only inches away.

Damn, I've offended her again.

Shawn straightened, then lowered his eyes. "By far the most distance I've seen accomplished by an Air."

Except Vayu. Shawn kept the thought to himself. He missed having that kind of competence on his side.

The right corner of her mouth twitched up. Apology accepted. She cleared her throat. "The weather patterns, which aren't actual patterns at all, follow a definite path. First was the forest fire in West Virginia. It had been a wet season; the conditions just weren't right for that large of a blaze." Her finger traced down a series of smaller rivers, and over the Ohio River to Huntington. "The earthquake here."

"No major fault lines," Shawn murmured.

Mary nodded her head. "There was another earthquake down the river, but they were too far apart, in both time and space, to be considered aftershocks. The anomalies end at the derecho, which ran us off from Fort Calhoun early. There hasn't been anything unusual since."

"They follow the rivers," Shawn said. "Coming directly for us; until they reached us."

Shawn stood and started pacing the room. He pointed to another admin clerk. "Were the numbers any different when we left Fort Calhoun? Or when we arrived in Denver?"

"No, sir. Same number. Except…"

"Except what?"

"One of the camps reported a missing person. But it never added up since the head counts remained the same. When we reached Denver we struck the missing person reports from the records as an error."

"Who went missing? Why was I never told?" Shawn slammed fist down on the desk of the man.

"I don't…we didn't…you never—"

Shawn was already walking away, his back to Mary. Sarcasm dripped from his voice. "What about the derecho, weather girl? Do you think that was human-induced or not?"

She spoke, tight-lipped, "It was far too late in the season for such a massive summer storm, sir."

Shawn closed his eyes and took a deep breath. It always amazed him how quickly his fragile grasp on a situation could shatter.

David stepped forward, notebook in hand. "But, if someone was aiming for One Less – why did they stop at Fort Calhoun?"

"Because they found what they were looking for." Shawn flexed his hands, refraining from shaking some sense into him.

"Sir?"

Shawn shouted over his shoulder as he slammed the door open out of the deli, "They found me!"

Chapter 50

It's a Date

After we parted from the Earths, Micah and I turned for the amusement park and our observation tower.

"That was very impressive." He nudged me with his shoulder, inching closer.

"Thanks. I'm glad I didn't freak. I hate bats." I laughed. "At least I didn't get pooped on."

He returned the laugh, throwing his arm around me. "All that guano – good fertilizer for the wheat field."

I eyed his hand on my shoulder. He made small circles, rubbing with the pad of his thumb.

I know this tune.

I tried distracting him. "I need you to call in my favor with the Earths."

"Finally going to build an army?" His hand went down to the small of my back.

"No. In fact, just the opposite. I want them to run away when I give my signal."

He furrowed his eyebrows. "Run away? Why?" Despite the frown, his hand slipped around my waist, pulling me into him.

"I'm sorry, but I don't think we should try it again – at least not this soon." I removed his hand, intertwining my fingers with his.

He stopped walking, pulling me back into him. I tried to avoid looking in his eyes, but he lifted my chin up.

"I think we should. You have more control over your powers because of it, don't you?"

My eyes floated away. "Yes, but—"

"And you will not take an army to the fight with you…" his sharp tone caused my eyes to snap back to him. "Although you claim to know you need all the help you can get."

I ripped my chin away from his hand. "What about you? You insist at being by my side, but if we do this – you won't even be able to make your way back to camp."

His hand fell. "Why is it so difficult for you to let people do things for you?"

I laughed. "Let them? I *let* your sister take Bee away from me. How much more 'let' do you need?"

He shook his head. "That's not what I meant."

"Well that's how it was taken." I clipped my words short. I crossed my arms over my chest, but in my own way, heaved a huge sigh of relief. We were finally arguing, and it felt good.

"What if I…" Micah trailed off.

I stayed silent.

"I mean, I might know a way for me to pass along the energy, then gain some for myself."

"How?" I asked, narrowing my eyes.

"We can ask for the help of some of the Elementals. And I think I've identified another Medwin; other than Shawn."

"Who?"

"Natasha." He took me by the arm, walking again. "Tomorrow is a free day at the One Less camp. I thought we could take it off and stay here. We'll do an energy exchange tonight then I'll try to recover some of it with Natasha tomorrow."

"Why don't we try the recovery first, to make sure it works?"

"I don't think we would truly know if it works – unless I was in a condition to really need it." He lifted an eyebrow at me, waiting for my answer.

I floundered, almost out of excuses. "But what if I need you? What if something happens and you can't even stand?"

I risked a glance at him. One corner of his mouth tipped up, but his shoulders drooped. For a moment, he looked like a heartbroken man. "The thing is…you don't need me. You seem to be the strongest when I am not around. We can't separate again – I won't do it. But, if I'm at least incapacitated, I figure you'll keep stepping up."

I shook my head and mumbled, "That's stupid." But was it really? I thought back to each of the times we were separated. Galapagos – I hadn't done much there. Though I had managed to send messages to Susan and Micah. And I had pseudo-escaped; who knows what would've happened if Micah hadn't found me lying unconscious on the rocks.

Then my time at the Chakra with Alex, when Micah traveled the world like a madman hunting down Shawn. What did I accomplish then? I tapped into the Athame…that was a power increase like no other. Then I left, right in the middle of childbirth. Hell, if I could do that on my own, what else could stop me?

"Fine." I leaned in to Micah. "We'll try it again. But we'll take it slow this time. I could use the energy to visit the Shades in the Chalice."

"The Chalice?" Micah asked.

"Like the Athame, but it keeps the Shades of men. Their blood filled the cup during the initiation ritual."

Micah nodded. "Banned before my time."

"But not before Cato's time…"

"He's there?" Micah's head snapped back to me.

"Yes…he's, well, I think he's on our side."

I let Micah run through the possibilities in his own head.

"Is there something you want me to tell him? Or ask him?"

Micah nodded slowly. "Yes – ask him if the mission of The Seven, according to the doctrine, supersedes family ties."

"Okay…" I wasn't sure if I really wanted to know the answer to that.

We made our way through the gates; I noticed Micah had doubled the guards. We stopped for dinner, then began the trek up the stairs. "You know, there is probably an easier way to do this. Like, with air, in the elevator shaft."

He laughed. "Maybe next time – look, we're almost to the top."

I sighed, pulling myself up the rest of the way with the railing.

Micah helped by pushing on my backside.

I laughed. "Get your hands off my butt."

"It's such a fine butt." He spun me around, pulling me close and keeping me there with a firm grip on my gluts.

He leaned in, nibbling at my ear as he walked me backward to his pillows. I giggled.

Someone cleared their throat from the other side of the room. We both jumped apart like teenagers caught in the act.

"Does this mean my shift is over?" One of the guards looked from me to Micah.

"Yes." Micah smoothed out his shirt, trying to recover some dignity. "Is the watch up top in place?"

The guard nodded. "Been there for an hour. Shift change goes at midnight." The guard glanced at me. "There isn't really any insulation between you and upstairs, so—"

"So keep the noise down," Micah finished for him. "Got it."

My hand went to my cheeks, they were hot.

What am I so embarrassed about? I am an adult for Christ's sake.

"Very well, then. Have a good night you two." The guard took his exit.

As soon as his silhouette disappeared down the corridor of stairs, I erupted in laughter.

Micah put his finger to his lips, then pointed up with his other finger, as if to remind me.

"Oh, please – like you wouldn't want to give them something to listen to." I put my hand on my hip, taunting him.

"Is that a challenge?" He stepped closer again, bending down so his lips were inches from mine. He lowered his voice, whispering, "Or a promise?"

I closed the rest of the distance, sealing the deal with a kiss. It was slow and reassuring and grounding.

This is what Micah does for me; he grounds me. He is my rock, my Micah.

"I love you," I whispered, even as our lips still touched.

"I love you too, Kaitlyn." He pulled away, looking into my eyes. "Let's get married."

That one took me by surprise.

"I'm sorry," he continued. "That just came out. Do you still want to?"

"Get married?" I asked.

He nodded.

"Yes. I mean, that's what we were supposed to do in the States. Will it be legal?" My hands squeezed his arms.

He shrugged. "There really isn't a defined 'legal' anymore, I don't think. I'm not concerned about the paperwork. Let's do it for us."

I smiled. "The winter solstice is coming up…"

"When the dark half of the year relinquishes to the light half," he said. "It's perfect."

"Next week then."

"It's a date." He took my hands, kissing them both at the knuckles.

I turned, leading him to the pillows. I made myself comfortable, folding one pillow in half and propping it under my arm.

Micah still stood. He took off his boots and socks, throwing them aside. Then he lifted the hem of his shirt, baring first his abdomen – then his chest.

"Turn around," I said. He obliged.

Last time, I hadn't gotten a chance to really look at him. He was much thinner than I remembered, but then again, everyone was these days. He had a few new scars. An angry, red welt ran from his shoulder to his hip. "What's that from?"

He turned the rest of the way to look at me, scratching his shoulder. "Ran into a small mob; somewhere in Missouri. Their weapon of choice was whips."

"Oh my God." I had never imagined what it must have been like for him, alone.

"I managed to get away, mostly intact. The couple I ran into down the road didn't, though." He shrugged and shook his head, as if trying to rid himself of the memory.

I do the same thing. "And that one?" I gestured to his shoulder where a patch of rough, pink scar tissue resided.

"Tried to convince a Fire to join us. He didn't agree." Micah unzipped his pants, turning to face me. "Let's not talk about my scars."

"Well." I toyed with the edge of a pillow. "I have to know what kind of man I am about to marry."

He removed his pants the rest of the way.

"Oh," I breathed. "*That* kind of man."

He was already hard, the evidence in the intimidating bulge of his boxers.

"Your turn," he said.

I shook my head, my smile teasing. "You're not finished yet."

One of his eyebrows went up. "Fine." He took off his boxers, throwing them at me.

I caught them right in front of my face. "So sexy." I laughed.

He dove onto the pillows, bouncing half of them up into the air. "*Now* it's your turn."

"Oh, I don't know." I rolled on top of him. "I think we can have some fun – even with my clothes on."

"Prude," he said, smiling.

I leaned down and whispered in his ear, "Slut."

He shivered.

My tongue darted in and out as I nibbled at his neck and down the length of his chest. Not breaking contact, I slipped out of my own clothes.

With his hands on my hips, he turned us both over. His body weight pinned me. "Let me take the lead, at least for tonight…"

He put both my arms above my head, pinning them down with only one of his. "Let me in, Kaitlyn."

I spread my legs. He didn't hesitate. I bit my lip, holding in my moan, until he was all the way in. He bent his head to my ear and began whispering. It was a foreign language; I couldn't comprehend anything he was saying. But it had a rhythm to it. Sounds rolled off his tongue effortlessly, and the low hum of his voice was mesmerizing. Something in my memory flashed. Men in grass skirts, doing groin thrusts back and forth in time to drums.

"A warrior's challenge," I whispered.

"What?" he asked.

"Nothing…keep going," I murmured. The pain was a welcome distraction. I was on the precipice of a nightmare.

He pulled back, just slightly, then pressed in. I held my breath, trying to concentrate on his foreign words. I lost myself in their tune. His chant washed through me, penetrating deeper, encouraging me to give myself to him.

He moved faster, and I raised my hips to meet him.

"Now," he said. I almost missed his switch to English. "Do it now."

I nodded, losing myself in his words again. As his whispers started to die off, I focused in on them, grabbing hold and refusing to let go - like I was stealing his breath. As he climaxed, I absorbed the energy. Ten seconds, then I released him. His body collapsed over me in an impossible weight.

He heaved in deep, slow breaths. Even with my help, he barely managed to roll himself off me.

"Are you okay?" I asked.

He nodded his head, grimacing at the movement.

"Should I get Natasha now?" My mouth turned down at the thought of running to another woman to fix what I had just done.

"No." He licked his lips, laying his head back down on the pillow. "Wait till morning, just…" He drifted off.

"Just stand watch." I finished the sentence for him. I kissed him on the forehead, stood, and stretched out my arms. I walked over to the windows, where my backpack was laying, and retrieved the Chalice. I sat cross-legged on the floor, staring at my wrapped package. I sighed – I wasn't in the mood for Cato. "Let's just get this over with."

Chapter 51

A Threesome

I was there before I knew it. The route was familiar to me now, and with the high I was riding, the netherworld bent to my will easily. Cato and Ted stood, waiting for me, the remaining men behind them.

"You've been gone awhile," Ted said.

"I've been busy." I walked toward them on firm ground.

"You've found Shawn," Cato concluded. "And you've found more power."

"Yes to both." I stopped in front of them. No need to divulge details. "Shawn is releasing the Shades in the Athame, as I am doing here. How will that affect his power?"

"He will be missing the knowledge they could otherwise provide. But his power will become more pure and controlled. He will be able to wield Akasha." Cato held nothing back.

I craned my neck, looking at the faces of the group of men. They looked anxious, but they would have to wait. "Before, with me, Shawn used The Great Rite to steal my energy. Is that partly what tainted his power?"

Cato flinched. "I'm sure of it."

"So if I used The Great Rite – would it do the same to me?"

Ted answered this time, shaking his head, "Not if both, or…" He cleared his throat, face going red. "All parties are willing."

I couldn't resist, "You mean like a threesome?"

The word 'threesome' echoed in the open space. Cato and Ted shifted on their feet, suddenly avoiding my gaze. A few snickers floated up from the group of men behind them, and some glares. I think I even saw one in the back crossing himself.

I stepped forward, Cato and Ted parting to give me way. "Don't worry." I glanced at Cato, "I'm not that desperate for power…yet." I continued to the group of men. "Step forward if you wish to move on – step aside if you wish to stay."

They hesitated, seeking guidance in each other's eyes. Finally, one brave soul stepped forward. More than half followed suit. Less than a dozen moved away.

I looked at the palms of my hands, already glowing in anticipation.

Would this one burn?

I chose the already injured hand. Burn marks on the palm, recovering dog bite on the wrist. Without warning, I flung my arm. Power burst out in a wide arc, from one end of the group to the other.

I exhaled the words of the spell, using air to intertwine my breath with Akasha, "In love and in trust, in peace and in wisdom, I release you." The men were gone in a wisp of smoke before I finished speaking. I lowered my arm, and my voice, "So mote it be."

It suddenly felt empty. I turned back to Cato and Ted. "And you?"

In perfect sync, they answered, "We're staying."

It was a little creepy, and I had to remind myself they were just ideas, or images of the men they had once been. I tried rubbing the goose bumps out of my arms. I glanced at my hand. There was no pain this time. Did that mean my conscious was clear?

"So what now?" I asked.

"Now, we prepare you." Cato said, stepping forward.

I stepped back, narrowing my eyes. "How?"

"Well, what do you need?"

I took a deep breath. "I need you to answer a question, first. It comes from Micah." I glanced at Ted, then back over to Cato. "Does the mission of The Seven, according to the doctrine, supersede family ties?"

Cato didn't hesitate. "Yes, it does."

"Oh," I mumbled. I was almost positive that was the wrong answer.

"However..." Cato continued.

My eyes snapped back to him.

"That doctrine no longer applies."

He was right, Susan had rewritten it, but after he had died. "Since when?"

Cato smiled. "If I'm honest, since the day you stepped into our lives, Kaitlyn."

That is a better answer – I think.

Cato asked, "You are trying to decide whether or not to trust me, which is understandable. After all – it is my son you are trying to kill."

"Micah stands with me; don't you consider him your son – or at least as much of one?" I snapped back.

"If not more so," Cato answered. "He was my natural choice to take over as Rais."

"Not Susan?"

Cato shrugged. "The Seven has never been run by a woman. But – times are changing."

"That they are," Ted mumbled.

I wondered if he was a former Rais.

"Let me share some of my knowledge with you." Cato held up his hand, palm out toward me. "You can decide whether or not to trust me later."

I hesitated. *Couldn't hurt, right?*

"What is your element of choice?" he asked.

I stepped forward, raising my good hand to meet his. I glanced into his dull, blue eyes. "Earth," I said.

Chapter 52

To Say the Least

Micah cracked open his eyes. His eyelids were heavy, and the light that crept in was blinding.

"Are you okay?" a soft voice asked. It wasn't Kaitlyn.

Micah tried again, squinting against the early morning sun. Details of a darkened form slowly emerged. Natasha.

Micah groaned. "I have to pee."

"Oh," Natasha glanced around the circular tower, eyes resting on a bucket. "Do you want me to—?"

"No, no. Sorry; it can wait. Where's Kaitlyn?"

"She…got restless, I think. Said she was going for breakfast." Natasha didn't look at him. She was concentrating.

For the first time, Micah noticed the tingling at his palm. His arm twitched.

"Hold still," Natasha said. "Almost done."

Micah glanced down, "Oh."

The barely detectable glow between each of their palms was the telltale signature of Natasha's energy transfer.

Micah looked back at her.

She wavered, sweat dotting her forehead, then toppled over.

"Natasha!" Micah pulled himself up, then rolled, using his arms to drag himself forward.

"I'm fine, I'm fine. Just…winded." She rolled over on her back, breathing hard.

He lay down next to her, doing the same. "We are pathetic."

She laughed. "To say the least."

"I'm still not sure I have the energy to even make it down the stairs." Micah sat up slowly, propping his back against the wall.

Natasha sighed. "I'm sorry…"

"No, no. I didn't mean it that way. It's just – I've got to find some way to keep up with her."

Natasha sat up, leaning against the wall, too. "We need more people. We can still make it work."

Micah looked at her with a wry smile. "Thanks, I—"

His eyes traveled outside the tower. "Wait, is that her?"

Natasha followed his line of sight, squinting. "I can't tell. Things are kind of blurry for me."

"Well, not for me." Micah made an attempt to stand. He couldn't get off his knees.

Kaitlyn was already past the train tracks, heading downtown.

He tried again, fell, and knocked over the backpack Kaitlyn left behind. Something clattered out. He sighed, mumbling, "I'll never catch her."

I'll never survive this.

"I have a headache." Natasha rubbed her temples. "I miss ibuprofen."

Micah stayed on the ground, bumping something by the backpack. He rolled over, picking up the object. It was the Chalice. His eyes lit up with an idea. "Natasha," he asked. "Do you have a knife handy?"

Chapter 53

Choosing a Name

I spent the night pacing the observation tower, stopping at every full circle to check Micah's ragged breathing. With all my pent up energy, I never felt so powerful – yet so powerless at the same time.

When dawn came, I was finally sitting still, looking out over the river. I closed my eyes, reaching out and practicing identifying Elementals in the area. I counted everyone at the amusement park and everyone at the One Less camp. I pressed further, testing the extent of my skill. Judging how far I went was hard, but I could at least pinpoint higher population areas. I scrutinized each form, finally realizing I was searching for the telltale signature of a Gaia. I was searching for Bee. I couldn't find her.

Good, I told myself, wiping a tear trailing down my cheek.

Natasha came in shortly after. I couldn't stand to watch her struggle to fix the damage I had done to Micah. I left.

I walked out of the observation tower, letting my skin drink in the gift of full sun, and took a deep breath. I made my way to the cooking fires. The smell of meat permeated the air.

What is that? Squirrel? Rabbit? I could really go for some wild dog, I smiled to myself.

The sound of laughter caught my attention. A group of kids, squealing and yelping, were playing tag around a dilapidated carnival game. A water gun horse race, by the looks of it. The horses had been torn off and were now in the kids' hands. Bee would've loved it.

We hadn't come across many kids in the past few years. Either they were kept hidden – protected, or not many survived the sudden push back into the dark ages. I laughed when a little blonde girl crouched down around a corner, then jumped up to scare the living daylights out of her older brother.

Another group of kids rounded the bend, the older children outpacing the younger. Toward the back of the group, a skinny, darker-skinned girl panted to keep up. A Fire. She snapped her head around, black braids swinging out in a wide arc.

I staggered back.

A Fire – those braids. I know this.

Pain ripped through my chest, settling deep in my stomach.

* * *

"Easy there, princess."

I turned, first meeting Shawn's blue eyes, then glancing down, into Ahi's brown ones.

I staggered back, almost tripping right into Akasha. I lunged forward and fell on my knees. Akasha rose; I turned again to Ahi. Chills ran down the length of my spine, despite the fire at my back.

Ahi had been the mist all along, on her knees in front of Shawn. He held a pistol to her head. I looked behind them for the other four swirls of mist. Alex was one, held to the ground by three larger men.

"Where's the baby?" Shawn asked, shoving the tip of his gun against the back of Ahi's head.

Shawn's finger was on the trigger, already squeezing. "Release. Your. Akasha."

Ahi shook, looking to me for help.

"Kaitlyn," Shawn asked, "is the baby mine?"

Above us, Akasha crested the treetops, chasing down Shawn's plasma.

Akasha or Ahi? Save the world or save Ahi? Why did it always have to one or the other? I was determined to make the right choice this time. I was determined to save both.

Ahi angled her head away from the gun. Blood dripped from a gash in the side of her head. "Help me, Kaitlyn."

Before the lump in my throat even finished forming, I shot my hand straight up into the air. Akasha rose, overtaking Shawn's plasma.

I looked at Shawn and whispered, "Too late."

Akasha burst as I released its energy. Bone-shaking thumps went off, and I dove for Ahi. I wrapped my arms around her as we tumbled, end over end, straight through the wall of fire, and back to Earth.

* * *

"Let her go! What the hell is wrong with you?"

I unwrapped myself from around the little girl at her mother's insistent screams. The girl was crying.

"Oh, shit – I'm so sorry. I...I was having a nightmare." *How else could I explain it?*

The girl and I were helped up, then pulled apart, her mother escorting her away. I was left to face the crowd that had gathered.

"Kaitlyn? Are you okay?" Someone touched my arm, keeping me steady.

"No," I answered honestly.

Kaitlyn, Chica, Mommy, Gaia, Lucy...

I chose the least painful of titles, blocking out the devastating memories the other names held.

I straightened, shaking off the touch at my arm. "The name is Lucy." I swallowed, "And I need to go for a walk."

"I think that is probably a good idea." The man gestured to the exit of the park.

My stride was quick; I never looked behind me though I could feel the weight of a thousand eyes boring into my back. I walked straight for downtown Denver, then the length of the 16th Street Mall, heading for One Less.

My nightmares had caught up with me, and I finally understood what I had to do – what I should've done all along. Akasha could reign, but not at the expense of human life.

I paused, eyes tearing up. Something dropped at my feet.

"Excuse me, could you please hand that up?"

I bent down, retrieving a piece of large red material, tied in a bow. I handed it to the woman standing on a ladder above me. She secured it to a lamppost, right next to a clump of gold balls.

Christmas decorations – already?

Other holiday paraphernalia was being placed up and down the outdoor mall. Good to know everything wasn't sacrificed in order to stoke the cooking fires. The air smelled of pine and cinnamon.

"There," she said, climbing down the ladder. She surveyed the rest of the decorations then smiled at me. "For the celebration of new beginnings."

I managed to smile back, then took my leave. Turning down the alley toward the entrance to the One Less camp, I stopped short. Two cars blocked the entire alleyway, sitting side by side, leaving an only very narrow space for passage. A guard stood on top of each of the cars, along with several in front. Each of them had their weapon pointed at me.

I did the only thing I could do. I raised my hands in the air.

"State your name and your business," one of the guards demanded, stepping forward.

"Lucy. Lucy Evermore." I pointed to the blue band on my arm.

"Check the list."

One of them lowered their barrel and began flipping through papers; probably some of the same papers I had drafted myself weeks ago.

My mind raced. What had happened? Had they found out about Micah's crew?

The shuffle of papers ceased. "She's on it."

I lowered my hands and stepped forward.

"Just a minute, you." The guard lowered his weapon and closed the distance between us. "Where were you last night? Everyone was accounted for once we went on lock-down. No one has been allowed to leave yet."

"Where I was, is none of your business," my tone was low and even.

"I've got orders to bring anyone found outside the camp straight to Shawn."

My entire chest constricted, though I kept my eyes locked on his. He said no more.

Is he giving me an out? If he wasn't, he'd already have me in cuffs.

I forced my lungs to take in air. "I don't like to be locked in; spent too much time in prison."

He narrowed his eyes, peering at my face tattoo. "You're that Earth – the one that killed the wild dog?"

I paused, then nodded.

His face broke into a smile. "Shawn doesn't have to know. I think we can work something out." He put his arm around me, leading me deeper into the alley.

I shoved it off. "I'm not going to go there."

He laughed. "Neither am I, sweetheart."

"Then what is it you want?"

"You'll be my entry into tonight's dog fight."

Chapter 54

A Promise

"A dog fight?" Erika choked on her coffee.

"Yeah – I got caught outside after the lockdown. I think it is the only way the guards won't turn me in. Unless you can pull a few favors?"

She shook her head. "My reach only goes so far. And the guards have gone all chauvinistic on me. Been turning away all my requests, even if it gets sent through someone else."

"What about you, Clay? Aren't you the head guard or something?"

He put down his breakfast plate, wiping his mouth with the back of his sleeve. "Not since I lost all the prisoners. But Kait—" He paused glancing at Erika. "Er, Lucy….have you ever been to a dog fight?"

"You mean like with pit bulls?"

Erika slapped her forehead with her hand.

Clay took a deep breath. "*You* are the dog."

"You mean I have to fight?" My stomach flipped. "Another person?"

"Usually a Fire. Not too many other Elementals volunteer." Erika looked at me. "I imagine you'll attract quite the crowd. Being an Earth, and all. Not to mention the fact you're already famous."

"Will Shawn be there?" I started picking apart my roll; I was no longer hungry.

"Shawn doesn't know about the dog fights. They're underground, so to speak."

I snorted. "That should give me an advantage."

Clay jumped in. "But there are usually dozens of each type of Elemental in attendance."

I caught his meaning. I wouldn't be able to use any of the other elemental powers, not even for a shield. People would notice. I set down my plate and rubbed my temples. "I don't want to go in blind. Erika – can you find out where the fight is going to be tonight?"

She nodded and stood. "I'm on it."

"And also who I'm fighting…" I called after her.

A few people looked my way with raised eyebrows.

I waited until she left, and lowered my voice, "Clay – when she finds out where it is, I'll need to know what's underneath. If it's slate, sand, or whatever."

He nodded, looking around. "Where is Micah? He might have some insight into this."

"Micah is…indisposed, and probably will be the rest of the day. It's better he doesn't know about this – he'd never let me do it. And if I don't, they'll turn me in." I swallowed the rest of my breakfast. "Should I walk away from this, Clay? I mean, is it worth keeping my secret? I could just, you know, hide out with Micah until we're ready."

Clay shrugged. "Winning one of these fights pretty much makes you a God among Fires. If you're trying to get Elementals on your side, this is how to win the flamers over."

I smiled. "Flamers?"

He laughed, but lowered his voice, "They hate being called that." Clay cleared his throat. "Seriously, though…I've seen a few of these fights, Kaitlyn. Nobody walks away, well, um…pretty."

I stood, glancing down at him with a wry smile. "Since when has pretty ever been on my priority list?"

* * *

I spent the rest of the day working in the gardens. Both Erika and Clay came to me several times with bits of information.

"You can dissolve the sandstone underneath the arena with pressurized water," Clay suggested.

"How long will that take?"

Clay shrugged. "I tried it once with a Water at the Chakra. The process sped up when I pushed acids and salt from the earth toward the area, then a Fire heated everything up."

I shook my head. "I can't use water or fire anyway. Besides, I'm not looking to have us all swallowed up in a sink hole."

I absorbed the other tips he gave me, working through a plan in my head while weeding, raking, and picking. The monotonous work was a welcome distraction from everything. From the dogfight and the black braids. I was not sure I could go back, and risk running into that girl again.

Not going back won't go over well with Micah.

Dusk came sooner than I was able to calm my nerves. I worked until the garden area was empty. Finally, I stood, taking a deep breath. The energy rush gained from being with Micah last night was already waning.

I turned and walked out of the gardens, past the eating area, keeping my eyes steady toward the Tivoli Center. Halfway in between 16th Street and the amusement park, the former college student union building was easy to find. A smoke stack jutted up out of the building, with 'Tivoli' painted down the side.

I approached one of the doors, trying not to glance toward the amusement park and Micah's observation tower. Two guards stood at the top of the steps. I paused, pushing my short hair back behind my ears. Certainly my face tattoo was recognizable – Lucy, the woman who killed the wild dog. I was adjusting the blue band at my bicep when I heard a whistle from around the corner of the building.

I peered into the dark, until a woman stuck her head out. Natasha. She motioned for me to join her.

I ran over. "Is it Micah?" I whispered.

She nodded.

"What – what happened?"

She took my hand, pulling me deeper into the shadows of two buildings, and straight into Micah.

I swallowed.

Goddamnit – this isn't going to help me right before a fight. I can't be Kaitlyn right now.

He put his hands on my shoulders. "I know what you're about to do."

I tried to step back, but his hold tightened. I sighed. "You can't change my mind about this, Micah. And you can't stop me."

"Don't you think I know that?" he hissed back. He pressed his lips together, then took a deep breath through his nose. He lowered his voice, annunciating each word, "I know that better than anyone."

"So what are you doing here?"

He glanced at Natasha, who had her back to us, giving us pseudo-privacy. "I can't go in there; it's invite only. But I want to give you a recharge."

"No!" I squeaked.

He put his hand over my mouth. I bit down.

"Ow!"

Natasha turned. "Shh!"

Micah examined his hand.

"It is a miracle you're even standing right now, Micah – I'm not going to take anything else from you."

"I don't matter right now."

His words stung, but I didn't argue.

He continued, "Let me help you, the only way I know how."

"We figured out a way to give most of his energy back," Natasha said, taking a step toward us. "It's a group effort, but we can do it."

She gestured behind me. I turned to see a dozen women, all I recognized from Micah's camp, standing toward the end of the Tivoli center.

"We'll take him back to the tower, and do it there," Natasha said.

I narrowed my eyes. "Do *what* there?"

"Not that, Kaitlyn." Micah rolled his eyes. "Remember what I said? She's like a Medwin."

I tried not to look at Micah. I felt the weight of his eyes, willing me to see it his way. I cleared my throat. "Is it safe?"

"The more that participate, the safer and easier it is." Natasha kept her face neutral, but I caught the tick at her mouth.

I crossed my arms. "Fine. Let's do this." I turned back to Micah. "But I'm only taking a little. Just enough to—"

Micah's lips pressed against mine, cutting me off. I stumbled back as he pushed forward. We finally collided against the brick wall, and he pinned me against it.

"Micah, wait."

I didn't want to do it here – in the open and in front of Natasha.

His hands snaked down my waist and to the inside of my thighs.

I yelped.

He immediately covered my mouth with his again. "We can't have that happening." I felt his lips curl up in a smile. He pulled on the blue band at my arm, removing it.

"What are you doing?" I whispered, looking around him for Natasha. I caught her silhouette disappearing around the corner where the large group had been.

He pulled the stretchy band over my head, positioning it in between my teeth. It wasn't going to muffle any moans, but damn – it felt sexy.

He pulled back my hair, and whispered in my ear, "The Great Rite works several different ways. As long as we are both aroused, there can be an energy exchange." One of his hands unzipped my pants. "I'm aroused Kaitlyn – are you?"

My eyebrows rose. I couldn't answer that. Not very well, anyway.

He shimmied my pants down past my hips, all the way to my ankles. I gripped the loose fabric of his shirt, ready to pull him up in case someone rounded the corner. When his fingers went to the elastic line of my panties, I squeaked.

"Shh," he said. "What? You think it's my turn to undress?"

I nodded.

"I told you, there is more than one way to do this."

And I'm sure we'll get to all of them, whether I like it or not. He was so stubborn sometimes – though I wasn't putting up much of a fight. Who would?

He tugged, and I was bare from waist to knee.

"We don't have a lot of time, so I'll just get right to the point." Micah stood, rubbing up against me; he was already hard. My hands went to his buckle.

He caught me at the wrists. "No, no, no. I'm in charge tonight. Don't make me tie you up." He lifted my wrists above my head, pinning them with one large, viselike hand. His other hand slithered down my torso, leaving a path of goose bumps, until he reached my outer thigh.

My whole body tensed as he made small circles with the tip of his finger, slowly working his way in between my legs. With each circle, my heart beat harder, rising into my throat.

I thought he was going to get to the point?

On cue, his finger traced my opening. Back and forth, back and forth. I tried giving him better access but my legs were shackled by my own clothing. It was pure torture.

"Stay still." His tongue darted in and out of my ear once, then again. "Just waiting for…"

He swished his finger once, the sweet sound of liquid accompanying the movement. "…that."

He thrust his finger inside me. I threw my head back in ecstasy, the rough brick catching strands of hair. His lips moved to my exposed neck. He withdrew his hand, tracing me again.

"Don't stop," the words came out slurred and muffled.

"I don't know Kaitlyn – seems like I give and give and give. Seems I need something in return." His mouth moved lower, closer to my nipple.

I groaned. "Anything, just…do it again."

"Anything?" He paused.

I couldn't nod fast enough.

"Good girl." He thrust two fingers inside, several times in a row. His teeth found my nipple through my thin shirt. Heat raced through my midsection, threatening to engulf me in flames.

He stopped again.

I gritted my teeth to keep from screaming in frustration.

"I decided what I want."

I opened my eyes. Even in the dark, I could see those green irises boring into me.

"You give me what I want…and I'll give you what you want." His hand in between my legs shifted, and I felt the tips of three fingers at my entrance. He lowered his voice even further, "Do you want this, Kaitlyn."

"Yes." I nodded. *Dear God, yes!*

"I want you to win this fight tonight, Kaitlyn. And I want you to come out alive and well."

I blinked. Technically, that was three things. He pressed his fingers in, a little bit at a time, then stopped. "Will you do that for me, Kaitlyn?"

Three for three; seemed fair. I nodded again.

He released my wrists in order to remove the band from my mouth. "Promise me, Kaitlyn. Out loud. Promise me you'll be okay tonight."

My hand went to his cheek. "Yes, Micah. I promise."

He bit the inside of his cheek, nodding – accepting my promise. His bicep flexed, and all three fingers entered me. I threw my head back again and moaned, not caring who heard me. My fingers curled in, scraping his cheek along the way.

"Faster," I huffed out, in between breaths.

"Start it now, Kaitlyn," he answered in reply.

"No – too soon."

"Do it, or I swear I'll stop."

I met his eyes. He wasn't bluffing. I opened a connection between us. The magic was mostly Earth, like the signal that went out to identify Elementals, only in reverse. The energy started to flow – I barely had to call it. I tried slowing it, meaning to take just a little this time. He probably couldn't stand to lose much more. It was a miracle he was standing at all.

"No," Micah said. "Take more."

Before I could protest, he bent lower and found my nipple again. The pinching sensation sent ripples of pleasure throughout my body. In a magnetic-like response, energy pulsated through the open connection. I rode the high until spasms froze me in place. In one final burst, energy shot through, and the connection closed.

My feet hit pavement – I hadn't realized I was in the air. I found Micah's eyes, using them to ground me while my orgasm subsided. Then he fell away.

I swiped, trying to catch the loose fabric at his chest. My fingers brushed cotton, but never caught hold. I watched in slow motion. His hands didn't move to protect him; he had gone unconscious.

The hard slap of skull against concrete never came. Soft, scarred hands slipped underneath just in time.

Natasha, good. Natasha... My eyes went wide with surprise. *Oh, crap.*

I bent, hastily tugging at my clothes. It wasn't just Natasha, it was her whole crew. They were all pawing Micah's unconscious body, trying to determine the best course of action. I narrowed my eyes at them while I zipped up my pants.

"Here, you lost this," Natasha shoved her hand in front of my face, holding out the blue armband.

My cheeks went red, half in anger and half with embarrassment. *How much did they see?*

"Psst, Kaitlyn."

I turned – Clay stood at the other end of the building motioning me over. *How much did* he *see?*

"Wait, I—"

"Go," Natasha interrupted me, practically pushing me toward Clay. "We've got this."

They already had Micah lifted, moving him away in the other direction. I caught a glimpse of his face. Deep scratches ran down his cheek. A new wound at his forearm was bandaged.

When did that happen?

The group turned the corner with their very handsome, very vulnerable patient in tow, and disappeared.

"Where have you been? The fight was supposed to start five minutes ago." Clay was at my side now, tugging me along.

I let him lead me away. I was riding Micah's high; it was hard to concentrate. Everything seemed cloudy and surreal. "Did you get the sand bags in place?" I asked.

He nodded. "Each bag has a few small holes poked in them, like you asked." We peered around the corner of the building at the main entrance. "You go through first. Contenders are supposed to arrive alone."

"Okay, wish me luck." I blinked, still a little dazed.

Clay raised an eyebrow at me. "You are practically glowing. I think I'm gonna need to wish the other guy luck."

I laughed, but it came out sounding strangled. I turned before he could see my cheeks turning red again, covered the distance to the brick steps in long strides, and marched up.

"Name," said the guard.

I cleared my throat. "Lucy."

"You're not on the list."

"Oh." This was…weird.

"Are you sure?" I tried again. "Lucy Evermore – I'm a contender." I straightened my back, hoping to heighten my appearance.

"Didn't anyone tell you?" He flipped his notebook shut. "You have to go in through that entrance." He nodded to a door down the length of the building.

"Why?" I squinted to see a dilapidated, rusted piece of metal barely hanging from its hinges.

He shrugged. "I guess because of the betting. Seeing fighters before the match gives the gamblers an edge. We have to close betting before you come into the ring."

"Makes sense, I guess." I had no idea others would have a stake in the fight. I tried running through how that would complicate everything in my head, when I caught the guard still looking at me. I went back down the stairs. "Like seeing the bride in her dress before the wedding." My laugh was nervous, and wholly unconvincing.

I stopped at the bottom of the stairs, and asked, "Just curious, who are you betting on?"

The guard looked me from top to bottom and back again, then said, "The other guy."

Chapter 55

The Dragon

I navigated the rusty door, wondering if my last tetanus shot was still effective. They had shoved enough needles in me the first few days I'd arrived at The Seven; one of them was surely tetanus.

The door slammed shut behind me, plunging me into darkness. A small flame unfolded on the other side of the room. Its owner moved it higher, revealing his face. "You're late."

Long, jagged scars ran from his temple to his mouth, pulling his upper lip in a permanent, cruel smile. He was missing several teeth on the same side of his mouth.

"What happened?" The question was out of my mouth before I could stop it. I still wasn't thinking straight.

He raised his eyebrows. "I was a contender."

I gasped. My hand shot up to cover my mouth – so far I was having a hard time being very contender-like.

The other side of his mouth curled up, completing the smile. "I was the winner."

My hand dropped, and the blood drained from my face.

He turned, motioning for me to follow down a long corridor. His body obscured the ball of fire he held above his palm, and for once I was thankful to be in the dark. The corners where wall met floor were blurry, no matter how hard I stared at them. My feet didn't feel like they were moving, but I kept up with the Fire just the same. My dreamlike reality didn't bode well for the fight.

We passed a dilapidated bar. Behind it on the wall was a faded spray painted word, "Sigi."

"Named after the building's founder," the Fire said. He pushed open a door. Deep, rhythmic chanting floated up the stairwell – getting louder as we descended.

"We are going to the catacombs of the Tivoli Center. Used to be where the beer was stored, then it was used as storage for the university."

"Now a convenient place for dog fights," I mumbled. My tongue felt thick and sticky.

He shook his head. "No. The fights are in a new place each time. Otherwise the Elementals would find some way to cheat."

I snorted. I'd still found a way to cheat. I wondered if my opponent had, too.

Our feet hit cement, and the chanting was loud enough to drown out any other thoughts. Even the walls seemed to reverberate in rhythm. My heartbeat picked up speed, matching the pace of the chanting.

The Fire stopped just outside of a double door. I peered through the foggy glass on my tiptoes. It was a sea of faces, all shouting.

"What's happening?" I tried jumping for a better view.

The Fire put his hand on my shoulder, leaning in so I could hear him better. "They just introduced your opponent. He is the title holder, for five fights now."

"Just five?" A small flower of hope bloomed in my chest.

He looked at me, eyebrows furrowed, then leaned in again. "There have only been six. It didn't take long for people to stop volunteering as contenders."

The flower went up in flame; the ashes leaving a sour taste in my mouth.

"Listen," he continued. "No one is allowed to interfere, magically. There are refs posted throughout and they will stop the fight and declare a winner. There are three rounds; each two minutes long. If you last the length of the fight, the refs will declare a winner. There are no tapouts..." The Fire's voice droned on about the rules; most of which I didn't understand.

I stared at the glass windows. The fog seemed to be spreading out, leaving a white film over the doors, across the walls and down to the floor. I watched the ghostly lines reach for me.

"Ok," the Fire's voice came back to me. "They're introducing you now," he smirked, looking at me sideways. "As Artemis, Goddess of the Hunt." He paused for two moments, then pushed on both doors. Our small cove was flooded with even more noise.

I floated forward.

"Welcome to the dog fights, Artemis," the Fire said, smiling as I moved past him.

The sea of people parted, revealing a tight, crooked path to a ring of overturned filing cabinets. I rubbed shoulders with people as I passed. Some leaned away, but all kept shouting. No matter how hard I squinted, none of their faces would come into focus.

Up and over the filing cabinets, and into the ring I went. The man in the ring with me bounced around on the opposite side, just as faceless as the rest. I tried to remember what Erika had told me about him.

I wonder if Erika is here now. I looked around at the screaming audience. *I wonder where Clay is.*

My questions barely had time to form in my head, when I heard a muffled dong of a bell. My eyes floated back to the other person in the ring, now walking toward me.

Has it begun?

I saw a flash of a fist, dull and huge, in front of me, then my nose exploded with pain.

When I opened my eyes, the arena was sideways. Someone was counting down.

"9…8…7…"

What happened to 10, I thought. *Did I get knocked out, already?*

"6…5…"

I sucked in the slobber protruding from my mouth, and tasted blood and dust. I propped myself up on one elbow. Anger lit through my body, overtaking even the pain in my throbbing face. Micah had given me everything he had, and now he was in the hands of multiple other women, trying to save him. And here I was, a few seconds into it, on the floor and losing.

"4…3…"

My ears honed into the sound of liquid drops hitting the floor. My blood.

"2…"

I hopped to my feet, removing my t-shirt, already covered in red. I wiped my face with it and tossed it aside. The crowd piped up; the shouts a mixture of encouragement and jeers. I could follow the sound of each shout back to its owner.

My eyes lifted to my opponent, taking him in with new clarity. His eyebrows lifted, and he was trying to hide a smile. He was relieved I'd recovered, not disappointed.

Age 28, a Fire who calls himself Dragon, and a logger before Daybreak, a memory of Erika's voice reached me. He was bigger than Micah, and thick with muscle. Maybe slower on his feet than me. *He's cocky, doesn't work much around camp anymore. Still riding his status as belt holder – no one challenges him, not even when he skips sentry duty.* His hands were not the hands of a worker. No cuts, and smooth, even skin. Dragon had become lazy with his new status. His hands did, however, have a spray of my blood across the knuckles. *Prides himself on physical fighting, he won't resort to his element until he starts losing.*

Dragon waited for me across the ring. He wasn't going to make the next move. It had to be me. I walked toward him. He met me in the middle. I lifted my hand, slowly, hoping he didn't mistake it for a punch. Then I extended it toward him, palm to the side. It stayed there, hovering in midair.

He glanced at it, then over at a man in a black shirt standing just outside the ring.

I rolled my eyes. "You forgot to shake, first."

"Um, that's not in the rules."

I sniffed, and tears stung my eyes from the pain. "Come on – it's just good manners."

A few snickers from those close enough to hear our conversation. Dragon glanced at the man in black again, then shrugged, and extended his own hand.

I lunged for the ground, the momentum carrying one foot back then up above my head. The sole of my boot connected with his nose. Before I was all the way up, I closed my fist, swinging it into his side. He was softer than I expected.

He doubled over, clutching at his midsection. Gravity still had my same leg in motion. I swung it up in front of me this time, my knee hitting its target – the nose again.

Dragon flew back, stumbling over his own feet. He crashed hard on top of a filing cabinet. The crowd roared; the sound echoing across the small enclosed room. It was almost deafening.

I turned, taking the opportunity to reach out and establish which Elementals were in the room. At least fifty Fires, and just a handful of each of the others.

"That's cheating!" Dragon yelled, lifting himself up then marching to the man in black. *The ref, maybe?* "Call the fight – she cheated!"

I stepped closer to the pair, staring down Dragon. "Sorry," I shrugged. "Shaking isn't in the rules."

Out of the corner of my eye, I saw the ref's mouth twitch.

"No call. Continue the fight."

Dragon wiped his nose, now also trickling blood. He turned toward me, face red, fists closed, and sweat beading down his temples.

There were no words. Just one step toward me, then a flurry of fists. I ducked under the first bout, spinning in a crouch. My elbow hit the same soft spot at his side. I felt his breath against the back of my neck, leaving in one, large, involuntary gust.

I spun back out and stepped away before he had the chance to grab ahold of me. If I let him do that, it would be over.

Dragon clutched his side, trying to get his breath back.

I could match him blow for blow, but my punches weren't nearly as powerful. There'd have to be more – and well-placed. If I could just keep at it, I could probably outlast him. I'd just have to take care not to get knocked unconscious.

Stamina, I told myself. *It will be a long fight. You should probably stretch.*

I bent down to touch my toes, then reached up high.

Again, snickers behind me.

I bent one leg, with the other just in front of me, extending my calves. No matter what the crowd thought, it wasn't a taunt, I was just being practical. Still, Dragon wasn't taking it the right way. He glared at me through lowered lids. A growl escaped his lips, then he charged.

He covered the distance quickly. I had just enough time to step forward – I feigned right, then spun out to the left allowing him to pass me. His hand shot out, just reaching the ends of my hair. My head jolted back before his fingers slipped through. Had my hair been any longer, I'd have been in trouble.

I turned. He was off-balance. I jumped, landing one foot in the middle of his back. He went down to his knees. Again, I stepped away, narrowly avoiding a swipe of his hand.

My heart raced; there had already been too many close calls. I had to be quicker.

He was on his feet again. He wiped his nose – the bleeding had already stopped. *Had mine?* I didn't want to check. Instead, I walked to the filing cabinet that still held Dragon's imprint.

I sat down, wiggling my backside. I looked up at Dragon as he walked toward me.

"My ass!" I shouted, forcing surprise in my tone.

He paused, mid-step.

"It's just so…comfortable." I didn't know if he could hear me. The people behind me sure could.

The smile on my own face was fake. Inside, I knew I needed to bring the fight to a whole new level. We needed to start using magic.

Chapter 56

Playing with Fire

Dragon moved to the middle of the ring, crossed his arms, and stared me down. I hopped up, keeping my senses open to the beginning weaves of flame.
Is this it? Is he mad enough?
I prepared myself, recalling Clay's intel on the earth below us. *We're on top of the Denver basin – a layer of sedimentary rock runs all the way to the eastern edge of the Rocky Mountains. Much of the basin is large, flat and reddish slabs of rock, the kind prevalent in the Red Rocks Park and Amphitheatre fifteen miles west of us. The basin runs deep, though. Before you reach it, there is sandstone and shale.*
Only rock, at my disposal. Rock, and nothing else.
Dragon put one foot back and his hands in fists, near his face – ready to parry a blow. My shoulders sagged. This wasn't it – he still needed some convincing.
So be it.
I lunged, hopping wide and to his left, then to his right. I could see his muscles tense as he tried to anticipate my next move, so I cartwheeled. Arms by my ears, legs wide, I completed a star pattern. Hand, hand, foot, foot. *My elementary school gym teacher would be proud.*
As soon as my second foot hit the ground, I ducked and sent a right hook into his soft spot. He winced, grabbing at it and turning away. I circled around, meeting him halfway with a spinning back

roundhouse kick. At least that's what Alex had told me it was. My heel connected with the same spot.

He stumbled away from me. "Damn it – stop hitting me there!"

I walked casually to the right, toward the ref. "Why, Dragon? Is that a rule too?"

I looked to the ref for clarification. He just shrugged.

Next I tried a somersault, not nearly as pretty as my cartwheel. I didn't expect the ground to be so hard. I managed to kick up as soon as I unfolded, but Dragon twisted, and it wasn't a direct blow. He stomped down. I rolled to the side. Another close call.

On the ground, facing away from him, there was no time to get up. His boot came down, hard and fast – aiming for my temple. I kicked back, and caught him behind his knee. With one leg in the air, he lost balance. I hopped up as he fell. With our situation reversed, I took the opportunity to kick him hard – in the side.

A long string of curse words came out of his mouth.

I stepped back, hoping that would do the trick. I let him pick himself up while I brushed dirt from my clothes. *Should've worn a leotard.*

Hung up on appearance, I barely had time to dodge the fireball. Its heat licked at my bicep as it passed. It flew into the audience, exploding across the chest of someone who didn't move quickly enough. The man started screaming, alternately hitting himself in the chest and rolling on the floor. Neither put the flame out.

I felt Dragon drawing some of the flame from the shirt, weave it into another ball, and wing it at me.

Now that I was on edge, it was easy enough to dodge. While I rode my energy high, the rest of the world moved in slow motion.

Before Dragon could react, I moved in, taking a shot at his nose and then again at his side. When he recovered, I held up his lighter for him to see. "Seriously, dude? Is this the extent of your fire?"

His neck went red, and his face actually shook. His mouth contorted in rage. He drew another fireball. I didn't even have to move for it to miss me. Anger threw off his aim.

The man rolling around on the floor continued screaming.

"For crying out loud," I picked up my shirt, discarded earlier in the fight, and threw it at his buddy. Within seconds they had the fire out.

Could no one else do that? Though, I suppose my shirt was already ruined.

I turned to Dragon and crossed my arms. "Your flame is weak, Dragon. A little too damp for you, down here in the catacombs?"

He put two fingers in his mouth. A loud, shrill whistle cut through the chatter, bringing the catacombs to a dead silence. A smile lit his face.

What is he up to?

After a few moments of nothing happening, he turned to the audience – staring them down. A few flinched, digging in their pockets for something. Another step toward them by Dragon, and they hurried to roll their thumb across a small gear, then hold the object up. Tiny flames danced atop each of the lighters. The fire spread across the room, most everyone holding up a lighter.

My mouth dropped open. I looked at the ref. Behind me, Dragon must have been spewing some unspoken threat, because the ref took out a lighter, too.

"You have got to be kidding me," I said out loud. The ref kept his gaze on the filing cabinet in front of him.

Further behind him, I felt someone reach for air. My eyes snapped to him. He didn't have a lighter. He sent his element out, starting to distinguish each of the flames near him first. I glared – I couldn't risk the match being called. The ref was obviously corrupt.

The Air continued, flipping his around like he was using an invisible lasso. It came to an abrupt stop when Clay grabbed him at the wrist, pulling the hand down. Lighters were relit without anyone thinking twice.

My eyes went back to the ref. His flame bent inward – directly toward me. My eyes followed the circle of people around me. Individually, the tiny flickering flames didn't seem so bad. But there were dozens of them, each reaching toward me – an ominous threat. Chills raked up and down my spine.

Out of the corner of my eye, Dragon swung his arm wide. Fire responded, growing longer and longer out of the lighters. The flames circled, joining together in a swirling mass above the ring. I felt the entire atmosphere pulsate out. When it paused at its peak, I dove for a filing cabinet. With my back to the floor, I pulled the cabinet on top of me, balancing it on my feet and hands. Intense heat hit the other side of the cabinet, while flame rained down around me.

I had no idea how Dragon was shielded from his own element, but I could hear his laughter over the crackling rush. It kept coming; I supposed there wouldn't be an end until the lighters ran out of fluid – or until all the air was sucked out of the room. I couldn't use water or air to help me here. Heat crept into my unwrapped palm – I looked at the filing cabinet I held above me. The entire thing was turning red. I didn't have much longer before my skin would start sizzling away.

I bounced it up slightly, testing the weight and repositioning my hands. I looked toward Dragon. He walked toward me. *Good.* He was walking slowly. *Bad.*

He needed to be closer. A few more steps, and my hands started to burn with pain.

Palms heal fast, I told myself. *Hang in there.* I would only have one chance at this.

"Now you know the extent of my fire." Dragon was still laughing. "Look at you cowering under there, like an earthworm."

My arms shook. I tried holding the weight with the edge of my hands. I blew air against my exposed palm, cooling it off. The bandaged hand would last a little longer. A few thin pieces of material made all the difference.

Dragon paused a few feet away. *Still too far, just by a bit.*

"By the time I'm done with you, you'll look like an earthworm that was left to shrivel up in the sun."

I rolled my eyes. "Yes, I get it. I'm a worm. Come here!"

"Was that the worm talking?" He leaned in closer, cocking his head and putting his hand to his ear.

That'll do.

I bent my limbs, then pushed all four of them up and out. As soon as my makeshift shield left me, I cowered – covering my head against the falling flame. I didn't see the filing cabinet hit him, but I heard it. The fire stopped all at once, and I peeked out. Dragon stumbled back, eyes dazed.

"Your hair!" someone squeaked behind me.

I rolled automatically. Even the once cool, concrete floor was too hot. I stood, checking my hair. Singed at the back. My shoulders were hot, but not enough to blister. The newly healed tattoos stung just a bit more; same with Shawn's mark.

I waited for Dragon to gain his balance, and to stop seeing stars. When his eyes finally focused back on me, I smiled. "My turn."

I sent energy straight into the Earth below us. I kept a tight rein on it, forcing it to circle. The entire room shook in response. The crowd gasped; a few near the doors bailed. Dragon was tight-lipped.

The filing cabinets bumped up. One after another, following the circle around. Just tiny hops, pushed up by the ground underneath. One near Dragon had enough momentum to fall over. Still hot from his fire, it singed his calf. He jumped away, then looked at me, wide-eyed.

I shrugged. "You play with fire and…well, you know the rest."

He turned to the crowd. "Light them!"

No one responded. Instead, they all looked at each other, shifting on their feet, scratching their necks.

"Light them, or I will strangle each and every one of you!" Dragon shouted. He kept a wary eye on me.

I put my hands in the air, signaling for him to proceed. My eyes scanned the room, locating the majority of the sand bags. This was going to be tricky, especially not being able to use air.

A series of barely distinguishable flicks, and the tiny, annoying flames were back. I sent out earth magic, but not into the ground. This time it was electric signals.

I sent it spinning around the room. The pressure increased, creating a weak, geomagnetic field. One by one, granules of sand were loosed from their bags. At first, you couldn't see them. But eventually, like static on a TV screen, they gravitated toward each other, blurring our vision. I watched as people covered the orifices of their faces with their hands. They didn't seem to notice belt buckles and watches pulling ever so slightly toward the center of the room.

I pulled apart my weaves, and sent out an oscillating tempo. The sand followed, and soon created thick enough strips to distinguish flames.

"Light them again," Dragon ordered, covering his own mouth.

"That sand – gets everywhere, doesn't it?" I moved one weave in, dousing him in the back of the head.

He tried pulling flame from the few lighters that were still lit. Sand moved in, extinguishing them.

Dragon growled, marched toward someone who still held a lighter, and took it from her. Right behind, I placed another kick into his side. The lighter flew up in the air.

I caught it, then turned to address the audience. "Light them again, and I will start shoving the sand down your throats!" It seemed convincing, even if I couldn't really do that, unless they each had a high dose of iron for breakfast that morning. I stared down the onlookers. The sound of several dozen lighters hitting the floor echoed across the room.

I turned back to my opponent. "How's the side, Dragon?"

He backed away, hands moving to protect his midsection. He bumped into one of the filing cabinets, falling back on it. As soon as his butt touched, he hopped back up. He craned his neck over his shoulder, brushing at his pants and checking for burns.

I laughed out loud. He definitely wasn't having fun anymore. I turned to the ref. "How does this end?" I noticed his lighter also lay uselessly on the floor by his foot.

He followed my gaze, then kicked the lighter away and cleared his throat. "Your opponent has to be unable to continue. He can't just give up – there are no tapouts."

I turned to Dragon, one side of my mouth tipped up in a smile. "Oh, good."

Dragon's eyes went double-wide. He took two steps back, then stumbled for the door. The crowd parted, but before he got there, two more shirts in black stepped in front of the exit. They held up their palms, each with a ball of fire levitating above. They threw their element down in front of them, creating a wall of fire.

Dragon backpedaled, skidding across the floor. He stopped just short of the flame. There were no more exits.

"Draaaagon...come back to plaaaay...." I taunted from the circle.

He shook his head violently, then followed the room around, pushing people out of his way. I adjusted my weaves, sending them straight down into the Earth. The sand granules hit the floor, skittering across the concrete – unable to follow the energy further.

The Earth responded, and a slab of rock jutted up. It just barely missed Dragon, but certainly caught his attention. He ran faster. I concentrated, trying again. The next one caught him under his foot. The rock shot up at least as tall as he was. Dragon was launched across the room. He landed hard on his back, right in front of me.

I took a step back, dropping to my knees, and sending the last bit of energy I could muster into the Earth. The room shook, people and filing cabinets alike falling over. Cracks crept along the walls and ceilings.

Dragon stood. With a wary eye on me, one foot lifted. He was going to try running again.

"I wouldn't do that if I were you," I said, looking up at him. "Just stay still and you won't feel a thing."

His whole body tensed. I had to be quick before he decided to bolt.

Just don't go too far...

My energy hit stronger stone, and shot off in a different direction – to the west.

Oops, too far.

I could feel it, even from here. Several miles, cracking hard stone all along the way. I used what was left, localizing it. Right as Dragon turned, preparing to run, a large stone shot up in front of him. Another came up behind him. The rest were easy; one after another, until he was encased in a five foot diameter stone cage.

His voice floated up and over, "Hey! Let me out – please? I'm...I'm...claustrophobic. I'm sorry. I think my nose is broken." No one answered his pleas. "I have to pee."

The ref laughed, coming up beside me. He took my hand, raising it in the air. "Winner!"

Cheers and shouts echoed across the room. It would have been much louder if half the room hadn't bailed. That was okay, maybe when they asked about the rest of the fight, the details would be exaggerated – make me look good.

The ref dropped my hand. I glanced at the lighter he held in his other hand. A zippo painted with the American flag. "I apologize for that." He shrugged. "Dragon – well, we all had our reasons for helping him."

I reared back my fist, hitting the ref square in the jaw. He went unconscious, slumping to the ground. The cheering stopped.

I turned to the crowd. "No more dog fights."

Everybody stared, but when I glanced their way, eyes flitted down to the ground.

I stepped toward the stone cage. "Do you hear me in there Dragon? No more dog fights! And if I catch wind of one, I'll intervene. Trap everyone involved – refs, contenders and audience alike in one of these stone cages!"

There was five seconds of silence and then a weak, "okay," from the other side of the rock.

Chapter 57

So Mote it Be

"Sir – there are some reports coming in. Weird activity northwest of here, within city limits."

Shawn paused on his way toward the stairs.

The Earth took that as a go ahead to continue, "A lot of fire—"

"You're on duty tonight?" Shawn asked, interrupting her.

"Yes, sir."

"Don't call me sir."

She clamped her lips shut.

He sighed, looking at the full moon lighting up the inside of the deli better than a dozen candles. A full moon meant better control over powers – everyone knew that. There was bound to be some unauthorized practicing. "Get one of each of the other Elementals to stand duty with you tonight. Let me know if it gets any worse."

She held out a stack of handwritten letters that had been coming in nonstop the past half hour. "But the reports—"

Shawn took them from her, and threw them back down on her desk. "Otherwise, see to it that I'm not interrupted." He himself planned to take advantage of the full moon. Tonight, he needed perfect control over his powers. It was finally time to see Sarah.

* * *

When his boots hit the cave floor, an eerie echo bounced off the walls. The last of the Shades, save Sarah and Arianna, had made it out. Releasing the final few was a blurry memory. Even thinking of it now caused his palms to pulse in pain.

And here he was again, back for more. *What do they call that?* "Pussy-whipped," Shawn mumbled under his breath.

"What?"

Shawn jumped at Arianna's voice behind him. "Um, nothing." He rubbed his nose with the back of his arm. "Mind showing your face? That gas cloud…it's weird."

Arianna took form in front of him. Her black hair had an extra shine to it. "How are you feeling?"

"Better." He smoothed his shirt then glanced at the cave high on the wall over his shoulder. "Nervous."

Arianna's lips turned up in an unexpected smile. "Whatever happens – things will be as they were meant to be."

That was hardly helpful. Shawn realized he was biting his fingernails. He hadn't done that since…well, since he was a boy. He pulled his hand down, his fingers brushed something small in his pocket. "Oh, I wanted to leave something here, if that's okay."

He pulled out a wrapped package and handed it to Arianna.

She glanced at him, then pulled apart the folded edges of thick paper to peek inside. Both eyebrows went up, and she folded the package again. "You think this will help?"

He shrugged. "I don't know. That's not really why I wanted to leave it. It just doesn't belong to me."

"Fine." She set the package down on the platform by her feet. When she stood, she folded her hands in front of her. "I am ready now, Athame Wielder."

He swallowed, nodding his head. He unwrapped the hand with the least amount of damage, staring at his open palm. He doubted it would ever really look the same again.

In front of him, Arianna's form flickered; a sign of her impatience.

Shawn licked his lips. "I just wanted to…" he drifted off as he looked at her. Arianna's large, brown eyes were boring into him. He scratched the back of his neck.

Why is this so hard?

"Yes?" she asked.

"Um…thank you, for…helping me."

Her eyebrows creased. "It wasn't *you* I was helping, Athame Wielder – what you seek to gain is just…a byproduct."

"Yeah," he mumbled, glancing down at his damaged hand again. "I know."

He took a deep breath, then extended his arm, palm over Arianna's head and whispered the words with a shaky voice, "In love and in trust, in peace and in wisdom, I release you, so mote it be."

A rush of wind circled around the cavern, picking up dust and water as it went. The stream tightened and converged where Arianna stood. Shawn squinted, ducking his head and shielding his open wounds against the elements. The noise was deafening. Finally, Shawn peeked over.

Arianna's large, brown eyes were still boring into him. He blinked. She was leaving, but on her own terms; not his. When he looked away, a final gust of wind rushed past and then all was silent. He straightened, resisting the urge to rub out the goose bumps on his arms. Drops of water hitting the still lake below echoed through the cave. Shawn didn't remember it being so…dark.

He took another deep breath. *And that was the easy one*, he thought.

Short, barely noticeable bursts of light danced across the wall beside him. They grew in size, highlighting Shawn's own, small shadow. He turned, squinting at the figure of light on the cave ledge. He sucked in his breath.

Sarah.

His lips refused to form the name out loud. He couldn't move, except for his unwrapped hand, twitching out of control.

Sarah's Shade descended. As she landed on the ledge in front of Shawn, his hand twitched faster.

"Okay, then." She took her human form, crossed her arms, and met Shawn's blue eyes. "Justify your actions."

Shawn swallowed. "What?"

She eyed him, tapping her foot. "It's why you're here, isn't it? You cannot obtain Akasha without a clear conscience."

Shawn pressed his lips together, tight. He knew he'd have to defend himself to Sarah; he just didn't think it would be right away. His practiced speech flew out of his head the moment he saw her. "It was the Great Rite," the words tumbled out of his mouth. He rubbed the back of his neck, looking down.

Sarah's eyes grew wide. "The Great Rite isn't about rape. It is supposed to be *consensual*. And usually done metaphorically – with a knife and a Chalice."

His eyes met hers. "That's not how we did it."

"This isn't about us any longer," her words were clipped and full of fury. "You made sure of that when you raped Kaitlyn."

"I was…I mean, I *am* trying to end the cycle," Shawn's tone slowly matched hers. "But to do that, I need to be able to wield the same power as a Gaia. You know what kind of magical energy the Great Rite can invoke. Kaitlyn is strong; I needed to take drastic steps in order to tap into her power."

"Oh, there is no doubt you tapped her – on several occasions."

Shawn's face grew red. "Yes, but it was always within the circle of elements, and it always raised the energy I sought."

Sarah's voice went soft, "Yet it wasn't enough. She escaped, and you continue to seek more energy."

He hesitated, trying to think back to the events before solidifying them with words. "It's like, I gained energy from the Great Rite – but so did she. I took precautions to make sure that didn't happen. I kept her weak. But, I don't know…" Shawn walked away, then back again, kicking the ground with the toe of his boot. "I keep going over everything in my head. I was wrong about a lot." Shawn's eyebrows rose, his clear blue eyes going glossy.

Sarah took a step forward. "We were right about some things, you know. The Seven did it all wrong. But there always has to be a balance." She laid a hand on his cheek.

He leaned into her touch.

Sarah continued, "It's a balance you can't maintain on your own; and neither can she. It takes both feminine and masculine energy. But you've tainted that."

Sarah morphed back into her gaseous form, and floated through Shawn. For a moment, her essence filled him, reminding him of what it used to feel like lying in bed, wrapped around one other until early afternoon each day.

She passed, leaving Shawn as empty as when he had lost her. He crumpled to his knees, hugging his chest as though he would fall apart any second.

Her voice echoed behind him, "You violated a sacred act, and it is not me that can offer forgiveness. You must seek it from Akasha herself."

Shawn nodded, throat too choked for words. He removed the Athame from its sheath on his hip. He wrapped the spell written down on a small piece of paper around the blade. He was right to think he would not be able to say it out loud – not this time. He touched the tip of the knife to the ground, his forehead, then his lips, and whispered, "Sarah."

Pain ripped through his abdomen and up to his chest. He held himself to the ground, resisting the urge to spin and grab hold of his former partner. There wasn't a roar as with Arianna, just a soft whisper of wind, and then he was alone.

* * *

Shawn returned to his body, feeling more hollow than ever. It wasn't supposed to be like this. He had freed the last of them, Akasha should be his. He slumped down on his bed, removing his shirt, shoes, and pants, then laying back.

Do I even want Akasha anymore, he wondered. *What's the point? Sarah is gone for good.*

He folded his hands behind his head, staring up at the ceiling, willing the ache in his chest to go away.

Just as he closed his eyes, the entire room vibrated. Shawn jolted out of bed.

An explosion?

No, the shaking continued, knocking his chair over. He left the room and ran down three flights of stairs in his boxers.

"What was that?" he asked the Earth on duty. "Earthquake?"

She turned from the window. "Kind of, sir." She stared at his bare chest.

"Don't call me sir, and what do you mean kind of?" He grabbed a spare jacket lying on a nearby chair.

She snapped her eyes away. "The movement started close by. There is a fault line under the Rockies, of course – but I'm not aware of any under the downtown area."

Shawn's blue eyes practically glowed in the otherwise darkened room. "Show me."

The pair went outside, followed by an Air, Water, and Fire.

"There." The Earth pointed southeast. They peered through two tall buildings and could just see the rise of the Tivoli center tower.

The Fire stepped forward. "My element was raging there just before the earthquake." He squinted into the night sky. "But I don't see any smoke."

"All right, let's go check it out." Shawn started for the Center.

"Sir?" the Earth asked.

"What?" Shawn snapped at her, barely turning his head.

"Your pants."

Chapter 58

Groupies

I pushed my way out of the building, taking a deep breath of cold air. It bit at my lungs, but felt wonderful after a steamy fight in the catacombs. I stretched, trying to reinvigorate exhausted muscles. A cold wind blew; the air tasted of snow. The sweat beading my body would turn to icicles soon. I looked toward our observation tower. Around it, grey smoke from several cooking fires rose steadily upward. Against the pitch black sky, you wouldn't see the smoke unless you were looking for it.

I wonder if there will be meat tonight. My stomach growled, and I started for the amusement park.

"Artemis, wait!"

I cocked my ear. *Artemis? Oh yeah.* I smiled. *Goddess of the Hunt.* I turned, and waited for a small group of Fires to approach. "The name's Lucy."

"Right," the one in the front said. Three of them stopped in front of me. "Look." He scratched his neck, glancing behind him as if to ensure the others were there. "We were sort of...Dragon groupies. For a long time. And now he is..."

A loser, I thought.

"...trapped behind stone, at least until someone frees him."

I glared at him. Some groupies they were.

"Hey, I'm just a Fire. Fire can't burn through stone – not very quickly, anyway."

I sighed, glancing at the doors. *Am I going to have to undo what I just did?*

"Don't worry," he said. "We'll take care of it. Anyway, in the meantime—"

"For crying out loud." The girl behind him pushed him aside. "What he's trying to do is ask if there is anything you need."

My gaze shifted to her. Her eyes went to her shoes as she fidgeted with the hem of her skirt.

Why are they all so nervous?

"Because, you know – we can get it for you."

"Now that you mentioned it," I began. All three heads snapped up. "There is something you can do for me. Do you know what Akasha is?"

The boy in the back, who had to be two heads taller than everyone else, spoke up, "Shawn mentioned it. Said it was the key to bringing power back to the world."

"He told you that?" the girl asked, eyebrows raised.

He shrugged. "I take care of his hands. He's always burning them."

I stuck my bandaged hand behind me, hoping no one noticed.

"I thought nuclear was his plan," said the girl.

"Yes but, without a way to get more uranium, something has got to power the plants."

I thought of Arnold, suddenly, wondering if this would convince even him. Accessing nuclear power without the risk of a radioactive byproduct. I furrowed my eyebrows. *Does using Akasha create radioactive waste?* I raised my good hand, wiggling my fingers. *Not glowing yet.*

The girl cleared her throat. They were all staring at me. "So, what is it you needed?" she asked.

"I need you to do something for me if you see Akasha," I said.

"What?" she asked.

"Run away."

Chapter 59

The Messenger

"You there, stop!" Shawn marched his way up the stairs with his small entourage of Elementals.

The Fire, in the process of padlocking the door, turned and did a double take as the chief of One Less approached. The Fire dropped the chain on the ground.

Shawn picked it up, slowly wrapping it around his fist. "Who are you?"

The Fire reached in his pocket, producing the blue armband.

"I see," Shawn said, continuing to wrap the chain around his hand. "The camp is on lockdown, no one is supposed to be out past dark."

Chattering and laughs broke the tension as a group of women rounded the corner. Each bore a blue band on their arm. They stopped in their tracks at the sight of Shawn, then turned tail, disappearing back the same way.

Shawn glared at the Fire. "What happened here tonight? How many were here?"

The Fire wiped his forehead with his sleeve, which came away damp. Shawn had to look up to talk to him, but the Fire was thin and gangly. The scar running down his face curled his mouth into a permanent smile.

The only thing scars prove is that their bearers had experienced a moment of weakness, Shawn told himself.

The Fire was still not talking. Shawn finished wrapping the chain. His fist was more than double the original size, with his bandages and the makeshift brass knuckles. For good measure, he glanced over his shoulder at his entourage. Almost instantly each of the elements were called, putting on an impressive, tiny display above their palms.

The Fire stepped back. "Ok, look – I'll show you. Just don't shoot the messenger."

Shawn smiled as the elements dissipated. "Do you see any guns?"

The Fire swallowed hard, then turned to enter the building. He led them through the hallways, past the dilapidated bar, and down to the catacombs. He explained as he went, "Dog fights. It's where—"

"I know what the dog fights are," Shawn snapped. "I also know there hasn't been any for a while – and I didn't think they would get revived right as the camp went on lockdown."

"We had a new contender."

"Who?"

"They called her Artemis – but her real name is Lucy."

"The one that brought in the wild dog?" Shawn asked.

"The very same." The Fire held the door open for Shawn and his crew; they all entered the small arena. "Don't touch the cabinets, they might still be hot."

They approached the large stones jutting up out of the ground.

"It's like Stonehenge," the Air said. He put his hands on one of the rocks, then his ear. "There's someone inside! I hear whimpering…"

Shawn nodded at his Earth. The Air stepped away and she stepped forward, sending out weaves. The stones vibrated, but didn't move.

Shawn glanced at her, then turned his attention back to the Fire while she continued. "Describe Lucy."

"Short, brown hair. Tattoos—"

"What kind?" Shawn stumbled as the ground shook. Still the rocks were going nowhere.

"Um…" The Fire scratched the back of his neck. "I don't know, a tree branch on her face." The Fire closed his eyes, recalling what he saw when she removed her shirt. "Leaves down her arms. An entire tree on her back—"

"You saw her back?"

"She was wearing one of those sports bra things." The Fire waited until another round of rumbling wore down. "A pretty cool looking compass on her shoulder blade – really detailed. Oh, and then the words Earth, Air, Fire and Water in the shape of a diamond."

"She's an Earth, right? Why would she get that?"

The Fire held out his forearm. "I have it, too. It's popular."

Shawn peered at it, then moved over to the Earth. There was a sheen of sweat across her forehead. He laid his hand on her shoulder.

She flinched.

"Don't move," Shawn said. "I'm just going to focus your power."

Shawn circled his energy around her magic. As he slowly squeezed it into a vice-like funnel, her whole body tensed. He kept a firm grip on her shoulder – and her magic.

The rock circle rumbled, bits of loose stone falling off. Shawn focused all their energy on just one of the thick, upright slabs.

She wavered. "I think it's going to explode."

"Just keep going," Shawn told her. He pulled on her, so they were taking one slow step back at a time. "Almost there. A little more..." Shawn coaxed.

The entire large stone vibrated. Shawn grabbed the Earth around the waist, pulling them both behind a filing cabinet. The rock burst, spraying sharp fragments out, following the energy path.

Shawn was the first up, heart skipping a beat, waiting to see what was inside.

As soon as the dust settled, Shawn was at the entrance to the stone circle. A large man sat in the middle, covering his ears and rocking back and forth.

Shawn's shoulders sagged. "I take it that's not Lucy."

"No." The Fire stepped up beside him, eyebrow raised. "Lucy won."

Shawn swallowed, glancing at Dragon, still rocking back and forth on the floor, mumbling about sand.

"Alright." Shawn pointed to the Water and Earth. "You and you help him. Get him to medical."

A radio crackled to life. The Fire on duty pulled out his handheld. "I think it's one of the patrols, but I can't get a good signal down here."

"So go up—" Shawn cut himself off. "What is that?"

"Well, that's Channel 9, what you told us to—"

"Not that! Can't you feel it?"

Both Fires behind Shawn exchanged glances. By the time they looked back, Shawn was racing out of the room.

They followed him up the steps, one of them passing along information as they went, "One of the patrol groups found a cluster of Elementals east of here. Near some underground silo."

Shawn burst out of the Tivoli Center, scanning the northern skies. As soon as the Fires and the Air caught up with him, he asked, "What's over there?"

"The amusement park," said the Air. "What happened? I didn't feel anything."

"No, you wouldn't," said Shawn. "It was Akasha."

Shawn squinted into the dark, pinpointing the tall observation tower. Moonlight glinted off the top. "Are those people?"

"Here, use these." The Air handed Shawn a pair of binoculars.

The Fire took his ear away from the handheld. "They've engaged, sir. Do you want prisoners?"

Shawn ignored him, focusing the lenses just in time to see someone running toward the edge of the tower. "Holy shit!"

The dark form jumped off.

"I think someone just committed suicide. Was it our Lucy?" Shawn's gaze went back to another person still on top. That was definitely a man.

"No – wait for it. I feel air being used." The Air pointed a short distance away from the tower.

Shawn followed with his binoculars. "Yes – there!" The dark form rose into the sky, wavering to get control. The body hung from a not-so-stable-looking miniature hang glider. It was definitely a woman. She kipped up, face disappearing into the apex of the glider.

"Can't be Lucy," said the Air. "That's an Air."

"No," said Shawn, lowering his binoculars. "That's a Gaia. She went east." He turned to the Fire with the radio. "Is that where the patrol is?"

The Fire nodded.

"Tell them to get out of there!" Shawn took off at a sprint toward his headquarters. "And call in the alarms! We're going west; initiate project red!"

"Sir?" the Fires asked in unison, trying to keep up with his sudden sprint.

"And don't call me sir!" Shawn yelled over his shoulder as he picked up speed.

Chapter 60

The Mark

I began the long trek up the stairs to the observation tower, resisting the urge to use air to push me up. Even after the fight, I had plenty of energy left, but maybe I could give it back to Micah. No need to hold onto it for nothing.

I halfway hoped Natasha and her group was still working on him. It would give me some satisfaction kicking them all out.

You shouldn't think like that. Natasha has done nothing but help you.

I reached the top of the tower, barely breathing hard. The tower was dark, and void of people. There weren't even any guards. I made a full loop just to be sure, tripping over pillows along the way. I lit a small ball of Akasha for light, looking for a clue as to where everyone might be. Nothing.

Quick, panicked footsteps moved across the roof above me.

Shit, I forgot about the guard up top. I sighed. *Better go talk to him.*

I climbed the short ladder to the roof, and pushed open the hatch. The hinges squeaked and it fell open with a clank. A hand extended to help me the rest of the way up.

"What was that?" the guard asked. "I felt something...weird."

I shrugged. "I was just practicing – my powers have been a little off lately. Do you know where Micah is?"

"Natasha brought him up a few hours ago, he wasn't looking too good. Whatever they were doing wasn't helping, either. She left this note for you."

I took the piece of paper he handed me.

Micah not responding well. Had to go underground.

Underground? Why would they have to do that? I thought of the quick-healing mud concoctions at the Chakra. Was there energy-giving soil nearby?

The map drawn underneath her note indicated a missile silo just east of Denver. I dropped the note, turning east. I didn't need a map – I had my own built-in radar to locate Micah. But first, I needed something else. I picked up a long iron bar that had been pried loose from somewhere on the structure, probably by a bored guard.

"Brr, it's chilly up here." I rubbed my bare arms from shoulder to elbow.

When he didn't say anything, I gave him a pointed look.

"Oh, right." He jumped to take off his floor-length leather duster jacket to drape it over my back.

"Thanks." I grabbed it before he could help me put it on. I slipped the bar through the inside of one sleeve, then the other.

"What are you doing? You can't stretch it – it won't go back into shape."

I didn't answer, taking quick steps toward the other end of the tower.

"Wait, slow down!" the guard called behind me. "You don't want to fall off."

"Oh, yes I do." I sped up my final few steps, then took a giant leap off the 250-foot tall tower. For several, heart-stopping moments, I was in a free fall. The long coat twisted around me. I feared the stench of leather would be the last thing I ever smelled.

Air came to me. It was easy when surrounded by the element. I pushed it up, forcing the coat into an even surface. The transition was so sudden, I almost lost my grip on the bar.

"Whoa…" As soon as I had a sure hold, I kipped my body up, settling the bar underneath my armpits. "That's better."

I peeked up and over the coat. I caught one glimpse of the guard on top of the tower. He was scratching his head. I smiled. *At least it'll give him something to talk about.*

I followed the river. Wind gusts were a little more predictable above it, with trees blocking either side.

The flight was short, compared to any other option. Ten minutes later I veered toward the only large group of Elementals I could find on the open plain. Access roads created a large, misshaped circle. I released some of the air, beginning my decent. I aimed for the Elementals.

My landing was not graceful, which was unfortunate because I had an audience. I let the end of the trench coat drag. It got tangled up in my feet just as the ground rushed up to meet me. I rolled, involuntarily. My backside seemed to find every rock jutting out of the hard, frozen ground.

I came to a stop and detangled myself from the mass of leather. Several pairs of eyes stared at me. I covered the distance, crossing a slab of concrete. It was cracked, with weeds pushing up through the gaps. As far as I could tell in the dark, there was nothing else around us, except for some sort of access door, antennas, and masts. I wrinkled my nose; it smelled like a farm.

Natasha stepped forward.

"Is Micah in there?" I asked as I glanced around at the doors.

She didn't respond.

My eyes went back to her. "Well?"

"He was but…they took him," she said.

"Who took him? And where?" I wanted to stomp my foot.

"Look there." She pointed to the double doors.

I walked around the group. In red spray paint, taking up almost the entire height of the door, was Shawn's mark. My scar began to itch while my blood ran cold.

"One Less," I whispered. "Was Shawn here?"

Natasha stepped up behind me, shaking her head. "No. But there were a lot of Fires."

Someone else piped up from the back of the group, "We are just a bunch of Earths. Rock doesn't stand a chance against fire."

I pressed my lips together.

These people weren't at the dogfight.

"Which way did they go? I didn't see them on my way here." Of course I was further north, following the river.

"Horseback. There are a few more horses, if you want one." She glanced at the crumpled leather jacket, and the bar hanging from my hands.

Hoofs and the sound of heavy breathing confirmed it. A few sideways steps showed a pen of horses. One ran in a circle; another threw up his front legs, kicking as if to ward me off. "No thanks, I'll take my chances with the..." I held up the leather. "...jacket."

"Wait," Natasha said, "you'll need help."

"I need help? There will be four times the amount of Fires than what were just here. What are your Earths going to do then?"

"That's not what I meant." Natasha crossed her arms, furrowing her eyebrows.

I stopped fiddling with the iron rod and jacket.

She took a deep breath. "Micah mentioned something about The Seven Chakras. We can help you access them."

Chapter 61

Prisoners

Shawn urged his horse through the mass of dead cars on 6th Avenue. He refrained from guiding the steed into a full gallop; it was still dark, and plenty of debris cluttered the way. Shawn looked over his shoulder. David was struggling to even stay on his horse.

Shawn growled, "Take everyone who has fallen behind and dig in there." Shawn pointed to a large sign signaling the entrance to a fairground. "If anyone else shows up, stop them."

Shawn angled his horse for the onramp of the interstate. Those still with him were much faster, keeping a tight column. They merged with another group on horseback.

"Whoa!" shouted the Fire, who had replaced David at Shawn's side. "It's a patrol."

Shawn reigned in his horse, signaling for the others to stop. He surveyed the patrol group. Several had minor injuries; bandages over their head or blossoming bruises. "What did you find?" Shawn asked.

"This, sir..." he motioned with his hand and the group split, allowing a few riders from the back forward. Each rider held a prisoner, bound and gagged, thrown across the back of the horse.

Shawn swung his leg around, jumping off his own horse. Three prisoners in all, a man and two women. He went to the women first, not bothering to remove their blindfolds, and checked each of their shoulders. He let out a disappointed sigh at the last one.

That would've been too easy, he thought.

He walked past the man, preparing to climb back into the saddle when something out of the corner of his eye stopped him.

Shawn walked back around, glancing at the prisoner's feet. *I know those boots.*

He removed the blindfold and blinked in astonishment at the face that glared up at him.

"This will be easier than I thought," Shawn said.

Chapter 62

Air

It was too cold – even for the bugs. But I preferred shivering over bug splatter against my face. This time when I took flight I followed the same path the horses took. The trail led me down a main road through town. I was focused on what was ahead, failing to take into account what was behind me.

A gust of wind knocked me sideways. Another forced me lower. I barely missed a tree branch leaning over the road. I looked behind me; three Airs followed, using actual hang gliders.

Another strong gust hit me from behind. They were going to bully me to the ground, or into the side of a building.

Hell if I am going to end up like bug splatter.

I let go of the element keeping me in flight. A moment later I was in free fall. For the second time in one night; it wasn't nearly as terrifying. As the ground rushed up to meet me, I spread the jacket back out, using a wind stream to stay up. My toes scraped asphalt.

I stayed low for three quick breaths. My splayed-out black leather jacket camouflaged me against the dark street. I flew straight up behind them and smiled. They were still searching the ground for me.

I let my fireballs fly, counting out two per hang glider. It was all the energy I wanted to spare. Tears in the fabric threw off their balance, and it didn't take long for the gliders to tip. If they could gain control of their element fast enough, they'd survive the fall, but it wouldn't be pretty.

I moved on. *Did Shawn know I was coming?* It couldn't have been the dog fight; I was careful not to use the other elements.

I lost concentration and dipped. "Whoa."

Focus, I told myself. *I can worry later.*

I barely avoided colliding with a large billboard that read, 'Jefferson County Fairgrounds'. I tried to prepare myself. *What could possibly lay in wait?*

"Trailers!" I squeaked out loud.

Releasing my energy for a brief second, I dipped again, narrowly missing a large RV spinning toward me in midair. One of the bars on the side-canopy caught me on the back. I buckled, just catching a glimpse of the source of trouble. A combination of Airs and Earths were using both of their elements to send a large row of campers up and out, directly toward me. Another was already airborne. I didn't have time to dodge it. The last thing I saw were the words, 'Open Sky', painted on moldy, off-white siding.

Chapter 63

Brothers

"Put him up here." Shawn pointed to the long, rectangular table top that served as a bar on the upper terrace of the open air amphitheatre. "Tie him down." Shawn took out his Athame, glancing at Micah. "You don't seem too worried."

Micah looked away, focusing on one of two 300-foot monolithic cliffs. The giant, sandstone towers provided near-perfect acoustics for the concert hall. He cocked his head, noticing a large crack up the side. Natasha had said there were some harsh tremors during Kaitlyn's dog fight, but would it have affected rocks all the way out here?

"Well it's no fun talking to you if you don't talk back, brother." Shawn ripped the duct tape off Micah's mouth. Shawn studied the prickly facial hair left behind on the gray strip of tape, then looked at Micah. There were deep lines around his eyes, and he had lost weight. "You look like shit."

Micah rubbed his cheek against his shoulder. "I could say the same about you."

Shawn shrugged, walking around to the other side of the bar Micah lay on. "It's this new world. No massage parlors. No over-the-counter drugs. No working bars." Shawn fiddled with the tap protruding from the table top, as if just to make sure. He glanced at Micah. "No fishing at the Chakra lake on Sundays."

Micah's eyes snapped back to Shawn. "Those days were long gone, even before Daybreak."

"They don't have to be," Shawn said quietly, keeping his eyes on the table top.

Micah looked up at the stars above him. "How exactly did you expect all this to turn out?"

"Oh, I don't know. Almost like this. Except you'd be right here…" Shawn took out his Athame and pointed to the empty space at his right hand side. "…instead of lying there."

"Even if Kaitlyn had never been chosen—"

"Kaitlyn!" Shawn interrupted. "She screwed everything up. She was supposed to be temporary."

"But then you couldn't resist her, and the power she held." Micah glared.

Shawn smiled his crooked half smile. "Neither could you, brother."

The Earth rumbled and basketball-sized pieces of the stone tower beside them crashed to the ground.

"You and I have different ideas of power." Micah said, looking out over the plains. In the distance, the chilling screech of twisting metal could be heard. Both pairs of eyes snapped northeast.

"She's coming for you, Shawn," Micah said, voice low.

Shawn nodded. "We'd better get ready." He pushed the tip of his knife into Micah's side.

Chapter 64

Fire

Pain crashed through my head in waves. I lay on hard ground. Everything was dark.

Probably because your eyes are closed.

I tried squinting one eye open, but it hurt too much. I decided to concentrate on something further away from my eye. I wiggled my toes inside my boots.

"Is she waking up? I think she's waking up," a voice said to my left.

I stopped moving.

"Who is she?" Another said to my right. "Is this the one we're running from?"

At my head, "No, stupid. This is Artemis – from the fight tonight."

"She can't be – she was using air. Artemis was an Earth."

"No, no," said yet another at my feet. I was surrounded. "That's Lucy – the one that brought in the wild dog. I recognize that ink – I helped put it on her."

More voices chimed in. There had to be a dozen, though it was difficult to tell with the chaotic waves crashing through my head.

If the swells wouldn't go away, I would have to embrace them. I waited for the next tide, it built slowly. First, tingling at the back of my neck. Then up my skull moving faster until my entire head was held in an unrelenting vise grip.

I used the adrenaline it caused, pushing it down into the Earth, and coming up with only stone. A platform broke through the surface, raising me up above the circle of people. I pushed up from the swell, back flipping off the rock and using air for a steady landing.

The group of people around the raised stone were trying to stay upright on top of the vibrating Earth. The crest of the wave was long past, but another was already coming. This time I used it to pull up more rock, surrounding the group. It caught all but one. A small guy, who stumbled back from the cage.

"Get her, David!" encouraging shouts came from inside the rock. They'd be able to get out eventually, especially if the Earths inside were worth their salt. I hoped it would hold until after Akasha.

David turned to me, pushing his glasses up on his nose, eyes wide. "Who...who are you really?"

I picked up the crumpled iron rod at my feet, gripping it with a solid fist. "All of the above." I swung it at him, connecting with the side of his temple. He fell sideways, unconscious.

I dragged him over to the rock cage, leaving his body on the opposite side from where I was headed. I placed my hand on the rocks. Energy was building up inside the cage as the group tried their various elements. I wiped dusty earth from my pants, and looked around. With the leather jacket nowhere in sight, and my energy quickly waning, I needed another form of transportation.

Over the Earth's vibrations, was a high-pitched whinny. I followed the rock cage around, peering out. The field just off the parking lot held a pen of horses.

Most were bucking, several throwing their front hooves in the air.

I looked at the only horse that was staying on all fours, on the far side of the pen. I approached him, hand reaching out through the bars. He looked at me out of the corner of his eye, sidling away. "Whoa, fella. There's a good boy."

He paused, extending his long face toward my palm. I rubbed his neck and mane, glancing at the other horses, still bucking. They were larger and stronger – probably faster. This one even had a twinge of gray on his mane. But right now I didn't need large and strong, I needed steady. I needed a rock.

I climbed halfway up the pen and pressed my forehead to the horse, nuzzling it. "I need Micah," I whispered, the lump bigger than ever in my throat. "Can you take me to him?"

The horse snorted.

"I'll take that as a yes." Climbing the top half of the pen, I jumped on his back, thankful he was saddled and ready to go. He headed for the gate and I kicked it open. He idled through the opening as I fit my feet into the stirrups.

"Giddy up," I said, leaning forward, anticipating the rush of wind that would accompany his speed.

He bent down to nibble on the grass.

I bounced up and down. "Get on now – go boy, go!"

His hooves stayed firmly planted. I sighed, hanging my head. It had begun to snow.

The horse perked up, jerking his head back.

"Whoa, you're gonna knock me out."

I looked north as a blast of heat swept through the snow flurries. Dust swirled up from the ground in the distance, revealing the outline of a pair of sister tornadoes. I watched in horror as fire entwined. The atmosphere crackled with a new weather phenomenon. Fire tornadoes.

The horse stepped away.

"Whoa, there. It'll be alright. We're not going that way."

I didn't say it out loud, but I was sure both the horse and I were thinking the same thing.

The tornados are coming this way.

"Kaitlyn!"

I shook my head. This had to be a nightmare; they were calling my name.

"Kaitlyn!" Natasha shouted, pulling me out of my shock. On horseback, she and several others gathered in front of me, partially blocking my view of the tornadoes. "We'll get this, then I'll head to the Chakra Center downtown, and wait for Akasha. You go get Micah!"

I shook my head. "No – I can't ask you…" I trailed off, my eye drawn to the fiery wind inching closer to us.

"Go!" Natasha shouted over the roar. "I'm telling *you*." She urged her horse forward, and slapped at the behind of my own ride. "Ya!"

My horse bucked, then shot off in the other direction. I looked back in time to see Natasha turn. As she stared at the fire tornadoes, the scarred side of her face was to me. She kicked her legs, and her horse lurched, straight for the flame. Straight for the same element that had marred her for life.

I angled my horse for Shawn. It was snowing harder, now. Fat, wet flakes brushed my cheeks as we flew down the road. The horse stretched his neck out, knees bent, low to the ground. He opened up his stride. I squeezed the reins, standing in my stirrups. The wind grew loud in my ears.

I scanned the horizon, spotting Elementals dotting the road. As we blew past them, they looked confused. I saw recognition in their eyes. They'd seen me around camp and let me go as one of their own. They turned toward the fire tornados, wondering who the enemy was. I raised rock along the way. Short but thick walls, near each Elemental, facing the way I was headed.

The inside of my legs squeezed against the saddle, and below that the horses mid-section. My hips, slightly raised, rocked with the rhythm of the powerful stallion's muscles. My heels pushed down, stretching out each calf. We both panted. My heart raced, beating in time to the pounding of hooves against asphalt.

Rumbling drew our attention to the mountains. One of the larger snow, covered peaks was shedding its white cloak. The avalanche was at a distance; no threat to us, but I knew all too well what it was like to be caught up in that beast.

Who is up there? Micah's people?

Shawn and Micah had their battle plans all along. Elementals were staged up and down the plains, and into the mountains. And I hadn't been privy to any of that information.

Why not?

Because I had never truly belonged to either army.

I leaned into the horse, next to his ear. "It's just you and me, pal."

He slowed, eyeing the mountains in the distance.

"Come on, now....what can I call you?" I kept talking, doing my best to distract him. "How about 'Rock'?" I rubbed his mane. "That's it. Get on, Rock – ya!"

He picked up speed, and I crouched down for fear of being blown off. The next Elemental we passed had his ear to a handheld radio. I snatched it as we flew past, making sure to leave a rock wall for him, too.

Shawn's voice blasted over the airwaves, "No one passes! Everybody is in place – anyone moving forward is to be considered a threat."

Shit.

The group coming up all had radios, too. They saw me, and struggled to call their elements. We passed before the first managed it. I wouldn't be so lucky with the next group. I merged onto an interstate, honing in on Shawn's signal and following it. It was getting stronger with every stride covered, like a game of hot, hot, cold.

The next group was ready for me. They stood as a wall across the road. A combination of Airs and Waters. Above us, the atmosphere swirled, and behind us heat from the fire tornados licked at our back.

The wind picked up, swirling the snow. Infused with more moisture, the snow hit me from every angle. Icy cold pelted the back of my neck, and sloshed across my face. Thunder rolled overhead. Rock whinnied, coming to a stop.

"Just a little thunder snow; can't hurt Rock," I coaxed the horse. I tried to exude enough confidence for the both of us. A draft moved upward, pulling the cold air to a higher altitude. More thunder.

"Take a break for a minute," I said, climbing off of him. I looked into the faces of the Elementals as I approached them. I stopped at one face I knew well.

Erika stepped forward. "Lucy – what are you doing?"

Chapter 65

Water

"Are you the one he wants us to stop?" Erika asked.

Can I lie my way past this one? I was sick of lies.

"Yes," I said.

"What is this – some sort of lover's quarrel?" She crossed her arms. "I *helped* you."

I blinked, Erika's face was changing – growing thinner and darker. Her hair grew out into long, black braids. Then it was Ahi standing there, glaring at me. "I *helped* you."

I was speechless; a lump formed in my throat. Her height dropped a full foot, and her sides expanded. Now it was Zola, holding her jar of dirt and mumbling, "I *helped* you."

I closed my eyes, shaking my head. "I never asked for your help."

It was Erika's face again. "Yes, you did. And I gave it! Time and time again." The black braids were back. "If I knew it was going to end like this, I never would have given it."

My face crumpled, tears streaming down my face. My heart broke in half – for Ahi and her mother, for Andres, for Zola, and for countless others. Everyone that had given their lives to help me. I'd spend eternity on Galapagos with Shawn if I could give back what I took.

Voices echoed in my head. They were all angry. I put my hands over my ears and shouted, "Stop!"

Behind me, Rock whinnied.

Erika took another step forward. "Why?"

I looked at her, eyes wide. Stripped of my lies, and all confidence – there was nothing left but the truth. "I am Gaia, and I have a daughter. She is two. I left her behind because…because Shawn is her father." The horse stopped sidestepping, calming under my voice. I put my hand to my stomach, it had nearly dropped to the ground at the mention of Bee. "Shawn created Daybreak. And it may have been better for the Earth, but…how can that continue with nuclear power?"

Erika looked over her shoulder at the rest of the Elementals.

I continued, "He needs a Gaia's power to run the facilities. And he won't stop at me and my daughter. The power is an addiction; he wants it for himself. And it doesn't matter how he gets it. He has to be stopped."

I glanced down the line of Elementals, trying to judge how they were receiving this. "I'm no longer asking for your help. All I want you to do is – get out of the way."

Erika closed the distance between us. "I can't do that. It's gone too far, now."

I bit my lips, squeezing my fists. "Please – I just need this one last favor."

She shook her head. "No more favors, Lucy."

My entire arm shook as energy gathered in my fist. "I don't want to—"

"What about the favor you owe me, Erika?" Someone stepped forward, out of the line of Elementals. Mike, from the group of Earths at the wheat field. I narrowed my eyes at the white splatter on his shoulder. *Was that—?*

"And my favor?" Layla, the tattoo artist also spoke up, interrupting my thought.

"That favor was for her!" Erika pointed at me, stomping her foot.

Layla shrugged. "You asked me to use the rest of my ink – and now I'm asking you. Let's do what Lucy wants." Layla winked at me.

"Any favor asked within reason – those were your exact words, Erika." Mike moved to stand next to Layla. "All she wants us to do is let her pass."

I crossed my arms, releasing the energy in my fist. I felt awkward enough for me and Erika both. Caught between me and the Elementals, she was backed into a corner. Would she fight her way out?

We all took a step back as Rock came forward. He nudged Erika with his nose. She fought her smile for a moment, but another nudge from Rock brightened her face. She rubbed the bridge of his nose. "Fine, but now we're even." She circled her finger in the air. "*All* of us."

I laughed, wiping my own nose. "Thank you."

Erika nodded and stepped away, motioning for the wall of the Elementals to do the same. Once they were out of the way, I climbed back on Rock and squeezed my knees into him. He cantered forward.

"Lucy! What should we do now?"

I looked over my shoulder at Erika. "Run. And when you see Akasha – take cover. And just so you know, my name is Kaitlyn!"

I gripped the reins, "Ya!"

Rock sprang into action. I was getting close; I could feel the familiar, sickly taint of Shawn's power humming in my veins. Micah was with him; I was sure of it now – I could feel them both together.

There were Elementals still left; but I didn't have time to stop and convince them all to run away without looking back. I took moisture straight out of the air, driving it into the ground around each Elemental. The water sunk in. Using Clay's suggestion, I pushed acids and salt found in the earth below us, heating them as they converged. The sandstone underneath dissolved at an accelerated rate. As the small space collapsed, I poured more moisture in. Those left still standing rushed to the aide of others in the sinkholes. I was no longer their concern. I left more small walls along the way.

I guided Rock off the interstate and down a thin, single lane road until we came to a small stone building. The sign read, 'Box Office'. I stood in the stirrups and swung one leg off. I walked around the building, making sure there were no Elementals waiting. Satisfied, I turned to Rock, rubbing his neck. "Thank you, sir."

He whinnied.

I flung my arm behind me, blasting open one side of the building. The horse skittered, but I kept a tight hold on his reins. "Shh, shh. That was the last one, I swear."

He pulled his lips back, crinkling the skin on his long snout.

"Okay I lied – there's going to be one more. A big one. I'm going to leave you here. It'll be safe, I promise. Just don't leave until after the blast, okay?"

He looked at me out of the corner of his eye.

"I know, I know. I'm stalling." I took a deep breath. "Okay, come on."

I led him into the tiny building, kicking stone and brick debris out of the way. There was just enough room for him. I tied his reins to a chair, then thought better of it and untied them. He looked at me again.

"Still stalling, I know – but I gotta keep you here, somehow." I looked around. There was a large plastic bin filled with files. I dumped it out; papers went everywhere. I walked over to the open side and set the bin down outside. Then I drew in moisture from the air; lots of it. I kept drawing until the bin was full, keeping a wary eye out for stray Elementals.

I dragged it back in, right under Rock's nose. He bent to drink.

"All life comes from water – right?"

He snorted at me.

"Okay, okay, I'm going."

I walked up the short hill. At the top, I looked toward where both Micah's and Shawn's signals were emitting. Several large, monolithic, red rock cliffs jutted up in a semicircle. Red Rocks Amphitheatre was obscured by the cliffs and hills surrounding it, but the energy that circled within could not be missed.

I glanced to my right, looking for Elementals, or more traps. My head snapped back to Red Rocks. Micah's signal was sputtering.

That's never happened before.

It sputtered again. I waved my hand behind me, encircling Rock's building with several more stone walls. They had staggered openings. If he did finish his water it'd take him some time to get out. I faced the amphitheatre and took a deep breath.

I'm coming Micah…

Chapter 66

Laughter

Micah grimaced.

"Stop whimpering; I'm barely scratching you." Shawn pulled the knife away as a fresh bout of blood spilled over Micah's forearm.

"Then why do it?" Micah asked.

Shawn took a step back and lifted his hands in a grand gesture. "For the show!" he said, voice booming throughout the amphitheatre, followed by his laughter. He reached down for his metal canteen. "And now for the special effects."

Shawn poured cold water over each of the cuts. It hampered the natural coagulation, and fresh blood pooled around Micah's body, just beginning to drip over the edges of the steel tabletop. With water mixed in, there was much less blood than there actually appeared to be. But Kaitlyn wouldn't know that.

Micah turned, watching the plains, waiting.

Shawn placed the tip of the knife at Micah's forehead, running it down the temple and just past the ear lobe. Micah flinched when it reached his neck.

"Just think…" Shawn said, pulling the knife away and adding water. "You'll have some really great scars."

"Untie me," Micah said.

"I don't think so."

He turned to look at Shawn. "I'm drained – I'm not going anywhere. Can't you tell?"

Shawn looked at Micah, wiping his nose with the back of his sleeve. He put the knife to Micah's wrist.

Micah flinched, expecting a deeper cut. Instead, the constricting bind around his hand was released. Shawn moved to Micah's feet and around to his other hand, slicing through the rope as he went.

Micah watched, keeping a wary eye on the Athame until his final limb was freed.

Shawn sheathed his knife, and narrowed his eyes at Micah. "What happened to you?"

"Kaitlyn happened to me," Micah said, closing his eyes. "Now what?"

"Now we wait." Shawn picked up the handheld and put it to his mouth. "Get those tornados closer."

"Tornados won't stop her."

Shawn leaned back against the bloodied tabletop. "I don't expect they will. But they'll sap her strength." Shawn ran his pinky through the thick, red liquid. When he pulled away, it held on like a stubborn leach. He dipped it back down, making small swirls. He laughed again.

"What?" Micah asked.

"I was just thinking, she had used wind when she ran from me on Galapagos. She even erupted the volcano. Now here I am, using wind and fire to keep her from getting to me."

"I thought you wanted her." Micah finally opened his eyes – the world swayed in front of him.

Shawn wiped his finger on his jeans. "I would've taken her – or the baby. Or found my own Gaia. Just not yet."

"When, then?"

Shawn started pacing. "Is this some sort of distraction technique? Twenty questions so she can sneak up behind me?" Shawn glanced around, then up at the monoliths. His crew stood guard at the top of the cliffs, and throughout the rest of the stadium.

Now it was Micah's turn for a crooked smile. "You'll know when she's here. She doesn't need to sneak up on you."

Shawn took out his knife again, spinning it in his hand while he paced. "I have nuclear facilities going up – several around the world, in protected places."

"Utah is protected?"

Shawn shrugged. "Mountain ranges on both sides to catch the fallout. I have more in each of the Arctics. I'd use a Gaia to power them."

"Just one Gaia?"

Shawn paused at the edge of the platform, looking down at the steps carved out of stone. "Well, okay. Maybe I would've taken her *and* the baby. And found ways to strengthen my own Akasha. But they would've been separated; safe. They would've been kept in check."

"When has Kaitlyn ever been kept in check? Besides, what do you know about babies?"

Shawn bowed his head. "I would've made a good father. I still might. Maybe just as good as you."

"Somehow, I don't think we'll ever get to find out." He grimaced. The pain was being replaced by numb. That wasn't good.

Laughter echoed through the amphitheatre once again.

"Stop laughing," Micah said through his teeth.

"That wasn't me." Shawn's eyes were wide, staring down the rocky steps toward the stage.

Micah followed his gaze. A lone figure stood, center stage.

Chapter 67

Elementals of all Four Persuasions

My landing on the stage was soft. I looked around; awed by the scene before me. I was at the bottom of a bowl, looking up at hundreds of rows carved out of the rock. At the rim of the bowl, two cliffs towered even higher to my left and my right.

The amphitheatre hummed with energy, and so did my veins – but I had never felt as small as I did right then.

It's not about me; it never has been. I laughed.

I focused on the people surrounding me. Elementals of all four persuasions. I honed in on their signals and they glowed blue, gold, red, and brown – though they didn't know it. They lit up the otherwise dark amphitheatre, splashing color against the reddish rock.

Then they began to call their elements, one by one. Magic swirled in the bowl, heightening my senses. There were Airs on top of the cliffs with their hang gliders. Fires stood at the rim of the bowl, ready behind large barrels tipped on their sides. When one accidentally let go of his, the barrel shattered on the stone steps. Liquid sloshed out and the smell of gas filled the air. Earths and Waters dotting the rows up jumped out of the way.

I know this, I thought. *Oh yeah - Donkey Kong.*

I was going to expend the rest of my energy just trying to get to Shawn, and I'd still have the big-ass gorilla to fight in the end. I eyed the dozens of

Elementals. They eyed me right back. I shook my head. *Nope – I'm done running the gauntlet.*

I sent energy up into the sky, past the thick clouds above us. Infusing cold moisture into the atmosphere, ice crystals formed. As the crystals fell, they punched a donut-shaped hole in the cloud cover. Moonlight shot through the temporary hole. There was a collective gasp around the amphitheatre as all heads turned skyward.

"It's a UFO!" someone shouted. He, along with several others near him, went for the nearest exit.

That was easy.

"No, wait! It's just a crazy weather thing – skypunch!" It was an Air spouting off, chasing down those trying to leave. I hit him with a blast of his own element. He went sprawling into one of many trees that lined the bottoms of the cliffs.

Movement above caught my eye. Hang gliders were taking flight. None of the Airs seemed fooled by my display.

Maybe something a little flashier for them, I thought. The skypunch hole closed, blocking out the moonlight once again. Clouds rolled at the disturbance. I infused more moisture into the atmosphere and charged the clouds with electrical energy. Next, I used opposite-charged energy to create a conductive path. Bolts of electricity shot down, aiming for the hang gliders and those left on top of the cliffs.

As lightning plagued the amphitheatre, I ascended the stairs. I used air when I could, giving me an extra push. I used earth for small ramps and springs, sending me up and over Elementals. I zigzagged, my silhouette giving my location away only occasionally with each flash of lightning.

I remembered Vayu, using a combination of wind, energy, and his own breath to create a spell. I copied it, speaking low, "Run...Akasha is coming." Air carried my words away, and they echoed throughout the amphitheatre.

More than halfway up, I paused behind one of the trees, surveying my progress. Red Rocks was in chaos. Lightning and snow rained down. Some Elementals held their ears, blocking out thunder and the sound of falling rock. Either that or the sound of my voice; I was not sure which they found to be worse. An unfortunate few didn't avoid the crumbling cliffs. Several more decided to leave. I followed the path of their retreat up the stairs and focused on the Elementals still standing at the top. Mostly Fires. Hot heads with something to prove. Dragon came to mind. In the end, it hadn't taken much to finish him off. Of course, I was fresh out of filing cabinets.

I took a deep breath and squared my shoulders. Sending out energy, I lit the barrels on fire. The Elementals behind them stumbled back in surprise. Someone went down the line, cursing and kicking the barrels down the stairs, adding to the chaos. Those still left in the concert venue got out of the way, fast. They continued to go, fleeing the area. For them, friendly fire was the last straw. I just hoped they would find cover fast enough, and far enough away.

As the last barrel made it to the bottom, shattering against the stage, I climbed my tree. I perched myself as high as I could, watching a driverless glider nose dive toward me. Rough bark scraped my back.

Micah proposed the handfasting ceremony to me in a tree.

The thought came out of nowhere.

Focus, Kaitlyn.

Three quick steps along a sturdy branch, and I leaped, grabbing hold of the glider's control bar. I didn't need to pull myself all the way up. A short burst of air sent me to the upper terrace. It was a large, flat area constructed with alternating slabs of concrete and stone. I landed on the railing separating the terrace from the stepped seating area.

One quick bend at the knees to balance myself, and I looked over at Shawn, and Micah sprawled out behind him.

Chapter 68

Two Peas in a Pod

"That.." Shawn cleared his throat, getting rid of the squeak that wanted to come out. He spoke up, loud enough to be heard over the heightening wind. "That was a good show."

The figure on the railing bowed. He walked a full semi-circle around her, leaving a wide berth. "Is that really our Kaitlyn? The princess?" He squinted, taking in her tattoos. The image of a woman with short hair working in the camp's gardens flashed in his mind – and another of the same woman chopping wood outside his headquarters. "You've been…right next to me for a while now." Shawn squeezed his Athame. If his palms sweated any more, he would lose his grip on it.

He walked back, standing to the side of Micah. She had yet to take her eyes off Shawn. He was counting on the gruesome display of Micah's crimson life-force throwing her off her game. Whether it be pure anger or a frightened little girl; Shawn could feed on either reaction. Shawn glanced over at Micah, ensuring he was still even there.

Eyes locked on Shawn, Kaitlyn jumped down from the railing. Without thinking, Shawn took a step back. Kaitlyn raised one eyebrow. The sound of quick, retreating footsteps made him glance over his shoulder. The rest of the Elementals were gone. It was just the three of them left under the stars, surrounded by rock. When he turned back, Kaitlyn was directly in front of him.

She glanced at his wrapped hands. "What have you been up to, Shawn?"

He lifted them, palms up, staring at them like he was lost in thought. She stepped toward him and began unwrapping one hand.

Shawn was too shocked to move. He even held the Athame in his other hand. *Was she not scared; not even a little bit?*

Once his palm was exposed, her fingertips hovered over the burn marks. "What have you done with the Shades?" she whispered.

He moved quickly, grasping her fingers. He squeezed, and turning her palm over. "Same as you," he said. "Only with…"

"The Chalice," Micah coughed out.

Shawn looked at him, then back to Kaitlyn. Her wide, brown eyes bore into him.

"You released them, safely?" she asked.

"What else do you think I would've done with Sarah?" He narrowed his eyes. "And you – they must have been male Shades, right? Did you release them safely?" His tone was mocking.

"What else do you think I would've done with Cato?"

Shawn's eyes bulged. "Cato? He was there?" Shawn squeezed her fingers tighter, trying to intimidate.

"He still is. I might need him for something else." She finally looked at Micah.

Shawn needed to gain the upper hand. He turned her wrist, following the words tattooed around it, reading aloud, "I am the hero of this story." He smirked. "Yeah, right."

Chapter 69

Akasha

"I can't believe you let Sarah go," I said, changing the subject.
What did he have to gain from it?
"Akasha," Micah chimed in.
Shawn tensed.
"Well?" I asked, a smirk twisting my mouth. "Do you have it?"
I felt him draw energy in, still holding my hand. I twisted, leaning back to bring my leg up. I kicked him in the chest. Our bond broken, we both went stumbling back.
When I steadied myself against the railing, he was still pulling energy together. Earth, fire, air and water, twisting and weaving the elements until they intertwined. It was shaky, with gusts escaping in large chunks that we both had to dodge. Finally, a light shined out from the middle. Flickering but definitely there. It grew to encompass the whole of the elements, right above his palm. My hand squeezed the cold railing, and a chill ran up my spine, stopping to pulsate at Shawn's mark on my shoulder.
Akasha's light danced across his scarred palm, making it look as if the exposed flesh slithered. It hit the dirt in his fingernails and threw strange shadows across his face. His arm muscles flexed, and sweat beaded his brow with the effort. The smirk on my face disappeared.

He wielded the power of Akasha; the power of a Gaia. Weak as it was, it was there. I knew only too well what more practice could bring.

Using the falling snow, I weaved together moisture in the form of an arrow, using air to shoot it straight at Akasha. The balance of elements thrown off, Akasha shattered around us and fizzled away into the night.

Shawn shook out his arm, then rewrapped his hand. He looked at me.

"What?" I asked.

He smiled. "You're nervous."

I tried to maintain a calm face, but my chin lifted slightly and the effort gave me away. His smile grew wider.

Chapter 70

A Toy

"Now you've done it." Micah said from his tabletop. His head lolled to the side to watch Kaitlyn seethe. Her fists were clenched, teeth gritted.

"Done what?" Shawn asked. His eyes darted between Micah and Kaitlyn.

Pause for dramatic effect, thought Micah. *1...2...3...* "You've pissed her off."

Shawn turned his head fully to Micah now, eyes wide. It gave Kaitlyn the chance she needed, and she took it. Air shot into Shawn's chest. He flew back, cracking his head and back against a small, square, stone hut. Temporarily dazed, Shawn sunk to the ground. A sign on the door, 'Family Restroom,' fell on Shawn.

He craned his neck up, fearing more falling rock. Instead he found Kaitlyn, squatting on top of the hut. She lobbed two fireballs in the air. They arched up, almost as high as the cliffs. Then she pushed Shawn with air again, out onto the open plaza. Making adjustments for his location, the fireballs began their descent.

Micah craned his neck to watch. It made his head swim, but this wasn't something he was willing to miss. The balls whistled and crackled as they came down. Shawn looked up with enough time to duck, covering his head. They hit his back. Gaseous flames splayed across his body then rolled to the concrete.

Kaitlyn was on the plaza, walking toward Shawn. She stopped, giving him a chance to put out the flames on his jacket.

"Now if you were a true Gaia," she said, pulling snowflakes together with energy. "You could do this." The moisture transformed into a sloshing sphere of water.

Shawn spared a hopeful glance.

"But, you're not. So..." Kaitlyn let the element fall. It splashed across the ground at her feet.

Shawn gave up at batting at the flames. He took off his jacket and tossed it aside.

"And since I am a Gaia...I'll just keep doing this." Kaitlyn threw out each hand, pitching more fireballs at Shawn.

They brushed his loose shirt. He whipped it off, over his head, attempting to throw it at Kaitlyn – and missed. Another well-aimed fireball licked at his bare bicep. The skin turned bright red.

"Aww." Kaitlyn pursed her lips. "Want me to get some mud for it?"

Shawn heard the hills rumble behind him. "No...don't!"

Kaitlyn concentrated on pulling loose dirt toward her and Shawn.

Micah's eyes widened. "Watch out!"

Before the dirt reached the dueling couple, Shawn tackled Kaitlyn. They rolled across the concrete and stone. Dirt sprayed across them.

Shawn ended up on top. He smiled. "I've been here before."

Micah's veins coursed with adrenaline. He pushed himself up; pain squeezed in on his head. He threw his legs over the side of the table and slid off.

Kaitlyn wriggled one knee in between her and Shawn. She bucked and kicked out. Shawn flew off, heals over head. He rolled.

They both got to their feet at the same time, while Micah fell to his knees.

Kaitlyn glanced at Micah. The distraction cost her. Shawn weaved energy, trying for Akasha, but not getting it together. The result was a wobbly, uncontrolled mass of various elements. He pushed it out, sending it toward Kaitlyn.

It hit her in the chest, throwing her back. When she stood, she was laughing. "You're losing, Shawn."

"You're the one that just got off the ground."

"No – I mean you're losing Akasha." Kaitlyn charged.

Shawn desperately attempted to call the elements again. They came in short bursts, mostly dissipating before he could weave them together.

Kaitlyn reached him, shouldering him in the midsection. They both rolled. Now Kaitlyn was on top. She pummeled his face. Punch after punch, his blood sprayed across her knuckles. She kept his arms pinned with her knees. When he no longer tried to dodge her strikes, she got up.

Shawn pushed himself off the ground, spitting blood. He glanced at the fire tornados, which were closer now, and then at the mountains, continuing to crumble under avalanche after avalanche. "Not all the Elementals have run off screaming."

Kaitlyn cocked her head. "No. I didn't have time to meet everyone in person."

Shawn stood up all the way, taking a deep breath. He tried Akasha once again. It never came.

Kaitlyn answered with her own magic, weaving a ball of Akasha, and shooting it straight toward Shawn. The charged energy slowed then stopped, midair. It was Shawn's tunnel – his only natural magic, and it was strong. Akasha remained suspended as Shawn squeezed the channel closed on his end.

Little by little, it began to move back toward Kaitlyn. Micah, still on his knees, forced himself forward.

"I still have this." Smiled Shawn, his face growing puffy.

Kaitlyn moved her lips. As words rode out on her breath, she mixed them with a tiny puff of wind. One wavelength and the magic floated by Shawn's ear. He shivered visibly. When the magic floated past Micah he heard, "Then you have nothing."

Moments later, Kaitlyn shoved another burst of energy toward Shawn. The tunnel pulsated out once, then again. It burst, spraying Akasha up and out. Shawn was thrown, landing hard on his back. Some of the spray hit Micah's bare skin. It felt like chemical burns.

Shawn stood. "I'll find her…you bitch! I'll finish you if I have to and then I'll find her. You can't hide a Gaia."

Kaitlyn went still. "What would you do with her?"

Shawn paced, limping across the plaza and rubbing his arm. Bruises blossomed across his body. "I'll find her and…and…I'll raise her. As a daughter. She'll be loved…and protected. And I can teach her."

"She has all those things now," Kaitlyn's voice cracked.

"I would die for her, Kaitlyn." Shawn squared his shoulders.

"Why wait?" Micah stood behind Shawn, a piece of rock lifted over his head. When Shawn turned in surprise, the rock came down. Shawn crumpled to the floor. Micah followed seconds later.

Kaitlyn rushed to Micah, kneeling down by his side.

"Why do you keep toying with him?" Micah asked, exhausted and shaky. "Just finish him off."

Beside them, Shawn groaned. His arms twitched but his eyes were shut tight.

"Because," said Kaitlyn, glancing at Shawn. "He's toyed with me plenty."

Chapter 71

Retaliation

Micah lay in front of me, clutching his midsection but breathing. His face was going white. He'd lost a lot of blood. A fact, up until now, I had done my best to ignore. I looked over at Shawn, who was just beginning to blink. His usual bright blue eyes were going dull. For the first time, I recognized Cato in him.

Still sprawled out on the ground, Shawn turned to me and swallowed. "What will you do?"

"I should kill you." My answer was instant, without thought.

"Why?" he asked.

"Why?! Because you *raped* me – repeatedly!"

He blinked, but didn't answer. I wanted to shake him.

"You hurt me Shawn." I tried to drill the pain I had incurred into him – willing him to understand what I had gone through. "You almost killed me. Not to mention everyone else who has died for your own selfish reasons. Power, control, greed."

He nodded, almost encouraging me. "How would you have me punished for your rape? How would you retaliate? You are the Gaia, Kaitlyn. How does Mother Earth retaliate when her children rape her lands, slicing down her trees and emptying her soil of precious minerals?" Shawn looked down, and picked up the Athame. "Here," he said, holding the knife out, handle first.

I got up and walked around Micah, then kneeled in between the two men, still on their backs.

I grasped the Athame; it quivered with energy. Shawn lifted his chin, baring his neck. I could see his pulse throbbing right underneath his skin. My hand twitched, itching to make a clean cut. One swipe, and it would be over.

"Kill me, Kaitlyn – because you are Mother Earth. You understand why natural disasters target the human population. This is what you were meant to do; stop those who harm you. For once – embrace everything that you are!"

Galapagos came back to me. Only this time, it was me standing by the bed, full of power and energy with that penguin by my side. Shawn lay weak and exposed, his energy raw and ready for the taking.

Micah lifted his head. "Kaitlyn, you know what to do."

My hand squeezed the Athame. A bead of sweat rolled down my temple.

Shawn closed his eyes, waiting.

The knife quivered even more in my hand. My eyes widened as I realized just how much Shawn was still manipulating me. He'd have me follow in his footsteps, even if he had to sacrifice himself.

I lowered the knife. When the tip scraped across the ground, Shawn opened his eyes. "What are you doing?"

I stood, wiping my forehead with my sleeve. I settled the knife in my other palm and glanced down at Shawn. "Embracing everything that I am," I said.

I touched the knife to my forehead. With the magical energy surrounding us, that was all it took.

As I fell back, losing touch with my conscious body, Shawn's smile was the last thing I saw.

Chapter 72

Another Shade

Micah's voice followed me into the cavern, "No, Kaitlyn!"

I landed on the platform like I had been doing it all my life. I looked around; it was completely empty. There were no glimmering life forms on the stairs or in the air. I walked to the edge and peered down at the water beneath me. No Shades there, either.

"Arianna?" I called out. My voice echoed off the walls.

I heard a scuffle above me. Still riding the high of power, I was connected to my physical body. Micah tried to shake me awake. Shawn pushed him away, then stood over my unconscious body, waiting to fend off further attempts by Micah.

Good to know they both found their feet.

Light gleamed out from a cavern high on the wall.

I thought Shawn released Sarah.

I leaped, covering the distance and landing solid on my feet. I threw my arm over my eyes, squinting at the sudden intrusion of light in the otherwise dark cave. The light rotated, sending alternating spikes of blue and white along the cavern walls, until it shimmered and pulled in on itself. A human form stepped forward and the light dwindled until it blinked out behind her.

It wasn't Sarah. It was me.

I stepped forward to meet her – to meet me.

Of course, I thought. *I was marked with the Athame same as any. Why did I not think my Shade existed?*

The woman before me was not a mirror image. She stood tall, with shoulders held back. Her skin glowed and her eyes sparkled.

"I have something for you," she said.

She reached behind her neck, unclasping a silver chain, and pulled a charm out from under her shirt. She handed it to me. I took it, rubbing the pad of my thumb across the smooth, blue butterfly. The gift from Micah to me, and something I thought I had lost in the waves of the Mediterranean.

"I didn't ask for this." My hand closed around the necklace, squeezing tight. "I didn't ask for any of it."

She smiled. "No one ever does. But you'll do what has to be done."

"Why?" I asked, in a whisper. Tears ran down my face.

"Because someone has to." She raised one hand, and paused, waiting for me.

I wiped my nose with my shirtsleeve. I took a deep breath, and raised my hand opposite hers. The light came back encompassing us both, growing brighter as our hands joined.

I clasped it, and our bodies merged, thrust together by the light.

* * *

"Get out of the way, or I swear I'll—"

"What? Bleed to death on me?" Shawn interrupted Micah's threat. He bent down to retrieve his singed shirt. "I might've cut a little too deep at your stomach. At least put some pressure on it."

Micah caught the shirt, then grimaced at the pain the sudden movement caused. "What do you care?"

"I watched my father die – I don't want a repeat with my brother."

Micah rolled onto his back. "Then close your eyes." The gray, turbulent sky was going darker. Micah was sure it wasn't part of the storm.

"Micah…Micah!" the voice echoed with varying degrees of volume.

"Micah!" This one was Kaitlyn's. It brought the world back into sharp focus. "Can you stay with me just a little longer?"

Micah shifted his gaze. Kaitlyn kneeled over him, using Shawn's shirt to apply pressure. She still held the Athame. Shawn stood behind her, hands hanging limp by his side.

"I…" her voice caught, and she swallowed hard, fighting back tears. "I still need you."

His hand went up to her cheek. She followed it with her own hand and something hard hit his knuckles. She relaxed her grip, and part of the lost butterfly necklace fell out.

His eyes darted to Shawn. Shawn didn't answer the unspoken question. Instead, he rubbed his neck and looked away. A stray wisp of Kaitlyn's hair drew Micah's eyes back to her. He tucked it behind her ear, then took the necklace from her hand. He clasped it around her bowed head.

When she rose, the butterfly fell to her chest just beneath her neckline. Blue swirls on the wings matched the angry swirls of dark grays in the sky

behind her. But her eyes, a deep brown shimmering with golden specks, were inviting; peaceful, almost.
"Beautiful," Micah said.

Chapter 73

Earth Falling

Power thrummed, and it was all I could do to keep it contained until Micah clasped the necklace around my neck. When the butterfly hit my chest, it was warm. It countered the cool burn I felt from Shawn's scar on the back of my shoulder.

A lump rose in my throat. Micah didn't have much longer. His eyes, a blend of rich greens, were infused with the amber-like spots. Spidery veins interconnected, laced through the color.

Like a leaf, I thought. *How did I never notice that before?*

I squeezed his hand. A static shock jumped from me to him.

Micah smiled. "Just like when we first met."

A smile spread across my own face.

Behind me, Shawn cleared his throat. "She wasn't there, right? I already sent her off…"

I turned, looking at him over my shoulder. "No, Sarah wasn't there." My thumb stroked Micah's cheek as I looked at Shawn. "What will you do now?"

He looked up at the sky. The clouds were beginning to dissipate, revealing the aurora borealis above. "I don't know. I'm very tired."

"There might be a way for you to get Akasha back." I swallowed hard, forcing the words out. "For good."

Micah moved under my hand, probably ready to protest. I squeezed his shoulder, reassuring him.

"How?" Shawn asked.

I held out my other hand to Shawn. "Help me."

He hesitated, but only for a second. What choice did he have?

Shawn's hand was cool. Shawn's cold to Micah's hot. Balance. Because too much of one thing was never good.

I closed my eyes, calling the elements and letting power envelope me. It threatened to tear me apart, but outside forces squeezed in, pressing against each other, holding everything together.

Akasha formed above us – a brilliant sphere, infused with color and charged energy. The three of us squinted as we looked up, our hands squeezing tight. I raised it, using more energy sent willingly by Shawn and Micah.

Akasha surpassed the height of the monolithic cliffs and peaked. I held it there, suspended, like a miniature sun in the sky. The rumbling avalanches and fire tornados ceased. With amplified senses, I felt Elementals retreating. Many took cover.

I pulled Akasha back down, bringing it in between the cliffs. I clenched my insides, forcing more and more energy up. I drew magic from the Earth. I borrowed it from the moisture-filled sky, and the wind that blew in. I called on what energy had almost dissipated from the fire tornadoes. All of it combined, and I made adjustments to Akasha along the way. It held together, expanding.

I was growing weak, and still needed more for the final infusion. "I need the rest of what you have," I told both Shawn and Micah.

I felt a boost from Micah almost immediately, but I held it back. Both needed to come at the same time.

"Will we survive it?" Shawn yelled over the howling winds.

"I...don't know," I answered honestly. I couldn't lie about something like that now – not with Akasha hanging over my head.

He looked at me, then nodded. He obliged with more energy. I would have happily drawn from him only, leaving Micah alone. But it wasn't about what I wanted – it was about what I needed, and I needed balance.

One final push, and Akasha burst out. The huge, monolithic cliffs of Red Rocks only contained the blast for so long. The intense inner core of Akasha rolled across the Rockies and the plains toward downtown Denver. Explosions shook the Earth. A deep cracking sound echoed across the amphitheatre. I looked up – the cliff to our right shifted.

Akasha was a magnet, attracting pockets of power. The increased energy sent Akasha further, miles and miles across the Earth. I recalled a spell I'd used to cleanse Shawn's Athame. I chanted, mixing the spell with the power of Akasha. "I consecrate you with earth; the Great Mother shall provide you protection." The hills rumbled as the avalanches started up again. Shawn's hand squeezed my own. I squeezed back, willing him to stay.

My voice was louder now, "I consecrate you with fire, so that you are empowered with the strength that burns in the core of the Earth." A surge of heat shot through Akasha like a wave. I adjusted the other three elements to maintain balance. Micah's breathing grew shallow. Still on one knee, I looked up at Akasha in a panic. I had to finish it.

"I consecrate you with air so that you may obtain the knowledge of infinite places." My energy began to wane, and Akasha flickered above us. What light left Akasha was balanced by a burst of power coming from the Chakra Center in Denver. My power extended further. More Elementals joined in. They were scattered, many behind the walls I left for them, but the blue, gold, red, and brown telltale signatures were strong. I had told them to run, but one by one, they sent their own energies, contributing to the strength of Akasha. Another surge, heavy with the element of air, extended my power, covering entire states now. Now the Chakra Center in Evansville joined. There were others along the way.

A large boulder smashed into the stage of the amphitheatre. All three of us looked up. The cliff hung at a precarious angle. It had to be the momentum of Akasha alone keeping it from falling on us.

"Hurry, Kaitlyn!" Micah coughed out.

I nodded, continuing with the last element, "I consecrate you with water so that understanding and wisdom of great mysteries will be yours." It was as if the oceans of the world became conductive. Our power combined with another.

"Galapagos," Shawn whispered, glancing at me.

I could almost taste the ash from the volcano that had erupted when I was trying to escape.

"And the Chakra," Micah countered through pasty, cracked lips.

He was right, the Galapagos had reached for its balance halfway across the world. The rest of the Earth's points of power were quick to respond. Our forest in Indonesia and its counter, Easter Island.

Then Heard and McDonald Islands and back to us. Six of the chakra points along the body of the Earth were accessed. There was just one left.

I glanced at Micah. He nodded in encouragement.

I finished the spell, chanting, "I consecrate this Earth with Akasha; cleanse it with my magical energy."

My whole body went stiff, then shook with uncontrollable spasms. I threw my head back, mouth open and eyes wide. My veins sizzled on the inside, taking my breath away. The rising tide washed through me and into the sky, powering Akasha and enveloping the world.

I sank back onto my heels as Akasha fizzled away, absorbed by the atmosphere, the oceans, and the Earth. The two hands I held went limp. I released Shawn's. He fell to his knees as I hovered over Micah.

Micah's eyelids fluttered, then he looked up at me. "Do you know what tonight was?" he asked.

I shook my head, not trusting my voice.

"The Winter Solstice." He turned his head east. The sun had just begun to rise. The brilliant orb crested the horizon. In a brief flash, its rays reached out, touching the Earth. I raised my hand, shielding my eyes. Then the whole of the hilly plains before us, and the Rocky Mountains behind us, were bathed in light.

I looked down. Micah's hand had gone limp. His light flickered out and his eyes fluttered shut.

The world went gray. I stepped back, away from Micah and Shawn. My heart hitched in my throat. I couldn't breathe. I turned away from Micah's limp body to the sun, closing my eyes, soaking in its heat, forcing away the cold that took hold of me.

I stepped onto the rail, balancing myself on top. I cleansed myself, willing the negative energy to go away.

This is all just a bad dream.

The sun's rays wrapped me in warmth, like Micah always had. But when I opened my eyes and turned, he was still lying there, turning whiter by the second. There was no more warmth.

Shawn was pumping Micah's chest. "Come on, come on." Shawn paused to check for Micah's pulse, then tilted his head back and breathed into his mouth. He resumed pumping, glancing up at me. "Help him!" Shawn's eyes were glossy. It was the second time I'd ever seen him cry.

Shawn didn't hear the subtle crack above us. And with his eyes glued to Micah, he didn't see Creation Rock begin to tip. I didn't call out. I didn't attempt to move.

The whole of the cliff smashed into the ground. Dirt and debris sprayed out. I shielded my face, missing the final few moments of the pair of brothers before me. They were both crushed. The entire Earth seemed to shake.

When the dust cleared, I jumped down from the rail. I splayed my hand across the monolithic cliff. It was warm but cool at the same time. I stepped forward, and hit something that clattered across the ground. I bent down to inspect. The Chalice.

Chapter 74

Our Solstice

Susan turned off the computer.

"Eat!" exclaimed Bee.

Alex laughed. "Just a snack, don't ruin your dinner."

"Otay." Bee was already rooting through the pantry.

"Well, that went better than expected," Susan said, gesturing to the computer. They just finished their first video conferencing session. Power was growing to be more consistent and stable, though they still had to deal with their fair share of blackouts, even on the hybrid power station.

"Give it some time," Alex said. "It'll get better." He wasn't referring to the power.

Susan sat, fiddling with the frayed edges of her shirt. "Do you think she made the right decision? Could it have been done any differently?"

Alex always treaded carefully around the subject. Susan still broke down at the loss of her brother from time to time.

Alex sat down beside her, kissing her on the cheek. "You've said yourself that since Akasha, the pH balance of the oceans have evened out. Acidification is a non-issue; something Daybreak didn't even fix."

Susan nodded.

Alex continued, "Whatever happened in the days after Akasha…well, let's just concentrate on doing what is best for Bee, and make sure her mother's sacrifice remains justified."

"Right." Susan swallowed hard then patted Alex on the knee. "I'll get dinner started."

* * *

During the video conference, I had taken more than a dozen screenshots of Bee. I stared at one now, tracing her outline with the pad of my finger until the screensaver came on, fading my daughter to black.

At one point during the session, when she had turned and I'd seen that her brown curls had grown past her shoulders, I almost lost it. It was elating yet crushing all at the same time. Most likely, I would never see her in person again; not if the Earth were to survive it.

"Excuse me, ma'am…"

I retracted my hand from the screen at the voice behind me, and turned. "Please don't call me 'ma'am'."

David cleared his throat. "I know you have designated a second, but…" he trailed off, again, as my second-in-command, Erika, entered the room. David rubbed the back of his neck and pushed his glasses up on his nose. "It's just that – I'm not sure this was the way Shawn meant things to be run."

"Shawn is dead," I reminded him, my voice cold. David was becoming annoying. He protested when I began using the aurora borealis to transfer nuclear energy to population centers, even though the underwater transfer cables had years' worth of development to go until they were safe. Hell, he protested when I used Akasha for the nuclear fission process instead of uranium.

Alex and Susan were hard at work on one of the hybrid power stations, dubbed Advanced Hybrid Industrial Units. AHI Units, named for all of the sacrifices made in the fight over power. But AHI Units also had years' worth of development ahead of them before they could support the new world. In the meantime, the Chakra Centers set up by governments around the world would help sustain our populations.

"Let me ask you, David, how do the carbon dioxide levels look?" I glanced at him, my finger tracing the spiral of life on the tabletop. It was our new symbol, plastered on almost everything the organization owned.

He opened his notebook. "Almost down to the preindustrial level."

I crossed my arms. "And Earth's temperature?"

"Also down – almost by .5 degrees Celsius." His cheeks went crimson.

"The Earth is fixing itself, David – thanks to Akasha."

Shawn had been right about one thing; nuclear was the most ready. But unlike him, I knew it wasn't the long-term option. Powerful, dangerous, convenient, necessary. Easter Island had already volunteered to serve as a site for a second nuclear station, and floating Russian nuclear reactors were being brought back online. All three would exist on sinkable islands, in case of emergency. All three wouldn't be activated until Gaias were found, and volunteered, to power them.

Coming to Shawn's plant in McMurdo Power Station on Ross Island in Antarctica was really my only option. It was almost exactly halfway around the world from Bee. Hopefully, whatever energy we each were manipulating would balance out. Besides, cold numbed the constant feeling of pain in my stomach, in my head, and in my heart.

"One Less doesn't—"

"And I've changed the name," I interrupted David. "To One More."

Both Erika and David arched their eyebrows.

"As in one more plant. We're going to plant things. Tell the Chakra Centers to get their shovels ready."

Erika did a fist pump.

David's other eyebrow went up. "Ma'am?"

I sighed. "I'll be in my room – do not disturb for an hour." My hand brushed the lump in my side cargo pocket, ensuring the Chalice was still there. "And David? Don't call me 'ma'am'."

* * *

I landed on the platform. My toes tingled as they touched down on glowing, not-so-solid ground. I looked up. The two men I had left last time were there: Cato and Ted.

"It is done then?" Cato asked.

I nodded, swallowing the lump in my throat.

"And not without its sacrifices…" Cato drifted off.

I looked up at him. The men glanced at each other, then slowly stepped aside. From behind them, two green eyes looked back at me.

A smile opened up my face as I walked toward Micah. I paused in front of him, stretching out my hand. He did the same. My solid to his translucent. He made an effort, and was able to solidify his extended limb. Our fingers intertwined.

I looked up into those deep pools of jade, sucking me in just as they always did.

"Hey," I said.

He smiled. "Hey, yourself."

"Shall we begin?" Cato interrupted the moment. Micah moved to stand next to me as Cato began, "Dearly Beloved, as we gather here today…"

Author's Note

I hope you have enjoyed reading The Akasha Series. Even more so, I hope it has inspired you to take a renewed interest in the health of our planet. I truly believe there is a little magic in all of us, even if it isn't in the form of flying fireballs. Simple acts of kindness, toward both humanity and the environment, can be miraculous.

If you like the series, please consider leaving a review on Smashwords.com, Amazon.com, BarnesandNoble.com, or on iTunes. There is a boxed set that contains never before published bonus content; short stories for each of the main characters (including Bee, twenty years in the future). Feel free to contact me at terra.harmony11@gmail.com; if you include links to a review for each of the four books in the series, I will email you the bonus content as a .pdf, free of charge, as a thank you for taking the time to leave a review and letting me know what you think!

About the Author

Terra is author of the eco-fantasy novels in the Akasha Series; 'Water', 'Air', 'Fire', and 'Earth'. The first book in The Painted Maidens Trilogy, 'The Rising', is also now available.

Terra was born and raised in Colorado but has since lived in California, Texas, Utah, North Carolina, and Virginia. Terra has served a 5½ year enlistment in the Marine Corp, has earned her bachelor's and master's degree and presently runs the language services division of a small business.

Terra currently lives in a suburb of Washington, DC with her husband of fourteen years and three children.

Connect with Terra:

E-mail: terra.harmony11@gmail.com
Facebook: http://facebook.com/terraharmony
Blog: http://harmonylit.wordpress.com
Twitter: https://twitter.com/#!/harmonygirlit

Discover Other Titles by Terra:

The Rising

Book One of the Painted Maidens Trilogy

Fifteen-year-old Serena is the youngest member of a dying race. The increasing acidity of the ocean is destroying her home, slowly eating away at the once thriving underwater landscape. But since the night of Serena's birth, it is an outside force that most threatens their dwindling population. Werewolves, who once served as protectors for mermaids in the Kingdom of the Undine, now seek to eliminate all who dwell in the ocean—and Serena is about to find herself right in the middle of the deadly conflict.

Given the title of Werewolf Liaison, Serena is determined to make things right for her people. When she ventures to The Dry, she meets Liam, the werewolf with hazel eyes, and her whole world gets turned upside down. As Serena discovers the real history between werewolves and mermaids, she is left wondering who her true enemies are.

Reviews for 'The Rising'

"It was a great ride. I devoured every page and loved the whole thing through." *by Ariel Avalon, Book Blogger*

"This is a wonderfully unique story." and "I recommend this if you enjoy mermaids or werewolves with some great action, mystery and a bit of romance." *by Darker Passions Book Blog*

"The book is fast paced filled with action that keeps you on the edge of your seat till the very end, add in a little romance and mystery for the perfect balance. The author has written a beautiful story that sparks the imagination. I loved everything about the story and can't wait for the next one to see what happens to both Serena and Liam as their stories unfold." *by The Reading Diaries Book Blog*

Printed in Great Britain
by Amazon